FRIEND ME

SYNERGY BOOK 2

MICHELLE MCCRAW

Enjoy!
Michelle

LAZY DOG BOOKS

This is a work of fiction. Names, characters, places, and incidents either are the products of the author's imagination or are used fictitiously. Any resemblance to actual persons, living or dead, businesses, companies, events, or locales is entirely coincidental.

Cover by Avery Kingston

ISBN: 978-1-7368294-1-7

To the caregivers, especially my mom, who give so much of themselves to those they love.

I'D WATCHED a lot of women come and go from Cooper Fallon's office, but this one was the worst. And she wasn't going quietly.

When her shriek—something that ended with "asshole"—escaped his closed office door to echo all the way down the hall to my desk, I pressed my lips together to hide my grin and pulled up the staffing agency's contact information.

Since his long-time assistant retired five months ago, the Chief Operating Officer of Synergy Analytics had gone through eighteen temporary assistants. Some stormed out, like this one was about to do, some slunk out, and some just didn't bother showing up the next day.

I swear, it was all his own doing. At first. After temp number five keyed the cherry surface of his desk on her way out, he asked me to select the next one. As a favor. And I just took advantage of his own high standards—and raging temper—to ensure that none stuck. I became the Statue of Liberty of San Francisco temps: *Give me your amateurs, your idlers, your novelists and poets yearning to slack off...*

So I might not have been the most impartial person to hire Cooper's assistant.

Because I had a plan. One that relied on, well, unreliable help.

As I composed the email to the agency—I had to be vague enough about why we were firing this one so they'd send us another just as terrible—a voice behind me asked, "Are they okay in there?"

I spun in my chair toward the familiar voice, banging my bare knee against the leg of my desk. I squinted at my work-buddy, Tyler Young, haloed in brightness from the hazy light coming through the converted mill's top-floor skylight.

I rubbed my knee. With Cooper bellowing from the corner office, I hadn't heard the soft approach of Tyler's sneakers. "I was just about to bust out the popcorn."

Flashing his adorable dimples, he came around to the front of my desk, as he always did so I didn't have to stare into the skylight. When Cooper's low growl cut across the temp's higher voice, Tyler shoved up his black-framed glasses and asked, "Are you sure? Do we need to—?"

I tilted my head to listen. The temp was giving as good as—or better than—she got. All the swearing was on her end. "No, they're pretty evenly matched. At least she's not a crier." I'd raided my desk drawer for chocolate and tissues to console the one he'd fired last week.

When the temp's shouting escalated into a high-pitched screech, Synergy's other founder, Jackson Jones, emerged from his office and ambled to my desk. "Hey, Marlee. Who picked"—he checked his Omega—"four o'clock?" My boss leaned his big hand on my desk and plucked a piece of candy from the ceramic bowl.

I snorted. "Someone down in payroll. I'm guessing she'll win it."

"Poor Cooper." He wadded up his candy wrapper and handed it to me to throw in the trash. "Not everyone can have San Francisco's best assistant. He's jealous I found you first."

My cheeks warming, I smoothed my rosebud-pink skirt.

Cooper, the COO of one of the world's hottest tech companies, demanded a lot of his employees. He was an alpha billionaire, just like in my favorite novels.

Total romance-hero material. I just wished he were mine.

That first day I'd met him, when I was still a part-timer figuring out what exactly analytics software did and how the building full of scruffy young programmers had made it onto the Fortune 1000, my jaw had dropped and my knees had gone weak. He was more than handsome; he looked like the model on the cover of the romance novel I'd been reading. Blond hair, blue eyes, the perfect amount of stubble, impeccable clothes—though lacking a broadsword—and tall as a redwood. I'd spent my first three days at Synergy staring at him. By the end of the second week, it was a full-blown crush.

Not only was he one of Northern California's most eligible bachelors, but he was a considerate, caring, honest man. He knew the names of all of his employees, from the executive floor down to the mailroom. He'd started a foundation to help kids from lower-income families go to coding camps. And most important—

"You going to get that?" Jackson asked, leaning a hip against the soapstone lab table I used as a desk.

Cooper's line was lit up on my desk phone, ringing, but since both people who should've answered it were screaming at each other, it was up to me.

"Cooper Fallon's office. Marlee Rice speaking."

"Hi," said a husky female voice. "This is Jamila Jallow. Is Cooper available? He's expecting my call."

He was? My heart thudded. Why was top-of-their-Stanford-class, could've-been-a-model, on-all-the-forty-under-forty-lists Jamila Jallow, Cooper's BFF, calling him today?

"No, I'm sorry. He's tied up at the moment. Can I help you?"

"Sure. Could you let him know my plans changed and I *can* go with him to Jackson's wedding?"

Holy Stephen Hawking.

"You can?" Although Jamila and Cooper had attended more than one industry function together, he never brought a date to Synergy events. And while my boss's wedding next weekend wasn't an official company function, I'd been sure he'd go stag.

"I can. But, you know, I'll just text him. Thanks, Marlee."

My ears buzzed. I'd figured Jamila would go to Jackson's wedding. They'd been friends since college. What did it mean that she'd go with Cooper? Was it a friends-date or a date-date?

It'd be just my luck if she snapped up Cooper right as I'd finally found the courage to do something about my three-year-old crush.

"Um, Marlee?" Tyler asked, straightening his glasses. "Are you okay?"

I blinked to focus. "Fine." I turned to Jackson. "That was Jamila Jallow. She says she's coming with Cooper. To your wedding."

His eyebrows shot up. "He never brings anyone to my parties."

"I know, right? What's going on?"

Cooper's door swung open, thumping into the wall, and the temp stormed out, her face as red as her silk blouse. I'd been a little afraid when the gorgeous woman had walked in on Monday with her designer clothes and shoes that cost more than my weekly salary, but she'd been too preoccupied with fluttering her fake eyelashes at Cooper to answer his calls. She snatched her buttery leather handbag off the desk outside and flounced past us toward the elevators.

"Bye, Lynley," I said.

"Fuck off." She veered right, yanked open the door, and disappeared into the stairwell.

I exchanged a glance with Jackson.

"Yeah," he said, "Cooper has that effect on me, sometimes."

Tyler said nothing. He hadn't spent enough time up here on the sixth floor to know that Cooper's moods were a summer thunderstorm: loud but quickly spent.

The man himself stepped out of his glass-walled office, his nostrils flaring, his jaw like marble. He shoved his hands into the pockets of his tailored black slacks and, gaze on the reclaimed-wood floor, approached us. I ran a hand over my pendant and sat up straighter in my chair.

Rubbing the back of his neck, he turned his crystal-blue eyes on me.

"Marlee?" He shifted on his feet. "It seems Lindsey—"

"Lynley," I corrected him.

He grimaced, showing straight white teeth. "She and I have agreed she's not a good fit for Synergy."

"That's one way of putting it," Jackson said.

Cooper's stare stabbed his friend. "If you'd just reconsider sharing Marlee with me…"

"I'd be happy to—" I began.

"Not happening," Jackson interrupted me. He stared at me, hard. "Marlee has plenty of work already. And you might as well ask to borrow my right arm. Find your own Marlee." He shrugged. "Or keep one of the temps she finds for you."

Before he spoke, Cooper took a beat to relax his hands, which had balled into fists. Then he looked at me. "Do you think you could—"

"Done." I clicked to send my email to the staffing agency.

"Thanks. You know I adore you, Marlee." And there it was, the heart-stopping smile that turned me to goo on the floor every time. I wanted to dance my fingertips over his strong, stubbly jaw and into his short, sandy hair. Run my hands over his gray striped dress shirt to touch the toned shoulders underneath. Drag my nails down his back and squeeze his—

"Anyway, Jay—" He turned to Jackson, and that was when I realized I'd been eye-fucking Cooper again. "Can we start our ride early? I have a foundation event tonight."

"I'll go change." Jackson shot me a look—he hadn't missed my wandering eyes—and then gripped Tyler's shoulder. "Let's talk tomorrow about your ideas for the fuel burn module." Because I was watching Cooper, I saw his gaze follow his friend's hand and then narrow at Tyler. Cooper tended to be the jealous partner in his bromance with Jackson.

"Sure thing." Tyler grinned at our boss, looking exactly like a Labrador Retriever who'd been told he was a good boy.

Jackson had created the company's flagship product—an automotive analytics package that made cars perform better and more safely—ten years ago in the dorm room he shared with Cooper at Stanford. A programming legend, he inspired admiration among the developers, and Tyler was president of the fan club. Though Tyler was a legit programmer himself. Jackson didn't have the patience to mentor many programmers, but he made time for Tyler.

When the two executives returned to their respective offices, I beckoned Tyler closer and checked that no one else was nearby. "I heard Sanjay's leaving."

"Yeah?" His lower lip pushed out into an almost-pout. "He's a good boss. I'll miss him."

"Sure, but..." I paused for effect. "That opens up a manager position. And I know a talented programmer who's ready for a promotion."

"Who, Grant?"

I snorted. "No, you dork. You."

He rocked back on his heels. "I'm not ready. I've been here less than a year."

"It doesn't matter how long you've been here. What matters is how much you know about programming and how good you are with people." And Tyler was good with people. Unlike most of his colleagues, he didn't look down his nose at me because I was an admin.

His eyes narrowed, uncertain.

"Think about it. HR will post the job next week."

He gave a noncommittal grunt. Plucking a peppermint from my candy dish, he twisted the ends tighter. He opened his mouth, took a breath, and then let it out slowly.

"Oh, right. The fuel-burn module. Want me to schedule a meeting with him tomorrow?" I clicked to Jackson's calendar and searched for a free slot. "How's two-thirty?"

A soft drumming was my only answer. His long fingers tapped out a rhythm against the side of his jeans.

"Tyler?" I prompted him again.

"Right. Sure." He dragged his gaze off my desk and met mine. "A few of us are—I thought you'd like, maybe, to, uh—"

"Yes?" I typed up the meeting invitation and sent it while he hesitated. I glanced at the clock in the corner of my screen. If Jackson was leaving now, I could just make the early train. Definitely a good idea, considering the problems we'd had lately. A few weeks ago, Dad had tried to help out by making dinner but had ended up burning through a pot on the stove and setting off the smoke alarm.

"It's three-dollar pint night, and…"

We both startled when Jackson slammed his office door and shouted down the hall, "Coop, get your ass in gear!"

Cooper emerged from his office, duffel bag thrown over his shoulder. Like Jackson, he wore a T-shirt that skimmed over his chest and ended just below the hip of a pair of tight-fitting bike shorts. My eyes trailed up his toned leg to the hint of a bulge just under the hem of that shirt. I swallowed.

"See you tomorrow." Jackson waved lazily in our direction before he jogged to the stairs and held the door for Cooper. "After the ride, let's—" The door shut behind them, cutting off Jackson's words.

I blinked hard and then turned back to Tyler. "Sorry, what did you say?"

He took off his glasses and rubbed them on his T-shirt. Without his glasses, his eyes were dappled with specks of brown, blue, green, and gold, like Earth seen from space.

"I was thinking about going to the pub on the next block after work. Want to come with?"

"I'm sorry, I can't tonight. Who're you going with?" When we hung out together at the quarterly Synergy parties, the other programmers orbited Tyler like satellites. Most of them were okay, but a few wouldn't even speak to someone without "developer" in her title. They scanned past me like I was some sort of exotic pink insect, completely beneath their notice.

"Oh, um. I hadn't invited anyone else yet."

I paused my packing. It was just like Tyler to build the gathering around me and my preferences. Such a sweet guy. If I were anyone else, I'd have jumped at the opportunity to spend time with him after work.

But I had responsibilities. And plans. "Maybe some other night?"

As soon as he nodded, I strode to the elevator and jabbed the button.

The doors slid open right away, and when I turned to press the button, I glimpsed Tyler's downturned mouth as he watched me go. I gave him an apologetic smile and finger-waggle.

He'd be fine. He'd go out tonight with his other friends. He was like most people our age who worked at Synergy—dedicated and hardworking with few responsibilities outside the office, and with plenty of cash to party when the work was done.

Even though we'd been friends for the better part of a year and best buddies for more than six months, Tyler didn't know I wasn't like him. I hoped he didn't think I was making up a fake excuse, like all my friends from college had. They'd slowly dropped out of my life after too many refused invitations, too many last-minute cancellations.

But from the moment he'd rescued me from that evil beer tap, Tyler had been different. He'd kept asking me places even though most times, I refused. He was a good friend. One worth keeping.

I'd take him to lunch the next day. But right then, I needed to woman up for my second job.

2

AS THE TRAIN pulled into my station in Oakland, I slid my book-mark into my library book and caressed the glossy cover. Some-day, someone would take me in his arms and kiss me the way the kilted hero of the romance novel had just kissed the heroine, all pent-up longing and a tangle of tongues. Would it be Cooper?

Not if he was in love with Jamila Jallow.

I looked up from the improbably waxed chest on the cover to see a man sitting across from me, smirking. I rolled my eyes and stood, shoving the book into my bag. If I'd been a guy ogling *Play-boy,* he'd have fist-bumped me. But because I was a woman reading a romance novel with a suggestive cover, he thought he could look down his nose at me. I made sure to ram his elbow—hard—with my pleather fuchsia purse on the way out.

Weaving through the crowd of people in the terminal, I made my way to the street outside. The air was still warm in the September evening, the sun just visible over the tops of the low buildings. I walked briskly along the broad, open streets, so different from the high rise–shadowed caverns of downtown San Francisco. I greeted the familiar faces I passed: old Mrs. Lukas clutching her bowling bag at the bus stop, burly Mr. Oliveras leaning in the doorway of his grocery, the little Park kids racing their matchbox cars on the front steps of their building. I'd lived in Oakland all my life, and although I'd gone to college and now worked in San Francisco, the East Bay was my home.

Just as I was about to let myself into our stucco bungalow, something clanked at the side of the house. My heart pounded in my ears. Our neighborhood usually felt safe, but it wouldn't have been the first time someone had tried to break in. This would've been a great time for my Highland hero to come to my rescue with his claymore and save me from the burglar, but all I had was Dad, and he used a cane, not a sword.

My hand shaking, I dug in my purse for my Taser—I hoped the batteries still worked—and, after easing down my bag and slipping off my heels, I tiptoed back down the steps and along the front of the house.

Metal scraped against metal just around the corner. Had the prowler decided to climb up onto the roof and come in through the window? I shuddered. My bedroom window.

I clutched the Taser in my fist and straightened my spine. Nope. I wasn't a helpless damsel in distress. I'd taken two self-defense classes at the Y, I was armed, and I wasn't afraid to protect myself and my home. Lunging around the corner, I swung the Taser in a high arc to catch the prowler in the face or neck as I'd been taught.

I dropped it like a hot potato, and it bounced off into the grass.

"Dad! What the hell?"

He looked down at me, one foot on the lowest rung of the ladder, his hands gripping the sides, and an ancient string of multicolored Christmas lights looped around his shoulder.

Crinkles formed around his slate-blue eyes. "Marlee! You're home! I was just about to hang the lights."

"Lights for what?" I rubbed my chest to keep my heart from beating through my breastbone.

He took one hand off the ladder to touch the wires hanging from his shoulder. "Christmas lights, of course."

"It's the middle of September. Don't you think it's a little early for that?" I edged closer, ready to steady him in case he took his other hand off the ladder.

His smile faded, and he looked at me blankly. Then the tips of his ears and his weathered cheeks turned red. "I thought I'd get an early start?" The uncertain way his voice rose at the end punched me in the gut.

"You know you're not supposed to use the ladder." I picked up my Taser and slid it into my jacket pocket before I put my arm around his waist. "Hold on and put your foot down."

He slumped his shoulders but obeyed. "My cane's over there." He lifted his chin toward the side of the house where it was still propped up against the stucco. I checked that he had two feet on the ground and both hands clutching the ladder before I released him long enough to grab the cane and tuck it into his hand.

"Let's go inside." I looped my arm around his waist and supported him as he released the ladder and pivoted toward the front of the house.

"I could have done it. I've been climbing that ladder since before you were born."

A fall from that very ladder had shattered his leg and permanently disabled him. I closed my eyes and pressed my lips together to keep myself from reminding him we couldn't afford another episode like that.

Instead, I said, "It's almost time for dinner, and, besides, we have two months before we need to hang the lights."

He limped along beside me to the front steps, where he paused. "On the bright side," he said, his eyes twinkling, "I've already ordered your Christmas present. It won't be late this year."

———

FROM THE FRONT DOOR, only six normal-sized steps—twelve of Dad's shuffling pace—separated the living room from the kitchen, which welcomed us with the spicy aroma of chili from the slow cooker. I left Dad leaning against the sink to wash his hands while I set my things by the back door.

He dried his hands and picked up the box of cornbread mix I'd left on the counter. "I guess I got sidetracked."

"Don't worry about it." Why had he decided to hang the lights? Had he seen one of those early Christmas commercials on TV and forgotten the date?

I aligned my heels against the wall before setting my laptop bag in the magenta cubby Dad had built next to the back door when I'd started kindergarten. He'd repainted it many times over the years, always in my favorite shades of pink.

I squeezed past him to wash my hands and then set the table. We no longer needed words at dinnertime; we'd prepared meals together so many times over the years that we anticipated what the other would do. I handed him a bowl, and he ladled on the chili. Repeat with a second bowl, which I carried to the round wooden table.

My college friends had thought I was strange for wanting to live at home, but Dad was the only family I had. I needed him. Now he needed me, too.

"How was school today?" he asked, settling into his creaky chair.

"Work, Dad. Work was fine. Cooper lost another admin, so I had to find him a new one for tomorrow."

"Another one? He must be hard on them."

"He is. He has high expectations." The fact that Cooper ran through temps faster than the Oakland A's ran through baseballs was a key part of my plan to win him. When my boss left for his honeymoon, it'd be just the two of us. I'd woo Cooper over cozy lunches.

"You give him unrealistic expectations. Those temps will never measure up to you." I had only a second to preen at his praise before he shot me with, "You could be doing so much more with your computer science degree."

My insides shriveled. I loved living with Dad, but this, right here, I could've done without. Most twenty-five-year-olds at least had the distance of a phone call; I had to look into my dad's eyes while he berated me about my underachievement.

"It's a steady salary, and I get my pick of special projects when I have time."

"But you never have time, do you?" Dad's no-BS teacher stare speared me.

"Jackson keeps me busy." I didn't add that rushing home to ensure Dad hadn't burned down the house or fallen—again—left me no time for special projects.

"When's he getting married?"

I blinked at the abrupt change in subject. "Next weekend."

"You taking anyone?"

I couldn't hide the fiery blush that spread from my cheeks to my forehead. "I don't know." For the ten-thousandth time, I wished my mother were still around to talk to about this stuff. Or to be a buffer between Dad and me. He tried, but—

"You should. Weddings are magical." Memory sparked in his eyes. "Ours was."

As many times as I'd heard the story, I didn't stop him. I loved it every time.

"We didn't have any money, but I knew it had to be special for my Maggie. So I borrowed plants from a landscaper friend—pots of roses in every color—and filled up Santos's back yard. Whenever I smell roses, it reminds me of our wedding. Is Alicia going to have roses?"

"No. Hydrangeas."

"No scent at all." He shook his head, but then, instead of scooping up more chili, he set down his spoon. "You'll find your magic at the wedding."

I'd hoped to, but with the Jamila development, my bravery had fizzled out. "Did she—were you scared she didn't feel the same way you did, at first?"

He chuckled. "Of course. I was the hired help. Every day while I was building that pool house, she came out in her swimsuit.

Sometimes alone with a book and her headphones. Sometimes with a friend or even a fella. I lost a thumbnail to a belt sander while I watched her swim with another guy." He smiled at the vision only he could see. "She was so beautiful. She looked just like you do now." He stared at the photo of my mother on the wall over what should've been her seat at the table.

He was mostly right. We shared the same thick, dark-honey hair—though mine wasn't teased up in a '90s do—and brown eyes. While her chin was rounded, I'd inherited Dad's square jaw and big grin. In the hollow of her neck rested a starburst-shaped pendant formed of tiny diamond chips. I stroked it where it lay now at the base of my throat.

"How did you know she was the one? And how did she know you were the one?"

He leaned back in his chair. "One day, we finished up early. I hung around, cleaning up, after the other guys left. I walked past the pool on the way out, and she asked me to hand her a towel. I was sweaty, covered in sawdust, but when I touched her hand, I knew. I knew I wanted to hold her hand for the rest of our lives." He smiled, but he didn't look at me. Instead, he looked back at her picture.

Why hadn't we talked about this before? The story was perfectly swoony. "And did she—was that when she knew?"

His sad smile turned into a smirk. "She told me she knew the first time I took off my shirt."

"Dad!"

"I think so. She finally saw that what she wanted wasn't those society boys with their floppy hair and their popped collars. It was me. Even though I was a little rough around the edges, I loved her like those other guys couldn't. A few days later, she handed me a beer at the end of the day, and we talked. And I finally worked up the guts to ask her out." He stared at his bowl, lost in the memories of a marriage that'd been cut too short.

When I looked away from his downcast face, the glint of metal caught my peripheral vision.

"Hey, Dad," I said, "how about we take the telescope out tonight? The sky looks clear."

He pulled his phone from his pocket and clicked a few times. "We'll be able to see Saturn. And the ISS transit is at 8:45." A broad grin spread over his face as he checked the charts.

The tightness in my chest eased. The Christmas lights were an anomaly. Dad was still as sharp as ever. "Tell you what," I said. "You wash the dishes, and I'll set up the telescope."

He stood, quicker than he should, wobbled briefly, but then snatched up his bowl. Leaning heavily on his cane, he shuffled to the sink. The telescope was too heavy for him to manage now, but I'd leave the adjustments to him.

When I carried my bowl to the sink, I kissed his stubbled cheek. "Love you, Dad."

"I love you too, Sunshine. But we can't stay out late tonight; you have school tomorrow."

I closed my eyes and let out a long sigh through my nose. Hefting the telescope case from its shelf, I clattered down the back steps into the lavender light of sunset. In the tiny backyard with its rosebushes and succulents, where we'd planted the Japanese maple for my mother, where Dad had taught me to throw and catch a baseball, and where we'd turned our gazes to the stars on countless clear nights, I breathed in the scents of home, the one he'd built for my mother and me.

My mother had died before their third anniversary, but at least she'd briefly known a perfect, fairy-tale love. Someday, I'd have it, too, and it'd make up for not having a mother to tuck me in at night, to give me the talk, to take a hundred pictures of my prom date and me. For not having a single memory of her.

Cooper hadn't even had to take off his shirt for me to fall for him. And sure, I'd touched him plenty of times, shaking his hand on my first day, handing him papers or his phone on many days since, and no spark yet, but a dance, a magical wedding dance, would bring us together. Like Cinderella and Prince Charming.

3

A SINGLE LINE from my best friend ruined my morning.

I'd just finished my Wednesday-morning code review—Jackson liked having me run through it first since I caught most of the errors he and his big-picture view missed—when a text popped up on my phone. Seeing Alicia's name, I figured she might want to go to lunch or had a question about Jackson's schedule. Harmless stuff.

Nope.

Alicia: I must've lost your reply card. Are you bringing anyone to the wedding?

It should've been easy to respond. Ten days before the wedding, I should've already handed my card to Alicia. I should've known for sure who—if anyone—I was taking.

I'd had a plan. I'd assumed Cooper and I would both go alone and I'd finally suck it up and tell him how I felt. I'd even hoped to catch a ride with him up to the vineyard. Tucked into the snug front seat of his Tesla, we'd finally have the one-on-one time that'd take us past colleagues to something more.

But that was before Jamila.

Now I had two choices: show up alone or bring my own date. Either way, it was a Morton's Fork where I ended up staring mournfully at him and Jamila instead of putting my plan into action.

And now my best friend had reminded me of how screwed my plan was.

I stared down the hallway at the glass wall of Cooper's office. After a second, he paced into view, headset on, one hand shoved into the pocket of his black dress slacks. He paused and rubbed one dark-blond eyebrow like his head pained him. Then he turned and strode back, disappearing from my field of vision.

Poor Cooper. He worked too hard, bore too many responsibilities. He picked up all of Jackson's slack. And Jackson left a lot of slack. He needed someone at home to ease his burdens, help him relax. Could Jamila do that? She had her own company, her own load of concerns. Maybe they bonded over that shared connection.

Another text flashed on my phone.

Alicia: You there?

Me: Can I have a couple more days to work out some stuff?

Alicia: No problem. I just need to get the count to the vineyard on Friday.

Two days. I had two days to come up with a strategy to respond to the Jamila development.

Glancing back at Cooper's office, I caught the flick of his pants cuff as he paced away.

Maybe it wasn't as bad as I thought. They could be going as friends, the way they'd attended so many galas before. All three of them had been close in college—Jackson, Cooper, and Jamila—so Jamila had her own invitation to the wedding. Maybe Cooper and Jamila were riding up together to save gas.

The stairwell door thunked shut behind me just before I heard the telltale drag of a sneaker on wood. Already smiling, I glanced over my shoulder. "What brings you up here?"

"Hey." Framed by the midday sun streaming through the skylight, Tyler stopped in front of my desk and stared at the corkboard to my left. When he didn't say anything more, I followed the line of his gaze to where it ended at the buttercup-yellow response card tacked to the board.

"She didn't text you to come up here and bug me about the wedding, did she? I said I'd tell her by Friday."

"Not—not exactly." He shifted his weight onto one foot and ducked his head.

My stomach rumbled, and I slapped my hand over it. Dad had still been sleeping when I left home this morning. Since I hadn't made him breakfast, I'd forgotten to eat anything myself.

"Want to go to lunch?" Tyler asked, grinning.

I'd also forgotten to bring my packed lunch. "Genius idea." I glanced at Jackson's closed door and shot him a quick message that I was leaving. He didn't respond, so he must have been in the coding zone. I grabbed my purse and stood. "Let's go."

When the elevator door opened in the lobby, Alicia stood chatting with José at the security desk. "Oh, good, you're ready to go."

"Go?" What had I forgotten?

My phone chimed with a reminder. *Alicia's final fitting.* I squeezed my eyes shut. Forgetful, hungry brain. "Change of plans, Tyler. We're going with Alicia to her dress fitting."

"Oh, no. Y'all had plans?" Alicia asked. "Don't worry about it. I can go alone."

"No way. You're not going up against the Dragon Lady by yourself."

"Dragon Lady?" Tyler asked.

"She's a real piece of work. But she can afford to be. She's the best." I shrugged.

"And a personal friend of Jackson's mother," Alicia said.

Together, we walked to the revolving door, and Tyler gestured for us to go first. "I can't wait to meet her."

The bridal shop wasn't far from Synergy's downtown office. As we walked, Alicia and Tyler talked about a project he was working on. I left my worries about Cooper and the wedding behind me at the Synergy building and let the September sunshine warm my face.

When we reached the shop, Alicia disappeared into the dressing room with the Dragon Lady.

"Don't forget, I promised I'd take a picture for Tiannah," I called after her. Tiannah, Alicia's best friend from home, was Alicia's official maid of honor. Since she lived in Texas, I'd taken up most of the local duties like dress fittings.

An assistant brought us drinks—a can of Mountain Dew for Tyler and a fancy flute of sparkling water for me—and we settled on a loveseat in front of a platform surrounded by three mirrors.

Tyler looked around the shop. "This is a first for me."

"You have all those brothers. And your sister. None of them is married?"

"No. One's engaged, though." He sipped his drink and swallowed like it was bitter instead of sweet.

I slipped off my shoes and tucked my knees under me. "When's the wedding?"

"Next summer, I think?" He looked away, drumming his fingers on his jeans. His dimple was gone.

I couldn't ignore the clear I-don't-want-to-talk-about-it vibes he was sending, but I could try to cheer him up. I set my glass on the table and squeezed his shoulder. "Be right back."

Crossing to the hat rack in the corner, I picked up an armful and carried them back to the loveseat. I set them gently on the low table and picked up a teal fascinator with peacock feathers and a cloud of netting. I set it on my head and raised my eyebrows at Tyler. "What do you think?"

One corner of his mouth curled up. "Not your color."

"Then it must be yours." I set it on his head and fluffed the netting. It made his hazel eyes turn blue.

He looked in the mirror and turned his head from side to side. "Damn, I look good."

"Modest, as well as handsome." I picked up a red one with fluffy feathers shooting off it like fireworks.

"That one," Tyler said, pointing.

I laid down the red one and picked up the one he'd indicated. It was simpler than the others, a trio of blush-pink silk roses nestled into a splash of pale pink netting studded with pearly beads. I settled it onto my head and glanced at the mirror. I nodded. "You're right. It's beautiful."

His eyes had gone dark under his ridiculous hat. "Beautiful."

The assistant's voice startled me. "Need a refill?"

Tyler snatched off his hat. "No, we're good."

She smiled at him, and then at me. "So when's the big day?"

"Alicia, you mean?" I nodded toward the changing room. Wasn't that her job to know? "It's—"

"No, I meant you two. You're going to look so gorgeous together."

"Oh, no. No." My laugh was too high, verging on unhinged. "We're just friends. Work friends."

"Just friends." Tyler gathered up the hats and carried them to the rack.

"Shame," the assistant said. Was she staring at his ass?

Okay. It was a nice ass, lean and tight under his jeans. I cleared my throat. "Friends."

Raised voices from the dressing room caught my attention. "Be right back, Tyler." I ducked behind the pink velvet curtain.

Alicia looked pale, the way she had before her morning sickness subsided a few weeks before, and she couldn't blink away all the tears that shone in her eyes. The Dragon Lady tugged at the zipper, frowning at the straining lace-covered silk.

"What's wrong?" I asked, sliding the heavy curtain closed behind me.

"It—it won't zip. I guess I've gained weight." Alicia sniffled.

"No tears on the dress," the Dragon Lady snapped. Her

nostrils flared, reminding me of why I'd named her the Dragon Lady. Aside from her sparkling personality, she always looked like she was about to shoot flames from her nose. She snatched a tissue from a box nearby and shoved it into Alicia's hand before she turned her attention to the zipper, which had stalled out at the dip in Alicia's spine.

Now I wished I'd accepted the champagne her assistant had offered.

"Of course you've gained weight," I said, clasping my hands to keep from clawing at the Dragon Lady's rigid blond beehive. "You're four months pregnant. Shouldn't the seamstress have planned for that?"

"We did. This is more weight than we'd anticipated," the woman snarled.

Alicia had the tiniest, most adorable baby bump. If it'd been mine and my true love's, I'd have lit it up in neon.

"What can we do about the dress?" I asked. My normally unflappable friend, who normally would've been able to solve this problem, was…flapped.

"Let me look into some"—the Dragon lady peered down her nose—"options." After she swished through the curtain, Alicia pressed the front of the dress to her chest. I could already tell the fabric wouldn't cover there, either. Her baby bump wasn't the only part of Alicia that'd expanded.

"See? It'll be fine," I said, taking another tissue from the box. "She said she had options."

A tear spilled over onto Alicia's cheek, dissolving some of her mascara. I blotted it away.

"They said I'd hardly show at four months. I should've eaten more salads."

"No, honey, your body is wonderful. You're growing a new life in there. Things are going to be a little weird. But it'll be fine." I'd make sure of it.

"Hey, y'all okay in there?" Tyler's low voice came through the curtain.

"Yes," Alicia said.

"No," I said at the same time, making Alicia crack a smile. "We'll be out in a few minutes. Maybe you could go grab some sandwiches...and chocolate?"

"On it," he said.

Alicia had just finished blowing her nose when the Dragon Lady returned. In one hand, she held a scrap of industrial-strength white spandex. In the other, she clutched a hanger with a limp-looking stretch lace mermaid gown.

She shook the spandex at Alicia. "Tummy-trimming body shaper."

Both Alicia and I stared at it in horror. If we ever got her into it, she'd have to be cut out with the Jaws of Life, which would drain the sexy right out of her wedding night. Assuming she didn't pass out at the ceremony from lack of oxygen.

"Won't it hurt the baby?" Alicia asked.

"We put these on brides all the time," the Dragon Lady said. She hadn't answered the question, but I wasn't about to take prenatal advice from her anyway.

"What's the other option?" I asked, eyeing the gown on the hanger.

"This is our emergency dress. It's very forgiving."

I lowered my chin and stared at it. Forgiving, maybe. Unflattering, definitely. That stretch lace would hide nothing. It was one thing to celebrate Alicia's pregnant body and another thing to highlight only her baby bump and supersized boobs. Jackson would probably love it. His conservative mother would be less enthused.

Alicia's fingers tightened on the bodice of her gown for a moment before she started pulling her arms out of the sleeves.

I laid a hand on her arm, stopping her. "No. There's got to be a third option." I gave the Dragon Lady the steely stare I used when I told Jackson he had to meet with the CEO. "Can't you let out the fabric in Alicia's dress?" She'd tried on dozens of gowns last spring when they'd gotten engaged, and this was the one she loved. I knew nothing about sewing, but—"I'm sure we can make it work."

The Dragon Lady pulled the gown away from Alicia's side to show me the inside seams. "There's no extra fabric to work with. And ordering the next size up would take two months."

In the mirror, Alicia's eyes went red-rimmed and glassy again.

"Then do a—a graft. You know, take some fabric from somewhere else and add to it." They did it with skin; surely there was a similar concept in alterations.

She curled her lip. "I suppose we could add a couple of panels at the sides. As long as you keep your arms down, it won't be too noticeable."

"You're the best bridal shop in San Francisco. I'm sure you can make it so it won't be noticeable at all," I said in a honey-sweet tone. "Audrey will be so pleased."

The Dragon Lady pursed her red lips, frowned at Alicia's torso for a moment, and then whipped the tape measure from around her neck. "We can't let Audrey down," she muttered.

The bell tinkled at the outer door. "I'll leave you two to work it out. We'll take the picture next time." I squeezed Alicia's hand and slipped out through the curtain.

Tyler met me at the loveseat, a paper sack in his hand.

I held out my hands, waggling my fingers. "Sandwich me."

"We don't need to wait for Alicia?"

"She'll be a minute."

"I got your favorite, turkey and avocado."

My stomach rumbled. "Thanks. You're awesome."

The first few bites of my sandwich were heavenly. He'd even remembered the spicy mustard I preferred to the disgusting mayonnaise that usually came on it. I only came up for air when Tyler spoke.

"I guess we won't have too many more days like this."

I glanced out the window at the September sunshine. "I guess not. It'll be fall soon."

"No." He set his sandwich on his lap. "I mean, the three of us."

"Why not? We've been friends since you two moved here." Unlike the other programmers, Tyler had been friendly—and not in a creepy, asking-me-out way but a treating-me-like-an-equal way—since I'd met him. He and Alicia had worked on a big project together in Synergy's Austin office, where they'd met Jackson. In Austin, Tyler had become Jackson's protégé, and Alicia his girlfriend.

Tyler had relocated at the beginning of the year, and we'd bonded at one of Synergy's quarterly parties. After Alicia had permanently moved here a few months later, we'd become instant friends. We'd been a triumvirate ever since, especially when Jackson traveled.

It was hard for me to keep friends since Dad took up so much of my free time, but these two had stuck for more than six months. As much as I loved my dad, I needed friends, too.

Tyler looked down at his sandwich. "I just figured with Alicia spending more time with Jackson, we three might not be together as much." He peeled a pickle off the bun.

I choked down the last bite of my sandwich. He was right: once they were married, Alicia and Jackson would spend more time as a family. Surely I wouldn't lose my friend entirely. We'd still hang out when she wasn't doing coupley things with her husband.

Wouldn't we?

I glanced toward the curtain. Next to it, a portrait of a double wedding caught my eye. Just like the sisters in the Colin Firth *Pride and Prejudice.*

It was too late for a double wedding, but double dates were always a possibility. It'd be perfect: Jackson and his best friend, Cooper, and Alicia and me. Maybe someday they'd be matron of honor and best man at *our* wedding. Cooper'd look yummy in a gray morning suit like the grooms in the portrait.

"Marlee?" Tyler's voice broke into my vision.

"What's that?"

"We'll always be friends, right?" He smiled at me, but his dimple was missing.

"Of course we will. I'd be so bored if you didn't come up to see me. And"—I narrowed my eyes—"when you get that manager position, you'll need to come up more often."

"I'm not ready for—"

"Of course you are. You just need to cowboy up and ask for what you want."

Just like I had to do.

It was time to get serious about the Cowgirl-Up-for-Cooper Plan.

4

I'D LEARNED a thing or two about our executives from working at Synergy for the past three years.

Harris Weston, our CEO, had a peanut allergy so severe that he couldn't fly on a commercial airplane.

Jackson, my boss, couldn't sit still for longer than twenty minutes unless he was coding.

And Cooper Fallon hit the gym at six-thirty every morning.

I pushed open the glass door to Synergy's first-floor workout room and almost bit my tongue when I saw him on the chest press. His tank top revealed the results of his daily use of the machine: broad, muscle-rounded shoulders, firm pecs, defined upper arms that belonged in a fitness magazine.

My face wasn't the only thing I had in common with my mother.

"Morning, Cooper," I called across the room.

"Marlee," he said on an exhale.

Whoa. It was too early to be this turned on. I ripped my eyes away from his deltoids and unrolled my yoga mat. When I'd first discovered his workout habit, I'd tried to share the weight equipment. Okay, I'd played dumb and asked him to teach me to use it until it'd seemed to irritate him. I wasn't proud of it. But yoga showed me to better advantage. No sweating or straining, and my yoga pants made my butt look cute. I started with a few stretches that allowed me to watch him as he pushed the handles in and out.

Da-amn.

I closed my eyes to shut out his distracting physique. Too bad it was imprinted on the backs of my eyelids. I took in a deep, cleansing breath and formed the intention for my practice: *Be strong for Dad…and graceful for Cooper so he'll really look at me.*

Not exactly what my yoga instructor had in mind.

I started my sun salutations, reaching up for the fluorescent lights and down to the pink surface of my mat. I did strong poses: Warrior, Crescent Lunge, Mountain. I sucked in my belly, expanded my chest, and stood tall.

Meanwhile, Cooper puffed out his cheeks as he pressed up the handles to lift the tall stack of weights. A drop of sweat rolled down his cheekbone and hung from his sculpted jaw. He furrowed his brow, focused on his reps.

His face had shown that same look of concentrated fury the day I'd fallen for him.

In my second week on the job, on the day he had a scheduled meeting with Weston, the CEO, Jackson had gone missing. Not just oversleeping, but gone. I'd never forget the thunderous look on Cooper's face when he growled, "We're going to find him."

I was terrified. Scared something had happened to my boss, worried I'd lose my job, and despairing I'd never be able to ogle Cooper again.

But we found him. Behind the sketchiest warehouse I'd ever seen. A mangy, brown rat had actually scurried along the wall behind Jackson as a lifted, blinged-out Escalade zoomed away.

I'd hovered just out of range of their whispered conversation. When Cooper clamped his hand on his friend's shoulder and Jackson returned a weak smile, both of their eyes glassy, I'd almost lost it right there behind that disgusting warehouse. I'd never had a friendship like that. I'd never had a friend who'd come searching for me in the seediest part of the city I'd ever seen and, without judgment, taken me back where I belonged.

After we got Jackson back to his office, Cooper turned his attention to me.

"Can I count on your discretion, Marlee?"

"Of—of course." I'd signed a nondisclosure when they'd hired me, but more than that, I loved working for Jackson. He was funny, kind, and energetic. And caretaking came naturally to me.

"Thank you. For that and for your assistance today." Cooper stared at his shiny wingtips. "Jackson has some…self-destructive tendencies. Authority—Weston in particular—triggers them sometimes."

What he said next burned itself into my brain.

"You and I"—he mesmerized me with his icy blue stare— "we're partners now in keeping him safe."

Partners. That had done me in. I'd have done anything he said, committed any crime, given him all the money I had—not that he needed any—to be his partner. To have him one day look at me the way he'd looked at Jackson, with love shining out of his eyes.

Because a man so devoted to a friend would offer his lover exactly what I craved: an epic romance. One where he'd ride to my rescue whenever I needed it. Where every day would be chocolate and flowers. A fairy tale become reality.

Partners. I'd dreamed of it since that day. That we'd become more than caretaker-partners. That he'd see me the way I saw him. As a soul mate.

I looked across the gym at him. He'd moved to the leg press, which put me directly in his line of sight. The pulleys whirred.

I dug one foot into the mat, lifted and gripped my back foot, and leaned forward into Dancer's pose, imagining how graceful our instructor looked when she did it. I tightened my belly and made a ninety-degree angle between my leg and my abdomen, continuing all the way out to my outstretched arm. I sighted along my extended fingers. My torso hovered over the mat. I was grace, confidence, poise.

Until I cut my gaze to Cooper to ensure he was checking me out.

The slight movement of my head overbalanced me. I flailed for a second, desperately windmilling my arms to regain my equilibrium, but it was no good. I toppled forward and just managed to hit the mat with my shoulder instead of my chin. An "oof" flew out of me. *Smooth, Marlee.*

Without pausing the rhythmic whirr of the machine, he called out, "You okay, Marlee?"

Trying to recover from my yoga fail, I straightened my arms, lifting my upper body into Cobra pose. "Fine," I squeaked.

———

LATER THAT MORNING, the glass wall of Jackson's office revealed the warning signs: the jiggling leg, the twirling pen, the vacant expression. Time to get him moving. After his ten-thirty left, I pushed open the door and poked my head into his office.

"Let's take a walk," I said.

Jackson looked at me as if I'd just told him school was dismissed for summer. "You're the best, Marlee."

"I know. Let's go." He needed to burn off some of his energy before his lunch meeting. He threw on a fleece over his Ramones T-shirt and walked beside me to the elevators. Outside, we turned toward the park. As the concrete turned to clover and grass, the tension eased from his shoulders, and the line between his eyebrows smoothed out.

"Anything you want to talk about, boss?" I asked. I kept my gaze on the paved path to avoid snagging my black kitten heels in the seams—the faux leather would peel right off—but he tensed.

"Not really."

That was his prerogative. I was his assistant, not his therapist, and if he didn't want to talk about the stress that was making his ADHD flare up, that was fine by me.

He stuck his hands in his pockets and headed off the path

toward a sculpture of a man and two bears—or dogs, I was never sure exactly what they were. He always meditated on a flat-topped boulder over there.

While he got his Om on, I sat on a bench and pondered my own problem: Cooper. And whatever was going on with Jamila. I'd borrowed a copy of a local tabloid from Cooper's new temp, and now I pulled it out of my bag. It covered a gala Cooper had attended with Jamila, and a large photo in the spread showed them on the red carpet. In her heels, she was as tall as Cooper, and her dark skin glowed against her white gown. He had his hand on the small of her back—something I'd imagined him doing to me at least once a day for the past three years—and their natural grins hinted that one of them had just told the other a secret joke.

But what caught my eye was the caption below: *With wedding bells ringing for **Jackson Jones** (left), will San Francisco's most eligible bachelor, **Cooper Fallon**, soon follow his partner down the aisle with tech queen **Jamila Jallow**?*

I spared hardly a glance for the smaller photo of Jackson and Alicia and its caption's speculation about her baby bump.

Wedding bells? What the hell?

I heard a scuff on the gravel, and Jackson rejoined me, a boyish smile on his face and his hands swinging free at his sides. He pointed at the tabloid I clutched. "Alicia looks fantastic."

I wiped the outrage from my face and smiled up at him. "She always looks fantastic, but you both look great in this one. Want me to get a copy from the paper?"

He peered at it over the top of the page. "Yeah. But what are they saying about Cooper and Jamila?"

I swallowed. "That you're giving them ideas with your wedding. Engagement ideas."

He snorted. "They're friends. Nothing more. No spark."

His words didn't comfort me the way they should have. When Jamila accompanied Cooper to functions, she was always gorgeous in a size-four evening gown with confidently cropped hair and a slender neck that showcased her glittering jeweled statement necklaces. So unlike me with my medium build, long brown hair, and one necklace. I caressed my pendant, tracing its sharp edges. She was the perfect partner for Cooper's lifestyle. There was no way I could compete with her if that was what he wanted. I crushed the tabloid closed.

"Look, Marlee." Jackson sat beside me on the bench. "I know you have…feelings for him. I think you two'd be great together."

I stopped breathing. We'd always danced around the subject before, sidestepping it the way I'd have avoided looking directly at the sun through Dad's telescope. I could have denied it, and he'd have backed off. But he was my friend as well as my boss. "Thanks."

"Since he's taking a date to the wedding, maybe you should, too? Dance a little? Show him what he's missing?" He nudged me with his elbow.

The image of Cooper and me going separately to the wedding but ending up together, just like Cinderella and her prince, had consumed me. But maybe he was right. Going to the ball with another date had worked for Amy Adams in *Enchanted*. And I'd already battled a dragon lady.

But who'd go with me? The wedding was nine days away. Since I'd met Cooper, I hadn't dated anyone seriously. No one had measured up to him.

"Think about it, okay?" He stood. "Andrew's not taking a date. He'd go with you."

A date with Jackson's brother seemed vaguely incestuous. But what other option did I have?

"I'll think about it." I threaded my arm through his as we walked back toward the office. "Now, what about you? Feeling better?"

Jackson laid his hand over mine. "Much better. I don't know what I'd do without you."

"Oh, I do," I said in a teasing tone. I ticked the items off my fingers. "You'd miss every meeting and they'd run the place into the ground without you. You'd starve because you'd forget to eat.

You'd go to jail for nonpayment of taxes. Oh, and you wouldn't be with Alicia."

As usual, he argued. "I was the one who actually did the groveling."

"But I gave you the idea. Without my amazing tips, you'd never have won her back." I wished I could've seen all my best romance novel grovel tips in action, but he'd done the groveling in Austin.

I walked through the revolving door, and he met me on the other side. "Point taken." He turned a hopeful eye to the delivery guy at the security desk. "Is there food?"

"Of course there's food," I said. "You have a lunch meeting with Mr. Weston."

His smile drooped. "Weston." The relationship between Synergy's CEO and Jackson was one I characterized in public as challenging. Really, they were like two wet cats in a sack.

"But I ordered your favorite chipotle-chicken sandwich. With fries. Carry it up for me?" I signed for the food, and Jackson took the bags from the delivery guy.

When the elevator doors closed behind us, Jackson looked up from the floor. "Any way you could—"

"Nope."

"But you don't know what I—"

"No." He was wrong. I did.

"But what if—?"

"Not a chance. You're going on your honeymoon in ten days. You have to meet with him before you go. And I scheduled him during lunch so you'd both be in a better mood. I ordered cookies."

Jackson's shoulders slumped. But then his face brightened. "Double chocolate-chip?"

"Of course."

"I love you, Marlee."

If only his partner felt the same.

5

AFTER I SETTLED Jackson and Mr. Weston in his office, I took my lunch and my novel into the sixth-floor breakroom. I poked at a square of my peanut-butter-and-jelly sandwich in its scarred plastic container, the same one I'd used when I was a kid. And just like then, I'd left Dad a matching sandwich. I hoped he remembered to eat it.

"There you are."

Thank Marie Curie it was Alicia and not Cooper who'd caught me with my sad-sack lunch. I beamed at my friend. "Hey. Did you need him? He's meeting with Weston."

"No, I came to see you." Although she wore a visitor badge, security never required an escort for Jackson's fiancée.

My stomach curled in on itself. "I promise I'll give you the reply card by tomorrow." If I'd just had the courage to ask Cooper to go with me, I might not be about to mark a sad *1* on the *Guests attending* line. Even sadder than eating lunch alone would be sitting abandoned at the head table watching Cooper dance all night with Jamila Jallow.

"No, I didn't come to pester you about that. Though, normally, you're not quite so...spontaneous." Alicia said it like the word tasted bad. Aside from falling in love with Jackson, Alicia, a planner to the core, had never done a spontaneous thing in her life. "I came to thank you for yesterday. I don't know what I would've done without you."

"It takes a bitch to fight one." I poked at my sandwich, and a little of the jelly oozed out.

"Marlee." She said my name so sharply I looked up. "You're not a bitch. You know what you want, and you do what it takes to get it."

I slumped in my chair. If only I were brave enough to get Cooper.

Her blue eyes were misty when she said, "But under that drive, you're the most kind-hearted, resilient person I know."

I smiled at my best friend. We had that in common. She'd taken in her nephew when she'd lost her sister. Alicia advocated for Noah, who also had ADHD, with a determination I hoped to one day emulate for someone I loved. She might look soft on the outside, but Alicia was all steel on the inside.

"Excuse me, Alicia." Cooper had come up behind her where she stood in the doorway. She stepped aside, all the warmth in her smile frosted over.

"How's your work for Jamila going?" he asked her. I froze at the name.

"Almost done. We'll wrap up the project before the wedding."

"Good." Cooper's blue eyes had been as cool and reflective as Millennium Tower, but they warmed when he noticed me. "Afternoon, Marlee." He reached into the refrigerator and pulled out one of his nasty green smoothies.

I snapped the lid onto my sandwich container and propped an elbow on it. "Hey, Cooper. How are you liking Kim?"

"Oh." His smile faltered. "She's fine."

She was not fine. Unlike her predecessor, the eyelash-batting, mouthy slacker, today's temporary administrative assistant had sat quietly at her desk all morning. But after four hours, she still couldn't spell Cooper's name correctly and had somehow managed to schedule him for a meeting with a key partner in

Boston while he was supposed to be at a conference in Los Angeles. She'd probably last a few more days, which was all I needed.

"Great." I gave him my most dazzling smile. "Good workout this morning?"

"Not bad."

Why couldn't I ever think of anything smart to say around him? In my mind, I'd be Katharine Hepburn to his Spencer Tracy, and everyone around us would be stunned by our witty banter. Or we'd have at least one meaningful conversation. Like, ever. In reality, we were finalists in the Most Awkward Coworkers competition.

"Well." He shot a side-eye at Alicia before lifting his smoothie toward me in a toast. "See you later."

When he turned, I watched those khaki-wrapped legs and tight ass stride across the hall until he sat behind his desk. After seeing him in his workout gear this morning, it was easy to imagine what was underneath the business casual.

I grabbed my book and fanned myself while I gave in to a few seconds of fantasy: me walking into his office, Cooper pressing the button on the wall to lower the shades. Me crossing to where he sat in his chair, him pulling me into his lap. The firm press of—

Alicia cleared her throat. "Marlee, this crush isn't healthy. I think you're holding onto something even you don't believe in anymore."

I glanced around to ensure we were still alone. "I felt it from the first day I saw him. True love. And I still believe in that. You and Jackson are proof."

She chuckled. "It certainly wasn't true love the first time I met Jackson Jones. He hated everything I represented, and I thought he was an ass."

"Jackson isn't exactly love-at-first-sight material. He can be a little…" I searched for the right word to describe my boss. I adored him, but others, especially Weston, found him challenging.

"Arrogant? High-handed? Prickly?"

"And you love him despite all that. Cooper, on the other hand, is faultless." I stroked my pendant.

"I think you might be romanticizing him a little. He's a block of ice until he explodes with that temper."

"He'd never turn it on me." She didn't share my admiration for Cooper. She respected him professionally, and she was cordial toward him. Even though she'd told me she thought Cooper resented her for taking his best friend away from him. I thought she was full of shit. Cooper Fallon was perfect. My fantasy brought to life.

"Besides, he's bringing Jamila to the wedding."

I ground my teeth. "I know." I shoved my sandwich back into my vintage Barbie lunchbox and led Alicia out of the breakroom and over to my desk.

Jackson's door opened. After watching Mr. Weston saunter out and cross the floor toward his own corner office, we both leaned against the edge of my desk. I could almost feel the heat boiling out of Jackson's office from their exchange.

"I think I'll go back to Jamila's office," Alicia said. "I'll call to check on him later."

"Good idea. I'll try to free up an hour or so this afternoon so he can have a little one-on-one time in the gym with the punching bag."

"You're a lifesaver, Marlee."

"It's what I do. See you tomorrow for lunch?"

"Oh." Alicia's smile faltered. "Jamila's getting an innovation award at a luncheon tomorrow. I told Jackson I'd go with him."

"Is—is Cooper going?"

"He is." Her lips tightened briefly. "I'm so sorry to miss our last Friday lunch before the wedding."

I waved my hand like it didn't matter. "Don't worry about it. Of course you should go with Jackson. Call me if you need any bridesmaid services this weekend."

"There's always something. I can't wait for it all to be over." She pushed off my desk and walked toward the stairs.

I watched her go, the lightness I'd felt before dimming like a brown dwarf star. Although she didn't want the lavish society wedding Jackson's mother had planned, she was marrying her true love. And Tyler was right: married Alicia would have less and less time for me as her life became interlinked with Jackson's. And Jackson's best friend.

If Cooper and I got together, it'd be so easy to spend time with Alicia. I'd go with him to the innovators' award luncheons. We'd go on double dates. Couples' weekends at the beach. Maybe our kids would play together someday.

But not if he wanted Jamila instead.

Sinking into my chair, I shoved my lunchbox into the drawer with my purse.

At a deliberate-sounding squeak on the floor behind me, I turned to see Tyler carrying a white paper sack.

"What are you doing up here?"

He held out the bag. "I—I had a cookie left over from lunch."

"For me?"

"It's double-chocolate coconut macadamia."

"That's my favorite!" He grinned when I snatched the bag and peeked inside. "Want half? Wait. You're allergic." I'd been careful to stock my dish only with candies processed in nut-free facilities since I'd found out. I broke off a chunk and popped it into my mouth. A buttery, creamy nut melted on my tongue. Heaven. "Why'd you get this kind?"

He pushed his glasses up his nose. "Um…" His gaze flicked to the distinctive yellow response card on my board and then back to me. The next few words tumbled out in a rush. "Alicia mentioned you didn't have a date for the wedding yet. I'm going, and I thought maybe—maybe you'd like to ride up with me. We could, um, hang out. At the wedding." He tapped his middle finger against his thigh.

Hang out? At the wedding? As in, go with my work bestie as my date?

I sighed. It was my own fault that this was what my life had become.

But then I cocked my head, considering. Which would be sadder: going alone or going with my friend?

Unlike the rest of the developers, he saw me. Listened to me. He was thoughtful. Considerate. Fetched me beers at company parties when I was busy. Brought me cookies. I swallowed the last delicious, nutty morsel.

My eyes burned to look at Cooper to know if he was observing me—us—but I couldn't. No sound came from his office. When hope flickered in Tyler's hazel eyes, I hardened my stare. "As friends, right?" I couldn't allow any more-than-friends feelings to get in the way of my Cowgirl-Up-for-Cooper Plan.

"Oh, um, yeah. Friends."

Maybe Jackson was right, and seeing me with a date would be the push Cooper needed to start thinking about me as something other than an off-limits coworker. Would he feel jealous when I walked into the room with Tyler, laughing at something he'd said? No, *Tyler* would be laughing at something *I'd* said. And I'd look over at Cooper, and he'd wonder what I'd said that was funny, and he'd want to hear it, and he'd ask me to dance. Cooper's hand in mine. Magic.

"Then, yeah, okay."

He flashed me a smile that creased his cheek in a dimple. "Great." He exhaled a gust of air. "Can I—?" He pointed at the response card. I handed it to him. He pulled a pen out of the cup on my desk. "Steak, lobster, or vegetarian?"

"Lobster." Alicia's wedding to the scion of the San Francisco Joneses was no backyard barbecue.

He showed it to me. He'd checked the box and scrawled at the bottom, *Seat with Tyler Young.* Shoving it into his jeans pocket, he said, "I'll give it to Alicia."

I nodded just as Jackson emerged from his office.

"There you are, Tyler. Stop flirting with Marlee and come in here." Still cranky from Weston, apparently. Jackson turned on his heel and went back into his office.

Red-faced, Tyler shrugged and hustled after him.

I straightened my necklace. My plan to woo Cooper wasn't derailed after all. In fact, it was just getting started.

6

AS THE HOURS before the wedding weekend ticked by, Cooper seemed…off.

Through the open door of his office, I watched him frown at his computer screen without touching the keyboard or mouse. His phone had rung several times, but he hadn't picked it up. Kim, the clueless temp, kept sending the calls anyway.

An anticipatory silence covered the sixth floor. The day before, Alicia and Jackson had left for the vineyard to finish the preparations on site. None of the other executives had come in; they were turning the wedding festivities into a three-day weekend. And the support staff were waiting for the clock to tick to noon to call it a day.

I'd made my own plan, written it in Sharpie on a piece of lined steno paper. I didn't bother to open my drawer to reread it since I'd memorized the simple list.

1. *Dance with Cooper at the wedding.*
2. *Act as Cooper's assistant during Jackson's honeymoon. Work late. Bond over takeout.*
3. *Kiss Cooper Fallon.*

Small, simple milestones, just as Alicia, the most organized person I knew, recommended. It started with a touch—I'd borrowed that from my parents' story—and it ended with a kiss. The camera focus would soften, the violins would soar, woodland creatures would congregate to serenade us. Okay, maybe not that, but it'd be a True Love's Kiss. Complete with sparks.

And then we'd live happily ever after.

His line rang. Again. Before the temp could pick it up and send it to Cooper, still frozen at his desk, I answered.

"Cooper Fallon's office. Marlee Rice speaking."

"Oh, Marlee, thank God. I didn't think I was ever going to get through. It's Jamila. Can you have him call me when he has a minute? I'm having a small crisis here." She chuckled, like she ate crises for breakfast.

I wished I hadn't picked up.

Then again, maybe the crisis was that she couldn't go to the wedding after all. Leaving Cooper date-free.

"Sure thing." After I hung up, I walked to Cooper's door. "Hey. You okay?"

He startled, actually jumped in his chair. "Shit, what time is it?"

"Don't worry, it's not even noon. But are you all right? You seem...distracted."

He blinked at me. "I'm fine."

"Nothing you want to talk about?"

"I'm good." The hard lines of his face softened. "Really."

I bit my lip. *Something* was bothering him. If only he'd tell me. I wished I could ask him about Jamila. But the question stuck in my throat.

"How are you?" he asked. "Ready for this weekend?"

You bet I am. "I don't have to do anything hard. Just smooth out the back of her dress at the start of the ceremony."

"And make sure she shows up." He glanced out the window as he chuckled.

"I don't think there's any danger of a runaway bride. Or

groom. They're soul mates." I sighed. "Just like my mother and dad."

"How is Will? Is he coming?"

"No, I thought a full weekend would be too much for Dad." Though he was doing better lately. Maybe he'd just messed up his meds that day he'd tried to climb the ladder.

"Too bad. I always enjoy talking to him about physics."

"And he loves talking to you." Two weeks ago, when I'd brought Dad to Jackson and Alicia's wedding shower, I'd found Dad and Cooper talking about quantum mechanics. Cooper hadn't blinked an eye when Dad couldn't come up with the term *Feynman diagram*; he'd just supplied it and kept chatting about bosons. And that was when I knew it was time to finally act on my crush. Not many men would accept a partner who came as a package deal with Dad and his health issues. But I knew Cooper would.

His phone vibrated on his desk. But he didn't reach for it right away. "Something you needed, Marlee?"

Oh. Right. "Jamila called. She asked that you call her back. Something about a crisis. A small one," I rushed to add as his eyebrows crashed together.

"Thanks."

I'd already turned to go when his voice stopped me. "You'll save me a dance at the wedding? First one after our toast?"

A joyful spark ran through me. *Play it cool.* Not even turning around, I said, as airily as I could manage, "Sure."

I may have put an extra swing in my hips as I returned to my desk. It didn't even bother me when his line lit and I knew he was calling Jamila. He'd asked me to dance. Step One was queued up.

I skimmed through the emails in Jackson's inbox, flagged a few for his response, and let the senders know he'd be away for the next three weeks. Fiji. Alicia had shown me pictures of turquoise water and sugar-sand beaches. Maybe someday Cooper would take me to that Caribbean hideaway he escaped to whenever he had the time.

His door opened and he emerged, the color back in his cheeks and a secret smile teasing at the corners of his mouth. His laptop bag hung from his shoulder.

"Heading out?" I asked, unnecessarily.

"Jamila asked me to stop by her place and pick something up, but we'll be leaving soon." He tipped his chin at my suitcase and dress bag. "Need a ride?"

My pasted-on smile wanted to turn over. He had a key to Jamila's home. He was familiar enough with it that he could locate her forgotten item. And he'd just asked me to be their third wheel. An image flashed into my mind of sitting not in the front seat but in the back of Cooper's Tesla while they talked and laughed until they remembered me and Jamila turned, pity in her eyes, to include me in the conversation.

The door to the stairwell thunked shut just before I heard the deliberate drag of a sneaker on the hardwood behind me.

"Hey, Marlee. Cooper." Tyler waited until I turned my attention to him. "Ready to go?" Instead of his usual T-shirt, he wore a white button-down with his jeans. The sleeves, rolled to the elbow, showed tanned skin and a dusting of golden hair.

My heart skipped at the sight of my savior from third-wheeldom.

"Yep." I faced Cooper, my smile no longer pasted-on but real. "Tyler's my ride."

"Oh?" His eyebrows arched up, and he looked between us.

I stood and plucked the hanging bag from the hook behind my desk. Tyler pulled up the handle of my roller bag.

"Wait!" I scurried to the kitchen and returned with a cold can of Mountain Dew I'd stashed in the fridge. I handed it to Tyler. "For the ride."

His smile broadened. "Thanks."

Tyler pulled my emasculatingly pink suitcase behind him to the elevator. The elevator doors opened, and we stepped inside. Tyler put a hand in front of the door. "Going down?"

Cooper frowned. "I'll catch the next one."

From inside the elevator, I glimpsed Cooper watching us, his brow lined and his lower lip caught between his teeth. As the door closed, he called, "Don't forget our dance."

A giddy shiver ran across my skin.

Then I looked at Tyler out of the corner of my eye. A mirror of Cooper's frown creased his face for a second before he turned to me. His posture was easy, but his knuckles on my suitcase were white. "You ready for this?"

"Am I ever." The countdown was complete, and my plan was a go for launch.

7

TYLER STARED straight ahead at the closed elevator doors. "You're into Cooper, aren't you?"

My face heated. "What? No. We work together, that's all." Only Alicia and Jackson knew about my crush. As Jackson's right hand, I had to protect a certain image, and I'd rather my coworkers didn't know about my less-than-professional feelings.

But, damn him, Tyler knew. "No, you *like* him." He grimaced. "I can see how you…you look at him. The way you did just now."

"It's just a crush." I fiddled with the zipper on my purse. "He doesn't even know. Or he pretends not to."

His voice was gentle when he spoke again. "Hey, we're friends, right?"

I faced him. He smiled when my gaze met his, but I couldn't tell if it was sadness or pity that drew down the corners of his eyes. "Yes. Friends."

He nodded. "Friends help each other out. Would you like me to help you?"

"Help me?"

"You know, act like we're…more than friends. Draw Cooper's attention to you. Make him see you the way I—the way everyone else does." One finger tapped against my pink suitcase handle.

"You mean we pretend we're *together*-together and try to make him jealous?" Was that the push Cooper needed? He was competitive; that I knew. I couldn't read Tyler's profile. Did he really mean it?

"Yeah."

"Really? You'd do that for me?"

His voice was tight. "I said I would."

If he didn't mind pretending this weekend, how could I turn down his offer? "Okay."

Another quick glance at me. "Okay?"

"Let's do it," I said. Maybe he and I could dance to the Beatles' "With a Little Help from My Friends."

"We should have a code name."

"A code name?"

"You know, if we need to say something and there are other people around. Same as for software projects."

"Oh. I'd been thinking of it as the Cowgirl-Up-for-Cooper Plan."

He wrinkled his nose. "How about Operation...Operation Prince Charming?"

I squeed and hugged myself. If it weren't for the camera in the elevator, I'd have kissed his cheek. "That's perfect! And thanks, really. I hope it's not too uncomfortable for you. You know, pretending to be my guy."

One side of his mouth quirked up. "I'll manage."

THE INN, with its backdrop of acres of neat rows of grapevines, looked just like the brochure Alicia and I had pored over together.

"Wow." Tyler leaned against the side of his Mustang and took it all in. She must not have shown him the brochures.

The two-hour trip to the vineyard had flown by with road-trip games. We'd played the singing game—Tyler knew *way* too many emo song lyrics; the movie game—I'd crushed him since I knew every romantic comedy ever made; and the classic alphabet game. I'd been almost disappointed at our turn-off to the wedding venue. But we were here now, and Operation Prince Charming was a go.

"I know, isn't it elegant?" I walked around the hood to stand beside him.

The two-story building's white stucco walls were broken by arched doorways and windows that revealed a wraparound porch with glossy red Adirondack chairs. Guests relaxed with glasses of wine, and a couple of waiters moved among them. Late-summer flowers in scarlet, lemon, and sunset-orange spilled from pots set in the windows and doorways.

"Jay's putting up everyone, not just me, right?" He popped the trunk.

"Uh-huh." Jackson had booked a nearby hotel for regular guests like Tyler, and the wedding party was staying at the vineyard's onsite inn. I pulled my dress bag off the top of the suitcases.

He walked up the steps and held the door for me. That was Tyler, my old-fashioned, southern gentleman. He held doors even when he wasn't pretending to be my date.

When my eyes adjusted from the dazzling sunlight outside to the darker interior, I saw something that made me extra thankful Tyler was there behind me.

Jamila Jallow spun to face us at the rumble of my suitcase's wheels on the tile floor. "Marlee Rice," she said, smiling, "it's good to see you again. Your style is to die for. I love your shoes."

"Thanks." They were just knockoff Manolo Blahnik pumps in petal pink. Nothing as fabulous as her spangled Jimmy Choos.

Cooper strolled up to stand at her side. I wished I knew if the key he handed Jamila matched his own or if they had separate rooms.

"Hi, Marlee. Tyler." He shook our hands. "Mila, this is Tyler Young, one of our developers. I won't tell you how talented he is. I wouldn't want you trying to poach him from us."

Her laugh was loud and brash. "Even I wouldn't try to steal one of Jackson's favorite programmers at his wedding." She clutched Cooper's arm. I wished I could have done that.

Tyler shook Jamila's hand. "It's an honor to meet you, Ms. Jallow. I read your blog post last week. Your ideas about machine learning are inspirational. I'd love to talk with you about it sometime."

"Please, it's Jamila or Mila. Cooper, look the other way." She slipped a card out of her tiny designer shoulder bag and handed it to Tyler. "In case we don't get to talk this weekend, call me and we'll set something up."

Tyler was making the same fanboy face he did in Jackson's presence. And why wouldn't he? She was brilliant, elegant, poised, funny, and too damned nice. I wanted to hate her, but I couldn't.

Cooper touched her arm, sparking a flame of jealousy in my heart. "Hands off Jackson's protégé. Come on, let's go get a drink before the rehearsal."

A look passed between them, and then she smiled at us. "See you later." They turned toward the stairs. No couple could be more opposite in appearance: Cooper's blond highlights, lightly tanned skin, and icy blue eyes contrasted with Jamila's ebony hair, dark skin, and deep, almost-black eyes. But they fit together, their regal self-assurance, their years of friendship binding them in ways I'd never experienced. They were perfect for each other. And I remained outside their bubble of shared history, of longstanding friendship, of privilege earned through intelligence and success. Why would Cooper choose me, the poor "before" version of Cinderella, over Jamila's glamour?

Tyler nudged me. His smile seemed forced. "Let's check you in."

"Oh. Right." I was here for Alicia, and I needed to dress for the rehearsal. Even if watching Cooper with Jamila made me want to hide in my room all weekend.

After I checked in, Tyler carried my bags up to my room. He

set my suitcase just inside the door before turning to go. The thought of watching Jamila with Cooper at the rehearsal—or worse, sitting at the dinner alone—sent a chill through me.

"I'll see you at the rehearsal dinner, right?" My voice was higher-pitched than I wanted it to be.

"Of course." His face was cautiously blank. "Unless you don't want to—"

"No!" I held out a hand. "We're friends, right?"

He clasped my hand in his larger one, his long fingers wrapping around the back. His warm, comforting grasp eased the tension that had constricted my ribs since our encounter with Cooper and Jamila.

His dimples made an appearance. "Friends. And wedding dates. And drinking buddies, right?"

"It *is* a winery."

"I think we're going to need a lot of wine to get us through this."

"What, you mean pretending?"

That expression he made sometimes crossed his face. I hadn't figured it out yet. A tightening of the eyes and mouth, almost like pain. But it was gone in a second, and his words didn't match it. "Nah, that'll be easy. I'm just worried about Jay's family. Alicia says they can be a lot."

"Aw. You're so sweet to worry about Alicia. She'll be fine. And we will, too. Like you said, the wine will get us through."

"Isn't that from 'You and Me Against the World' by Helen Reddy?"

"That's one of my dad's favorites. I thought you only knew emo alt-rock music. But I believe she said it was memories that'd get us through."

"Memories, wine, friends. It's all good."

That grin. Those dimples. Yeah, we'd make it through. Even if Cooper was with Jamila, a weekend with my buddy Tyler was going to be a blast.

8

MY VISION BLURRED. Living with Dad during college, I hadn't played too many drinking games. All I knew was I didn't understand this one, and I'd already lost.

"Jasmine."

"Nectarines."

"Petroleum," Tyler said with a confident smile.

"Show-off," Jamila said.

I sniffed my glass. Wine. I knew if I tasted it, it'd taste like… wine. Though I might've burned my taste buds off with everything I'd already drunk. I shoved the glass to the far side of my dessert plate. Shit, was that where it belonged? I stole a look at Jamila's place setting. She'd set her wineglass on the other side of her water goblet. I corrected my mistake. The rehearsal dinner with all of its fancy forks and glasses was way out of my league.

"How'd you learn about wine?" Jamila asked him. "Your parents?"

"No." He chuckled. "My family is more Shiner Bock than Riesling."

She set down her glass and leaned forward. "Texas?"

"Dallas, born and bred."

"You're far from home, cowboy. Do you miss it?"

"Nah. I love it here. The opportunities. Plus, home was always a little crowded."

"Tyler comes from a large family. Four brothers and a sister," Cooper said. "Most of them were college athletes, and one is a pro baseball player." Cooper could do that, pull up interesting facts about almost anyone at Synergy. He cared so much about the company. So thoughtful and generous.

But when I turned to Tyler, he wasn't glowing with admiration like I was. He took his glasses off and inspected them, his lips in a tight line.

"Which team?" Jamila apparently hadn't noticed that Tyler's happy bubble had burst.

"Minnesota," he said.

"Mom and Dad must be so proud."

More tension crept into his jaw. "They are. Though they'd be happier if he played closer to home."

"They just missed the playoffs this year," was Jackson's brother Andrew's addition to the conversation.

Jackson's sister Sam dragged up a chair and plopped into it. "Sammy!" Andrew turned to her. "You escaped Bachelor Number Twenty-Two?"

"Why would she think I'd hit it off with a banker?" She tugged her skirt to cover her knees.

"Because she's tried entrepreneurs, CEOs, CIOs, CTOs, even a couple of trust-funders. She's getting desperate."

"I'm only twenty-four. And maybe I'm not interested in part-nering up. Now or ever. I introduced him to Nat and snuck off." She waved her hand across the room where, sure enough, the youngest Jones chatted up a cute guy in an expensive-looking suit.

Huh. I knew there were women like that—Alicia said before she'd met Jackson, she'd been one of them—but it was hard for me to imagine not wanting true love, the kind that made you feel sparks when you touched, the kind that made your toes curl when you kissed.

"You know Mother. She's always looking to expand the Jones empire, either organically"—Andrew nodded at Alicia at the next table, resting a hand on her belly—"or through acquisition. Besides, what's the harm? Maybe one of them will be a hidden gem."

She rolled her eyes. "The only gem I'm interested in is the Ruby programming language. Our mother can keep her white knights and Prince Charmings."

I jumped when Tyler whispered in my ear. "I think that's our cue."

"Our cue?"

He stood and hauled me up by our joined hands. I wobbled and sagged into his side. Whoa. I was more unbalanced than I'd thought. *Stupid wine.*

"I need to put Marlee to bed." And he actually waggled his eyebrows in Cooper's direction. "Big day tomorrow."

I glanced at Cooper. His own heavy eyebrows arched. "Goodnight. See you tomorrow."

Damn. Aside from the eyebrow-arch, he was unfazed.

As we turned away, Tyler whispered in my ear, "Okay if I touch your hip?"

Was this part of the fake date? Or was he being my friend and keeping me from falling? Everything had blurred at the edges. "Um…okay."

His hand slid from my shoulder to the small of my back, where he paused. The alcohol must have screwed with my nerve endings because a tingly trail of sparks followed his hand to where it came to rest on the upper swell of my ass. He guided me between the tables toward the door as if he touched me like that every day.

"Okay?" he murmured in my ear, his warm breath making goose bumps pop up on my neck.

"That's not my hip," I whispered.

He looked back over his shoulder. "I think it worked, though. He's staring at your ass."

Probably because it was glowing from the tingles Tyler's touch had created. It had been too long—three years—since I'd let anyone get this close.

The whole situation was weird. I'd gone out with guy friends before, including Tyler. Baseball games, bars, even a fancy-dress fundraiser with Jackson once. But I'd never fake-dated anyone. Were we doing it right? It felt right—physically—since my skin did a happy dance whenever Tyler touched me. But deeper inside, past my tingling nerve endings, it felt wrong. Even if it worked and Cooper told me he and Jamila were only friends and he could love me, would I come to regret the lie I'd told to push him along?

When the restaurant door shut behind us, I stepped away. Or tried to. When I left the safety of Tyler's support, I bumped up against the wall. He reached for me but stopped when I held up a hand and remained standing, propped up by the wall.

"Thanks," I said. "I'm good." Holding on to the rail, I trapped my tongue between my teeth and picked my way up the stairs. *Stupid wine. Stupid heels.*

I managed to stay upright and crossed the tasting room to the door, which he opened for me with a flourish. Outside, I took a deep gulp of the fresh night air to sober up. It didn't work. Without Tyler's support or my new best friend, the wall, the horizon tipped and I wobbled in my heels.

"Gotta sit." Not caring about dirt on my consignment-store dress, I sank to the top step of the porch.

"You okay?" The step shook when Tyler flopped down on it.

"I'm more of a beer girl. That wine went straight to my head." I looked up at the stars to ground myself and spotted Pegasus. Its diamond shape reminded me of something we'd talked about earlier.

"So your brother's a pro baseball player? Why didn't I know that?"

I turned my gaze away from the sky just in time to see his jaw harden. "I don't talk about my family a lot."

"Oh." I rubbed his arm. "Sorry I brought it up. Did you play a sport, too?"

He leaned into my touch. "Nah. I mean, I liked playing with my brothers. And on my high-school teams. But once I started programming, I knew that was it for me. Getting a job at Synergy, working with Jay, that was a dream come true. My version of the Olympics."

"I'm sure your family is proud of you, too. You're a star programmer at a fast-growing company. You've done well for yourself."

One corner of his mouth tightened. "It's not easy being the geek in a family of athletes. Sports are a lot easier to understand than software." He sipped his wine. "Didn't help that I told my brother to finish his degree before going into the draft."

Oh.

Sure, Dad nagged at me for not reaching my potential, but he'd never compared me to anyone else. He'd have supported me even if I'd had a superstar sibling. And he'd ridden me hard to finish my degree, even after Jackson had hired me.

"*I* understand software. And I know you're killing it at Synergy. Do you think you'll stay for a while?" Programmers in the Bay Area tended to be transient, scrambling up the salary ladder.

"Yeah. I can't imagine wanting to leave."

"Good. I still think you should apply for that manager position."

He ducked his head. "I don't know. I've got a lot more to learn about software before I start telling other people what to do. But what about you? Ever thought about coming to join us on the fourth floor?"

Of course I had. But programming in an official capacity meant less flexible hours. "Can't. Gotta get home to Dad."

"Why's that?"

Shit. I sucked in the cool night air to make my brain work better. I hadn't meant to tell Tyler about Dad's problems. When I told friends I needed to care for him, they never believed me. Even if they met him on one of his bad days, they asked me why he was my problem, why he couldn't live in a nursing home. Regardless, they thought I was making excuses and stopped inviting me out. No one understood. Except for Alicia, who had her own nephew to care for. So far, Tyler had been persistent. He kept asking me to happy hours and softball leagues and parties. But maybe if I told him about my home life, he'd give up on me, too. And I wanted to hold on to Tyler. Especially with Alicia's life changing.

"Oh, you know, he gets lonely all day at home. If I don't go home on time, he might start watching cable news. And then I'd have to start caring about politics."

Tyler chuckled. "Can't have that."

Crisis averted. I stood. "Walk me back to the inn?"

He cast an assessing glance over me that sent shivers down my neck.

I whacked his arm. "I didn't mean it like *that*, you—you. I'm not sure I can make it back without twisting an ankle."

"Of course, Lady Rice." He rose to his feet and gave me a mock bow and another flourish with his arm while he cocked his elbow for me. I slipped my hand through and squeezed his biceps. His rock-hard biceps.

The night was clear with a waning gibbous moon to light the path back to the inn. A cool breeze sighed through the vineyard to our right, stirring up the sweet aroma of fallen grapes that'd missed the harvest. Tyler's mass and warmth protected me from the chill I hadn't anticipated when I'd left the inn earlier in my thin dress.

The lights of the inn glowed ahead of us. How did one end a fake date? With a fake kiss? Or a real one? My brain, sticky with wine, stalled on the question. What would his lips feel like on mine? Would there be a spark like when he'd touched my ass?

I bit the inside of my cheek to focus. No, this was Tyler. There would be no kissing. Or any more wine to jumble up my thoughts.

At last, we reached the inn's porch.

"Well, this is me," I said, releasing his arm and leaning on the stair rail for support.

He shoved his hands into his pockets. "Do you need me to walk you to your room?"

"No." I jutted out my chin and, as proof, let go of the rail. Surprising even myself, I remained upright. "Thank you."

"Just asking." In the lamplight, Tyler's pupils had all but consumed the hazel irises.

"You won't try to drive back to your hotel, will you?"

"Nah, I'll get a ride with someone. Don't worry about me." He looked down at his Vans.

Now I was sorry I'd been so curt. We'd had fun, and it hadn't been awkward...until now. And that was my fault. "Friends worry about each other. So be safe tonight. I wouldn't want anything to happen to my wedding date."

That made him look up and grin. "See you tomorrow, wedding date."

I couldn't help smiling back. "Good night, wedding date."

"Drink some water," was the last thing I heard as I climbed the steps, clinging to the rail.

9

FOUR HUNDRED PAIRS of eyes watched us where we stood on the stage in the reception hall, me in my strawflower-yellow bridesmaid gown and Cooper looking good enough to lick in his tux. Despite his years of practice speaking in front of audiences, Cooper's smile looked forced, frozen. Maybe he was feeling the aftereffects of last night's wine, too.

I gave him an encouraging smile and murmured, "We've got this."

Tiannah, sitting next to Alicia at the head table, and Andrew, on Jackson's other side, had already given their toasts. Now, it was our turn, the moment I'd been planning for weeks.

Raising my glass of ginger ale, I leaned into the microphone. "We're here tonight to celebrate the marriage of Alicia and Jackson with the help of so many family and friends, including the entire Synergy board." I gestured to the table of VIPs to my left and paused for the polite applause.

"And *we're*"—Cooper laid an arm casually around my shoulders, making my stomach flip—"here as Jay's oldest friend—"

"—and Alicia's newest friend." I grinned at her. The poor thing was surrounded by Jackson's intimidatingly wealthy family and San Francisco's tech elite, and she couldn't even loosen up with champagne. But the stress of an unexpected pregnancy, a new city, and a new family that lived their lives in the business magazines didn't weigh her down tonight. She practically floated with bliss at being joined with her soul mate.

"I've known Jay since we were college roommates. Through Jay, I've developed an appreciation for European sportscars"— Cooper paused for the burst of laughter from the crowd—"and because of me, Jay knows every word of *Casablanca*. Together, we built Jay's idea into a Fortune 1,000 company with offices around the world. And of all the software companies in all the towns in all the world, Alicia walks into Jay's." He paused again for the guests' appreciative chuckle. "While it was highly inappropriate for him to fall for a consultant—"

"—it was also incredibly romantic," I said. "When I saw them together for the first time, I knew they were smitten."

"Jay's not known for his focus," Cooper said. "I think the only thing that got him through freshman English was my pantomimed summaries of the books he wouldn't read."

Jackson called out, "You should've seen him do *The Kite Runner*."

Cooper's smile was fond as he turned back to the crowd. "But since he met Alicia, he's shown new dedication. Last year, he and Alicia led our team to the most successful product launch in the history of Synergy." Cheers erupted from the tables of Synergy employees and from the board. The stock price had risen by twenty-five percent over the past nine months. "Alicia's the only person I've ever met who can keep Jay in line. I know I never could."

"Like every couple, they've had their ups and downs," I said, "but I've never seen two people more in love, not since my own mother and dad. So I couldn't be happier that my boss has met such an excellent partner, and that my friend has found the love of her life. Let's all raise our glasses to many years of happiness to come."

Cooper said, "Here's looking at you, kids."

The guests all raised their glasses in the toast, Jackson and Alicia kissed, and the buzz of conversation resumed.

When we stepped off the stage, I turned to Cooper, lifted to my tiptoes, and hugged him, trying to make it seem spontaneous even though I'd been planning it for days. "Thanks so much, Cooper. I couldn't have done it without you," I whispered in his ear. Sweet Ada Lovelace, he smelled good. Spearmint and champagne and romance-hero perfection. After a too-long hug, I reluctantly lowered to my heels and stepped away from him.

The singer stepped up to the microphone, the band started to play, and Jackson twirled Alicia onto the dance floor.

"They look so happy." I'd never seen Jackson so relaxed, so content. Alicia was like the music in his headphones, calming him, focusing him. Could I be that for Cooper? Someday, would the little frown line between his eyebrows smooth out when I was near?

Not tonight. The furrow was deep when he said, "Do you think so? I think he looks…tired."

"No! Well, maybe a little." Alicia was the one who looked tired. I'd seen her before the stylist had covered up the dark shadows under her eyes. "They've worked hard to put this together and to wrap up work so they can get away to Fiji."

"And I'm the one who'll have to pick up the slack while he's gone," he grumbled.

Ah. *That* was what was making him so cranky.

"I'll help you while he's away." All part of the plan. "Isn't it worth it to see them so happy?"

Tyler walked up to us, and I grabbed his arm to pull him closer. "Tyler, don't you think they look happy?"

"Happiest I've ever seen them." He lifted his glass of champagne. "May we all marry the loves of our lives." In the light over the dance floor, the green edged out the other colors in his hazel eyes.

"Hear, hear." I stole a glance at Cooper. His glass dangled from his fingers at his side, and he frowned at the couple.

The song ended, and while everyone around clapped, Alicia and Jackson beckoned to us to join them on the dance floor.

Tyler touched my arm. "Shall we, wedding date?"

"Oh. I, um." The regret on my face was real. I'd much rather have stayed and talked with Tyler, who actually seemed to be enjoying himself, than with cranky Cooper. But it was step two of the plan. "This is my dance with Cooper."

For a moment, the corners of Tyler's mouth tightened, but then his expression cleared into his regular genial one. "Fine. But remember, Fallon, Marlee's my date tonight."

The tips of my fingers tingled. Tyler was *good* at this fake-date thing.

Apparently, I was not. I shook out my fingers.

When Cooper held out his hand, I took it and followed him to the middle of the floor. He raised our clasped hands and put his other hand on my back. On my bare back above my low-cut satin gown. His eyes widened as he slid his hand lower, finally finding fabric at the dip in my back, just above where Tyler's hand had grazed my ass last night. Under the weight of his hand, the thin fabric clung to my sweat-damp skin. That probably explained why I wasn't erupting in the same shivers I'd had last night when Tyler had touched me there.

"Wouldn't want to make your date jealous, would we?"

I forced a laugh. Ugh. The irony.

"I suppose tonight is not the time to warn you about the challenges of dating a coworker." His eyes were fixed on Alicia and Jackson.

I tilted up my chin. "It worked out fine for them. They're happier than a pair of heliophysicists during a solar eclipse."

"Right." He looked down at me. "I'm telling you this because I care about you, Marlee."

"You—you do?" I held my breath and waited. Could he be about to tell me he had feelings for me?

"Like an older brother."

Shit. Well, I could work with that. "Jackson's like my brother.

You're like my brother's best friend." One of my favorite romantic tropes. And if the heroine was persistent, the brother's friend always fell in love with her at the end.

Clearly, Cooper hadn't read any brother's-best-friend romances. "Anyway, if something were to…to happen between you and Tyler, it would be difficult—uncomfortable—for you to see him at work every day. It would hurt to be that close to him and know you can never be with him."

My feet stopped moving. Was he warning me about coworker relationships because that's what was holding *him* back? Had he avoided starting something with me because he was afraid of the work fallout? Was Jamila only a distraction for him? My heart— every organ in my body—filled with promise. "I'd hold out hope. That we could work it out and be together. Someday."

His ice-blue eyes melted a little at that. "That's what I love about you, Marlee. You're a ray of sunlight in dark times. Thank you." He leaned in to kiss my cheek. I held in a squeal. He'd said "love" and kissed me, even though his lips were cold and wooden.

The song ended, and I tore myself away from him to clap for the band. My head whirled, and I couldn't feel my feet. I floated back to Tyler at the edge of the dance floor.

"Thanks, Tyler, for indulging me. And thank you, Marlee." Cooper nodded, almost a princely bow.

Tyler laid a possessive hand on the bare skin of my lower back —*zing!*—and kissed my cheek. The other one, not the one Cooper had just kissed, and closer to my mouth so my own lips buzzed with anticipation. The tenderness in that brief touch made me melt. Cooper could learn a thing or two.

"Great job on the toast, by the way. Everyone's talking about it," Tyler said. He pulled me into his side and looked back at Cooper, eyebrows raised, in just the right balance of friendly and *hands-off-my-girl*.

"Thanks," I said. "We work well together, don't you think, Cooper?"

Cooper's eyes lingered on Tyler's hand on my hip. "Hmm. I need to find Jamila. And a drink. Have fun." He turned and stalked toward the bar.

That hadn't ended so well.

Tyler massaged a circle on my lower back. "You looked like you had a moment out there." He nodded toward the dance floor.

My dance buzz faded. "I don't know. He called me a 'ray of sunshine.' What do you think that means?"

Tyler eased his stiff posture. "I think it means you look fantastic in that dress. With your hair up, you look like, um…that princess—my sister had a doll who wore a big yellow dress."

"Belle? From *Beauty and the Beast?*"

"That's the one."

"Aw. You're the sweetest wedding date ever." I hugged him.

He pulled away. "Sweet?"

"Definitely."

"No guy wants to be called sweet. Or nice."

"But you're both of those."

He rolled his eyes up to the spotlights over the stage. "Dance with me?"

"Sure."

Just before we stepped onto the dance floor, I spotted gangly, eleven-year-old Noah sitting alone at a table. His grandmothers had joined the dancing: Alicia's mother with Jackson, and her stepmother with Alicia. There were plenty of other kids at the wedding—a bunch of young Jones cousins—but they clustered around the cake table, leaving Noah by himself. The evening must have been strange for Noah, marking the official transition for him and Alicia into the Jones family, and my heart ached for the kid who'd undergone so much change in the past year. And who'd lost his mother, same as me. I stopped next to Noah, pulling Tyler to a halt.

"Hey, Noah," I said. "Tyler and I are going to dance. Want to come with?"

His ears turned pink, and he shook his head, making the long dark-blond strands fly over his face. "No, thanks." Noah, Alicia had told me, had had a tiny crush on me since I'd been his babysitter a few months ago.

Tyler squatted down in front of him. He spoke softly, but I heard him say, "Look, my friend, when a pretty girl asks you to dance, you say yes. She might not ask you again."

Noah gulped and nodded, his eyes wide. I stretched out my hand to him, and he took it and followed us onto the dance floor, where the band played a poppy '60s tune. Tyler launched into a ridiculous frat-boy shimmy, and Noah and I giggled and bopped along.

While we danced, my eyes landed on Alicia and Jackson, who'd partnered up again, slowly swaying out of time with the fast song. They reminded me of my parents' wedding photo. Their wedding hadn't been opulent at all, but the expressions on their faces were so similar to my friends'. Pure love shone out of Alicia's blue eyes as she looked at her husband. I full-body sighed.

A few songs later, I was sweaty and my hair was starting to escape its sprayed-stiff updo when the band transitioned to "Something" by the Beatles. Alicia approached and asked Noah, "Hey, buddy. Dance with me?"

"Sure." Alicia grinned her thanks at me over his head as they twirled away.

Tyler moved closer and grasped my right hand. He hesitated for a moment and then slid his arm along my back, pulling me in until only a few inches separated us. "Okay?" he asked.

"Fine." But it was more than fine. Tyler was just as warm as I was, and his white collared shirt, unbuttoned at the neck, stuck to his skin. The scent of his cologne—cedar and citrus—bloomed at close range. I looked up into his eyes, a kaleidoscope of emerald, amber, and sapphire. A hint of stubble softened his strong jaw. When the lights from the bandstand struck his face, his good looks hit me like a dodgeball in my gut. I'd never really *looked* at him before. Certainly not from this close.

"Mmm-hmm."

"What's that?" he asked.

"I was just agreeing with you."

"I didn't say anything."

"Oh." If I'd been drinking, I'd have blamed the wine. Then I noticed we'd closed the few inches between our bodies, and the yellow silk covering my breasts pressed right against the thin cotton of his shirt.

Tyler looked over my shoulder. "Get ready for phase two."

"What?"

"Operation Prince Charming. Phase one was dancing." He led us into a quarter-turn and took a deep breath. "Ready?"

"For wha—"

He kissed me.

And the world stopped.

I mean, the world kept going around us, and the singer crooned, "Don't want to leave her now," and the other couples kept swaying, and the colored lights zoomed. But for me, everything faded except the soft touch of Tyler's lips on mine and his arms holding me up on that dance floor. It could have been five seconds or five minutes or five hours because time ended while my eyes closed and our lips met.

At last, he eased away, and I opened my eyes. My right hand was tangled in the hair at the back of his head, and he stared down into my face. His chest heaved like he'd run up a flight of stairs. Or maybe it was my chest heaving.

Then his eyes flicked to my right, where Cooper watched us over Jamila's shoulder.

10

AS TYLER and I rotated in the center of the dance floor, perspiration dampened my forehead and my feet ached, but I couldn't remember the last time I'd felt more like the star of a Rodgers and Hammerstein musical. If I could've carried a tune, I'd have burst into song.

Dad never had money or time to send me to dance classes, but he'd rolled up the living-room rug and taught me the basics to Anne Murray's "Could I Have this Dance." As much as I fantasized about being a princess at a ball, I'd have required Mia Thermopolis–level lessons from Julie Andrews to get me there. But that night, Tyler was my own Fred Astaire, twirling me around like I was Ginger Rogers.

The band lurched into Elvis Presley's "Can't Help Falling in Love," and Tyler spun me out and back against him. My gauzy yellow skirt flared around my ankles and twisted up in his pants legs.

"Are you some kind of wedding gigolo?" I asked him.

"What?" He shot me a puzzled smile as he deftly dodged a whirling pair of flower girls.

"Do they hire you to dance with the bridesmaids and spinster aunts?"

Tyler hummed and led me into the spotlight in the center of the floor.

"You're a fabulous dancer. I'm a terrible dancer, and you've made me look good all night."

"You already looked good." He spun us into a fast turn. "I just made you look graceful."

I snorted. Gracefully.

"My mom," he said.

"What?"

"My mother taught all of us boys to dance. She said she didn't want us to embarrass her at the school mother-son dance."

I imagined Tyler and four lookalike brothers dressed in suits and lined up like a buffet. Tasty. But still—"Your poor mother."

"We were better at blocking and tackling than the foxtrot, but we did okay."

When the song ended and the singer announced a fifteen-minute break, my dance high evaporated, making my feet throb in my spindly sandals.

"Gotta sit down," I groaned.

"Oh. Right. Sorry." Tyler held out an arm for me to lean on and led me to a table.

"No reason to be sorry." I sank into a chair. "I can't remember ever having such a good time at a wedding."

He grinned. "Water or champagne?"

"Water, please."

"Be right back."

I watched him walk to the bar. His dress shirt clung to his skin, wrinkled where my sweaty palm had gripped his shoulder. His face was flushed, but he smiled, his posture relaxed and easy. Until Cooper walked up behind him and said something. Tyler spun around.

My phone vibrated in my dress pocket, and I pulled it out and thumbed open my text app.

```
Dad: Going to bed. Hope you're having a good
time at the party.
```

```
    Me: I am. Good night. I'll call you tomorrow
                                            morning.
```

Even the throbbing in my feet lessened. Dad had done great this weekend. All those little slip-ups he'd had over the past few weeks were perfectly normal parts of the aging process. And here I was, at my friends' wedding, dancing like any other twenty-five-year-old, not sitting at home like some friendless shut-in.

"Fantastic party." Jamila Jallow eased into the chair across from me, pulling my attention from my phone. Her form-fitting magenta gown showed no wrinkles, and only the gleam of her skin hinted that she'd danced almost as much as I had.

"It's like a fairy-tale ball." With my feet, I scrabbled under my chair for my sandals. I found them and poked my toes in. I couldn't talk to elegant Jamila while barefoot.

She leaned back in the chair, hooking her arm over the back-rest. "I like you, Marlee. And from what Cooper says, you're smart as a whip."

"Thank you." I sat up taller.

"Can I be straight with you? One professional woman to another?"

I blinked. Jamila Jallow, CEO of her own company and all-around superwoman, wanted to advise me? "O-okay."

She leaned forward, her elbows on her knees. When her gaze crawled over me, I was transparent, exposed. "Software is a man's world. For now. That means you have to use that head. And those pretty brown eyes." She paused for a few seconds.

This was the strangest career advice I'd ever heard. "Mmm-hmm?"

"I think some fantasy is keeping you from seeing what's in front of you. And what could be."

Was she talking about my crush? "Why do you think it's only a fantasy? Don't you think I could—"

"I think Cooper Fallon is a complicated man. But you're young. Talented. That brain of yours is wasted on managing calendars and filling out expense reports." She echoed my dad.

"That's not all I—"

"You could do more." Her tone shut me down. I imagined it worked in the boardroom, too. From her clutch, she pulled a business card and held it out to me. "Whatever you need—advice, mentoring, a new job"—she waved away my protest—"call me. When you're ready."

I slipped the card into the pocket of my skirt. I wouldn't need it, but it was kind of her to offer.

She glanced toward the bar, and I followed her gaze to find Cooper and Tyler coming toward us, drinks in their hands. "You haven't asked for it, but I'll give you some personal advice, too. Hold onto Tyler with both hands. That guy is special."

She stood just as Cooper reached the table. He handed her a glass of champagne.

"You know what would go great with this? Another slice of cake." Were those doe-eyes she was making at him?

"Of course," he said. He nodded at Tyler and me and walked away, his arm around Jamila's narrow waist.

Had Jamila just warned me off Cooper under the guise of career advice? Was she trying to spare me hurt because she and Cooper were together or trying to divert me because she felt threatened? Or was she trying to poach me from Synergy? Pain pinched my forehead. I took the glass of water from Tyler and gulped it down.

"You okay?" Tyler eased into Jamila's chair.

"Fine." I guzzled more water and watched him over the rim of the glass. *Special,* she'd called him. He was sweet. A little goofy. The complete opposite of Cooper Fallon. Confidence wrapped Cooper in a golden aura. He assessed each situation and then acted with command. He even moved with the smooth grace of a lion.

Tyler rotated his champagne flute on the table. He followed Jackson around like a puppy. An ungainly one with too-big paws. He listened more than he spoke, and too many of his sentences rose up at the end like questions. It was adorable in a friend, but in a lover? Not what I wanted.

No matter how much fun we were having, or how excellent a dancer Tyler was, there was just no comparison.

————

AFTER WE GATHERED to send off Alicia and Jackson, the pinch in my forehead grew to a full headache, so I limped to the head table to escape the loud music. Tyler went in search of ibuprofen.

I pulled my phone out of my clutch. No new messages from Dad or our neighbor, Alma, who'd spent the evening with him. She'd have told me if Dad had any problems he hadn't told me about.

When I looked up from my phone, Cooper stood a few seats down, fingering a boutonniere. At first I thought he'd just taken it off, but then I noticed his was still pinned to his lapel, bruised from dancing. With Jamila. The one in his hand had a white calla lily in it, marking it as Jackson's.

"Do you think he'll want that?" I asked. I doubted it; the only things Jackson collected were vintage T-shirts. And cars.

Cooper startled and looked up. He rubbed the back of his neck. "Hmm, maybe." He tucked the flower into his breast pocket. "I'll keep it for him, just in case."

He's so thoughtful. Even though Jackson would probably laugh at his sentimentality, Cooper was going to save this memento of his wedding for his friend. One more thing we had in common: I kept my dried prom corsage in the drawer under the window seat in my bedroom.

We both had other dates, and it was almost midnight, but I couldn't pass up this chance. Ignoring the ache in my feet, I walked the few steps to his side. "Want to have a drink later at the inn? We can talk and relax." His frown told me he had something on his mind. Maybe we'd finally move past the awkward conversations we always seemed to have and talk about something meaningful.

"Thanks, but no." His gaze rested on Alicia's bouquet, also abandoned on the table. "Mila needs to get home tonight."

All my happiness from dancing dissipated, leaving me with a heavy lump in my stomach. He was going home with Jamila.

"You aren't staying? Alicia and Jackson will miss you at the brunch tomorrow morning. You won't see them before they leave on their honeymoon."

"No, I—I can't." He tore his gaze from the flowers and met my eyes. "Tell Jay to have a good trip. I'll see you in the office Monday."

I nodded but balled up my fists. My plans to talk to Cooper, to finally confess my crush and see if he felt anything close to what I did, had gone completely to hell. All I could do was move on to step two of the plan on Monday.

"Drive safely." I forced a smile.

He turned and strode to the table where Jamila stood, tall, elegant, and, unlike me, still wearing shoes, talking to some Synergy executives. He put his hand on the small of her back and leaned to whisper in her ear. She twined her arm around his waist and presented her cheek for a kiss. Damn. They looked so comfortable together. Like lovers.

"What's wrong?"

Unclenching my jaw and my fists, I tried to smile at Tyler, who'd approached while I was staring at them. "Nothing." But I glanced toward where Cooper and Jamila stood, arms around each other.

He followed my gaze and tilted his head to the side, watching them. Then he held out two orange tablets and a bottle of water.

I swallowed the pills, wishing they could numb my jealousy, too.

"Let's sit down until those kick in." His tone was so gentle it made my eyes tingle with tears.

"Okay."

Tyler sat in the chair next to me and pointed at my feet. "Mind if I—?"

"You want to touch my feet? But they're sweaty."

"And they hurt." He reached for my ankle and set my heel on his knee. His hand stroked over the red furrow on my ankle where the strap had dug in. "Okay?"

"Y-yes." His hands were warm, and he applied the perfect amount of pressure to ease the ache the evil shoes had left.

He continued down the top of my foot and smoothed his hand over the strap mark above my toes. I leaned back in the chair.

"Head still hurt?" he asked.

"Mmm-hmm."

He pushed a thumb between my big toe and second toe and applied pressure. Letting a friend, a coworker, touch my feet was weird. But as he pressed between my toes, the pain in my head lessened. Since when did ibuprofen work so quickly?

"What—what are you doing?"

"Do you want me to stop?"

"No! It's helping."

He grinned. "Thought so. You can trust me."

And I did. His thumbs moved over the top of my big toe, and then underneath to the ball of my foot. The band's music faded, and so did the other wedding guests. The tension left my muscles, and I melted into the chair.

He'd surprised me twice tonight. First with his dancing skills, and now with the professional-grade foot massage. What other hidden talents did he possess? What else didn't I know about my friend, Tyler Young?

Leaving my now-boneless foot on his knee, he reached for the other, caressing my calf. He used the same long strokes down my ankle and over the top of my foot, easing the taut muscles beneath.

He moved his hands to my instep and worked a spot there. Gently at first, then slowly increasing the pressure. The muscle eased and became pliant. I didn't know a thing about bioenergy, chi, or prana, but something mystical was going on in my foot.

Not only my foot. A tingle crept up my ankle and held at the juncture of my thighs. Pulsing. Warming. I looked down to check that his hands were still on my foot and hadn't traveled up my skirt, where phantom fingers touched me. As I shifted in the chair, my skin heated.

"Feels good?" He kept his head down, eyes on my foot.

"Yeah." My voice came out high and breathy. I let my eyes drift closed while I pressed my thighs together. Slickness slipped past the insufficient barrier of my thong, and I dared to squeeze a little harder. Tyler's hands shifted from my instep to the center of my foot. His thumbs pressed up toward my toes. The tingle intensified. My pulse roared in my ears, and I gulped in air. This was no relaxing foot massage. It was pure foreplay.

He continued kneading the bottom of my foot, and when he simultaneously pressed on my instep, my empty core clenched. And clenched and clenched again until warmth spread across my lower belly.

I let out a shaky breath. This was massage sorcery.

Tyler stilled his hands on my feet. "Better now?"

"Gnnh."

I kept my eyes closed, but I heard the cocky smile in his voice. "Ready to call it a night?"

"I'm not sure my body works anymore. That was some foot massage."

"I could carry you back."

I cracked an eye open. With those surprisingly strong arms, he could, too. And—a thrill ran through me—it'd cause all kinds of ridiculous talk. But then I remembered Cooper had left. Operation Prince Charming was over. The little thrill fluttered and died.

"No, I'm okay." I gathered up the evil shoes—I'd enjoy burning them later—and my clutch. I could manage the short walk back to the inn barefoot.

He offered his arm. "Shall we, wedding date?"

That's all he was: a wedding date. Temporary. Time-boxed. We'd ride back to the city together tomorrow, but only as friends. At work on Monday, I'd see him in the cafeteria, perhaps, and wave. No more dancing or shockingly intimate foot massages. Definitely no more kissing. Better to stop the pretense now. I kept my arm at my side and squared my shoulders. "Let's go."

Outside the desperate melee of the remaining partygoers, the world was dark and silent. A soft breeze rustled the dried leaves on the grapevines and raised goosebumps on my arms.

"Would you look at that." Tyler stopped walking, and I halted, too.

"What?" I peered down the path, thinking he'd spotted a couple making out. That's where *my* mind was.

"I haven't seen so many stars since I stopped hanging out in pastures."

I raised my eyes to the night sky. Away from the fog and lights of the city, even the smudge of the Milky Way was visible. Like Dad had taught me, I oriented myself. "Look, there's Andromeda."

"Where?"

"See the Milky Way? Now look down, and you'll see a *W*. That's Cassiopeia. Just to the right, seven or eight stars make kind of a curved triangle with the point down toward the horizon. See it?"

"Yeah. Are you cold?"

"Just a little." I was freezing. Tyler's jacket, warm from his body, draped over my shoulders. It even smelled like him. I snuggled into it.

"What's her story?" he asked.

"Whose?" My mind had gone all Milky-Way blurry.

"Andromeda. When we studied mythology in English class, I was too busy looking at Vanessa Brown to pay attention."

I blinked. "That's too bad. You missed a good story. And it even has a happy ending."

Tyler snorted. "Vanessa was a lot more interesting than my English teacher. Besides, I thought all the mortals got turned into swans or bears."

"Some did. Not Andromeda."

"Tell me about her." He moved closer, his body solid against my arm.

"Andromeda was a princess and the daughter of Queen Cassiopeia."

"Why is Cassiopeia a *W*? Was she turned into a snake?"

"Huh? No, she's sitting in a chair. I'll get to that."

"Okay."

I clutched his arm to steady myself as I looked up into the sky. "Cassiopeia was very beautiful and also very vain. She bragged about it and made Poseidon angry."

"Poseidon was the god of the sea, right?"

"Right. So Poseidon sent a sea monster to terrorize her people. Cassiopeia found an oracle who told her the only way to defeat the monster was to sacrifice her only daughter, Andromeda. They chained her to a rock on the beach, and Andromeda waited for the sea monster to come devour her."

"That doesn't sound like a happy ending."

"Shush. Just in time, Perseus came. That's him to the left of Andromeda—he looks like a stick figure missing its arms—and killed the monster. He freed Andromeda, fell in love with her, and they sailed away to live…happily ever after."

"Far away from the evil mother-in-law. Perfect." His arm came around me, over his jacket. "So why is Cassiopeia sitting in a chair?"

"Poseidon was still angry at her, so he chained her to a chair in the sky."

"Kinky." His breath tickled my ear.

"What?"

"Nothing." He pulled away, leaving my body chilled despite his jacket, but he grasped my hand in his larger, warm one. He started walking down the dark path again, and with one last look up at the stories in the sky, I followed him. We stopped just outside the pool of light surrounding the inn.

"I had fun tonight," he said.

"Me, too." While I loved weddings, receptions usually made me miserable. The couple spent the night in a bubble of happiness, and I was stuck outside. Tonight, Tyler and I had made our own bubble.

"Maybe we could…do it again sometime?" I couldn't see his face in the darkness, but his tone lifted with hope.

"Do what?"

"Pretend to be dating. Or go out. For real."

Damn. "Tyler—"

"Don't say it." His voice was a low rumble.

"But—" I didn't want him to be angry, or disappointed, or whatever that growl indicated. As I stepped closer to him—I didn't know if it was to catch his hand or to hug him because my body just *went*—my foot sank unexpectedly into the soft lawn, and I stumbled. Catlike, he clutched me and wrapped me in his arms. Being this close to him was even more intoxicating than wearing his jacket. I flashed back to the kiss on the dance floor. It had been a sweet, mouth-closed, for-public-consumption kiss. But it had been anything but chaste. Heat had simmered just under the surface. I wondered if that heat would burst into flame if we tried it again, here in the dark.

I rocked back on my heels. I couldn't. I wanted Cooper, not my friend, no matter how cute, no matter how magical he'd made tonight. I had to keep my eyes on my goal. And my lips to myself.

But Tyler had turned out to be so much more than I'd thought. *Special,* Jamila had said. An unexpected mix of Gene Kelly and Tantric masseuse, the most attentive date I'd ever had, even though it was all pretend.

That kiss. Had it been only for show, or were his lips really as bewitching as they seemed?

It was wrong, but I had to know.

I pushed up on my toes.

And I kissed him.

I was so right. There had to be an enchantment on his lips. It made my entire body tremble and my knees stop working. Tyler might have been holding me up. Or else I was floating because Poseidon had stuck me up in the sky.

His tongue tentatively touched my lower lip, and I let him in. He tasted like he smelled: citrus and champagne and desire. I slid one hand behind his back along the smooth fabric of his dress shirt, caressing the firm muscles underneath. With the other, I traced the arc of his neck before I tangled my fingers in his hair. He pulled me closer, and I was lost.

I don't know how long we kissed while the stars turned in the sky around us. Tyler pulled away first, leaving my lips buzzing. We were both panting, his breath warm on my face.

"Was that okay?" he asked. If it hadn't been so dark, I was sure the answer would have been clear in my glassy eyes and flushed cheeks.

"Better than okay." I ignored the flashing red lights, the sirens that told me to stop, and I went in for more. More fireworks. More brain-melting pleasure. I pressed up against him, shamelessly rubbing my soft parts against his corresponding hard ones. As sensitized as that foot massage had made me, I could probably get off fully clothed. Something I hadn't done since...well, since that sexy foot massage. But before that, high school. I trailed my hand down his chest, my jelly-brain ignoring my previous resolution to stay focused. What'd be the harm in a little make-out session between friends, really?

Just as my hand reached the waistband of his pants, he gasped and stepped away. "Wait. Stop."

"Stop?" My heartbeat said, *go-go, go-go.*

"We're friends, right?"

"Friends." I nodded.

Wrong answer. "Friends." The moonlight illuminated his bitter smile. "G'night, Marlee."

Turning his back to me, he shoved his hands into his pockets and headed down the path that led to the parking lot. The cold breeze pushed in through the open front of Tyler's jacket, chilling my heated skin and dousing my desire. I trudged up the stairs to my lonely room at the inn.

11

NO, I didn't toss and turn all night. I drifted off into the blissful sleep of someone with a clear conscience. Not someone who'd tried to add some benefits to her friendship with a sweet guy seconds after she'd said she couldn't date him.

"Marlee, are you okay?" Andrew asked as I grabbed a chocolate-chip muffin from the brunch buffet in the common room at the inn.

"'M fine," I mumbled through a bite of muffin. Jackson's brother was the third person who'd asked me that in the five minutes I'd been downstairs at the post-wedding brunch.

He peered at the blue shadows under my eyes that had made my concealer throw up its hands in defeat. "Can I bring you a cup of coffee?"

"The biggest one you can find. Please."

Now that he'd left, I could crawl into a corner and be antisocial. I wouldn't have to talk to Jackson or Tyler or—

A hand gripped my arm, pink fingernails curling around the sleeve of my cardigan. "There you are."

Alicia.

She marched me to a pair of wing chairs in the corner, away

from the crowd at the buffet. But her voice was gentle when she said, "You look—tired."

I was so freaking tired of people telling me that. "So do you."

She snorted. "I have an excuse. Everyone expects a bride to look exhausted the morning after her wedding night."

I widened my eyes. "Ooh. *Did* he keep you up all night?"

Her cheeks went bright red, but then her eyes went all fuzzy. "We slept a little this morning."

"Okay, I'm going to need some details." So maybe I lived my sex life vicariously through Alicia. At least one of us was getting some that didn't require batteries.

She shook her head. "I need to know what's going on between you and Tyler."

"Oh." I swallowed to try to dissolve the lump in my throat.

She swiveled her head side to side. "Look, I don't know how long we can talk without being interrupted. When Tyler gave me your reply card, I thought 'seat with Tyler' meant that you two were coming to the wedding as friends. And then you—he—he kissed you. What's going on?"

"You saw." I'd hoped she hadn't. That she'd been so enclosed in her happy bubble with Jackson that she'd been oblivious.

Her lips pressed into a thin line.

Now it was my turn to check that no one was listening to us. I lowered my voice anyway. "I was—we were trying to make Cooper jealous. By pretending we were…together."

"Tyler agreed to this?"

"He suggested it!" I hissed.

She slumped in her chair. "I don't think he—"

Irrational, blazing-hot anger rippled through me. I leaned toward her and hissed, "You don't know Cooper. We had a connection when we were dancing. It was like he was telling me the only reason he couldn't date me was because we're coworkers." I clutched my pendant, warm against the hollow of my throat.

"You know he has a point."

"Oh, it's fine for you but not for me?" How could my friend, my best friend, crush my dreams this way? "Don't you think I deserve the fairy tale? All I've wanted my whole life was the kind of love my parents had. The kind you read about. And Cooper is it for me. You know I've crushed on him for years. And now it could all finally come true."

"Marlee." She curled her fingers around my hand where it gripped the armrest. "You know I want you to be happy. And to find your perfect someone the way I did. All I mean is that Cooper's less flexible about company policy—about everything, really —than Jackson is. The appearance of...of fraternization might stop him from pursuing someone."

And that's what he'd said while we'd danced. Was he really so cold that he could shut down his feelings for someone—me— because of company policy?

"I don't even report to him." My voice was weak, thready.

She gave me a sad smile. "It wouldn't matter."

A relationship with Jamila had no such barriers. "Do you think he and Jamila are together?"

She shook her head. "I don't know. I always assumed they were just good friends. But friends can become more." She let that settle in my brain for a few seconds and then said, "Speaking of—"

She didn't have to finish the sentence for the muffin to become an infinitely heavy black hole in my stomach.

"Either you and Tyler are better actors than I'd ever have believed, or there's a genuine spark there."

I looked down at my pink floral skirt. "There's something, all right. And I—I kissed him. Later. Privately. And I tried to—I think I upset him."

"But why, Marlee? Why would you kiss Tyler if you're interested in Cooper?"

I traced a rose on my skirt. "It's been three years since I've been that close to a guy. My hormones overpowered my brain."

Those hormones were going to fuck up our friendship if I didn't get them under control.

"There you are." Andrew held out a cup of coffee.

I took it from him. Black. I sipped it and shuddered at the bitterness. "Thank you."

Alicia said, "Andrew, would you mind getting me a glass of juice, please?"

"No problem. Sis." He grinned and took off.

Her smile disappeared when she looked at me. "The kiss? The private one?"

I set the bitter coffee on the end table. "He gave me a foot massage. I think it was some sort of voodoo. Is that a Texas thing? I could swear it felt like he put his hands on my—" I looked down at my lap.

"He didn't." Her blue eyes blinked wide.

"No! Of course not." Though, for a second there, I'd wanted him to.

"And then you tried to—?"

"Climb him like a tree. But he stopped me." I smoothed down my skirt. I'd taken things too far and pissed off my friend.

"You're my friend, and I love you, Marlee. But Tyler's my friend, too." She gripped my hand harder. "Don't hurt him."

"I won't. I promise." And the only way to keep that promise was to put Tyler in the friend zone. And keep him there. With no visitation privileges to the more-than-friends zone.

My promise was still floating in the air between us when Tyler and Sam walked up. Holding a can of Mountain Dew in one hand, he extended a cup of coffee to me. "Morning."

He didn't look much better than I did. Scruff covered his cheeks and chin, and his eyelids drooped over bloodshot eyes. He wore a plaid shirt unbuttoned over a navy V-neck T-shirt, exposing a few dark brown hairs at the bottom of the vee. I wondered if they covered his entire chest in a mat or if they were sparse, strategically scattered across his pecs and…below. I pressed my thighs together and looked down into my coffee.

He'd lightened it with milk and—I took a sip and sighed
—sugar.

"Morning," Alicia said. "Sam, did you have fun last night? I
didn't see you after the pictures."

"Oh, I went back to the inn. I had an idea for my research. So,
yes, I had fun."

Alicia laughed. "What about you, Tyler? Fun night?"

I kept my eyes on the fluid dynamics of the swirling lipids in
my coffee, not daring to look up.

"I did. Marlee's a good"—*don't say it, don't say it*—"dancer."

I blinked at him. A smile teased his lips when he returned my
gaze. Friends. Maybe we could manage it.

"Tyler!" Jackson had approached from the other side, making
me slosh my coffee. He gripped Tyler's hand and pulled him into
a bro-hug with the other arm. "Did you just get here?"

"Yeah."

Jackson rubbed his hands together, grinning. "So. Who did
something they regret last night? I'm only getting married once,
so I need the stories to be epic. I want people to be talking about
this weekend for the rest of our lives. Tyler? Marlee? Not you,
Sam; I don't want to hear about my little sister's debauchery."

Before I could mumble a lie, Andrew bounced up with a glass
of juice, which he handed to Alicia. "Watch out, Sam. Mother's on
the warpath. She heard you left the reception early last night."

"I was working on my dissertation project. That's much more
important than yet another party. No offense, Jackson."

"There was wine and dancing. It wasn't just another party, was
it?" Jackson turned to Alicia. She set a consoling hand on his
forearm.

Andrew nudged his sister. "Hey, Sam, maybe you could tell
Mother you snuck off with Tyler. You guys are both computer
geeks. She might buy it."

She stepped away from him, wrinkling her nose. "Tyler's with
Marlee."

"Tyler and Marlee?" Jackson chuckled. "They're just friends."

He must've been the only one who missed our dance-floor kiss. What was I going to say? I couldn't lie to Jackson. "We—"

"Friends make the best lovers, I think."

We all turned wide eyes to Sam, who'd said it. I'd known her for three years, and she'd never had a serious relationship. What did she know about lovers?

"Someone who knows you and likes you already. Who cares about you as a person. And then you add on the romantic and sexual components. It's like having a program that already functions well and adding on a new feature. What could be better? I'd want to be friends with my partner."

I couldn't—wouldn't—look at Tyler. I'd tried to bolt on a feature to our relationship, but it was one that didn't belong. Like trying to add a weather-forecasting feature to a note-taking app.

"I need—I mean, I'm going to get a drink." Leaving his soda on a nearby table, Tyler stalked away without looking back. Without looking at *me*.

Jackson turned to me, eyebrows arching toward his hairline. "What's going on?"

"Nothing. I...Excuse me." Alicia could tell him all about it. I had to make things right with my friend. I followed Tyler outside to the porch.

He stood at the rail overlooking the vineyard. Stepping up beside him, I took a deep breath of grape-scented air.

"Last night I—I went too far. I made a mistake." I swallowed. "Our friendship is important to me, and I shouldn't have done that. I'm sorry."

"I'm sorry, too. I crossed a line by kissing you. I got caught up in Operation—"

"I know. It's okay. And if you don't want to keep it up anymore, I'm okay with that." Operation Prince Charming had sounded like just another fun game when he'd proposed it at the start of the weekend. But it had turned out to be dangerous fun. Like playing with matches.

"No, it's fine. We're friends. Friends help each other. I want to help you." When he turned toward me, he looked like my friend again. No angry lines between his eyebrows, no sad droop to his lips. He smiled, though the dimple didn't show.

Was the fake-dating helping? I replayed the shock on Cooper's face after Tyler had kissed me. It hadn't been quite jealousy, but it was a good start. Maybe if I spent some quality time with my battery-operated boyfriend substitute, I could keep my hormones in check and my hands off Tyler. And then Cooper would realize we were perfect for each other.

"Thanks. You're the best."

"Carly Simon, 'Nobody Does It Better.'"

For the first time that day, I laughed. But it reminded me that we had to spend two hours alone in a car, driving back to the city. How awkward would it be? Worse, could I trust myself not to reach for his hand over the console?

Distance. That was what I needed. And a solo orgasm or two. Then I could be his friend and pretend-girlfriend in front of Cooper.

"Hey, you don't mind if I catch a ride back with Sam? She offered while we were getting dressed yesterday." It wasn't even a lie. We'd geeked out over sci-fi TV, and she'd asked me if I'd watch an episode or two of *Battlestar Galactica* with her Sunday night.

Tyler's grin faded. "No problem. I was thinking about heading back early anyway."

My heart twinged, but I said, "I've got some final bridesmaid duties to wrap up. See you at work Monday?"

"Sure thing." He turned on the toe of his sneaker and walked to the steps that led to the parking lot. No smile, no hug, not even a friendly shoulder-squeeze.

I deserved it. But I'd try to make it up to him. Starting Monday.

12

"UM, COOPER?" I leaned on the doorframe of his office at eight thirty on Monday morning.

He kept his eyes on his screen and tapped a key on his computer. "Yes, Marlee?"

"I have good news and bad news."

He snapped his head up, eyes wide in his pale face. "Jackson's all right? And Alicia?"

"Oh." I grimaced. "Of course they are. It's nothing *that* dramatic." He eased back in his chair. "The good news is that Kim, the temp you hated last week, called to say she's not coming back. The bad news is that means you don't have an assistant today." I fought the giddy laugh that tried to bubble out of me. Step two of my plan had fallen into place almost too easily.

He rested his elbows on the glass-covered cherrywood desktop, bowed his head, and tugged at the dark-blond roots of his hair. Seeing him so vulnerable made me want to go over, pull his head back, and give him a long, slow kiss. I wondered if his lips would taste of citrus like Tyler's did. I shook off both thoughts—especially the memory of Tyler's kiss—and took a few steps into his office, my heels sinking into the plush antique rug. "Why are you so hard on them, anyway?"

"Who? The temps?" When I nodded, he rubbed the back of his neck. "It's your fault, really."

I drew a breath to argue. I'd been nothing but kind to each of his temps, taking time away from my own work to train them and to help them with Cooper's outrageous demands. The man demanded perfection from everyone—well, everyone but Jackson, who was a lost cause at anything except coding; for everything else, he had me—and it was too much to ask of a temp who was making eighteen bucks an hour and going to night school.

"How dare—"

He stopped me by raising his hands, palms out. "All I meant was that the bar you set is too high. They all seem incompetent compared to you."

I almost, *almost* felt guilty about setting them up for failure. "It's hard starting something new. You have to give people a chance." *Give me a chance.*

He shook his head. "You've been great since day one. On your first day"—Cooper ticked off the items on his fingers—"you tracked down Jay at his apartment where he was sleeping off a hangover, made him shower and dress, and had him here, on time, with coffee in hand, for a board presentation. *I* couldn't have done that, and I've known him for over ten years."

I couldn't believe he remembered. "I figured I had to. If he was fired, I was out of a job."

"If I could just clone you…"

"Well, you can't. Don't even ask me for a cheek swab. But I have an idea." Having accomplished step one, the success of our dance still to be determined, it was time to leap into step two: forced proximity, one of my favorite romance tropes. "Since Jackson's away for three weeks, I'll be completely bored. So while he's gone, I'll be your acting assistant. I'll get you organized. I'll even screen some candidates for you. Maybe we can finally find the right one for you. Permanently."

"I don't have to do anything? You'll take care of it?"

"You don't want to interview the candidates?"

He glanced at his screen. I was sure twenty emails had popped in during the five minutes we'd been talking. "Not if I don't have to."

"You trust me to hire a permanent assistant for you?" Now I really did feel bad about his misplaced trust in me.

"Absolutely."

"Okay then. I'll find you someone great. I promise." I'd make up for the sabotage.

His face brightened. "And in the meantime, I get you for three weeks?"

You could have me forever if you'd just ask. I fingered my pendant and nodded, thinking of ice cubes and winter breezes to keep the blush from my cheeks.

"Deal," he said.

He looked back at his monitor and then up at me, a wry smile on his lips. "Coincidentally, I have a meeting in the northwest conference room in ten minutes. Can you load the presentation and videoconference in the Austin team? Please?"

I held in a sigh. "Sure thing." I turned to leave.

He called after me, "Lunch is on me."

I peeked at him over my shoulder. "While I'm your assistant, lunch is on you *every* day. *With* dessert."

He chuckled. "You drive a hard bargain, Miss Rice."

"I'll show you hard," I muttered under my breath as I stepped out into the hallway and almost collided with a broad chest in a faded green Donkey Kong T-shirt. Crap, why'd he have to catch me coming out of Cooper's office?

"Sorry," I squeaked, pulling up short.

Tyler's jaw tightened for a second, but then he smiled. "Hey, glad you made it back. How was *Battlestar Galactica?*"

"Good. Sam had a lot of opinions about it. We had fun." It wasn't like hanging out with Tyler or Alicia, but making new friends was a good thing. Especially after you'd kissed your friend at your other friend's wedding.

We turned together and walked toward the conference room,

talking about the weather, sci-fi, anything except how we'd almost ruined our friendship by taking things too far.

He settled into a chair while I set up the presentation and got it up on the screen. After a few minutes, Cooper strode in. "We good to go, Marlee?"

"Ready. Just click the call button." I scanned the room one more time. Everything was in order.

Just as I prepared to slip out, Tyler leaned back in his chair. "Marlee, did you bring in my jacket?"

My blush was natural as I shot a glance at Cooper. "It's at my desk. Thanks again for letting me borrow it."

"Anytime." Tyler infused his gaze with heat, and it fed the fire in my cheeks. He was so good at this fake-dating thing, he was making me good at it.

Easing the door closed behind me, I gripped the cool handle for a second, trying to slow my pulse and stop glowing like a red giant. We were back to playing the game, that was all.

An hour later when everyone emerged from the conference room, I had Cooper's schedule organized, color-coded, and both printed and updated to his phone. I'd blocked out an hour for "Lunch with Marlee" every day he was unscheduled. I wasn't kidding about the lunches. I was going to make the most of my three weeks with Cooper. With Alicia and Jackson's side-eye gone, I'd finally get up my nerve to show Cooper how I felt about him, and lunches away from the office—and takeout dinners working late—were the perfect opportunity.

Tyler made a big show of picking up his jacket as he passed by my desk, and he gave me one of his Texas winks. But a colleague waited for him at the door to the stairwell, so he didn't linger at my desk.

Instead of going directly to his office, Cooper rested a khaki-clad hip on my desk. He held up his phone. "Thanks for syncing my calendar for me."

"No problem. Jackson also likes a printed copy, so I put that on your desk. Let me know if you don't want a printout going forward."

"It's fine, thanks." He glanced over my shoulder at the door to the stairs, where Tyler and his team member stood, talking. In a low voice, Cooper said, "He looks exhausted. Is that your fault?"

My fault? He looked better than he had Sunday morning. He'd even given me that flirty wink. "What do you mean?"

"Did you keep our boy up too late?" he asked, staring pointedly at Tyler's suit jacket, draped over his arm.

Sweet Sir Isaac Newton.

I reached for my bottle of water but missed and tipped it across my desk. Shooting up from my chair, I grabbed a roll of paper towels from my drawer and started blotting up the mess.

"I can't believe—" I said, much too loudly, before Cooper gave me a "simmer-down" gesture. I continued in a whisper-shout, "First, it's none of your business who I—" Though I wished it were. "Second, we are *not* sleeping together." The door to the stairwell slammed behind me, and I winced.

"Really." Cooper's voice was flat, skeptical.

Fake-dating was one thing. Fake-sleeping-together was a step too far. Cooper was too much of a gentleman to break up a serious relationship. "Really. We're casual. Seeing if we want to be more than friends."

"It looked like you two hit it off with all that dancing."

Was that a gleam of jealousy in his eye? Had Operation Prince Charming actually worked?

"We, ah, we're taking it slow." That was true. I hoped we could forget how I'd tried to screw it up by turning our fake kiss into a real make-out session. I couldn't let that happen again.

He shrugged. "You looked happy."

Cooper was giving me whiplash with his don't-date-coworkers speech followed by "You looked happy." But had I been? I still hadn't sorted through my emotions from the weekend. They lay jumbled inside me like the photos on my phone, unreviewed. I threw the soggy paper in the trash and glared at him. "Don't presume."

He grimaced. "Marlee, you know I—"

My phone rang, and a glance told me it was Jackson's line. I held up a finger and picked up the receiver.

A sneeze came through the phone, followed by a wet sniffle. "Marlee, it's Audrey Jones. I need your help."

Why was Jackson's mother calling me? A chill shot through me. "Are Jackson and Alicia all right?" Cooper had pushed off my desk, about to return to his office, but he froze.

"Of course. I'm sure they're fine. It's me"—she sneezed again—"who isn't."

"What's wrong?" I shooed Cooper away and mouthed, *They're okay.*

"We're keeping their cat, Tigger, while they're on their honeymoon, and my—my"—another sneeze—"my allergy medications aren't working. Would you mind keeping him for us?"

A cat. In our house. With Dad. I squeezed my eyes shut and shook my head. But Alicia loved that cat. So I said, "No, Mrs. Jones. I wouldn't mind at all."

"Thank you. Can I send him with a driver to your office? Do you think you could leave the office early to take him home?"

I'd miss my first lunch with Cooper, but I pictured Alicia, worry-free at last, on the beach in Fiji. "That'll be fine. Thank you."

After we hung up, I knocked on Cooper's doorframe.

"Sorry, I'm going to have to take a rain check for lunch. Jackson's mother is allergic to Tigger, and she's sending him home with me. Now."

He frowned. "Poor Audrey."

"Poor Marlee. What am I going to do with a cat?" We'd never had so much as a fish.

"Have you met Tigger? He loves everyone. And he sleeps all the time. Just set up his bed near a sunny window, and you won't hear a sound from him for three weeks."

I made a noncommittal noise. I hoped the cat wouldn't cause trouble. I had enough to handle at home.

I turned to go. "Call me if you need anything."

"Mm-hm." He already had his nose back in his computer screen.

I dragged back to my desk to pack up. The score was Fate - 2, Marlee's romantic plans - 0.

───────

THAT NIGHT, as I washed my scratched-up arms in the kitchen sink, I mentally calculated the hours I'd have to spend with Tigger until Jackson and Alicia returned from their honeymoon. Under the kitchen table, the cat nonchalantly licked a paw and rubbed it over his ear.

"Four hundred fifty-six hours, cat. Can't we be friends for that long?"

He swiveled his ears back and hissed at me.

Maybe I should spend more time at the office. That'd minimize time with Tigger and maximize time with Cooper. But then who'd take care of Dad? "Okay, maybe friends is too much to ask. Can't we just ignore each other?"

He stood up, turned his orange-striped back, and plunked back down, his twitching tail facing me. I closed my eyes and sighed through my nose.

Dad walked in. "Sunshine, who were you talking to?"

"Just the cat."

He furrowed his brow. "We don't have a cat."

That familiar feeling zapped me like a Taser to the chest. "Dad, remember, I told you about Tigger when I came home. We're watching him for Jackson and Alicia."

His expression didn't change, but he said, "That's right. Well, good night."

A minor slip-up. That's all it was. He'd been fine over the

weekend. Fine all day. I wasn't losing my dad. He was tired, and he'd forgotten.

I stared at the cat who didn't want to be at our house any more than I wanted him to be there.

"Troublemaker," I growled. If it weren't for Alicia and Noah, who loved that cat, he'd be out on his furry butt. Thank goodness for Operation Prince Charming. It'd give me the distraction I needed to get through the next nineteen days.

13

"THANKS, MARLEE. I APPRECIATE YOUR HELP." Cooper didn't look up from his monitor when he spoke.

As of Wednesday afternoon, I'd made zero progress with him, even as his unofficial admin. We'd spent plenty of time together, but the meteors of affection I lobbed his way kept burning to ash in the thick atmosphere of professionalism he surrounded himself with.

Standing in front of his desk, I tilted my head to the side. "Need anything else?" He didn't look nearly as stressed as he'd been before the wedding. But there was something in the slump of his shoulders—shoulders he always held back like a four-star general—and the way his chest seemed to cradle his heart. I wanted to comb my fingers through his hair, smooth the lines on his forehead. I wished I could pull off his wingtips and offer him a Tyler-quality foot massage, but I had Muggle fingers.

Had Jamila hurt him? Had they also argued at the end of the wedding weekend? Even I couldn't convince myself of that. She'd called him every day although their conversations had been brief.

That had been Cooper since the wedding: brief. At lunch today, we'd been fine as long as we'd spoken about work. He'd talked about his upcoming trip to the East Coast offices until I'd almost face-planted into my Cobb salad. But when I'd asked him what he did after hours while he was traveling, he'd looked at me with his head cocked to the side and said one word: "Work."

I'd pressed him. Surely he had a favorite restaurant or bar in New York. Someplace he and Jackson had gone on one of their many trips. But his mouth had gone tighter than the door seal on his Tesla, and he'd mumbled about having no time for play.

He cleared his throat.

Oops. How long had I been standing there, staring? "So nothing else?"

"No. Thank you."

Clutching my tablet to my chest, I turned and walked across his plush rug to the door. That was exactly what he needed: play. To let loose, relax. I could help him with that. If only he'd let me. How could I convince him to let me help with Operation Hakuna Matata?

Focused on my thoughts, I didn't notice the visitor standing at my desk until I was right on him.

"Tyler! I didn't know you were coming up."

"Hey." He picked up a cherry candy from the bowl on my desk and twisted it between his fingers. Those fingers. I'd never given them a second thought before, and now I fixated on them at the oddest times. Why?

I blinked and sat in my chair, keeping my eyes on his face rather than those dangerous hands. "What can I do for you?"

He met my gaze and, after a second, the corners of his mouth turned up. "I haven't seen you in the cafeteria lately. How've you been?"

"Good. Busy. Um"—I checked over my shoulder that Cooper's office door was closed—"still working on Operation Prince Charming. We've been going to lunch together."

He popped the candy into his mouth and spoke around it. "Good. Glad it's working."

"I don't know that I'd say it's *working*. I haven't made a lot of progress." I logged back into my computer and glanced at the dozen emails that'd come in while I was in Cooper's office.

"Anything you need me to do?"

Tyler's fingers drummed against the side of his leg. *No fingers!* This sexual dry spell was really doing things to my head. Maybe I needed a new vibrator. My last few sessions with The Cooper—yes, I named my sex toys—had been lackluster. "No, thanks. I'm going to keep trying. It's only been a few days."

"I won't keep you, then." But he didn't leave. He opened his mouth and then closed it again. And that drew my gaze to his lips. Stained pink with the cherry candy, those lips had kissed me senseless on Saturday night. *No! Absolutely no thinking about kissing my friend.*

By the Kepler Telescope, where *could* I look? His nose. I had no sexual feelings at all about his nose. He had a nice nose. Straight. It'd press into my neck while he—

I swallowed and straightened a stack of papers on my desk. "Tyler, what do you need?"

"A-a group of us are going out tonight. For happy hour." He tapped against his thigh. "Want to come? Not—not if you're busy. Then you should go do that."

"Do what?"

"Whatever you have planned."

"Oh." I used to be spontaneous. Back when I was in college, I'd go to a friend's dorm room after class and play video games. Or get a beer with Jackson after work. But on Wednesdays, Alma went to choir practice, and I hated the idea of leaving Dad alone. Plus, he'd never remember to feed Tigger. And who knew what evil a hangry Tigger would get up to?

But the thought of telling Tyler no just as we were repairing the friendship I'd almost shattered over the weekend made cold prickles erupt in my belly. He'd made an effort by asking me to join him and his coworkers. I had to try, too.

"I can't tonight. I have to plan ahead to make arrangements for Dad and Tigger." He blinked a few times, but before he could voice the questions I saw forming behind those hazel eyes, I rushed on. "How about tomorrow? I could ask my neighbor to look in on them."

His shoulders slumped. "My brother's coming to town tomorrow. We're going to dinner."

"Oh. Well, then—"

He shook his head. "Come. Come with us. Raleigh's not so bad."

"Which one is Raleigh?"

"Played football at SMU. Now he's in sales."

I didn't want to be a third wheel at his dinner with his brother. But I also didn't want to tell him no.

"You really don't mind?"

His mouth tightened, but then he said, "No. I'll make him promise to be on his best behavior."

"Okay."

"Okay." His tone lightened. "I'll come get you here tomorrow at six."

I nodded. When he turned and walked to the stairs, I deliberately turned away. Raleigh wasn't the only one who needed to watch his behavior.

———

THE FOLLOWING EVENING, Tyler arrived at my desk five minutes early, and I wasn't ready. Not because I needed to primp to go out with my work-buddy and his brother. Not even because I wasn't emotionally ready to be in a social setting again with my friend after he'd triggered my sex-starved hormones. Okay, that might have been a lie.

What made me most not-ready was that I wasn't sure Dad was okay.

He'd been fine since I'd returned from the wedding. In fact, this morning, he'd told me to have a good day at *work*, not school. But when I'd called him about five-thirty, half an hour before our neighbor Alma was supposed to come over, he'd asked me three times when I was coming home.

I'd called Alma and asked her to go over early to check on him. After about twenty minutes, she'd called and assured me he was fine. From the false cheerfulness in her voice, I suspected she'd done something to make him fine, like coax him out of bed or help him find his cane—maybe both. And the annoying part? I could hear that asshole, Tigger, purring at her in the background. She'd called him lindo.

So when Tyler came up the stairs just as I hung up with Alma, I wasn't ready to be the fun work friend I needed to be. And it showed.

"What's wrong?" He tapped his fingers against his jeans.

"Nothing. I'm fine."

"Something's wrong. You can tell me."

"It's my dad. He sounded off when I called to check on him." I still hadn't told him anything about Dad's slip-ups. If I said it out loud, it might sound worse than it was. And it might even be true.

"Off?"

"Just—confused. It happens to him sometimes."

"Do you need to cancel tonight?" He shoved his hands into his jeans pockets.

I could've. Maybe I should've gone home to check on Dad myself. But then I'd be breaking my promise to my friend. Besides, Alma had said he was fine. And she had my number in case that changed.

"No, I'm good. Where are we meeting your brother?"

"An Italian place between here and his hotel. It's not far. Want to walk?"

I looked up at the skylight. No rain. "Sure."

Outside the Synergy building's revolving door, fog had started to roll in, cold and sticky. Taillights from traffic-mired cars glowed in the mist. Office workers and tourists pushed past each other on the sidewalk.

Tyler crooked an elbow toward me. "Let's go."

I threaded my hand through, pulling myself into his comforting warmth. He led me toward the park, the same direction I'd walked with Jackson a couple of weeks ago. Maybe we could find our way back to how we were then, before I'd made things weird.

"You can tell me to butt out, but what's wrong with your dad?" he asked.

Or maybe not. I pulled my hand away and nestled it into my own coat pocket. But if we were going to trust each other, I had to share.

"You met him at Jackson and Alicia's engagement party. He uses a cane. Because he broke his leg a couple years ago, and it didn't heal quite right. He tried to go back to work, but he—it didn't work out. His pain medicine makes him confused sometimes. So he's home all the time now. I worry about him."

We stopped at the intersection, and Tyler peered at me, his eyes dark in the dusky street. "Would you feel better if you went home?"

Yes. No. "He's fine, really. Our neighbor's with him."

"But how are you? Taking care of a disabled parent is a lot."

"Me? I'm fine. He's always taken care of me. Now it's my turn. We do okay." I took a deep breath. I'd never told him the rest, either, always managing to change the subject before she came up. "My mother died when I was little."

The light changed, and we crossed the street. When we were on the other side, he stretched his arm across my shoulders and side-hugged me, just for a second, like guys did with each other. Then he put his hands in his coat pockets. "I'm sorry."

"Thanks." Talking about my dead mother was always a buzzkill, so I said, "You have a big family, right? Four brothers?"

"And a sister." He stared ahead, down the sidewalk. "Raleigh—in fact, my entire family—can be a little..." He blew out a breath, visible in the chilly air for a second before it merged with the fog. "Much. We joke a lot, usually at each other's expense." He stopped in front of a glass-fronted restaurant where servers floated among white tablecloths and shiny metallic accents. "This is it. Just—" He grimaced. "Ignore everything he says."

He held the door open for me, and I walked in. I didn't even have to guess who Raleigh might be. Standing in the small waiting area of the restaurant was Tyler's twin. Well, not a twin, but a bulkier, slightly older version. Instead of Tyler's open expression, a smirk twisted his lips.

"Ty!" Raleigh stretched out his arms to embrace his brother, thumping him on the back. When he looked at me, his eyes were a solid brown, no flecks of color like Tyler's. "Who's this?"

Tyler pushed out of Raleigh's bear hug. Keeping his hands at his sides, he said, "Marlee, meet my brother Raleigh. Raleigh, this is my friend Marlee Rice."

Not wanting to get wrapped up in Raleigh's meaty arms, I stuck out my hand. "Nice to meet you."

He shook it more gently than I'd expected. "Well, well, well."

"Should we get a table now that we're all here?" Tyler asked. Without waiting for an answer, he stepped up to the hostess. She took us directly to a table in the back, where Tyler and I faced off against Raleigh.

While we looked over the menu and ordered, the two brothers exchanged news. Raleigh was in town visiting his company's headquarters as he did three or four times a year. He'd seen their parents the previous weekend and reported that they were in good health but missed Tyler. How long had it been since he was home? Weeks? Months? More? Raleigh implied it was on the *more* side.

Tyler told Raleigh about his place in the Excelsior—a shithole, he called it with an apologetic glance at me. I'd never been there, but it couldn't be that bad. San Francisco real estate was expensive, but Synergy paid developers well. And he told his brother about his job. He was doing okay, he said. I opened my mouth to correct him—Tyler was Jackson's protégé, which said something about his talent and prospects—but the server arrived with our meals, and our talk turned to food and the brothers' favorite restaurants in Dallas.

Raleigh put down his fork and swallowed his bite of rigatoni. "The rehearsal dinner's at Carolina's. Bella wanted something chichi."

Tyler mumbled something into his chicken.

Figuring Raleigh deserved a better response than that, I said, "You're the one getting married?"

He nodded. "This summer. My college girlfriend. Though I knew her before that. Went to the same high school, but she's a couple years younger. Your class, right, Ty?"

"Yeah." He curled over his plate and shoved a bite of chicken with his fork.

Raleigh leaned back in his chair. "Though, now that I think about it, I remember her being at our house sometimes. She was friends with somebody. Maybe went with one of us to prom?"

Tyler dropped his fork onto his plate with a clang that rang out into the noisy dining room. Glaring at his brother, he spat out, "Friends. I dated her for six months, asshole."

My heart stopped. Raleigh's smile froze on his face, and his eyes went wide. I had time to run through two scenarios of leaping between them without getting marinara on my oyster-pink skirt—sadly, both utter failures even in my imagination—when Raleigh started to chuckle. Then he escalated into a full-on belly laugh that caused people at nearby tables to shoot him amused looks. Raleigh had a great laugh. Too bad he was an utter tool.

"I knew that. I was just fucking with you."

"Shit-for-brains," Tyler mumbled. Then he glanced up at me. "Sorry."

"Justified," I whispered. I'd never had a sibling, but Raleigh had to have broken the code by dating his brother's ex. And then he'd *joked* about it? What a—

"Though if you'd gone out for sports like the rest of us, maybe you could've held onto her."

I clamped my mouth shut and breathed in through my nose.

"This guy"—Raleigh wagged his fork at Tyler—"could've played for UT."

Tyler rolled his eyes.

"But he preferred sitting in the library in front of a computer to going to practice. Or mixing it up with the rest of us."

Tyler leaned back in his chair. "I was always your goalie, catcher, center. You never let me play forward or shortstop or quarterback."

Raleigh shrugged. "We never knew you wanted to. You could've said something."

Tyler set down his water glass with a thunk. "I did."

"Pssh. You should've said something louder."

Maybe I'd been wrong all those years when I'd wanted a sibling. I checked my phone. Nothing from Alma. And I still had plenty of time before the last train. I glanced at Raleigh. *Unfortunately.*

He chewed, his gaze unfocused, and set down his fork. "Though maybe if I'd spent more time in the library, I'd have a cushy desk job like you."

"You have a great job," Tyler said. "You make plenty of money, and you've traveled everywhere. New York, San Francisco, Singapore…"

"Yeah," Raleigh said. "But Bella hates it. She wishes I was home more. She wants babies." He grimaced.

"And you don't?" I asked him.

"I don't know. Maybe. Not yet. With three younger siblings, I kinda had my fill of kids. You know?"

I didn't want to feel sorry for the asshole, but maybe he had a point. He'd probably changed his share of diapers, at least for the two youngest.

Raleigh crossed his fork and knife on his empty plate, and a busboy whisked it away. A gleam came into his brown eyes. "So. How long have you two been together?"

"We're not," Tyler growled.

"Nope, just friends." My voice was too high.

Raleigh reached across the table and cuffed Tyler's shoulder. "Dumbass." They exchanged some sort of unspoken brother-language with their eyes.

Finally, Tyler looked down at his half-eaten dinner. "I think I'll take this home."

"That's my brother Tyler. Always watching his girlish figure." Raleigh patted his flat stomach.

"You should watch yours," Tyler said. "You've put on a few pounds, old man."

Tyler could dish it out, too. I smiled and pulled out my wallet. "I need to make a call. Can I give you some cash to settle up?"

Raleigh looked at me like I had two heads. "I don't know what this numbnuts does out here on the Left Coast, but I wasn't raised to let a lady pay for dinner."

Tyler rolled his eyes. "I've got it, bonehead."

"I'll expense it."

Leaving them arguing over the check, I slipped on my coat and went outside, where I stood under the dripping marquee and called Dad.

"Hey, are you doing okay?"

"Of course, Sunshine. I had dinner with Alma, and now Tigger and I are watching baseball. He likes baseball, don't you, big guy?"

"Dad." Damned cat. "Will you be okay if I stay in the city a little longer?"

"Sure."

"Will you check that the doors are locked? And the stove is off?"

He chuckled. "Yes, ma'am. I'm the father here, remember?"

"I remember." He sounded good. And I really shouldn't treat him like a child. "Good night. I'll see you in the morning."

"G'night, Sunshine."

I put my phone away. Tyler and Raleigh had come outside and

were talking quietly. When I approached, Raleigh was saying, "So what do I tell them?"

"Tell them I don't know."

I put a hand on Tyler's shoulder so he'd know I was there.

"Mom'll bawl her eyes out if you aren't home at Thanksgiving."

Tyler's shoulder tensed. "I'll think about it."

Raleigh pressed his lips into a flat line. Then he extended a hand to me. "Marlee, it was a pleasure."

"Mmm." It'd have been a lie to reciprocate the sentiment.

He wrapped Tyler in another bear hug. "See you, man." He turned and walked away.

"Yep. Just as bad as I thought it'd be." Tyler mirrored my half-smile. "Do you need to go home right away?"

I checked my watch. I had a couple of hours before the last train. After that miserable dinner, I couldn't leave Tyler alone. His shoulders still slumped like Raleigh'd hit him with a baseball bat. "Not right away. Want to get some dessert?"

He chucked his takeout container in a nearby trash can. "Best idea ever."

———

ON THAT CHILLY night near closing time, we were the only patrons in the ice cream shop. Tyler asked the teenage employee which flavors contained tree nuts, and after sampling a few nut-free flavors, he went for a double scoop of malted milk chocolate and fudge ripple with caramel sauce. I chose a scoop of creamy strawberry-mango sorbet. We sat near the front window, where the fog licked at the glass.

I dragged my spoon across the top of my sorbet. "Is he always that way?"

He jammed his spoon into his ice cream. "They all are. Why do you think I live two thousand miles away?" But his smile was wry. "It's family."

"Doesn't it hurt?"

He shrugged. "Sometimes."

At dinner, he'd looked like Dad that time he shot a staple through his index finger.

"You should tell them. Stand up to them."

He worked a spoonful out of his cup. "What he said was true. I was always second-best in sports. And Bella only dated me until it was clear I'd never be a varsity athlete."

"That's awful!" I set down my cup.

He shrugged.

I shook my head, glad for once to have been an only child. "Well, I think she underestimated you. All of them did. And it's not fair. Plus, your brother's an ass."

I popped another spoonful of sorbet into my mouth and looked up to see him watching me as I slid the spoon out of my mouth. His Adam's apple bobbed when he swallowed. My own throat suddenly dry, I dropped my gaze to the table. I really needed to order that new vibrator soon.

Luckily for me, the cranky teenager who'd served us called out, "Sorry, guys, we're closing," and flipped the sign in the window.

Ambling out into the dark, foggy street, we dodged tourists and late-evening commuters. Tiny droplets condensed and sparkled on the ends of my hair and the sleeves of my coat. Clammy air crawled over my face and crept into the open collar of my coat. I shivered.

"Cold?" Tyler asked.

That was one of the things that had gotten me into trouble after the wedding. I had to resist exposure to Tyler's scent, the heat of his body. "No, I'm good. But I think I'll take a cab to the train." The station was only a few blocks away, but it'd been a long day, and my defenses were melting like the ice cream we'd had.

He coughed. "I'll get a cab home and drop you off."

"The train station isn't exactly on the way."

"I don't mind. I'm not in a hurry."

Before I could protest again, he waved at a passing taxi and, when it stopped, opened the door for me. I told the driver the name of the station, and Tyler, sliding in behind me, gave his address as the second stop. Even this late at night, traffic crawled along the streets. It would've been faster to walk, but the cab was warm and dry. I stared out the window, watching drops of water tremble and trail down the glass.

Tyler touched my hand where it rested on the vinyl seat. "Thanks for coming with me. It was better with you there."

I turned away from the window to smile at him. Flipping my hand over, I twined my fingers with his. "Anytime you need emotional support against your jerk brothers, you let me know."

"Promise?" He cleared his throat.

"What?"

He rolled his lower lip between his teeth. "You see, I have this wedding to go to this summer. All of my jerk brothers—and my sister, who's also a jerk—will be there. Maybe we could do the wedding-date thing again."

Summer was months away. But thinking of poor Tyler at his brother's wedding to his ex, I couldn't say no. "If you're not dating anyone you'd rather take, I'll go with you. That's what friends do."

Instead of flashing me his easy smile and taking me up on my offer, he frowned and rubbed at his throat.

"What's the matter?"

He worked his mouth before he spoke, like he was testing it out. "I feel itchy. Weird. Like I'm having a reaction."

"But you didn't eat any macadamia nuts. Any tree nuts at all." My brain was slow, like a computer when its memory was overloaded.

"Do you remember if any of the flavors near the chocolate had nuts? Maybe they used the same scoop."

"There was a Nutella-flavored one in the same case." I remembered because I'd considered trying it but ruled it out due to Tyler's allergy. "That has nuts, right?"

He swallowed with difficulty. "Sure does."

"Hey," I said to the cab driver. "Can you take us to the closest hospital, please?"

"No." Tyler's voice had a rasp to it. "I've got an epipen at my apartment. I'll be fine."

The driver slowed. "What'll it be?"

My heart was going to beat out of my chest, but I understood not wanting to go to the hospital unnecessarily. Tyler probably had the high-deductible coverage like me. "Take us to his apartment. In the Excelsior, please. And hurry." I gripped his hand like that'd help.

The five-minute drive to his apartment seemed to take five hours. Tyler sucked in air, wheezing and gasping like an emphysema patient. He used one hand to massage his throat. The other squeezed my hand, as if to reassure me. It didn't work. I was breathing hard enough for both of us by the time we pulled up in front of his place.

When he stumbled, I ducked under his arm and supported him up the stairs to his place. He unlocked the door and flipped on the light. I'd never been inside his apartment, but I had no time to look around. My heart tripped in my chest like I was the one having the allergy attack.

He staggered through an open door and flicked the light switch. The bathroom was just big enough for a tub and shower combination, the toilet, and a square cabinet for the sink. He leaned over the sink, pulled open the medicine cabinet, and grabbed a plastic tube, which he set on the counter. Closing the lid on the toilet, he fumbled with his belt. "Sorry," he gasped, right as he dropped his jeans to the floor.

"Don't worry about it." Holy Hippocrates, he was worried about dropping trou in the middle of an anaphylactic reaction? I stood at the sink, my hands dangling, numb.

But Tyler knew what to do. He sank onto the toilet lid, and

with steady fingers, pulled the device from its tube. He popped off the top, set it against the outside of his thigh right below the leg of his boxer briefs, and pressed down until it clicked.

"That's it? It's done?"

His hands shook when he set the device on the counter. He cleared his throat. "Yeah."

"Now can I call 911?"

"No, I'll be fine."

"It says right on there to seek immediate medical attention." The words were printed above the evil-looking needle.

"I'll be fine. I've been through this a few times." His face was sweaty and pale, but he was breathing easier now. His lips had already turned from blue to pale pink.

When he stood, I stretched my arms toward him like I could catch him if he fell. "Really, I'm fine." He pulled up his jeans. "Sorry about all this. I'll call you a ride home."

I crossed my arms. "I'm not going home. I'm not leaving you alone tonight. What if your symptoms come back? Or you have a reaction to the medicine?"

"I'll be okay. Really."

I didn't move. "I'm staying."

"Fine." His lips twitched. "Mind if I go lie down?"

"Oh. Sure. No problem." Now it wasn't just my hands that were useless; it was my entire body. I backed out of the bathroom and trailed him through another door into his bedroom. He slid open the closet door and pulled down a pillow and blanket. He carried them to the living room, which had a single long couch set up in front of a coffee table and a television. The apartment was small, not quite as big as our house's tiny first floor.

He tossed the pillow onto the sofa and flopped down onto the cushions. "You take the bed."

"Absolutely not. You just had a medical emergency. You're sleeping in your bed." Tyler was stubborn, but not as stubborn as I was. I grasped his hand and tugged until he stood. "Go on. I'll give you a minute to settle in."

Frowning, he trudged into his bedroom. I called home to check on Dad, and then I spent a few minutes in his bathroom washing my face and brushing my teeth with his toothpaste and my finger.

When I walked into the bedroom, he flashed me a sleepy smile, and my heart rate finally slowed. "Feeling better?"

"Yeah." The covers were tucked up to his chin. "I'm breathing fine now. Really, you can go home."

"Not a chance." I sat on the other side of the bed, on top of the covers, and stretched out beside him, covering myself with the blanket he'd thrown over the couch earlier.

"What are you doing?" The smile had disappeared.

"There's plenty of room here. I'm going to make sure you sleep okay."

"Really, I'm—"

"I know, I know, you're fine. Still, I'm staying." I didn't know what I'd do if anything happened to my friend. And I was not about to find out.

He flicked off the lamp, and we lay there in the silence.

"We're never going back to that place again, you know," I said.

"The ice cream place?" He chuckled. "Shame. My ice cream was really good. Until it tried to kill me."

I laid a hand on his chest so I could feel his heartbeat. It seemed fast, but it was steady. He set his hand over mine. "Too soon?"

"Definitely too soon. No more jokes. Go to sleep."

His fingers tightened. "Thanks, Marlee. For taking care of me."

I knew he didn't mean only his allergy attack. He'd taken care of himself just fine. He meant with awful Raleigh.

"Anytime." And I would take care of him anytime. Just like I'd do with Alicia. I shoved the thought of what could've happened to him out of my brain. I knew I'd have trouble sleeping if I thought about that scary cab ride.

Instead, I watched his chest rise and fall in the dim light that filtered in at the sides of the blinds. His breath steadied and slowed and soon, mine did, too.

14

I WOKE in the gray light of dawn, warm and safe. But it wasn't my pillow under my cheek; it was someone else's skin.

Oh. My. God. What had I done?

I lifted my head, and my cheek came away from Tyler's chest with a soft sucking sound. I stared at the expanse of skin before me. A tattoo marked his golden shoulder, a curved V with a little pentagon on one end and a triangle on the other. It looked vaguely familiar, but I couldn't figure out what a V on Tyler's shoulder would signify. Maybe it was a Y for Young? Or had he started a tattoo that actually looked like something and had second thoughts?

He sighed and stretched his other arm back behind the pillow. The arm that wasn't snug around my waist. My—*oh, thank Gregor Mendel*—fully clothed waist. Although I'd sprawled over his chest, my lower half was still on top of the comforter. Some nurse I'd been. I'd fallen asleep on top of my patient.

By the faint light coming in through the blinds, I took a second to admire the curve of his triceps, the flat plane of his pectorals, the ridges of his abdominals. For someone who sat at a desk all day, he had a lot of muscles going on. But I kept my fingers curled into my palms. Friends didn't touch friends' naked chests. And they certainly didn't peek under the sheet that covered his lower half.

But I didn't have to peek to see that the lower half was equally...surprising. Not that I was surprised Tyler had a penis. Of course he did. I'd just never had a reason to think about it before. Until this morning, when his erection made a tent under the sheet big enough for—

I shut my eyes. But they flew open again. The soft jersey sheets clung to him, outlining the shape in graphic detail. I swallowed hard and dragged my gaze away.

The furnishings in his bedroom were spartan: a dresser and a single nightstand with his glasses resting next to a clock, its LED display telling me it was well after six. *Crap.* It was Friday, Cooper had an early meeting, and I needed to get to the office.

I slid carefully out from underneath his arm. A frown crossed his face, and I moved the hand that had been on my back onto his stomach. He murmured, "Princess," and I froze, waiting for him to open his eyes, but he didn't. No time to wake him; besides, after his allergy attack, he needed the rest. Instead, I eased myself off the bed and tiptoed out into the living room.

I spotted my handbag on the floor by the door where I'd dropped it during last night's mad dash for the epinephrine. I dug out my phone, hoping Tyler's clock had been wrong about the time, but it was half past six. No time to go home and change. I'd be stuck wearing yesterday's clothes to work. While I ordered an Uber, I tugged at my bra to dig the underwire out of the gouge it'd made in the side of my boob while I'd slept. Ouch.

Where had I dropped my coat? I circled the small room until the rosy light filtering in from the window illuminated a splotch of light fabric against the dark sofa. I walked over to grab it off the cushion, but a hiss startled me, making me snatch my hand back. The corner of my blush-pink coat peeked out from under a lump of dove-gray fluff.

Malevolent blue eyes—they were almost the same color as Cooper's—blinked at me from a dark gray face. It hissed at me again. Tyler had a…cat? One who, apparently, hated me just as much as Tigger did. Had I been a cat-abuser in a previous life? A dog? And how did I not know my friend had a cat?

"Pretty kitty," I whispered. "C'mere." I beckoned toward myself. The cat's stare didn't leave my face. "Shh. It's okay." I didn't know if I was talking to myself or the cat. I stretched a tentative hand toward the corner of my coat. The cat growled, and I tucked my hand against my wrinkled blouse. Nope. My coat wasn't worth the loss of my typing fingers.

A rough voice came from behind me. "Morning."

"Hey." He was still shirtless, wearing only last night's jeans, unbelted and drooping low on his waist. Lightning-fast, I averted my gaze. "I have an early meeting, and your cat's holding my coat hostage. Can you—?"

"Oh. Sorry. Sure." He scooped up the cat, and I plucked my coat off the sofa.

"Thanks."

"This is Subha. She's pretty laid-back." With one arm, he cuddled the cat against his bare chest, and she purred. I didn't blame her. He had a comfy chest. And oh-my-sweet-Leonardo-da-Vinci, how sexy was a muscular chest with a fluffy kitty snuggled against it? *No.* My friend was *not* sexy. Okay, fine, he was, but I wasn't attracted to him. At all.

"How are you feeling?" His color was better than it had been last night. His lips were pink and no longer blue-tinged.

"Better. Thanks," he said. When he smiled, the tightness in my chest eased. "Sorry about all the cat hair. Want me to run a roller over it?"

I checked my phone, like time could have miraculously started to run backward. "No time. Cooper's got an early meeting."

"Then I guess breakfast's out, too. Give me a minute to get dressed and I'll drive you."

"No, thanks. I called an Uber. You should go back to bed." I fought the urge to go to him, hug him, kiss his cheek. Sure, he was standing there, healthy, and not lying in a hospital bed with a breathing tube. But if I touched him, even if it was only to reassure myself he was okay, I was afraid I'd take more than our friendship allowed.

Keeping my eyes off his bare skin, I shoved my arms into my coat and swung my purse over my shoulder. "See you later."

I unbolted the door and slipped out. As I ran down the stairs, I tried to forget our panicked race up the stairs the night before. I hadn't been so scared since Dad fell off that ladder. I was glad I'd been with Tyler last night. Though, if we hadn't been together, he never would've eaten that contaminated ice cream. Next time, I'd watch to make sure the server used a fresh scoop. I'd take better care of my friend.

At the office, I clutched my coat around me and raced past security with a cursory wave. *Nothing to see here.* Upstairs, I glanced down the hall to Cooper's office—still dark—grabbed my workout bag, and dashed to Jackson's private bathroom.

A few minutes later, I was fresh-smelling and reasonably presentable, enough for a Friday at Synergy. I scurried back to my desk, shoved my bag in a drawer, and dropped into my chair just as the elevator dinged and Cooper walked out in his pressed and pomaded perfection.

He did a double-take at my desk. Normally, that would've been a good thing. Today I didn't love the extra attention. He took in my ponytail and "Yoga Girls Are Twisted" T-shirt over yesterday's rumpled pale-pink skirt.

"Feeling okay, Marlee?"

"I overslept." In a manner of speaking. A backwards way. I stared into his eyes, daring him to call my bluff.

He scratched the back of his neck. "I know Jackson isn't a stickler for dress code, but I'd prefer that my assistant represent me in a professional manner. Even on a Friday."

The blush started at my chest and barreled up to the roots of my hair. "Sorry, Cooper. It won't happen again."

"Okay, then. Can you start the conference call?"

"Sure thing." I pulled up the meeting application on my

screen, thankful not to have to look him in the eye. He turned, walked into his office, and shut the door.

I called the London office, conferenced in Cooper, and disconnected my line. Then I collapsed into my chair and blew out a breath. It was going to be a long day. I pulled out my phone to call Dad and found a text.

Tyler: Everything OK?

Hysterical laughter bubbled up behind my closed lips. Everything was *not* okay. My crush had called me out on our nonexistent dress code. I'd nearly gotten my friend killed and then ended up sleeping on his naked chest. Plus, I'd left Dad home alone all night.

But none of that was on him.

Me: Yep

I called Dad.

"Hi," I said when he picked up. "Sorry again about last night. I needed to help my friend."

"Maggie?"

I winced and rubbed my temple. "No, Dad, it's Marlee."

"Sunshine! You're all right?"

"Yes, fine. How are you?"

"Good, good. Playoff game this afternoon. How do tacos sound for dinner?"

The sharp pain at my temple eased a little. "Great. I'll see you at home tonight, okay?"

"See you later, sweetheart."

I set down my phone and leaned over my desk with my head in my hands, grateful, so grateful he was okay. But what if something had happened to him? I was truly a terrible person. As penance, I'd do nothing but work and stay home with Dad.

Wait. Staying home with him shouldn't have been a punishment. The man had cared for me for my whole life. I was an ungrateful daughter. I tugged on my ponytail.

Finally, I groaned and turned my attention to my computer.

Lost in my morning code review, I didn't hear the footsteps approach and jumped when a to-go cup of coffee and a paper bag plunked onto my desk. Tyler stood over me, a bottle of Mountain Dew in his hand and a bright grin on his face.

Just as he opened his mouth, Cooper loomed into view.

I wrenched my eyes from Tyler's face and flashed Cooper a tight smile. "What can I do for you, Cooper?"

His gaze took in Tyler, the cup of coffee, and my yoga shirt—again. His eyebrows rose. "Morning, Tyler." He smirked.

"Morning," Tyler grumbled.

I tilted my chin toward the coffee he'd brought me. "Thanks. I'll see you later."

The corners of his mouth tightened before he turned and walked back to the stairwell.

After the door shut, Cooper waggled his thick eyebrows at me. "Overslept, huh?"

I narrowed my eyes at him. Cooper didn't seem jealous at all. He seemed...gleeful. "I slept over at Tyler's last night. Unexpectedly."

His eyebrows rose. "So there *is* something going on."

I lifted the coffee to my lips. It tasted of pumpkin spice and dishonesty. Even though everything I'd said to him was true, it felt like I was lying to Cooper. A relationship built on a lie wouldn't stand. Before he left on his trip, I was going to come clean. About Tyler and about my feelings for Cooper.

Those laser-beam eyes scrutinized me again like they were trying to burn through my bullshit. At last, he blinked and leaned a hip on my desk. "Hey, I've got tickets to a musical, and I was wondering..."

Holy Hubble Telescope. He was finally going to ask me out. I stilled, waiting for him to say the words.

"They're for next week, and I'll be away. Would you like them? I know you're a musical theater fan. You could take Tyler."

I slumped. Even though I'd wanted forever to see a professional musical performance. "Sure. I mean, yes, that'd be wonderful. Thank you."

When he frowned—probably at my ingratitude—I dropped my gaze to my desk. My phone lit up, and I snatched up the handset, grateful for a reprieve from that laser-blue gaze.

José from security said, "Marlee, your visitor is here."

"Visitor?" Who'd come to see *me*?

"He says he has an appointment."

I pulled up my calendar and found the entry for an interview with another candidate for Cooper's assistant position. I'd been so caught up in everything that I'd forgotten. At least today's candidate was a guy. A man wouldn't notice my less-than-professional T-shirt and wrinkled skirt, unlike the women I'd been interviewing all week.

"Thanks. I'll be right down."

Cooper still hovered in front of my desk. "I'm interviewing another candidate for you," I said, plucking my folder of résumés out of the file sorter. "Want to come with?"

He shuddered and stepped back. "No, thanks. I have a lot of work to do."

I shook my head at him, and he turned and scurried back to his office. Coward.

Snatching up the coffee Tyler had brought me—he had to be the best friend ever—I peeked into the bag. Inside was the paper pastry sleeve I'd expected, lying on top of a plastic-wrapped pet-hair roller. I snickered.

But as I rode down the elevator to the ground floor, the smile died on my face. If today's candidate was qualified, he'd replace me in my temporary role as Cooper's assistant. No more one-on-one lunches, no more excuses to pop into his office, no chances to help him with late-night work.

My time was running out.

OF COURSE she'd come to Synergy on the day I was wearing a T-shirt and had my unwashed hair up in a ponytail.

Jamila Jallow, her legs looking endless in a pair of high-waisted trousers and a Burberry raincoat open at the front to reveal a cashmere sweater and silk scarf, leaned against the security desk, chatting with José.

"Morning, Jamila."

"Morning, Marlee. Can you escort me up?"

I'd planned to interview the candidate downstairs, but I supposed I could bring them both up to the sixth floor. "Sure. Let me just grab"—I looked at the résumé in my hand—"Ben."

A guy about my age sprang from his seat on one of the uncomfortable chartreuse leather chairs in the lobby. "Marlee?" he asked, already extending his hand. He wore a blue checked button-down shirt under a gray sweater and dark chinos. His lace-up ankle boots matched the soft-looking brown leather of his satchel.

I strode over to him, wishing I looked as put-together as he did. When I shook his hand, I tilted my head up only slightly to look him in his whiskey-colored eyes. Not monstrously tall like Cooper and Jamila. "Hi, Ben. I'm Marlee Rice. Let's go upstairs."

While we waited for the elevator, Ben leaned around me. "You're Jamila Jallow, right?"

She smiled and extended a long, slender hand. "I am."

"Ben Levy-Walters." He shook her hand. "I read your blog post this week about user experience design. It was inspirational."

Did the entire population of San Francisco read Jamila's blog? Ugh.

While we rode up, they continued their conversation about user interfaces. I kept my mouth shut and listened. The guy was smart, holding his own with one of the industry's brightest stars. Hmm.

On the sixth floor, I parked Ben in a conference room and walked Jamila to Cooper's office. When I knocked and opened the door, his frown of concentration disappeared and a grin broke over his face. A grin he'd never shown *me*.

"Mila! I didn't know you were coming in today."

"I thought I'd surprise you. Check in."

I closed the door and trudged back to Ben. What did I have to do to make him see me? Smile at me?

But I cleared Jamila out of my head when I sat across the table from Ben. As we traded pleasantries, I scanned through his résumé. I remembered that his credentials had been only so-so: two years as a receptionist and three as an executive assistant at a single company. No college degree. But his cover letter had been stellar.

"So, Ben," I said, starting the official part of the interview, "tell me why you applied to this position at Synergy." I sat back and prepared to be snowed about the *amazing opportunity* and *perfect fit* as I had been by every other candidate.

"Honestly?" He leaned forward, his palms on the edge of the table and his fingers splayed toward me. His whiskey-brown eyes were wide. "The startup I'd been working for cratered last month. I didn't even see it coming. My boss said we were fine, and I believed him. Story of my life. Anyway, I sat in a dark room for two weeks eating Häagen-Dazs." The corner of his mouth quirked up. "Then my sister told me about this position. She works here in accounting, and she knows I'm a total fanboy of Cooper Fallon."

So that's how his subpar résumé had gotten through HR's filter—he was an employee referral. "Really? Tell me what you know about Cooper and why you're a fan."

He leaned back in his chair. "Not many people know Cooper was a computer science major. They all assume Jackson was the programming brains and Cooper was the business guy. That's true, but Cooper helped with the initial product development." He folded his hands in his lap. "He doesn't give interviews about his life before college, and he's active in foundations that support at-risk kids. So I assume he had some trouble growing up. Like me." He bent toward me slightly. "I want to learn from him. Someday I'd like to help kids, too."

I nodded at him. He could learn a lot from Cooper. I was starting to like Ben, but he needed to know what he was getting himself into. "He can be…challenging to work with."

He chuckled. "I know the position's been vacant for months, since his old admin retired. None of the temps have worked out?"

I grimaced. No need for him to know why. "No. And he's been too busy to interview for the position until now."

His gaze was steady, assessing me. "And *he's* not interviewing me now; *you* are. Why is that?"

"Oh, he's been traveling and working on—"

"Excuse my French, but bullshit." He ran his eyes over me, from my ponytail to my faux leather booties. "I think it's *your* fault."

I cocked my head. "Really." This guy had known me for all of twenty minutes, and he was going to diagnose my relationship with Cooper. Ha.

"Everyone knows Jackson Jones is a—a bit…distracted. But you've been able to pull him together into a contributing executive at the company."

I'd have loved to take credit for that, but he'd changed for Alicia. "Well, actually, it was—"

He interrupted me. "You let him focus on what's important. You're the Wizard of Oz, making the magic happen from behind the curtain. You're *too* good. Cooper sees what Jackson has and wants the same thing."

I shifted in my chair. This wasn't supposed to be about me. If only Ben were right and Cooper *did* want me. But I was not going there with this too-observant man.

When I didn't object, Ben continued, "I suspect Cooper isn't like Jackson. He seems to have it together."

"He does." I compressed my lips to avoid babbling about all of Cooper's good qualities. I didn't need to sell him.

"What *does* he need?"

I sat back in my chair. Who was interviewing whom? "What do *you* think he needs?"

A slow smile spread over Ben's face. Like me, he must have liked challenges. "A guy who, in ten years, has grown a company from his dorm room to a Fortune 1000 company. A guy whose cofounder is brilliant but scattered and whose CEO is, from"—he checked that the conference room door was shut—"certain reports, a bit of a…we'll say, a difficult personality."

A dick was more like it. But Ben was at a job interview.

"Yet Cooper Fallon still manages to support various foundations and keeps his company growing every year. He maintains a grueling travel schedule. He needs…"

I leaned forward in my chair.

"He needs someone to protect him from himself. While it's important to support this company and its employees, he needs someone to keep him from giving away too much of himself. Before he burns out."

I remembered the dark shadows under his eyes that hadn't gone away after his return from Asia. Operation Hakuna Matata. I leaned back in my chair. "Exactly."

"Excuse me for saying it, but you look like you could use someone to do that for you, too."

I narrowed my eyes at Ben. This man saw too much. I had no doubt we'd hire him; he was exactly what Cooper needed. But I'd have to watch myself around him.

15

WHEN I OPENED the front door that night, Dad was watching *Nova* in his battered old recliner.

"Hi, Dad," I called over the blare of the television.

"Sunshine! Good day at work?" When he beamed at me, the flickering blue light of the television cast shadows on his face so that it looked like a grinning skull.

"Fine." I shook off my shivers as I crossed to the kitchen and flipped on the light. I hoped we had some beer. Or wine. That'd be even better. After dinner, I'd sneak upstairs and finally order that new vibrator. Something more...lifelike.

Hiding my burning cheeks from Dad, I set down my bags and toed out of my heels. That's when Tigger's uncharacteristically full bowl on the floor caught my eye. He normally scarfed down his meal in seconds. Was he sick? I really wasn't in the mood to take the cranky kitty to the vet tonight. I would, of course. No way would Alicia's beloved kitty be in less than perfect condition when I handed him back in a week. I looked under the table, where he loved to hide from me, but only an orange dust bunny sat there.

I padded back into the living room, but Tigger wasn't snuggled up with Dad, either. I went into his room, lifted the corner of the bedspread, and peered under the bed. More dust bunnies—I added vacuuming to my mental to-do list—but no cat.

Tigger's hatred for me was so fierce that he refused to set his dainty paws on the second floor, but I ran up the stairs anyway and checked my room. No sign of the ferocious fluffball.

I trotted back down the stairs, my heart racing, and stood between Dad and the television.

"Have you seen Tigger?" I tried to keep the panic out of my voice. No sense in upsetting him.

"Who?"

I snatched the remote and muted the television. "Tigger. The cat."

He scrunched his forehead. "We don't have a cat."

I closed my eyes and inhaled a few yoga breaths to calm myself. "Alicia's cat. He's been here for almost two weeks."

When I opened my eyes, Dad's face registered no understanding. *Shit.* After one last glance around the room, I returned to the kitchen. I found my sneakers on top of the washing machine, slid them on, and grabbed a jacket, a flashlight, and my phone. The corpulent kitty couldn't have gone far, but he'd be hard to find in the dark. And I had to find him. Alicia loved that goddamned cat.

TWO HOURS LATER, my hands shook as I poured myself a tumbler of red wine. I flopped into a kitchen chair and looked down at myself. My pale-pink skirt and my T-shirt were smeared with dirt and blanketed in orange and white fur, and my hands and arms were cross-hatched with scratches. Most of them weren't deep, and I'd washed them out well, but the gouge across the back of my hand had bled a bit and was starting to form a scab. The side of my face felt puffy around the shallow scratch that started on my cheekbone and trailed all the way down my neck. Still, I smirked—*ouch*. I'd emerged from our battle victorious.

My heart had pounded, my entire body tense and shaking as I'd wandered up and down our neighborhood streets. I wasn't sure whether I should call him or try to sneak up on him, considering how much Tigger despised me. Eventually, my voice had faded to a croak, making it a moot point. I'd already started to imagine finding his crumpled body in the street and mentally composed what I'd tell Alicia when I'd heard a rustle of dry leaves and lit up a pair of yellow eyes in the beam of my flashlight.

I'd chased him across a couple of yards until I cornered him against someone's steps and grabbed him around the middle. It wasn't until the demon scratched my face that I had the idea to take off my jacket and bundle him in it. After that, he was relatively docile, letting out only the occasional yowl as I carried him home like a running back who'd just scored the winning touchdown. I'd suppressed my urge to spike him and dab when we were safely inside the kitchen.

Now the little monster was safely snuggled up against Dad in his bed. Meanwhile, I wished we had something stronger than wine to tame my shakes so I could go to bed myself. And as much as I didn't want to think about it, my relief at finding Alicia's cat unharmed wasn't the only reason my hands trembled. The slack incomprehension on Dad's face when I'd asked him about Tigger terrified me. I couldn't deny it anymore: something was wrong with my dad.

16

BACK AT WORK on Monday afternoon, dressed *appropriately* in a black skirt and pink cowl-neck sweater, I stood to stretch my back. Working for Jackson gave me more opportunities to move around; he always needed a walk or help hunting down something in his office. Working for Cooper involved a lot more sitting at my desk.

When the stairwell door opened, I grinned. Tyler bounded out, hardly out of breath, and strolled over. Over the past week, he'd made a habit of coming up to my desk in the late afternoons. He leaned his hip on the desk and crossed his arms. "Hey."

"Good weekend?"

"It was okay. Yours?"

"Same old stuff." I smoothed my hair. "Dad and I watched sports."

"Wait. What happened to your hand?" He reached down, took my hand in both of his and rotated it toward the skylight. I'd been able to camouflage the mark on my face with my makeup, but the scratch on my hand was deeper. No one else—not even Cooper, and we'd eaten lunch together—had noticed it.

I snorted. "Tigger happened. He escaped on Friday and told me I'd never take him alive. But I did—he's fine. Please don't tell Alicia."

He examined the long scratch, running a finger lightly beside the dark red scab. Goosebumps sprang up on my forearm. He looked from my hand to my face, his eyes the velvety brownish green of moss on a tree trunk.

My message app pinged, jarring me out of the moment. "Hey. Just a sec." I gently tugged my hand out of his and glanced at my screen. "Oh! Ben accepted our offer."

"Who's Ben?" He picked up a piece of watermelon candy and twirled it between his fingers.

I tore my gaze from the candy back to my computer screen to tap out a response to the HR associate. "He's going to be Cooper's assistant. He starts the week after next."

"That's good for you, right? Less work, especially with Jay coming back."

"Right." What it meant was that I was out of time. Cooper was leaving on his trip tomorrow and wouldn't return until Ben's first day. I had to make my move *now*. Fortunately, I'd already made arrangements for Dad so I could work late.

"We could—we could go celebrate. That Mexican place down the street does Monday Margarita Madness."

That did sound fun, but—"Sorry. I promised Cooper I'd help him with his presentation for his East Coast trip."

"Tonight?"

I shifted in my chair. "He's been in back-to-back meetings ever since the wedding, taking on Jackson's workload. He's been working on it in the evenings on his own. I'm just helping him put the finishing touches on it." He was such a good man. So responsible. A tiny shard of guilt twinged me for the incompetent temps I'd hired. All for a good cause.

Tyler was silent for a moment. "I guess Operation Prince Charming is still in progress."

I lowered my voice. "I'm going to lay it on the table tonight."

"Tonight?" He took a half-step back like I'd taken a swing at him, but then he gave me a weak smile. "I mean, are you actually going to lay it"—he gestured at my torso—"on the table?"

"Ew. Don't be gross. I'm talking about feelings. You've heard of those, right?" Ugh, why was I being a bitch to my friend?

His jaw tightened. "Sure. Though I'm not sure he has." He squinted at Cooper's closed door.

He was no fan of Cooper Fallon, but I tried to make him understand. "Maybe he comes off as cold. Initially. But he has feelings, too. Passion. I think the right person could make him ease up a little. Melt a little of the ice." I'd dreamed about it once or twice or maybe a thousand times. How that mask he wore would crack when I told him I cared. Just like the alpha billionaire in the romance novel I'd read last week, who only needed a good-hearted woman to show him what love was.

"The right person. That's you." His voice was flat, almost as cold as Cooper's. "And he's your right person."

"Of course." I nudged my pencil cup into place. If only Cooper could see it. Then I'd get my sparks. And true love's kiss.

He dropped the piece of candy back into my bowl. "Afternoon, Cooper."

I spun in my chair, whacking my knee on the leg of the table. Starbursts of pain cartwheeled across my vision. But sure enough, Cooper had come to my desk.

"What's up, Cooper?" I rubbed my knee.

He glanced between us. "I almost forgot to give you these." He handed me an envelope.

"What's this?"

"The theater tickets I promised you. You and Tyler could go together. Work out this lovers' spat you're having." He circled his hand to indicate the two of us.

He could probably feel the tension that rolled between us like the fog outside. I opened the envelope and pulled out two tickets, center orchestra, of course, to—"*Hamilton?*" I squeaked.

"Have you seen it?"

"No." The tickets were for Friday night. I couldn't leave Dad and Tigger. I shoved them back into the envelope. "I can't—"

Tyler spoke over me. "We'd love to go. Thank you."

"Fantastic. You'll love it." Cooper smiled like a proud uncle, the first time I'd seen his face crack its stern expression all day. "You about ready to start on my presentation, Marlee?"

A thrill ran through me. This was it. Operation Prince Charming, ready for takeoff. I nodded, not trusting my voice.

"My office, ten minutes?" His voice was low and sexy.

Maybe I would be literally on the table. Or splayed out on that big buttery sofa in his office. I imagined that laser gaze of his getting closer and closer as his lips descended over mine. His woodsy scent surrounding me. The heat of his body radiating through his expensive shirt. Surely up close he'd be warm and not frosty like he always seemed. "Sure," I squeaked.

With a nod, he turned and strode back toward his office.

Wow. I blinked.

"He's leaving tomorrow, right?"

"Yes." I sighed and pushed the envelope with the tickets toward Tyler. "You go. I can't get away."

He didn't touch the envelope. "You're dying to see *Hamilton.* You won't need to work late since both Jackson and Cooper will be away. Why can't you go?"

"It's complicated." I still couldn't make sense of why Dad had forgotten about Tigger. Staying late tonight was bad enough. Though he'd seemed fine when I'd called him just before Tyler had come up, two nights in a week was asking for trouble.

"Anything wrong?"

"Just—just my dad is all. I don't think I can leave him alone."

"When we went out with Raleigh, you said he seemed off. Has he gotten worse?"

"Maybe." He had; I knew he had. His slip-ups were getting more frequent. And the one on Friday night—letting Tigger out—could've had serious consequences.

"Can you ask your neighbor to watch him again?"

"I feel bad always asking her. He's my responsibility."

"Even caretakers need a break sometimes," he said. "Ask her.

And if she can't do it, I'll find someone to hang out with him. You know you're dying to go."

One corner of my mouth lifted. "Okay. I'll text you tonight to let you know what she says."

"Perfect." He turned away. "It'll be great. Just you wait."

Now I full-on grinned. I'd played the soundtrack in the car on the way to the wedding. "You've been listening to it."

"Maybe." He rolled his lower lip under his teeth. "See you tomorrow."

The next second, he'd disappeared into the stairwell.

I stood and picked up my tablet. When would I have another chance to see *Hamilton?* I'd kick myself if I missed this opportunity. I'd been dying to see the show for years. Dad would be fine. Wouldn't he?

Tyler would be fine, too. Though I couldn't figure out why he'd gotten so pissed-off earlier. He'd been on board with Operation Prince Charming before. He'd be happy for me when Cooper and I were together, right? Even if Tyler and Cooper weren't exactly besties, I'd figure out some way for us all to hang out. We'd stay friends after.

Flinging my hair over my shoulder, I all but skipped to Cooper's door. Phase two of Operation Prince Charming was on.

Two hours later, we sat in the leather club chairs in his office with a spread of Thai takeout on the coffee table in front of us.

I set down my chopsticks and empty plate—with Cooper, one couldn't eat directly out of the takeout containers; he kept china plates in his credenza—and curled my legs under me in the chair. My heels had come off an hour ago.

He broke the silence that had stretched between us while we'd been eating. "How's Will?"

That was Cooper. So considerate, always conscious that his employees had families and lives outside Synergy. "He's okay. The colder weather always makes his leg sore."

"That's too bad. Does he need anything? A referral to a specialist? An advocate?"

"No, we're good, thanks."

"He's lucky to have you around to take care of him."

I lifted my mug from the table and cradled it in my hands. "I think I'm the lucky one to have him."

"You did win the Dad Lottery."

"Oh, is that a thing?" I smiled. "I guess I did."

Cooper cleared his throat and tilted his chin down to give me a mock-serious look. "And what does Will think of young Tyler?"

I narrowed my eyes at him. "They haven't met. Why would they?"

"With his visits up here and your sleepover last week, I figured things were getting serious."

He'd noticed Tyler's visits? Who did that, other than someone who was jealous? But after over a week in close proximity to Cooper, I was able to play it cool. "What are you, my sorority sister?"

"I'm just interested."

My heart beat faster. Interested? In me? It was time for honesty. To tell him how I felt. "We're friends. That's all."

"You went to Jackson's wedding together."

"*You* went with Jamila."

He raised his mug to his lips but didn't drink. "She's always my plus-one when I need one. We've been friends since college."

Friends with benefits? Or friends becoming more? She'd spent more time at Synergy over the past two weeks than she had the three previous years combined. I wish I knew how he felt about her. And how he felt about me.

Maybe he was waiting for me to make the first move because he hadn't wanted to insert himself between Tyler and me. And it was up to me to show him how I felt. Exactly what Amy Adams told Patrick Dempsey in *Enchanted*.

"So? You and Tyler?"

I looked him directly in the eye. Operation Prince Charming—and the associated fun and games—was over. Now we were in the endgame. "We didn't have dates to the wedding, so we went together. Friends do that."

"He kissed you. In public."

And in private. I dropped my gaze. Raising my mug of tea to my lips, I hoped the steam would hide my blush. "We got carried away."

"Last week's sleepover?"

"He had an allergic reaction. I stayed over to make sure he was okay."

"You're a good friend. And a good daughter. A stellar assistant. You excel at everything, Marlee."

At that, I looked at him. *Really* looked. We were so alike. Both of us strove for perfection, or at least to put up a perfect façade. We both hid things under that front—I hid my struggles with Dad, and he never talked about his past before Stanford. We were both driven to achieve our goals. He'd gotten what he wanted: a multibillion-dollar company. Was I on the cusp of what I wanted, my own happily ever after?

He was the Prince Charming I'd always dreamed of, handsome and successful and kind. Understanding about Dad. If he could only see *me*, not as a Synergy employee, but as a woman sitting in front of him. A woman who could love him if he only gave me a chance. We'd be great together. Did he suspect the same? Had he accepted my help tonight to ask about Tyler and ensure the path was clear? Why wouldn't he make a move, then?

Because, as I'd told Ben, Cooper was too busy taking care of those around him to take care of himself. I'd have to take care of him.

I unfolded my legs and stepped around the coffee table. He watched me, his face unreadable, as I perched on the loveseat next to his chair. I took his hand in one of mine. "Cooper," I began softly, "I need to tell you—"

My pulse leaped when he set his other hand on top of mine and pierced me with his stare. The Eagle had landed. He was going to tell me how he felt. I widened my eyes, my ears, every pore to catch his words. Hope surged through my bloodstream in the brief, glorious moment before I told him I cared about him. That someday, I could love him, too.

"Marlee, stop." He pulled my hand off his and set it on the cool leather arm of the loveseat. In one smooth movement, he rose from the chair and strode to the window. He stood there, his back tall and straight and cold.

"I've got it from here. Thanks for your help. You should go home now."

My heart fell into my stomach, where the spicy Thai food started to erode it. Painfully. I couldn't believe he'd shut me down when we'd come so close to something more. "But, Cooper, I—"

"No, Marlee." He didn't even turn. "You are a Synergy employee. I am the Chief Operating Officer. Even if I—"

I jumped up from the loveseat and marched over to him, facing his stiff back, trying so hard to hold in my anger I vibrated with it. "Don't you ever do anything just because you want to? Bend the rules? Even flaunt them sometimes?"

He was a block of granite. "No. Unlike Jackson, I take my responsibilities very seriously. You, of all people, should under-stand that."

"There are important rules like...doing right by people. Respect. Showing others you care. Jackson does just fine by those. Other rules"—*don't fall in love with your coworker*—"can be sacri-ficed to stay true to the more important ones."

"All rules are created for a reason, Marlee. They're all important."

Inside my head, I called him an obstinate jackass and a few other choice names. But continuing the argument, even after hours, would've been futile at best. In the mood he was in, I wouldn't have put it past Cooper to write me up a formal warn-ing. He'd probably include not wearing proper footwear in the office.

"Good night, Cooper," I said. "Have a good trip." *Stubborn...conventionalist.*

"Good night." He held up his hand in a sort of wave but didn't turn around to look at me.

Snatching up my shoes, I kicked the door shut behind me. Hard. I hoped it startled him. I hoped he regretted blowing me off. I hoped he had blue balls for the next week.

I froze midway between his office and my desk. *Sigmund Freud on a stick.* Now I was one of the batshit women leaving Cooper's office. If I ever saw that bitch, Karma, I'd zap her with my Taser.

17

RAIN PATTERED AGAINST THE SKYLIGHT, turning everything inside the office so gray I couldn't tell if it was morning or afternoon.

Not that it mattered.

I glanced at the closed door to Cooper's unlit office and then quickly away. How could I avoid going in there ever again? Every time I looked at it, my belly burned with shame. At least it made me feel something. I was an asteroid, spinning through space, pulled by only the weakest of forces. Hollow. Numb.

I yanked open my drawer and dug out my old plan. I'd crossed off step one, our dance. I hadn't bothered marking through step two since bonding over takeout had turned into such a colossal failure. And step three? There would be no magical kiss for me.

Slamming the drawer shut, I trudged to the copy room and fed the list into the shredder. But even its noisy grind didn't satisfy. Maybe I should've burned it.

When the shredder turned off, silence pressed against my ears. In fact, except for the drumming of the rain on the skylight, the sixth floor was remarkably quiet. Probably because Jackson's and Cooper's outsized personalities were missing.

Which should've been a relief. Seeing Cooper would be uncomfortable at best after he'd turned me down last night, even after my anger had dissolved, replaced by emptiness. And having Jackson see me, pale under my makeup with blue shadows under my eyes? He'd have the whole, humiliating story out of me and do something ridiculous like buy me flowers.

And as much as I loved flowers, pity flowers were the worst. What kind did you get for someone who'd crushed on someone for three years and been turned down cold? One of those horrible bleeding-heart funeral arrangements, with red ribbons dripping down like blood.

The door crashed open behind me, and the squeal of Tyler's sneakers rang out on the empty floor. "Marlee, aren't you coming?"

I turned to face him. "Coming where?"

"The town hall meeting. It's about to start. Everyone's there."

I glanced around the empty floor and then back at my computer screen, which should've reminded me. Oh, right, it'd gone into sleep mode while I moped.

I grabbed my phone and stood. But instead of leading me toward the elevators, he put his hands on my upper arms. Even through my cardigan's sleeves, I felt that thrill, same as at the wedding. Just another sign of how screwed-up my romantic life was. Tingles anytime a guy so much as touched me. Go figure.

He squeezed my arms gently. "Are you okay?"

I couldn't look at him. My spine felt like a wet noodle, and I couldn't muster up the energy to project the bad-ass image I needed to shield myself from those who either scorned me or feared me and my power at Synergy.

"I'm fine," I muttered, staring at Ms. Pac-Man's bow on his T-shirt.

"Your dad's okay?"

"What? Of course." Still, I glanced down at my phone. No messages or texts. He'd been up and moving in the kitchen when

I'd kissed him on the cheek and walked out the door this morning.

"Then what's—" He glanced toward Cooper's office. "Oh."

The wound was too fresh to talk about, even with my friend. "Let's go."

He gripped my hand and strode toward the stairs. "Elevators are full."

My heels weren't made for the concrete stairs, and he took it slowly, holding my ice-cold hand and letting me clatter behind at my own pace down the four flights to the second floor, where the auditorium was. We paused in front of the metal door.

Footsteps thumped above us, and one of the developers, Grant, came around the bend in the stairs. "Hey, Tyler, you coming?"

He peered into my eyes. "Just a minute."

"Save you a seat? Or are you sitting with her?" I heard the sneer in his voice.

"I'm with Marlee. I'll see you after."

Grant walked around us and opened the door. The beats of Weston's signature song, DJ Khaled's "All I Do Is Win," filled the conference room on the other side. The door swung shut behind him, muffling the music.

Even in the dimly lit stairwell, the gold flecks in Tyler's eyes gleamed. "You want to go in?"

I gave him the best smile I could muster. He'd turned down his friend for me. "I guess."

He lifted a hand to my face and tucked a stray strand behind my ear. I couldn't help it; I leaned into his touch, warm and safe. Tyler would never hurt me. He'd stick with me, no matter what.

Tyler ran his hands down my arms. "You're shivering. Are you cold?"

I was, like an exoplanet, too far from the sun. "I'm sorry, I— you're being too nice. And I know you hate being called that, but it's true."

He put his arms around me, and I buried my face in the heat of his chest. I wanted to stay there forever, but the music ended, and Weston's voice came faintly through the door.

"We're missing the meeting. And I'm getting makeup all over your shirt."

"Don't worry about it." He rubbed circles on my back. "Let it all out."

Oddly, I had no tears. But I soaked up his warmth like the light side of the moon while he whispered soothing nonsense into my hair.

We didn't make it to the town hall. Maybe Weston told the employees we were all going to be laid off.

I didn't care.

I only cared that my friend was a giant teddy bear, making me feel a tiny bit better, convincing me I wasn't completely unlovable, that someone cared about me. While he held me in the stairwell, he pressed mute on all my problems—my dad, Cooper, even evil Tigger—and let me be myself, messy emotions and all.

Finally, when I felt almost human again, I squeezed him one more time and raised my head. All the colors of my face—pink lipstick and blush, peachy foundation, black mascara—remained on his white shirt, right above Ms. Pac-Man's face. I rubbed at the stains for a second before I gave up.

"Thanks for being such a good friend."

He put a knuckle under my chin and lifted so I'd look him in the eyes. They were brown that day, like sun-warmed soil. "I'm always here for you, Marlee."

I gave him a wobbly smile. "We still on for *Hamilton* on Friday? My neighbor said she could come over and stay with my dad."

"Wouldn't miss it for anything."

"I'm sorry about your shirt." I tried again to rub the stain off with my thumb. "And I look hideous with my makeup smeared like this."

"With or without your makeup, you're the most beautiful woman in this office."

I had to hold on tight to Tyler. I'd never find another friend as good as him.

—————

WHEN TYLER SHOWED up at my desk late on Friday afternoon, I had some seriously unfriendly feelings toward him. After a long day of work, how the hell did he pull off full-on smoking hot?

Maybe it was the jacket. Instead of his usual T-shirt and jeans, he wore slim khaki pants and a dress shirt somewhere between blue and green that brought out the cool colors in his hazel eyes. Over it, he wore a dark blazer, maybe the same one he'd worn to Alicia's wedding. Under my desk, I pinched the skin between my thumb and forefinger, using the pain to remind myself that, no matter how hot he looked that night, we were just friends.

"Ready to go?" he asked, and damn me if those dimples didn't make me stumble as I stood.

"Yeah." Why was my voice so breathy? This was just Tyler, my friend, and we were going to *Hamilton* together. It wasn't a date. It was two friends going on a friendly trip to the theater. A gift from Cooper. Who'd broken my heart. That must have been why I felt so weird around Tyler. My heart—and the part of my brain that regulated it—was as defective as the Schiaparelli lander and burned-out as the crater it left on Mars. I cleared my throat.

"Got the tickets?"

"Mm-hm." I patted my purse.

"Everything all right? Your dad's okay?"

The setting sun chose that moment to sink low enough that its rays beamed between the neighboring buildings into Jackson's office, and a spear of salmon pink shone through the glass wall directly onto Tyler. It gilded the tips of his hair and made the afternoon whiskers on his jaw sparkle.

"Marlee?"

"Yep, I'm good." I blinked hard and headed toward the elevators.

"And your dad?"

"He's fine." I'd called him, and he and Alma were in the middle of a game of gin rummy. He sounded the way he used to —strong, steady, smart. Good days like today made me hope the bad days like last Friday were like quantum particles observed in an anomalous state, to be smoothed out into more normal behavior over time. Maybe I'd ask Dad what he thought about my theory on one of his good days.

When we stepped into the elevator, I caught Tyler's cologne— cedar and citrus—and was back outside the inn, wearing his jacket, encircled by his arms, his lips—

I held my breath. If only I could stop breathing until the doors opened. That was the only way I was going to get through the evening without doing something completely inappropriate with my friend. Damned dry spell was turning my brain inside out.

Six floors was a long way, and the Synergy elevator was leisurely. My chest tightened, and spots danced in front of my eyes. But I would not let Tyler's intoxicating scent make me do something stupid in that elevator.

Tyler must have thought I was having some kind of mental-health crisis when I shoved out into the lobby before the doors fully opened, gasping in breaths of pine-scented industrial cleaner. The cleaning guy sure did when I almost tripped over his floor buffer.

Tyler gripped my elbow to keep me from face-planting onto the slick floor. "You sure you're okay?"

"This is weird, right?" I shouted over the buffer's motor.

"What's weird?"

I led him, still clutching my elbow, to the front doors where I didn't have to shout. And shouldn't—the night security guard, Howard, didn't need to hear this. "You and me. Going on a d— going to the theater. Together, I mean. The two of us." I pressed my lips together to stop the flow of words.

"No." He scrunched up his forehead. At least the dimples

were gone now. "We do stuff together all the time. You sure you're okay?"

Ah. So it was just me. "Yeah. I'm fine."

He held the door open for me, and we walked out into the golden light of sunset, the air surprisingly warm for the middle of October. I followed him toward the parking garage.

On the way, I spotted my favorite tamale cart. I smiled at Diego as he cranked the canopy closed. The lingering spicy scent beckoned to me, making my mouth water. It had been a while since I'd had tamales. All those stiff lunches with Cooper, and I'd made zero progress. Now, it hardly seemed worth the missed visits to Diego's cart. I'd come by for lunch tomorrow.

Tyler stopped right in front of the cart. "These are your favorite, right?" he asked me.

"Aren't they everyone's? I'm sure there aren't any left."

But Diego pulled a steam-softened sack from the toasty depths of the cart. "Here you go. Have a nice night." He winked at Tyler. "Hasta luego, Marlee."

"See you, Diego." Tyler tucked the sack under his arm and continued toward the garage. "I thought we'd have a picnic, if that's okay."

He hated hearing it, so I didn't say it. But Tyler was sweet to remember that I loved Diego's tamales. My stomach growled at the aroma coming from the sack of tamales. "Sounds great."

In the car, the scent of the tamales covered up Tyler's cologne, and I could think again. Clearly, my old vibrator wasn't working. It was time to step up my game and order the fancy one that promised to blow my mind with screaming orgasms. And buy some earplugs for Dad.

"So tell me about—"

I cut him off. "Are you going home for the holidays?" I wasn't ready to talk about how Operation Prince Charming had gone down in flames on Tuesday.

He furrowed his forehead. "You mean Thanksgiving?"

"It's a little over a month away. You need to buy a ticket if you're going."

"I wasn't going to. You met Raleigh. The rest of them are the same. Alicia said I could hang with them if I'm staying here."

Even though it was just my dad and me, holidays—especially Thanksgiving—were for family. "You should go home. Tell them off the way you told off that jerk, Raleigh."

He chuckled. "You told off Raleigh. I'd need to take you with me."

Silence dropped over us like a blanket. And not the comfortable, friendly, soft kind of blanket.

"I mean, hypothetically," he said. "In the upside-down world where I went home. Which I'm not doing."

"Of course. And I'd bring my phaser—set to stun, of course—and go to town on any of your siblings who tried to put you down. Pew! Pew!" I pretended to shoot at the other cars.

"Phasers don't go pew-pew. That's a *Star Wars* blaster. On *Star Trek*, they're more like a wah-wah-wah-wah sound. Or, in the newer shows, a zee-ot."

"A zee-ot." And we were back in safe territory.

When we parked at the Civic Center, Tyler retrieved a frayed blanket from the Mustang's trunk before we ascended to the grassy area outside City Hall. He spread out the blanket, and I tucked the flared skirt of my dress, another pink floral print, under me. The white-columned building and its dome rose behind him, dusted coral by the sunset.

He handed me a bottle of water and cracked open a Mountain Dew.

"They don't allow wine in the park, but I figured the atmosphere was worth it," Tyler said. "Better than some stuffy restaurant."

I leaned back on my hands. Tyler was the opposite of stuffy. What you saw was what you got: open, honest, true. I couldn't say the same about Cooper, whose enigmatic, opaque nature had been a puzzle to me the three years I'd known him. I'd hoped that someday I'd crack it, and the mysteries of his universe would be laid bare. Not anymore. My chest tightened in a perfunctory twinge.

Tyler passed me a fork and a couple of tamales on a paper plate. "Buen provecho."

I took a bite. "Great Galileo, these are good. Have some before they get cold."

He unwrapped a couple of tamales and laid them on his plate. "Why is this weird?"

Oh. I'd thought he'd chosen to ignore my awkward verbal fire hose in the lobby. And in the car. That probably would've been better. If we didn't talk about it, it wasn't real.

Why was it weird? Sitting on a blanket in the park eating tamales with him didn't feel weird. Even though we were dressed up, we were still two friends sharing a meal. Outside. In public. Unlike in the elevator, I didn't want to wrap myself in him, kiss those soft lips. And he didn't want to kiss me. He sat across from me, poking at his tamales, not even looking at me. A man meandered past us, pushing a rattling shopping cart. Nope, we were safe out here.

"I guess it's not weird." Maybe I was the only one who lost her mind when we got too close.

"Good, because that's not how I feel around you. I feel like... like all the colors are turned up. Like it's always sunrise or sunset around you." He held up his hand, turning it to examine the orange where the setting sun hit it and the dusky blue shadows on the other side.

"Tyler, we—" My heart pounded like it wanted to leap out of my chest and straight into his. No. I couldn't let myself get sucked in by poetry. We were friends hanging out. Soon, the sun would set, taking away the golden magic and leaving us in the cool blues and grays of twilight. What would that do to Tyler's eyes? Would they fade to dark, or would the golden flecks glow like a cat's?

I needed to get him back under the fluorescents that washed out his vibrant shades and turned him back into my everyday work friend.

I set down my plate. "We're friends. And I don't want anything to ruin that." Cooper had been right about that while we'd danced at the wedding. As long as I maintained a safe distance, like a satellite in orbit, I'd be fine. But if I nudged closer to Tyler, our friendship would burn up like a fiery meteor in the atmosphere and leave behind only a cold hunk of metal. I couldn't destroy our friendship like that. I wouldn't.

He took a breath to say something but then blew it out. Instead, he lifted the green bottle to his lips and drank. "I don't want to ruin our friendship, either. It's special to me. You're special to me."

I smiled. "Our friendship is important. Especially with—" I couldn't even say it. If I didn't say the words, Alicia's marriage wouldn't change our friendship. She, Tyler, and I wouldn't change. We'd still be the three outsiders who, when we were together, helped each other feel like insiders.

"I get it." He laid his hand on my knee, over my dress, just for a second, before he speared a bite of tamale and popped it in his mouth. He rolled his eyes up while he chewed. "You're right. These are the best."

"I know, right?" I picked up my plate and dove into my second tamale. We were back in the safe zone. "Stick with me. I've got plenty more to show you."

He snorted. "I'm sure you do."

———

MY HEART WAS BREAKING. Again.

It was one thing to listen to the soundtrack through my earbuds. It was something else entirely to see it acted out on the stage, especially from three rows back, where I could plainly see Eliza's anguished expression as she cradled her son in her arms. And when she cried out, a sob hiccupped out of me.

I only remembered I was still in a theater full of strangers when I caught a flash out of the corner of my eye. The lady next to me turned, her diamond earrings catching the stage lights, to give me a comforting smile.

From my other side, a handkerchief brushed against my hand. I smiled my thanks at Tyler, whose eyes were glossy, too. But I had actual tears running down my cheeks, and probably mascara, so I didn't try to give it back. At least my tear ducts were operational again. And these were good tears. Sad, but for someone else. Not myself.

I blotted my eyes and returned my attention to the stage, where the drama marched to its inevitable conclusion.

I knew the ending. Everyone does. Still, I was glad I had Tyler's handkerchief.

Cooper would've loved the show. Though he'd probably already seen it on Broadway. Sure, he was a workaholic, but he was also a musical theater junkie. If he'd been with me, instead of in Boston, we could've gushed over the music, the costumes, the performances. In front of the stage, where there was plenty of room for his long legs, would he have passed me a tissue? Held my hand? Laid an arm over the back of my seat?

Maybe.

Or maybe not. He was more the silk pocket square type than the cotton handkerchief type. And he was never a fan of PDA, even if it was only to comfort a friend.

The lady next to me gathered up her coat before she turned to me. "Is Cooper all right? He never misses the shows."

Of course. These were his season tickets. They'd probably been sitting together for years. "He had to travel. For work."

"Tell him we missed him. And Jamila, too."

Jamila. I drew my stiff cheeks into a smile and said, "Of course I will."

"But I'm glad you could come. I can tell you enjoyed it. Drive safely, now."

"You, too."

She nodded and followed her companion down the aisle.

I turned to find Tyler standing so close I could've bumped his chin with my nose. "Ready to go?" he asked.

"Yeah." It'd been a magical evening, but it was time for Cinderella to return home where she belonged. I walked down the now-empty aisle, clutching my playbill to keep from finding comfort in Tyler's hand.

Outside, the sun was gone, leaving the sky a hazy charcoal. The lights reflecting off the theater's façade lit up the short distance to the subway stairs. I stopped under the yellow glow of a streetlight. "Thanks for coming with me. I had a great time."

"Want to get a drink? It's not late. There's a place near here—"

"No." I laid a hand on his sleeve. "I've got to get back. Alma's probably ready to go home."

He drummed his fingers on the side of his leg. "I'll drive you."

I shook my head. "The train station's right here, and Oakland is completely out of your way. It'd take you over an hour to get to my place and back home."

His dimples disappeared, and he seemed to shrink. "Are you sure? It's late for the train."

I smiled. "You just said it wasn't late. You can't have it both ways." I lifted onto my toes and kissed his cheek, right where the dimple had been. Tyler froze, like I'd gotten him with my imaginary phaser. But I kept moving, making sure not to breathe him in. A quick peck and a quicker exit.

"I'll see you at work on Monday," I said, already passing him to get to the subway stairs.

Just before I took my first step down, I looked back to where I'd left Tyler. Still standing where I'd left him, he raised his long-fingered hand in a wave.

I waved back, then descended the stairs.

We could stay friends. I didn't want anything more. Need anything more. Not from him. We needed to stay in the friend zone. He'd said that was important to him, too.

Still, on the train ride home, I finally ordered that new vibrator. If I was going to stay friends with Tyler and get over Cooper Fallon, I was going to need it.

18

MONDAY WAS QUIET, so I spent the morning cleaning out Jackson's office. I didn't dare touch Cooper's. Not that anything was ever out of place in his sanctuary.

When Tyler asked me if I wanted to go to lunch, I insisted we go to the employee cafeteria. No more dangerous one-on-one time. We'd hang out together in public places until Alicia came back and we had a chaperone again. In the noisy bustle of the cafeteria, we were simply two colleagues sharing a meal. Those dimples that showed just before he laughed could've been for anyone; they weren't for me to jealously collect and catalog.

Last week's unseasonable warmth was gone, and that evening, the chilly October mist wrapped me as soon as I stepped out of the BART station in Oakland. I buttoned my coat against the tiny drops of moisture beading up on the wool and dampening my hair. I couldn't wait to get home, put on my cozy pajamas, and lose myself in a novel. I hoped Dad hadn't accidentally turned off the heat again.

But as soon as I stepped through the front door, I knew something was wrong. Tigger twined around my ankles, mewling. The television was off, the house was dark, and the recliner was empty.

"Dad?" I called out. Silence. I yanked off my damp boots and padded into the kitchen, flipping on the light. Tigger's meows grew desperate, so I paused to fill his bowl and almost lost a finger to his ravenous, sharp teeth.

Then I saw the phone—Dad's phone—lying on the kitchen counter.

"Dad?" I called again. I walked to his bedroom, but it was also empty. The bathroom, too. I knew he wouldn't be upstairs—couldn't be—but I ran up anyway. When I saw my bedroom undisturbed, a lump caught in my throat. I looked through the window into the yard. He wasn't there, either. Not on the bench under the Japanese maple, not sitting on the steps.

I pulled my phone from my pocket and called Alma. "Have you seen my dad?" I asked as soon as she answered.

She understood what I didn't—couldn't—say. "No, mija. I'm on my way."

My hands shook so badly that I couldn't press the disconnect button. I was frozen, unable to think of what to do. Where could he have gone? How could I find him? I was thankful we'd sold the truck last year. He couldn't have gotten far on foot.

I didn't know how long I stood there, but Alma's voice from downstairs broke me out of my trance. I ran down and hugged her. After a moment, she disengaged from my embrace but held my arms, reassuring me with her touch.

Her dark brown eyes searched mine. "I'll stay here and wait for Will to come back. While I'm waiting, I'll make some calls. Do you know where he might have gone?"

I shook my head. Panic fogged my brain and scattered my thoughts.

"He used to go to the YMCA, right?" she asked.

I nodded. He used to swim as therapy for his knee in the afternoons.

"Check there, but on your way, ask at the bar down the street and the restaurants on the next block. He might have gotten hungry."

I couldn't think through my rising terror, but I could follow her directions. A horrifying thought struck me. "You'll call the—" I couldn't say the word *hospital,* but her look of comprehension told me she understood.

"Yes. But I won't call the police—yet."

Cold prickles crawled up my spine. An official report might take him away from me. I turned to the door.

"Wait," she said. "You shouldn't go out alone. Do you have a friend you can call?"

I ran through my mental list. Alicia and Jackson were in Fiji until Friday. Cooper was still in Boston. All my friends from college had moved away or moved on. I started to shake my head, but then I thought of Tyler. He was my friend. He'd help me.

I found his name in my phone and pressed it before I could reconsider.

After six rings, I'd already pulled the phone from my ear to disconnect when he spoke.

"Hey, Marlee." He sounded breathless, like he'd run to answer it.

"Tyler," I squeaked. I stopped to clear my throat.

"What's wrong?"

"My dad"—I cleared my throat again—"My dad's gone missing. I—Could you—?" The words wouldn't come out.

But he didn't wait to be asked. "Where are you?"

"I'm at home. But I'm going out now to look for him."

"I'll call you when I get to Oakland and we'll meet up. Be careful, okay?"

"Okay."

He must have heard the quaver in my voice because he said, "It'll be fine. You'll probably find him before I get there."

Unable to speak past the hysteria gripping my throat, I hung up. A few seconds later, my phone pinged. Tyler had used an app to send me his location, and it was asking me to share my location with him. I clicked *Yes,* hopeful that technology could help me find Dad.

Twenty minutes later, I emerged alone from a restaurant a few blocks from the house. The rumble of Tyler's vintage Mustang as it pulled up in front vibrated through my chest. My racing heartbeat slowed a fraction when he leaped to stand before me on the sidewalk. His arms twitched like he wanted to reach out to me, but he kept them at his sides. Lines of concern bracketed his mouth, and his eyes flicked between mine.

I couldn't show the same restraint. I stepped into him, wrapped my arms around his solid back, and tucked my head under his chin. I breathed in his familiar, comforting scent. "Thank you. Thank you so much for coming."

His arms came around me. After a quick squeeze, he released me and stepped back. He looked around us. "What's the plan?"

I no longer trembled, and my voice surprised me with its steadiness. "I've searched the restaurants here. I was on my way to the Y. My dad used to exercise there."

"Okay. I'll drive." He opened the door of the Mustang and closed it behind me. When he slid in, he reached across the console for my hand and held it, keeping me from falling over the edge.

I didn't wait for him when we pulled up in front of the YMCA. I jumped out and ran into the lobby, where I pushed to the front of the line and accosted the woman at the membership desk. "Have you seen my dad? Will Rice. He's fifty-three, walks with a cane or else a limp, short white hair, a little thin?"

She eyed me, wary of the wild-eyed woman who'd burst in on her peaceful evening. She shook her head. I pulled out my phone and showed her the photo I'd used at the other places I'd looked.

"Are you sure?"

"No, miss."

I turned away and scanned the lobby myself as if he'd be lurking there, somehow unseen by the receptionist, but I didn't see his cropped white hair anywhere. I bit my lip.

Tyler jogged to my side and put his arm around me. "Hey, we'll find him. Where should we go next?"

My panic came rushing back. I had no idea. I opened my mouth to tell him that, but my phone vibrated. When I saw it was Alma, hope fluttered in my chest.

"Hola, mija. Señor Oliveras from the grocery called. He said someone saw your dad at the train station."

"When?"

"About ten minutes ago. Hurry."

I grabbed Tyler's hand and pulled him toward the exit. "He's at the BART station. Let's go."

In the car, he held my hand again as I directed him. "You don't think—"

"I don't think he can get anywhere. I doubt he has any money with him. Of course, I didn't think he'd wander off…" I stared out the window, unable to continue. He squeezed my hand.

Tyler left the Mustang on the street with its hazard lights flashing while we ran inside the station. I almost collapsed when I spotted the familiar shape in front of the ticket machine.

"Dad!" I called to him. When I reached him, I threw my arms around him and hugged him tight. "You scared me. Why'd you leave the house?"

"I wanted to go see Maggie," he said, as if it were the most reasonable thing in the world to take the train to see my dead mother.

I released him and slipped my hand into his as I'd done so many times when I was little. But this time, I spoke like the parent. "Dad, you can't wander off. We've been looking for you everywhere."

He smiled down at me and cocked his head to the side. "I was right here."

How long had he been there? I'd come through the station a little more than an hour ago. Surely I would've walked past him if he'd come straight there from home. If only I hadn't been stuck in my own head, focused on myself…

I looked him over from head to toe. His hair was slicked to his head, and the bottoms of his pants were wet to the ankles as if he'd been walking for a while in the misty rain. With the fuzzy state he was in, I'd never know exactly where he'd gone.

I'd almost forgotten Tyler was there until he put a hand on my back and extended his right hand to my father. "Mr. Rice, I'm Tyler Young, a friend of Marlee's."

Dad shook his hand and straightened to his full height so he was almost at Tyler's eye level. "Will Rice." He sounded so normal. But then he said, "I was going to visit Maggie."

Tyler raised his eyebrows at me. I shook my head. "Come on, Dad," I said. "Let's go home." I walked beside him, gripping his free arm as he leaned on his cane and shuffled out behind Tyler.

I wedged myself into the tiny back seat and marveled at how easily Tyler engaged Dad in conversation as he drove us home. They talked about baseball, and even I could tell that Dad was jumping back and forth between this year's playoffs and some series from ten or twenty years before, but Tyler followed his leaps without comment. Still, I was glad for the ride to be over when we reached our house.

While I hugged Alma and told her what had happened, Dad went to bed. The lines around his eyes and mouth told me he was exhausted, even if he wouldn't admit it.

I felt it, too. My knees trembled, and my limbs were heavy. My head was packed with mud, the thoughts struggling through it. The stress that had tightened my spine and kept me going for the past ninety minutes—had it been only that?—left me all at once, and I collapsed, boneless, on the couch.

Tyler stood in the middle of the living room, hands on his hips, making the room look smaller even than it was. "Mind if I make us something to eat? I haven't had dinner yet, and I imagine you haven't, either."

The last thing I wanted to do was haul myself into the kitchen, but it was the least I could do for Tyler, who'd been so strong through my ordeal. "Give me a minute, and I'll—"

"No," he cut me off. "Stay there. I'll find us something. That is, if it's okay with you?"

I tried to muster the energy to be the hospitable friend I should've been. I just—couldn't. "Fine." I stretched out on the couch. I'd rest for a few minutes. Then I'd go into the kitchen and help Tyler find something to cook.

A hand on my shoulder nudged me awake. I groaned as I sat up. I hadn't meant to fall asleep, but those dreamless, worry-free minutes had soothed my jangled nerves. Tyler sank down at the other end of the couch—he left an entire cushion between us—with a plate. He tilted his chin toward another plate in front of me on the coffee table.

"I made us sandwiches. I hope that's okay."

"Thank you." I pulled the plate onto my lap. Tigger hopped up, stretched out along Tyler's thigh, and stared at me, unblinking. We ate in silence. Until—

"Who's Maggie?"

I finished chewing and swallowed with difficulty. My mouth had gone dry. "My mother, Margaret."

"You told me she died. Was your dad going to visit her at the cemetery?"

"No. She was cremated. She's over there." I waved my hand at the small round table in the corner of the room with the floral-patterned, ceramic urn on it. Then I took a big bite of my sandwich so I wouldn't have to say anything else.

Tyler was silent for a minute, but then he continued, "Does he have episodes like this...often?"

I set down my plate and drank from the glass of water Tyler had placed on the table in front of me. I wished it were something alcoholic. "Not this bad." I drank again and set down the glass. "But last week, it was Dad who let the cat out. He forgot Tigger was staying here."

I stole a look at Tyler. He set down his sandwich, and his mouth tightened. He rotated toward me, splaying one knee toward the back of the couch.

"My grandpa had Alzheimer's."

I froze. Alzheimer's? I'd thought about it a couple times, but that was only for old people.

He shook his head rapidly and held out his palms to me in an "easy-there" gesture. "I'm not saying your dad has it. Although people can develop it in their forties and fifties."

His fingers tapped his knee. "It started out small, forgetting appointments or telling the same story over and over. We made fun of him sometimes, and he laughed about it." Tyler pulled at a frayed thread in the sofa. "But eventually, he got so bad we couldn't leave him alone. He'd forget to turn off the stove. One time, he left the bathtub running, and it overflowed. Ruined the ceiling of the room below. And a couple of times, he wandered off. Like your dad. Couldn't explain why he'd done it." He smoothed down the thread and looked up at me. "After we found him standing in the middle of a busy street, we had to put him in the memory-care unit of a nursing home."

I crossed my arms, suddenly cold. "I couldn't do that." I flicked my gaze to Mom's urn, surrounded by candles and the flowers I'd picked up at the grocery store. I couldn't lose him, too. "I'll—I'll hire someone. To take care of him while I'm at work."

"Sure, that's fine." Tyler's voice soothed me like honey in hot tea. "You're taking good care of him."

Tears prickled behind my eyes, and I reached for the plates on the coffee table.

"I'll do it. You've had a hard night. Don't worry about anything." The blanket from the back of the sofa draped over my shoulders, and the cushion heaved as Tyler stood. While he clattered the dishes, my mind raced.

Why had Dad wandered off?

What was happening to him?

Dad used to take care of both of us. He'd been so sharp, so capable. Now I couldn't trust him to stay home alone.

With help, I could take care of him, couldn't I?

I'd been sure I could...until Tyler agreed with me in that half-hearted way.

I shivered, even under the blanket. I'd find a way to take care of Dad. I was strong and independent, and I had the Taser to prove it.

Tyler came back from washing the dishes and moved toward Dad's recliner, where he'd thrown his coat when he'd come in. He stood there for a few seconds before picking up his coat. "If you're okay, I'm going to go."

Strong. Independent. "I'm fine. Thank you again for coming over. I don't know what I'd have done..." I tried to swallow down the lump in my throat.

He crossed to the sofa where I huddled under my blanket. "Anytime you need help, call me, okay? I'll always be here for you."

I blinked away the sudden wetness in my eyes, and my chin trembled so much I couldn't get out another thanks.

He bent and kissed the top of my head, lingering a moment. Maybe I could get through this. Especially if I could call on my friends.

"Call me tomorrow, okay? Tell me how he's doing?"

"Okay. Good night."

I stood and bolted the door behind him. The stairs to my room were too far away. Besides, I couldn't let Dad slip past me. I lay down on the squashy sofa, curled up under the blanket, and closed my eyes to welcome sleep.

19

I WOKE IN THE DARK, my heart racing. *Dad. Is he still here?*

I galloped down the hall, paused to catch my ragged breath, then tiptoed into his room. The moonlight shone on his sleeping form through his open curtains. Tigger, snuggled into the bend of his knees, blinked his yellow eyes at me but didn't hiss, for once.

I closed the door softly and went to the kitchen to make coffee. Early as it was here, it was three hours later on the East Coast. Cooper would be up. Probably having already worked out in the hotel gym, showered, and dressed in one of his perfect business casual slacks-and-sport-coat ensembles. I could almost smell his aftershave.

I texted him.

```
Me: I won't be in the office today. Have to
take Dad to the doctor. Text me if you need
                                     anything.
```

My phone dinged as the first splash of coffee hit the stained bottom of the carafe.

```
Cooper: Is he OK?
```

So thoughtful of him to ask, especially after I'd thrown myself at him in his office.

Me: He had an episode yesterday. Need to get
him checked out.

Maybe he'd check out fine. Maybe the doctor would tell me this was normal behavior and I'd overreacted. Or he'd adjust his meds again.

Cooper: Do *you* need anything?

My heart fluttered. He was too kind.

Me: Send chocolate. 😉

Cooper: On it. Meetings are going well here. I
won't need you. Take the rest of the day off.

Like I said, thoughtful. Caring. But not mine. Not able to share this burden with me.

Me: Thank you. See you Monday.

I looked at my phone every five minutes for the next hour, and then every half hour after that, but he never responded. He was busy. I knew that. Besides, I'd told him everything was fine. Even though it wasn't.

———

THE UMPIRE HAD JUST SHOUTED, "Play ball!" when our doorbell rang.

"What the hell?" Dad grumbled. "Who'd come over during the World Series?"

I reached over and patted his knee. "Don't worry about it, Dad. I'll take care of it." It was probably UPS delivering my package of essentials. I hadn't wanted to leave Dad alone in the house even to run to the store for tampons. Or—I bit my lip and glanced at Dad—the discreet package I was anticipating.

But when I opened the door, Tyler stood on my front porch, clutching a pizza box. He scanned my face, and then his gaze dropped to my faded college sweatshirt and yoga pants, all the way down to my flip-flops. I curled my toes to hide my chipped polish.

"Tyler! What are you doing here? I mean, I'm glad you came." A smile stretched my face wide. I loved my dad, but it was great to see another person.

"Hey. I know you said you were fine, but I—I brought pizza." He waved the box toward me. "You sure he's okay? And you, too?" His eyes searched mine.

I stepped out onto the porch and pulled the door shut behind me. Even though I knew Dad couldn't hear me with the TV blaring, I kept my voice low. "I took him to the doctor yesterday. Without running the expensive tests, he told us it's probably early-onset Alzheimer's. So yesterday I—I hired someone to watch him while I'm at work. She starts Monday."

"Oh. That's good, right?" He raised hopeful eyebrows.

No, dammit, it wasn't good. My fifty-three-year-old father shouldn't need a nurse. Or a babysitter. He should be enjoying early retirement, hanging out with friends, going for a beer at the corner bar. He shouldn't be stuck inside, being watched by someone trained in CPR and bulky enough to stop him from leaving the house. And I shouldn't have had to make that decision. I shrugged and looked down at Tyler's Vans.

"Hey." He put a knuckle under my chin until I looked him in the eye. "It'll be okay. You're getting him the care he needs. You're a good daughter."

I sniffled. "Stop being so nice."

He set the pizza box on the wide porch railing and tugged me to him. "Sorry, I can't. You're my friend." He held me tight, and it had to have been the pressure that squeezed the tears out of me. I rubbed them on the soft cotton of his Galaga shirt. It smelled like citrus and sunshine, and I wanted to wrap it around me like a blanket. But, too soon, he stepped back.

"Want me to leave this and go?" He waved at the box.

Go? And leave Dad and me alone again? "Don't be ridiculous. Come eat with us."

"You sure?"

Dad shouted from inside the house, "Marlee! You still out there?"

"Yeah! Just a sec." I grinned up at Tyler. "You coming? We have beer."

He picked up the box. "Sold."

I opened the door. "Dad, you remember Tyler from the other night, right?"

Dad looked up quickly but then focused back on the game. "Tyler from the train station. Tyler with the muscle car. Sit the fuck down and be quiet."

Tyler froze. I laid a hand on his forearm. "He's always like that during baseball," I whispered. He'd never been a big swearer, but nowadays TV sports brought it out in him.

"But Oakland's not even—"

"Shh. Doesn't matter. It's the Series."

"Ah." He snapped his mouth shut. He set the pizza on the coffee table and took a seat on the end of the sofa closer to Dad.

Be right back, I mouthed and went to the kitchen for plates, napkins, and three bottles of beer. In the plus column, I'd tidied the house this morning. Too bad I'd picked up my novel instead of showering, brushing my hair, or putting on makeup. I didn't usually let people from the office see me when I was less than put-together. But Tyler had seen me the other night at the theater with mascara tear tracks. It couldn't get much more real than that. I finger-combed my hair and put it back up in a ponytail.

When I returned, a commercial played, muted. The men

looked away from each other, Tyler at the floor, his cheeks pink, and Dad at me, smiling too brightly.

"Thanks, Sunshine. Nothing better than beer, pizza, and base-ball. I like this one." He pointed with his thumb, and I hadn't thought it possible, but Tyler's cheeks went even more blotchily red.

I handed Dad a beer and then a slice of pizza, supreme, my favorite. *But supreme is everyone's favorite.*

I passed another slice to Tyler and took my plate to the other end of the sofa. The game came back on, and Dad turned up the volume.

"Who's your team, Tyler?" Dad asked at the next commercial. No one had to ask him who *his* team was. He'd been cheering loudly for them.

"In this Series? I don't really care. I'm an Astros fan."

"Bunch of cheaters."

Tyler blinked.

"Dad! Be nice!" I scooted closer to Tyler to whisper, "He gets really emotionally invested in sports."

"Didn't Marlee tell me you're from Dallas?"

On his good days, he was sharp as a tack.

"I am."

"Then why aren't you a Rangers fan?"

Tyler's lip curled. "My brothers are all big Rangers fans. I guess I just wanted to be different."

"Good thing," Dad said. "When's the last time the Rangers won the Series?"

"Exactly." Tyler clinked his beer bottle against Dad's.

At the next commercial break, Tyler asked Dad about the house, and soon they were talking about power tools. Dad even got so caught up in a tribute to his dear departed tile saw—I'd sold it on eBay to pay off a hospital bill before we met our deductible—that he missed an at-bat. We finished the pizza and another round of beer, and by the time the game ended, I was using Tyler's shoulder as a pillow, and Dad was yawning.

He levered himself up from the depths of the recliner. "I'm turning in early. You kids have fun." He winked. "But not too much fun."

"*Dad.*" I sat up. "Tyler and I are *friends.*"

"Oh, right," he said, smirking.

Tyler stood to shake his hand. "Good night, Mr. Rice. Thanks for letting me watch the game with you."

"Anytime. It's refreshing to watch with a true fan."

I rolled my eyes at his pointed look in my direction.

While Dad shuffled off to bed, Tyler remained standing. "Did you want me to—" He inclined his head toward the door.

At eight o'clock on a Friday night, most twenty-five-year-olds would just be heading out to dinner or stumbling home from happy hour to rest for a couple of hours before hitting a club. The long, lonely night stretched ahead of me.

"No, stay. Please? Unless you had...other plans." Maybe he had a date. *Please don't let him have a date.* I ached for company.

Tyler quirked his lip. "Nope. I brought my game system. Want me to get it?"

"Sure. I'll just clean up."

While he went out to his car, I washed the plates and chucked the empty bottles into the recycling bin. When I returned to the living room, I carried a tray with beer, a bowl of pretzels, and chocolate. The white chocolate that Cooper had sent. It was kind of him, but when someone says she needs chocolate, she *never* means white chocolate. It's not even really chocolate. It'd taste okay with the pretzels, I supposed.

As I set down the tray, Tyler muttered at the back of our ancient television.

"Trouble?" I asked.

"No, no, I got it." He seemed to have an entire compartment in his bag for cables. "Aha!" He yanked one from the bottom of the bag, plugged in some sort of adapter, connected another cable, and threw the switch on the game system. The TV flashed up an animated video.

He tossed the extraneous cables into his bag and then flopped onto the sofa. I handed him a beer and sat on the other end, splaying one knee on the cushion toward him.

"So, tell me. What'd my dad ask you that was so embarrassing? While I was getting the plates."

Checking the battery compartment of one of the controllers appeared to require his attention for several seconds. "He asked me what my intentions were. Toward you."

That made my cheeks hot. "You told him we're friends, right?" Without waiting for him to answer, I said, "He had a good night. Today he seems like himself. Except for the swearing."

His mouth turned down at the corners. "He called a drill an 'electric hole-puncher.' He might not show symptoms all the time, but there's no cure. The neurons he's lost won't regenerate." His gaze turned introspective, like he was thinking about his grandfather. Then he blinked. "You're doing the right thing by getting help for him."

I picked at the label on my beer bottle. "I know. I wish—"

He reached across and caressed my shoulder with his big hand. "I know."

I sniffed and blinked the tears back. "Are we going to play or what?"

He squeezed my shoulder and then withdrew. A chill crept from where his warm hand had rested and frosted my heart. I reached behind me and pulled the blanket over my shoulders. Still not as good as his hand.

"I think you'll enjoy this one. We have to work together on the missions. And we're gonna blow up a lot of stuff. It's my favorite game for relieving stress." He handed me a controller. "Have you used this system before? Need anything explained?"

It had been a couple of years since I'd played, but the device felt familiar in my hand. "No, I'm good."

"Great." He shot me a grin and then returned his attention to the screen. "Let's go."

He was right. Watching our enemies explode in front of us was strangely satisfying. Working together with Tyler, I was in control, part of a team. He didn't criticize me when I was clumsy or too aggressive; he let me try again until I'd mastered it. I couldn't stop smiling, and hours later, my face and stomach muscles ached from laughing.

"Watch out!" My warning came too late. Tyler's character collapsed under fire. "How could you have missed that huge tank?"

I glanced over at him. *Oh.* He was watching me, his own controller forgotten in his slack hands. I ignored the unmistakable sounds of my own character's demise. Now I regretted having sat at the far end of the sofa from Tyler. It'd be so nice to lean my head on his shoulder, have his arms come around me, and just relax into his embrace. Friends did that…right?

"You never told me what happened with Operation Prince Charming."

It felt like he'd dumped cold beer on my head. I pulled the blanket tighter around myself. "It…it didn't go so well. Cooper has reservations about having a relationship with someone who works for Synergy." Okay, fine, that was my spin on what he'd said. "So it's not going to work out." I shrugged.

Friend or not, I didn't want to talk about it with Tyler. I didn't like the way his mouth pinched whenever I said Cooper's name. I dropped the controller onto my lap and blew on my sweaty hands. "Remind me to do some warm-up finger exercises next time."

"*Reservations* doesn't sound so bad. Are you going to wait? Keep trying?"

I kneaded my palm with my other thumb. "I don't think so."

"I've never known you to give up on anything." He ducked his head to catch my gaze.

I stared at the TV. "There's a difference between having a crush on someone and being a stalker. I'm trying to let it go." Though Cooper Fallon had held a place in my heart for so long, the space he'd left felt empty.

"Marlee." He scooted toward me until our knees touched. "Remember the first time we met? Really met?"

I knew what he meant. Jackson had introduced us on Tyler's first day, when he was showing him around the office. But we'd gotten to know each other weeks later. "You saved me from that evil keg tap."

"You had beer in your eyes and your hair."

"And all over my shirt. You gave me your sweater to cover up."

He chuckled. "I lent it to you. And you never gave it back."

"What? I didn't?" I'd worn it every weekend last spring. It was too soft and cozy to give back. Even after I'd washed the beer out of it, it smelled incredible, like nothing else in my drawers.

"You didn't. But I don't mind." His voice had gone all deep. "Even covered in beer, you were the most beautiful woman I'd ever met."

"Aw, thanks. You're sweet." But in the flickering light from the television, his pupils had swallowed up his irises, leaving only a glint of gold. He didn't look sweet. He looked dangerous.

"I didn't say it to be sweet. I said it because it's true. And now that you and Cooper aren't getting together, I think we—" He cleared his throat. "I think we should think about being more than friends."

I tugged the blanket tighter around myself. "I can't just go from being in—from crushing on Cooper to dating someone else. My heart doesn't work like that." I'd thought Cooper was my One True Love, like my mother had been for Dad. If that was true, I'd be pining for a long time. Years. Decades.

"But I—"

"We're friends. I can't think of you like that." What if Cooper's warnings came true? What if a relationship turned out to be too weird, and I lost my friend? I couldn't let that happen.

He looked like I'd slapped him. "Okay." He clasped his hands between his knees and stared at them like they held the key we'd been hunting in the video game. "Okay." He stood. "I'll get out of here, then."

"No, Tyler, I—" *Shit*. Why the *fuck* had he ruined everything by saying that? "I want to stay friends."

"Of course." He looked like he'd stepped on a rusty nail and was trying to smile through the pain. "Friends. See you Monday."

"Okay." But were we?

I watched him walk out, his back stiff. The engine of his Mustang roared to life. It was only after the rumble died away down the street that I refocused on our living room and realized he'd left his gaming system connected to our television.

I let out a shaky breath. It meant he wanted to stay friends. That he'd be back, and we'd play again. That, regardless of what he'd said earlier, he wanted to hold together our precious friendship and not risk it by trying to make it more.

Because what I needed most, after snuffing out my crush, while Dad needed more care than I knew how to give him, was a friend.

Staring at the game console, I hoped Tyler would be that friend for me.

20

BEN STIFFENED at first when I hugged him in the lobby on Monday morning, but then he relaxed and patted my back.

Releasing him, I said, "I'm sorry. I'm usually better about respecting boundaries at work, but I'm so glad to see you."

He tilted his head to the side. "Did you think I wouldn't show?"

"Maybe." I took the temporary badge from José at the security desk and handed it to Ben. "You wouldn't have been the first." He clipped the badge to his belt loop and smoothed down the caramel-colored sweater that matched his eyes.

I led him to the elevator. "After you're done in HR, I'll bring you up to speed and get you started. Cooper's in meetings all morning, but he's taking you to lunch, and you can get to know him then. Jackson's coming back from a trip today, so I'll need to spend some time with him. But other than that, I'm available until four o'clock." I dreaded the conversation I needed to have later with Jackson about my new schedule.

After I dropped off Ben in Human Resources, I walked up to the sixth floor. I had about an hour to prepare for Ben's training and catch up with Jackson. Even though I'd worked remotely the two days I'd been out, I was behind where I wanted to be for Jackson's first day back.

I emerged from the stairwell and glanced at Cooper's door, glad it was still shut. He shouldn't need anything while he was in meetings. I cringed, remembering the last time I'd been in his office, when I'd thrown myself at him and we'd argued. Now I was glad he'd shown more restraint than I had. Seeing him today was going to be awkward enough.

My boss's door was open with the light on. Poking my head inside, I smiled at him. "Hey, stranger."

"Marlee, my savior!" His tan skin told me he'd spent time at the beach. He'd grown out his stubble until it was almost the full beard he'd had last year. Alicia must've finally told him she missed it.

He clicked his laptop into its docking station and walked out from behind his desk, arms wide. Guilt about what I needed to tell him twanged through me, but it could wait until after I'd greeted him properly. He folded me into his arms, and I hugged him back.

"Good trip?" I asked.

He smiled down at me. "The best. Fiji is amazing. We were in a bungalow right on the beach." He released me and pointed at the club chairs by the window. He sat and crossed an ankle over his knee. "You wouldn't believe how many stars we could see at night. We thought of you when we were trying to figure out the constellations. I know you know them all, but I may have tried to convince Alicia that one of them was SpongeBob SquarePants."

I smiled at Jackson's casual use of *we thought* as if he and Alicia even shared a brain now. Had my parents talked like that? Would I ever talk that way about someone?

"I've never seen the southern hemisphere's constellations in person," I said. "You should've brought a star map. Or used an app on your phone."

He leaned back in the chair and folded his hands behind his

head, elbows spread wide. "Didn't need it. I was *plenty* entertained."

I held out my palm. "No. I don't want to hear about the business part of your honeymoon."

"What?" His eyes went innocently wide. "Alicia's going to tell you all about it. I've heard you two cackling."

"About *my* love life, not hers. You're my boss. I have boundaries." It was a lie. I knew all about—and envied—Alicia's and Jackson's fantastic sex life. But I didn't want to hear the details from him. That was over the line.

"Fine." He raised an eyebrow. "I'm sure you maintained *boundaries* with Cooper while I was gone."

The blood drained from my face. "Did he say something?"

Jackson stood and walked to the other window. "No. I haven't seen him yet. *Did* something happen?"

"No." I tried not to sigh as I said it.

"Ohh-kay." Jackson had known me too long not to be suspicious. "Anything you want to talk about?"

My stomach clenched. "Actually, yes. But not about Cooper. About my dad."

Jackson's forehead crinkled. "Is he okay?"

I gave him a wry smile. "Not really." I told him about our adventure at the BART station in as little detail as possible. "The doctor recommended I hire a caregiver during the day while I'm at work. And so I—" I faltered. "I need to cut back my hours so I can be home before she leaves. I understand if there's a salary reduction."

Jackson snorted. "You expect me to dock your salary just when your expenses are increasing?" He shook his head. "You've supported me too long and too well for that. You do what you need to do to take care of your dad. We'll work it out."

I let out a shaky breath. "Thanks. I won't let you down. If you need me after hours, I'll be happy to put in more time from home."

He clasped my hand. "That's great, Marlee. And let me—let *us* —know if there's anything we can do to help."

I blinked away the moisture in my eyes. "You're the best. Thank you."

With one last press of my hand, he stood and walked back to his desk. His back to me, he said gruffly, "Now, shouldn't you be telling me where I need to be this morning and what I need to be doing?"

I smiled. Jackson had never been good with gratitude. Or tears.

I pulled up his calendar on my phone and started filling him in. Maybe this wouldn't be as bad as I'd feared.

———

I'D JUST FINISHED CLEANING off Ben's desk when he emerged from the stairwell with his brand-new laptop bag slung over his shoulder. Another set of footsteps to learn. Ben's were stiff but quiet, the rubber soles of his urban combat-style boots muting his purposeful strides. I waved him over.

"Are you ready to start?"

He rolled his eyes. "I have a ton of online compliance training to do. But can I please do some actual work first?"

I chuckled. "Cooper's a fanatic about our respectful, harassment-free work environment." Well, except when faced with the incompetent temps I'd hired. But they'd have brought out the worst in almost anyone. "Plus, there's all the legal stuff. It's not a lot of fun, but Cooper and the lawyers are sticklers for it."

He compressed his lips and looked at his new boss's closed door. Doubt flickered in his narrowed eyes. Crap, we couldn't lose him this early. He was exactly what Cooper needed. "But he's a great guy," I rushed to say. "You'll love him."

He tilted his head to the side, watching me, but then he looked down at the desk. "So this is me?"

Relieved, I gave him a quick smile. "Yes. Let's fire up your laptop, and I'll set you up with Cooper's calendar and email."

Two hours later, Ben had mastered his new boss's calendar, and I'd filled him in on Cooper's work habits and preferences. When the light finally blinked out on Cooper's phone line and his office door swung open, we stood to greet the man himself. He emerged looking more formal than usual in a slim-fitting charcoal suit with a crisp cornflower blue shirt that matched his eyes. No tie. Like always, I couldn't hold in a tiny sigh at his gorgeousness. Ben's gaze flicked to me and then to Cooper. I wondered what his too-observant eyes saw.

Cooper strode over to us and extended his hand. Ben shook it, leaning in a little.

"You must be Ben. I'm Cooper Fallon."

"It's great to meet you, Mr. Fallon."

"Please, call me Cooper."

Ben's pupils dilated, and his nostrils flared. I held in a smug smile. Cooper had that effect on everyone, not just me. Their hands separated.

"God, you're tall," Ben blurted out. "Taller than you look in the photos." He blushed. "Not that I've been stalking you online or anything." He pressed his lips together.

"He's always standing next to Jackson, and you think they're both normal height, but they're not," I said, trying to ease his awkwardness. Jamila was an Amazon, too, especially in heels, but I wasn't about to bring her up.

Cooper had been staring at Ben, flexing his right hand at his side. He raised it in front of his chest and rubbed it for a second with his left hand.

Something odd was happening here. "Cooper, can I talk to you for a minute?"

I didn't think it was possible, but Cooper's jaw became even more rigid. Sweet Darwin on the *H.M.S. Beagle*, I wasn't going to try to jump his bones *now*.

"Just—just for a minute," I said.

He followed me over to my desk and stood, hands in his pockets.

I whispered, "Look, Ben is very qualified and a great guy. Do. Not. Screw. This. Up. Give him a chance."

His forehead creased. "I will. Of course I will."

I narrowed my eyes at him. "Good. Behave yourself at lunch."

Leading him back over to Ben's desk, I asked, "Where are you guys going?"

Cooper named a trendy restaurant nearby. He asked Ben, "Do you know it?"

"I do." For some reason, Ben's color deepened. He was a blotchy blusher like Tyler. Adorable.

"Will that be okay?" Cooper asked.

"Fine."

"Let's go." Cooper turned and led the way to the elevator doors.

I shook my head. I hoped they'd work out their weirdness. Cooper was plenty awkward around me, but I'd never seen him so inept. Ben was perfect, and I wanted him—needed him—to stay. I couldn't be picking up extra work from Cooper anymore with my new responsibilities at home.

Back at my desk, I checked my phone. No texts or voice mails from Sylvia. I'd already called her that morning to check on Dad, and she'd assured me they'd be fine. I was afraid I'd piss her off if I called again. I needed to make it through the day without upsetting the fragile balance of my new reality. So I texted Alicia.

Me: Free for lunch?

Alicia: Sorry, having lunch with Jackson. Can I come by your house tonight to pick up my sweet boy?

Me: Yes! Come for dinner.

Sweet boy, my ass. The little demon had hissed at me again as I'd left. He'd seemed indifferent to Sylvia, but they'd probably be best friends by this afternoon. I was the only one he hated.

My stomach made a Tigger-like sound. But the thought of taking my sad lunchbox to the empty kitchen was enough to take away my appetite.

I could've gone down to the cafeteria. Tyler would probably be there with his table full of programmers. Would we be friendly or awkward? We'd been friends less than a year; still, I couldn't imagine my life without Tyler in it. His dimples and the cute flop of his hair. The squeak of his sneaker on the old wood floors. The way he'd drop whatever he was doing to help me when I needed it.

Maybe I needed to make the first move, show him that things between us didn't have to be weird.

As I pulled my lunchbox from my drawer, the stairwell door slammed open and Tyler bounded out, flushed and out of breath. He saw me and froze, his hand still on the push bar. "Marlee! I lost track of—but I didn't—would you like to—" His face fell. "Are you going out?"

I gave him a wry smile. The poor guy had been coding all morning and lost the power of coherent speech. "I was just going down to the lunchroom. Want to come with me? Or did you need something from him?" I tipped my head toward Jackson's closed door. *Please say you came up here for me. That we're still friends.*

He let the stairwell door swing shut. "No. Yes! Actually, I was wondering if you wanted to go out to lunch?" His voice rose on the question, and his face scrunched up in an adorably hopeful expression.

My skin tingled, like after I'd crossed my legs too long and the blood finally started flowing again. It wasn't going to be weird.

I held up my lunchbox. "But I packed."

"I'm buying," he said. "Save it for tomorrow."

I couldn't suppress my grin. We were going to be fine. "Okay."

21

WHEN WE REACHED the bright sunshine out on the street, Tyler asked, "Want to eat in the park? I saw a food truck."

In the second half of October, the weather had turned fall-like, but the day was sunny, a last reminder of summer. And of our pre-theater picnic. "Sure."

He held out an elbow, and I took it. Just two friends on their way to the park to get a sandwich. Friends just like we'd been before Operation Prince Charming. Friends who didn't need or want anything more.

On the short walk to the park, we passed by other business-casual office workers, tourists wearing San Francisco sweatshirts they'd picked up to ward off the morning chill, and hard-hatted construction workers taking a break from the ever-present rehabs going on in the city. We passed the garlicky Italian restaurant, the curry aroma of an Indian place, the heavy scent of fried fish. Soon, the towering buildings opened up onto the park square and its spiky green hedges.

Tyler asked me about Dad, and I told him he was doing fine. That having Sylvia at home to take care of him eased my mind while I was at work. Overall, things were pretty good in my world. Jackson and Alicia were back, and I'd spend time with my bestie that night. We were getting rid of her evil cat who'd caused me way more stress than I'd needed. Plus, we'd hired an awesome assistant for Cooper who'd ease my workload.

While we waited in line at the food truck, I closed my eyes and let the sunshine warm my face. My life had changed a lot over the past week, but I still had Dad, my BFF, an awesome boss, and my buddy Tyler.

When I opened my eyes, he was smiling at me. The same tender smile he'd given me when we'd played video games the other night. When we'd stumbled in the moonlight from the rehearsal dinner to the inn. When we'd danced together at the wedding. Just my good buddy, Tyler, who didn't care that I was doing a job I was overqualified for, who didn't think I was weird for living at home at age twenty-five, who knew how important family was to me. Who saw the real Marlee and liked her.

But despite all that and the supernova of a kiss we'd shared at the wedding, I had too few friends left to endanger this one.

"Thanks," I said. "This was a great idea." Last week, I'd have thrown my arms around him and hugged him, but today I held back.

He grinned, but it wasn't as broad as usual. Maybe he missed that ghost-hug, too. "I have lots of great ideas."

"I have a great idea. How about you apply for that manager position? They haven't found anyone they like yet."

He stared at his sneakers. "Don't you think I'm underqualified? I've only worked for the company for a couple of years. And I've been in my current job for less than a year."

"Of course not. And you'll never know if you don't try." I'd taken my own advice with Cooper and had disastrous results. But if I hadn't, I'd still be pining for him. Still obsessed with him. And between Jackson's return and Dad's care, I needed focus. Moving on was the smart thing to do.

When we got our sandwiches, we walked away from the

crowded lawn where the other cube dwellers soaked up the sunlight to a bench in a shady grove of trees. The area was quiet except for the birds and the squirrels, who chittered and squawked at each other—or maybe at us for disturbing their lunchtime peace.

I unwrapped my sandwich and took a bite of the warm, gooey cheese that oozed out between the crunchy slices of sourdough. "Mmm," I moaned. "*So* much better than peanut butter and jelly."

"Better scenery than the cafeteria, too." Tyler shot me a sly look and took a huge bite of his own sandwich.

I rolled my eyes. "Have you talked to Jackson yet?" I knew he hadn't, but I needed to steer the conversation onto a safe subject.

"Not yet. I don't meet with him until tomorrow."

"He said they had a great time in Fiji."

He snorted. "Who wouldn't?"

"I know I would. A warm, sandy beach sounds perfect today." As I finished my sandwich, I shivered. Under the shade of the trees, a chilly breeze reminded me it was October. I wished I'd ordered hot coffee instead of water.

"Are you cold?"

"A little."

The words weren't even fully out of my mouth before he was tugging his gray sweater off and slipping it, warm from his body, over my head. I thought about protesting, but as soon as I had his sweater on, I was too cozy to consider taking it off. Maybe I could steal this one, too. He rubbed his hands over my upper arms.

"Better?" he asked.

His thin, almost see-through gray Burger Time T-shirt stretched over his chest. If I squinted at him and swapped out the ancient T-shirt and jeans for an unbuttoned dress shirt and slacks, he looked like the man-candy on my current romance read. I dragged my gaze up to his face, wanting to trace the dimple that bracketed his smile, run my fingers through his hair, pull his face to mine, and—whoa. This was Tyler. Firmly in the friend zone. I needed to build a fence around him with some *Keep Out* signs and barbed wire. Possibly with a shark-infested moat. Because when I was so close to him, so wrapped up in his scent, with his warm hands on me, I couldn't remember my own name, much less why Tyler needed to be nothing more than my friend.

Why was that, again?

"Yeah, I'm good now. Thanks." I hunted through my purse for my compact and lipstick then smeared the creamy pink over my lips. *No kissing.*

Tyler stared at my lips. Rosy blotches bloomed on his cheeks. "I wasn't trying to—"

"I know." I wedged my bag between us on the bench.

After a few seconds, he moved his arm from the back of the bench to reach into his back pocket. He pulled out a sheaf of glossy paper and extended it to me.

"What's this?" I read the word *Care.*

"I visited a few facilities over the weekend. I figured you'd be too busy to do it, and, well, it's expensive, but it's about the same cost as in-home care. Easier on you, too."

His sweater wasn't enough to protect against the frost that swept through me. He was holding brochures from Oakland-area memory-care nursing homes. Dad wasn't ready for that. Not yet. Neither was I.

I shoved my hands between my knees. If I didn't touch the papers, it wouldn't be real. I stared at the tree across the path. "We don't need that."

After a minute, he said, "Maybe not today, but he will."

"No. I can keep him at home. He loves our house." I touched my pendant. "He and my mother bought it together. And he doesn't want to leave."

"But—" I heard him inhale and then let the breath out. He touched my shoulder, a light caress. "Someone your age shouldn't have to deal with all this. Your dad doesn't want you to miss out on your youth because of him."

I shrugged off his hand. "He was only a little older than I am now when my mother died and left him to take care of me. What would I have done if he'd decided he couldn't handle it?"

He recoiled. "You'd still be taking care of him. And you could visit him all the time."

"Visit?" My nostrils flared. "He doesn't need me to visit. He needs me with him all the time."

"Marlee, I—I think you may be romanticizing your dad's condition. He's going to need full-time care. And no matter how much love you give him, it's not going to make him any better. He's going to get to the point that he doesn't even know you."

I couldn't sit there for another minute. I'd been wrong. He was just like all my college friends. Former friends. He didn't get me at all. I sprang up from the bench, scattering the pamphlets. "My dad and I belong together because we're a family. Your relationship with your family may be screwed up, but mine isn't. I love my dad. And he loves me. He could never forget me."

I didn't even care that his face paled and his jaw went slack. Anyone who wanted to separate me from Dad wasn't friend material. I was just glad I'd figured it out before—before...*nothing!* There was no *before* here. Maybe not even an after.

Grabbing my purse, I whirled and stomped away down the path. I gripped the sharp edges of my pendant until an imprint remained on my cold fingers. Dad was the most important person in my life. Tyler, whatever I'd thought of him before, was not.

I'd almost reached the office when I heard the staccato slam of sneakers on sidewalk and my name. Tyler. I slowed my steps and stopped in front of the revolving door.

He put a hand on my arm. I looked at his fingers, long and powerful. Still magical? It didn't matter. I didn't want any part of them.

"I—I'm sorry. I didn't mean to upset you."

I looked up into his eyes, no longer sparkling with kaleidoscope colors but churned into a muddy brown. "Well, you did. I don't think I can—I need—"

From our left, a throat cleared. Without looking, I stepped out of the way of the door. Tyler still held my arm, so when I tugged, he came with me. Stumbling, he grabbed me by the elbows to steady himself, and we ended up half-hugging. I edged away, but he tightened his hold on my arms, his eyes pleading with me not to continue what I'd been saying. To reconsider.

Over his shoulder, I glimpsed Ben and Cooper standing side-by-side on the sidewalk, staring. What did they think of us, with Tyler holding me and my cheeks angry red? I took another step back and brushed Tyler's hands off my arms, and that's when I realized I was still wearing his sweater. His oversized, drab gray sweater that covered my hands and couldn't be mistaken for mine.

Ben's wide eyes dashed any hopes I'd had of playing it cool and confident. So much for making a good impression on his first day. Cooper tilted his head to the side.

"Hey, Ben. Hi, Cooper. Did you have a nice lunch?" I didn't wait for their response before I pushed through the revolving door. The three men followed. I'd already shrugged out of Tyler's sweater by the time they emerged into the warmth of the lobby. Refusing to look at his face, I shoved it toward him with one hand and smoothed my hair with the other. "Thanks."

He took it from me. While we waited in front of the elevator bank, he extended his right hand to Ben. "I'm Tyler Young. I'm a developer on the automotive analytics team."

"Ben Levy-Walters. Cooper's new assistant. Today's my first day."

"Welcome to Synergy. I'm sure Marlee's told you everything you need to know, but if you ever need anything from the programming team, come find me."

Ben shot me a look as the elevator door opened. "I sure will." He bit his lip, and as I walked past him, he whispered, "Yum," and unsubtly popped his lips.

I lifted my chin and stepped onto the elevator. After straightening my blouse, I busied myself with my phone—Jackson had texted—until Tyler said a casual "See ya" and walked out on the fourth floor.

I refused to look up. I wasn't here for their assumptions or judgments about Tyler and me. Hell, I didn't know what to think about Tyler at this point. Could we still be friends after what he'd said?

When the elevator doors opened on the sixth floor, I smoothed my skirt and sailed out. I grabbed my laptop from my desk, but before I could make it into Jackson's office, my boss sauntered out into the hallway.

"Coop! Sorry we didn't meet up yesterday. Alicia and I were jet-lagged and fell asleep on the couch." What started out in a handshake turned into a hug and a back-slap.

When they disengaged, Cooper's hand rested on Jackson's arm for just a minute before he shoved his hands in his pockets and rocked back on his heels. His smile looked strained now. Maybe the past three weeks had been more stressful on him than he'd let on.

"I—I'd like you to meet my new assistant, Ben Levy-Walters."

"You have a new assistant?" Jackson's posture straightened, and he extended a hand to Ben. "Welcome aboard. Everything okay so far? This guy"—he jerked his thumb at Cooper—"hasn't been too hard on you, has he?"

"No, not at all," Ben said, his voice low and smooth. "Cooper took me to lunch. And everyone's been great today, especially Marlee."

Normally, I would've loved the praise, but when their eyes all turned to me, I wanted to cover up my rumpled blouse and wind-tangled hair. I gave Jackson a wobbly smile and said, "Ready to tackle your email?"

Jackson took a deep breath and let it out in a huff. "Marlee, you're such a taskmaster." He smiled at Ben. "Nice meeting you, Ben. Let me know if I can do anything to help." He turned to Cooper. "Come over for dinner tonight. I'll grill some steaks and we can catch up." Then he gestured toward the open door of his office. "After you, Marlee."

I hugged my laptop to my chest and walked into the safety of Jackson's office. Jackson snapped the door closed.

"So, Marlee," he said, grinning mischievously, "what'd I miss?"

22

I'D BARELY CLOSED my bedroom door when Alicia asked, "What's going on with your dad?"

She hadn't missed his calling me Maggie twice during dinner. Or how he'd been stumped by the coffee maker. The coffee maker he'd used twice a day for at least five years. I'd finally asked him to sit down and made his coffee myself.

I sat on the bed and gestured for her to do the same. Tigger leaped up and curled into her side like he belonged there. "He hasn't been himself lately." Leaving out Tigger's grand adventure the night Dad let him escape, I filled her in on Dad's trek to the BART station, his diagnosis, and the new health aide.

Alicia's eyes crinkled with sympathy. "I'm so sorry. Is there anything we can do to help?"

I reached out and flicked her hair over her shoulder. Growling, Tigger glared at me with his yellow eyes. "Jackson's letting me leave early every day so I can take over from Sylvia, his caregiver. We'll be fine."

Alicia searched my face. "Will you?"

I was tempted, so tempted, to spill my guts to my friend, to tell her that, no, I was terrified I was about to lose the only family I had. But then my phone rang, and I glanced at the display. Butterflies with razor-sharp wings shredded my stomach. "It's Tyler."

She rolled her eyes. "Aren't you going to answer it?"

I bit my lip. "No. I'm—I'm not ready to talk to him yet. We had a fight. About Dad, actually. He brought me some pamphlets about memory-care facilities."

"Wasn't he just trying to help?"

"I guess so." My hand crept to the pendant around my neck and I zipped it along the chain. "But it made me see that we don't want the same things. That I value family, and he doesn't. Tyler moved across the country to get away from his family. I've never wanted to move out of this house. We're so different I'm not sure we can even be friends anymore. I mean, I can't avoid seeing him at work, but that's it." The ringing stopped.

"Friends can be different. It's not like you two…" Her eyes widened. "*Did* you?"

"No. No! Though he…he said we should be more than friends. I said no, and we were okay, but now we're not."

"That's too bad. He's a good guy. A good friend."

A good friend. I didn't have enough of those. What if he stopped coming to my desk and going to lunch with me? I'd miss those dimples. And his hugs. Still, every time I remembered those pamphlets, icicles stabbed my heart.

"What's this?" Alicia reached down to where her boot brushed the floor and tugged the box out from under my bed.

"Wait!" I leaped off the bed and scrambled to stop her. But her ridiculously long arms snatched it out of my reach.

"Oh!" She snapped the lid back on the box. Then she opened it again. "Ohhhh."

"That's not—" My face had reached the same temperature as the surface of the sun.

"I like this one." She pointed at The Tyler.

I collapsed onto the bed, hiding my face. "You can take it out. It's clean."

From its silky nest, she pulled the new long, purple, lifelike dildo with its obscenely bulbous head. Then, of course, she found The Cooper shoved underneath. She pulled it out, too. It was smaller, curved and featureless, made of sparkly silicone, a no-nonsense vibrator for getting business done. Until it hadn't anymore.

She held one in each hand, eyebrows raised.

"What? Can't a girl have a selection for different…experiences?"

She flicked on The Cooper. I'd left it on its highest setting, and it whined with effort. She winced and turned it off. Then she flicked on The Tyler, and it started a low pulse that made me squirm from three feet away.

"Different experiences." The problem with having a best friend is that sometimes, she knows your business better than you do.

"The Coo—" I froze. "That one wasn't meeting my needs."

"You named your dildo after Cooper?"

I grimaced. "No?"

"And what'd you call this one?" Setting The Cooper back in the box, she ran a manicured finger over the veins and ridges of the other one.

"The Tyler," I mumbled.

"You named a sex toy after your platonic friend, who might not even be your friend anymore."

I curled my knees up to my chest. "It's complicated."

"Hmm." At last, she took pity on me and changed the subject. "Jackson wants to have a party next weekend."

I looked up at her. "A party a week after your honeymoon?"

"That's what I said! He wants to throw a welcome-back-slash-Halloween party at our place. We, um"—I could see her struggling to tame the smile that wanted to break out over her face—"we have special associations with Halloween."

She'd told me about Jackson's party last year in Austin, when he'd kissed her for the first time. Her happily-ever-after had started a little over a year ago, and now she was married to her true love. I sighed.

"You'll come, right?" she asked.

"Of course. I wouldn't miss it. Will…will Cooper be there?"

The corners of her mouth tightened. "Yes, he'll be there." She paused. "Jamila, too. And Tyler." She compressed her lips. I could tell she was holding something back.

"Marlee?" Dad's voice came from downstairs.

I frowned. He'd already gone to bed—he slept a lot lately—and I was surprised he was still awake. "I'll be right back," I said.

It took a few minutes to resettle Dad. He wanted a glass of water and couldn't find his cane, which had rolled under his bed. I returned to find Alicia scanning the titles in my bookcase.

"You have all of my favorites from when I was a kid." She ran a finger over the bent spines. *"Anne of Green Gables, The Princess Diaries, The Baby-Sitters Club."*

"I couldn't give them up. Dad said he used to tell me stories— fairy tales—while my mother was pregnant with me. And when I was little. Then I graduated to those. I guess that's where all this came from." I waved my hand at my frilly pink-and-white room. I pointed to the now-dark dormer window with its cushioned seat. "When I was a kid, I'd sit there and read and then act out the stories with my dolls. I still love to curl up there under a blanket with a romance novel."

Alicia stroked her sweater over her baby bump. "Maybe we'll build a window seat and some bookcases. You can advise us on reading material."

"It's a girl?" I squealed.

"We just found out this morning."

I hugged my friend. "I can't wait to buy her a pink dress. With ruffles! And I'll read her *The Secret Garden.*" Visions of princess tea parties with Alicia's daughter danced through my head. I'd be the best auntie ever.

The doorbell rang, breaking into my visions of princess mani-pedis.

I headed for the stairs. "It's probably our neighbor Alma checking on us. I'll be right back."

I ran down the stairs, unbolted the door, and opened it. But it wasn't Alma. Tyler filled the doorway.

"What are you doing here?" I blurted out.

He ducked his head, and I winced. "Sorry," I said. "I didn't mean it the way it came out."

The corners of his mouth lifted just a little. "You didn't answer your phone, and I was in the area." He looked at his sneakers and scuffed them on the stoop.

No one from Synergy was ever "in the area" of Oakland. I crossed my arms.

He looked up, and the light from inside glinted off his glasses. "Listen, I'm sorry about—about our fight earlier. I overstepped. And I'm sorry."

My back stiff, I said, "It's okay."

"Can we go back to being friends again?"

"I—okay." Friends was a reasonable request. But nothing else. And I wouldn't be confiding in him about Dad anymore.

"You should take your game system, though." When I'd come home from work, I'd disconnected it and jammed it into a grocery bag, intending to drop it at his desk tomorrow. This way, I'd be saved from lugging it onto the train.

"Oh." The corners of his mouth turned down, and the golden sparks disappeared from his eyes. "You're sure?"

"Positive. It'd be best if you didn't—if we kept our friendship in the office."

A meow sounded behind me. I whirled to block Tigger from escaping, but he sat on the rug and meowed again at Tyler. Tyler crouched and held out a hand. Tigger stood, stalked past me, and, purring, rubbed his traitorous little face on Tyler's hand.

Tyler crooned, "Good boy."

I heard footsteps on the stairs and sighed. *Caught.*

"Oh, hi, Tyler," Alicia said in an insinuating singsong.

"Hey, Alicia." His cheeks didn't flare red like mine had. He looked like being caught on my porch by our boss's wife was no big deal.

"Thanks for coming by. I'll see you tomorrow, Tyler." I couldn't look him in the eye as I said it.

I didn't miss the hurt in his voice. "Um, okay. See you tomorrow." He grabbed the bag with his game system, turned on his heel, and walked back to his blue Mustang. Tigger gave a last, forlorn meow after him.

When I met her gaze, Alicia's expression was troubled. "You're sure you can't—"

"I'm sure." I couldn't give him what he wanted. And I couldn't want what he'd give me.

ON THURSDAY MORNING, I padded downstairs holding my boots so I wouldn't wake Dad, but he was sitting at the kitchen table with a cup of coffee.

"Morning, Sunshine."

"Morning, Dad. Feeling good today?" I poured coffee into my travel mug.

"Great. I think I'll carve the pumpkin this morning. If you don't mind, that is. I know how much you used to love Halloween, but you're so busy these days..."

"You'll use the kit with the little saws, right? Not the big kitchen knives. And Sylvia will help you."

"Is that any way to talk to your father? I've been using knives *and power tools* since before you were born."

I froze in the middle of screwing the cap onto my travel mug. "You won't use power tools on the pumpkin, will you?" He couldn't. I'd locked them in the shed, and I'd hidden the key.

"I was only saying..." He heaved out a sigh. "Of course not. I'll use the tiny saws."

I found the plastic bag with the kit and set it on the counter. "Thanks, Dad."

I heard a knock at the front door, and then it opened. "Good morning," Sylvia called.

"Hey, Sylvia," I said. "Look who's already up."

She smiled at Dad. "Hey, Will. You must be feeling good today."

"I was," he grumbled into his coffee.

"He said he wants to carve the pumpkin today. It's sitting on the back porch. Here's the carving kit." I pointed to it on the counter.

"That sounds like fun." She nodded at me, a promise she wouldn't let him slice off any digits. "Oh, Marlee. My cousin says she can stay with him Saturday night so you can go to your party."

I couldn't help myself; I did a little dance before I reached out and hugged her. "Thank you. That's great." I didn't want to miss Alicia and Jackson's party, but Dad was getting to be too much for Alma to handle. Sylvia's cousin was a nurse.

I bent to kiss Dad's cheek. "Have fun today. Be good."

He said nothing but stared into his coffee. Shaking off his moodiness, I headed to work.

23

STRAIGHTENING MY WIG, I rang Alicia and Jackson's doorbell.

Noah opened the door. The eleven-year-old was dressed in the bottom half of a dinosaur costume, complete with stuffed, spiky tail; a striped shirt; Wolverine claws; and an old-style hockey mask pushed up to the top of his head. He snapped his teeth at me.

"Okay, I give up. What are you dressed as?"

"I'm the Jabberwocky. We read it in class. Lewis Carroll never describes it, except for the 'jaws that bite'"—he snapped his teeth again—"and 'the claws that catch,' so I made up the rest. And you're Princess Leia."

He sounded let-down at my generic costume. To be honest, I was a little disappointed, too, considering all the thought Noah had put into his.

"You got it. I even have a blaster." I showed it to him.

"We're not allowed to have toy weapons at school."

"Oh." I hid it in a fold of my white gown. Clearly, I was losing points in his eyes. Maybe Tigger had rubbed off on him.

"You staying up for the party?" I asked.

"Just for the first hour. Then I have to go to bed. I have tae kwon do tomorrow morning." He stepped aside to let me in.

"Hey, have you met Sam? She's my aunt or something." He screwed up his face like he was trying to hide a grin behind a scowl. "She's pretty cool."

"Sam, Jackson's sister? Yeah, I know her." Had Sam replaced me in Noah's affections? A tiny pang pierced my heart. I shouldn't be jealous of an eleven-year-old's crush, should I? I sighed. I'd done stupider things for love. Like, tonight. I shoved my blaster into its hip holster.

"Let's go find her. She's in the kitchen." He darted ahead of me through the open-plan living room into the kitchen, where Alicia, Jackson, and Sam stood in the way of a couple of uniformed caterers.

I walked behind the island to hug Alicia. She was dressed as Alice in Wonderland, her blond hair pulled back behind a black headband. She wore a blue dress, white tights, and black Mary Janes. "Everything okay?"

"Yes, I guess." She glanced at the caterer sliding a tray of bacon-wrapped scallops out of the oven.

"Hey, Sam." Sam wore a pair of black cargo pants, an over-sized faded black Bon Jovi T-shirt with a sword-pierced heart on it, and a crown made of playing cards, all hearts. "You're the Queen of Hearts?"

"Yeah! You like my costume? Noah and I made it. I don't usually come to Jackson's parties, and I didn't know it was dress-up."

"Sam." Jackson, the White Rabbit in white T-shirt, jeans, and floppy ears, noogied her head in the open center of the crown. "I told you at least three times about the costumes."

"Fine. I didn't want to dress up. Costumes are scratchy. But this isn't so bad." She plucked at the T-shirt, which I recognized as his.

"Whoa." Cooper's deep voice sounded behind me. I whirled to see one of the servers grappling with a tray. It looked like he'd narrowly missed knocking into her. Odd. Cooper was usually so careful, almost graceful. I'd never seen him trip or fall or knock into anyone. Not like the position he'd found Tyler and me in last week after our fight at lunch. Or the time I'd fallen while doing yoga in front of him.

"Sorry. Are you all right?" he asked her.

"Yes. Sorry." She set down the tray.

Automatically, I checked behind Cooper. No Jamila. But that didn't spark the pleasure it would've a month ago.

The kitchen was getting crowded. "They've got it under control in here. Let's move out of the way." I shooed the party hosts and guests out of the kitchen. Tugging Alicia by the hand, I led her into the living room and sat next to her on the sofa. Sam and Noah headed toward the dining room, where I heard the sound of dice shaken in a cup.

Jackson carried over a tray of glasses of orange punch. He handed one with a maraschino cherry on top to Alicia. Then he passed me one with a twist of orange rind. "You get our special Halloween punch." He winked.

"What is it?" I sniffed it, and bubbles fizzed into my nose.

Cooper eased down onto the sofa next to me. His lightsaber handle poked me in the thigh, and I scooted a few inches away. "Just a recipe Jay and I made up in college. Try it."

Disappointingly, my glass held the only fizzes, even with Cooper's knee touching mine.

"Cheers," I said and clinked his glass.

"Cheers."

I sipped the drink and shuddered when it burned my throat. "This is potent," I choked out between coughs.

He tried a cautious sip. "Wow," he wheezed. "You're not kidding. I guess it's been a while since college."

"Hey, guys." Tyler looked impossibly tall in a royal-blue embroidered satin coat, waistcoat, and breeches. On his head was a shaggy wig with horns that curled out of it. But he was no Beast. His familiar grin wavered when he took in Cooper's and my coordinated costumes.

"Tyler!" I wanted to jump up and hug him, but I was trapped

between Cooper and Alicia, a drink I didn't want in my hand and no way to lever myself out of Sofa Canyon. I knew I was supposed to be angry with him, but it wasn't anger—or the booze —that warmed me up from the inside.

"Hey." His wave encompassed the three of us wedged onto the couch, and I deflated a little when he turned to Jackson for a bro-hug with shoulder smacks. Damned person-eating couch.

Cooper nudged my shoulder. "Drink up. You're matching me tonight, Ms. Rice."

In more ways than one. I took a tiny sip and then another. Now that I was used to the high alcohol content, I could taste the sweet orange flavor. "It's not so bad after the first sip."

Cooper drank again. "You're right." He rested his glass on his knee. "Nice costume, by the way."

"Great minds think alike." I smirked and patted the braid coiled over my ear. Damn, the wig was hot. I'd only chosen my costume—out of habit and a lack of inspiration—to match Cooper's Han Solo one. Now I was just...disenchanted. And overheated. In retrospect, pestering Ben to find out what Cooper was wearing seemed silly.

I turned to check on Alicia, but her gaze was directed over my head. "Jamila. So good to see you." She set down her glass and pushed her hands into the cushion to stand.

"Don't get up." The scent of jasmine floated over me as Jamila bent to hug Alicia. She straightened. "Hey, Marlee. Good to see you."

By pushing against Alicia's and Cooper's knees, I levered myself up so I wouldn't be staring at the short hem of her blue Wonder Woman skirt. Now I was at bustier level. Great. I ripped my gaze from her gorgeous boobs to her equally gorgeous face. "Good to see you, Jamila."

She tugged forward the woman who'd been hovering behind her. "This is Jenny." As she finished making the introductions, I glanced at Cooper, who was staring at the women's clasped hands. *Uh-oh.*

I nudged his knee. "Drink up."

He did.

———

TWO HOURS LATER, the room—or I—had started to tilt, and everything made me laugh. I stood next to the bar with Jackson and Cooper. Jackson had one arm slung around Cooper's shoulders and one arm around mine. I'd lost track of the number of times he'd refilled my cup with the toxic orange punch.

"You're my two best friends," Jackson slurred. His bunny nose and drawn-on whiskers were just a smear of pink and gray after two hours of hugging his guests and drinking.

"What about Alicia?" I asked. Drunk-Marlee found it suddenly important that we not forget my friend sitting across the room, talking to Sam.

"Right, she's my best friend. And Noah. And the baby. Then you guys." The last word was drawn out in a buzzy hiss.

Cooper frowned. "The *baby's* above me? I've known you for fourteen fucking years, and your baby's not even born yet." His voice rose. "How can a *fetus* be a better friend than me?"

Uh-oh. That Fallon temper was going to ruin Alicia's party. I shushed him and reached around Jackson to lay a gentling hand on his forearm. "Of course Jackson's going to love his *baby* the most. The baby's family, silly. You're not." Jackson nodded slowly.

That orange punch was *evil* and if I ever see it again, I'll set it aflame. Because Cooper, who'd had at least one too many, if not two, collapsed onto Jackson's shoulder, and I saw his back heave up into a hiccup—or a sob. He mumbled something I couldn't hear.

Jackson patted his friend's back. "'S okay, Coop."

On the other side of the room, Alicia's mouth tightened.

No way would I let Cooper upset her at her own party.

"I've got this, Jackson. Why don't you go check on Alicia?" I helped him disentangle himself from Cooper, who was still muttering, and draped him over my own shoulders. I rubbed his back while Jackson made his escape.

"Hey, now. Why don't we get you some water?" People around us were starting to stare, so I led him toward the kitchen.

"Never be the same," he mumbled.

"Oh, sweetie, you'll be fine tomorrow. I'll make sure you have some water and ipo—ibo—iboprufen. Ibuprofen, I mean."

I'd thought the kitchen was empty, but it wasn't. In the corner, where they wouldn't be visible from anyone in the adjacent living room, Jamila pressed Jenny up against the countertop. As she bent over the shorter woman, her scrap of a Wonder Woman skirt rode up, and I caught a flash of her perfectly toned ass, barely covered by her red panties—and one of Jenny's hands. Jenny's red Captain Marvel boot hooked around Jamila's calf. Their lips fused together.

That vile orange punch tried to make me toss out a snarky comment about a DC-Marvel crossover, but I clamped down my teeth just in time. No need to draw attention to the scene in the kitchen. If we could just sneak past them, maybe Cooper wouldn't see them. Jamila had seemed so nice. How could she do this to him?

I dragged Cooper toward the laundry room. But his feet stopped moving, and he stared at the women. Crap. Were they just drunk and fooling around? Or was Jamila cheating on him? This was going to go bad. Fast.

"Hey, Mila. Jenny." His tone was conversational, friendly. My eyes widened, my tipsy brain trying to puzzle out the situation.

Jamila turned her head, her temple still pressed against Jenny's forehead, her lips puffy. "Hey, Coop." Jenny waggled her gauntleted fingers at him.

Finally, he let me push him into the laundry room. Under the fluorescents, he looked green. "Are you okay?" I asked.

When he shrugged, he overbalanced and wobbled. I grabbed his biceps. "Cooper?"

"Yeah, I'm good." But he didn't look at me. His blue eyes stared at something, maybe nothing, behind me.

"I'm so sorry you saw that. Maybe Jamila isn't it for you, but you'll find someone." Why hadn't I just left him in the living room while I fetched the water? I tightened my grip on his arms to prove to him how serious I was—or to ensure we both remained upright. "You're gorgeous, smart, successful. I know the right woman is out there for you."

His eyes were red-rimmed and bloodshot, and he smelled like orange soda and tequila. Still, he was the most beautiful man I'd ever met. Even young Harrison Ford could only wish to look as good in a Han Solo costume.

He looked at me, his blue gaze hot as a gas flame. "Maybe she's been right here all along." And he leaned forward and kissed me.

I'd dreamed of this moment. I'd built it up, embroidered it in my imagination so that I anticipated the tingle that would follow the warm brush of his lips over mine. I prepared to swoon from the hot rush of blood from my brain to my soon-to-be-throbbing lady parts. I gripped his arms, preparing for my knees to weaken.

But it was only a kiss. Orange punch–scented. Closed-mouth. A press of lips. Nothing hard pushed against my hip except his plastic lightsaber. No angels sang. No tingle. No clench in my core. No pulse rushing in my ears. Zero sparks.

For the first time in three years, my heart didn't thump at Cooper's nearness. My fingertips didn't go numb, and my breath didn't quicken.

I truly wanted him to find someone special. Someone who'd set his heart on fire, someone who'd make him long for her the way I'd longed for him for three years. And, even in my alcoholic haze, I knew that person wasn't me.

And I deserved someone who wanted me, who loved me back, who made me freaking tingle. Who, when we were together, made the world narrow to us two, blurring the world around us.

If that had happened when Cooper kissed me, I wouldn't have heard the sound.

A squeak on hardwood. A squeak I knew.

I pulled away from Cooper and looked toward the doorway just in time to catch the flash of a princely boot sole. *Great Galileo.*

My hands still rested on Cooper's arms, and I shook him. Gently. Orange punch barf would be hard to get out of my white gown.

"Hey. Are you okay?" I needed to talk to Tyler, explain what he'd seen. That hadn't been a no-big-deal squeak. If a boot squeak could be angry, that one had been.

"No," he groaned and slumped back against the washing machine, his normally tan skin pallid.

"Water," I said. "Don't move."

In the kitchen, I waved at the still-lip-locked women. "Don't mind me." I grabbed a glass, filled it from the tap, and scurried back into the laundry room.

I pushed the glass into his hands. "Drink."

While he chugged the water, I called a car for him. His color was better when he handed the glass back to me, but his glassy eyes and clumsy movements told me he was either drunk or heartbroken—probably both. Walking him past Jamila would be cruel, so I took him outside through the garage.

The cool air slapped my cheeks, and so did my good friend, remorse. Why had I stood so close and let Cooper kiss me? Why had I done it where anyone could see? And why had fate, that cruel bitch, made Tyler walk by just then? I glanced back at the house. I'd have to find him, talk to him. And say what?

I looked up at the sky. More to myself than to Cooper, I said, "Too bad it's too foggy to see the stars tonight." A hazy glow lit the sky where the moon should've been. No stars, not even a planet, were visible. I could've used the companionship of the constellations.

"Whazzat?" He dragged his gaze from the street to my face.

"No stars tonight. It's foggy."

He didn't even look up. "Can't ever see stars here. Too much light polloosh—pollution." He belched softly.

I closed my eyes for a moment. When I opened them, headlights swept the curb. *Thank Copernicus.* I guided Cooper into the backseat of the car and watched it drive away.

When I turned back toward the house, Tyler sat on the front steps, arms looped around his knees. His long coat pooled around him on the step. My heart skipped in my chest. At least we'd be doing this without an audience of partygoers. I didn't owe him an apology, but I owed him an explanation after I'd told him I wouldn't be chasing Cooper anymore.

I trudged up the stairs and sat next to him on the cold wooden porch. The breeze fluttered my long white skirt around my ankles.

Staring out at the street, I said, "Look, I—"

At the same time, he said, "Congratulations."

I blinked at the bitterness in his voice. Where had sweet, sunny Tyler gone, and who was this snarling doppelganger? "What?"

"Operation Prince Charming. Looks like it worked. You're welcome."

I'd never seen him this angry before. Had something upset him at the party? Or before? "No. It's not like that."

He stood, and his right-hand fingers tapped out a furious rhythm against the satin of his breeches. "We were friends, Marlee. And you used me to get what you wanted. And the worst part is I let you. I can't believe I fucking let you."

It was late October, and the weather had turned chilly. But that didn't explain the cold that gripped me like I was on the ice planet Hoth instead of a street in San Francisco. I had to tell him I'd been wrong to use him, that I didn't even want Cooper anymore. But if I was on Hoth, he was on Tatooine. His face had gone all blotchy red in the porchlight. Heat radiated from him.

"I'm done. No one can compete with Cooper Fallon." His arms fell to his sides, and he looked down the sidewalk toward Cooper's abandoned silver Tesla. In a low voice, he said, "I can't."

When he walked away from me, I was in the Death Star's

compactor, hardly able to breathe through the weight compressing my chest. And I didn't want to think about why.

R2-D2 couldn't save me. This princess had gotten herself and her friend into this trash heap. And now I needed to find a way out.

24

MONDAY WAS about what you'd expect: a 7.5 on the debacle scale.

Cooper walked in minutes after I did—late for him—and set a cup of coffee on my desk. I could tell from the delicious aroma that it was a caramel macchiato, missing the shot of pumpkin spice syrup I always added in the fall, but I couldn't expect him to remember that.

He rubbed the back of his neck under the collar of his raincoat. "Marlee, I—I don't even know what to say. I was upset and drunk and—what I did was inexcusable. I'm sorry. Can you forgive me?"

I blinked at him and lifted the cup to my nose. Heaven. "It was just a kiss. No big deal."

"But you—you didn't care?"

"No." I grinned, thankful that I didn't. A month ago, I'd have been crushed that it wasn't true love's kiss for him. But when I'd finally gotten what I'd been waiting three years for, I hadn't wanted it.

Irony is the worst.

"Do you want to talk to HR?" he asked. "I'll give them a statement."

I tried hard to keep from rolling my eyes, but I probably failed in the end. He'd have been justified in reporting me to HR, based solely on the eye-fucking I'd done during the first three years of my employment at Synergy.

"No need. But if you want to bring me more coffee, I'm down with that. Or flowers. Flowers are nice."

The corners of his mouth inched up like it'd been so long that he'd forgotten how. "Thanks, Marlee. For understanding. For being a good friend."

I returned a wry smile. "Anytime, Cooper."

As he walked away, I called, "Pink peonies. They're my favorite."

Not looking back, he gave a thumbs-up.

That was Cooper. Except for that ill-timed, drunken kiss on Saturday night, he was an upstanding guy. He'd had his heart broken, and he was worried about hurting *me*. The next time I saw Jamila, I'd give her a piece of my mind.

Jackson, his face pale, dragged in about ten. He mumbled something that included "Tequila" and "thirty" and "sucks" and closed his office door. Gently.

So far, I'd emerged unscathed from my Saturday night of debauchery. But then things got real.

As in, real bad.

Ben came upstairs after his midmorning beverage run with a stormcloud face. And no coffee for me. "Marlee, can we talk in the conference room?"

I stood, the coffee Cooper had brought me earlier curdling in my stomach. He wasn't going to quit, was he? Because I couldn't handle that. With Dad's problems, I didn't have the energy—emotional or physical—for finding a replacement and all the extra work an assistantless Cooper would require. Plus, Ben was not only helpful and efficient, but after only a week, he was becoming a friend. I mentally shook my fist at Karma. Sabotaging Cooper's assistant search had finally come back to bite me.

I trudged into the conference room behind him and shut the

door. He stood, his back to the window, and bit the inside of his lip for a second before he spoke.

"The other admins are saying you left Jackson's party with Cooper."

Cold prickles washed over my face. "What?"

"That you two are together." He crossed his arms. "I know we don't know each other all that well, and normally I wouldn't poke my nose into your business, but this is a bad idea, Marlee."

How had he heard the gossip before I had? He'd been at Synergy a week. I'd been there three freaking years. Those meddling admins should have come to me first. I stared at him in silent shock.

Uncrossing his arms, he reached for my hand and rubbed my fingers. His words had drained the warmth out of them. "Cooper's...complicated. You're a beautiful girl, and you'll make some deserving guy very lucky. Don't waste it on Cooper Fallon."

If only he'd been around three years ago to tell me that. Not that I'd have listened. Thinking of all the time I'd spent wishing and planning made my body heavy, like I was trying to walk on Jupiter.

He watched me, sympathy in his light-brown eyes.

At last, I found words. "No, it's not true. I-I took him to the kitchen to get him some water, but, um, someone else was there. So we went to the laundry room for a couple of minutes. To talk." My cheeks burned. "He kissed me, but it was just friendly, I swear. And then I called a car for him and sent him home. Alone. We both had too much to drink"—*damned evil punch*—"but that's it."

His grip tightened on my hand. "You're sure that's it? Friendly? He brought you coffee this morning." Ben never missed anything.

"Apology coffee." I twisted my lips into the best approximation of a smile I could manage. "We're cool. But thanks. Thanks for caring enough to talk to me."

He raised his eyebrows and lifted his other arm, and I stepped into his hug. "Anytime, honey." He squeezed me once and then let go. "And don't worry about the gossip. I'll try to clear it up."

I took a deep breath. "We'd better get back out there. I have a hungover executive to manage."

"I have a lot to do, too. Cooper's headed back out on the road."

I opened the door and led the way out. "Europe this time, right?"

"Yeah. A week. He's asked me to be on call during European business hours."

"Ugh. Better than Asia, I guess."

After lunch, I returned to my desk to find it covered in a gigantic arrangement of bright pink peonies. Seriously, the thing was three feet tall.

Ben ambled over, leaned on the corner of my desk, and flicked one of the blooms.

"Apology flowers," I said, gritting my teeth. How many of the gossiping assistants had watched the over-the-top bouquet come up from the ground floor? I scowled at all three dozen peonies.

"That's some apology. This is, like, an entire peony bush. Are you sure you didn't do anything more than kiss?"

I glared at him.

His mouth dropped open. "Mr. Weston."

I whirled, and sure enough, our CEO had approached silently and stroked a soft pink petal. "That's quite an arrangement, Ms. Rice."

"It's—it's gorgeous, isn't it?"

His sharp green eyes speared me. "I understand it's from Mr. Fallon. I hear you two attended a party together Saturday night."

"Not...not together." My heart rabbited in my chest. Why did I always feel like prey around him?

"And yet, he sent you flowers. Interesting." His gaze lingered on me for a second, scanning me right down to my bones. Then he turned on his silent heel and stalked toward Cooper's office.

"Mr. Weston, he's on a—" Ben's mouth snapped shut when

Weston, without looking back, flung up a hand like he was shooing a fly and walked right into Cooper's office without knocking.

Ben's face was pale. "Holy shit. That man is terrifying."

I shuddered. "Tell me about it."

The stairwell door closed behind me, and I heard the characteristic squeak of Vans. I whirled around, keeping my body in front of the flowers, but there was no way I could cover up the colossal arrangement.

"Tyler, hey," Ben said, his voice still shaky.

There was no dimple today. Not even the hint of a smile. His hair was flat on the top like he'd been wearing headphones and unruly in front like he'd been tugging on it. His slouch hid the muscles I'd drooled over—literally and figuratively—that night I'd slept in his bed.

Still, he was heartbreakingly beautiful.

And in my chest, I felt a ping, like a hairline fracture in my heart. I didn't want him to scowl at me. I wanted him to smile, to break out that dimple. To walk toward me and stand in that spot that blocked the sun from my eyes. To lean on my desk while we compared the number of painkillers we'd taken to lessen the aftereffects of that evil punch. To tell me about the elegant bit of code he'd wrestled into being that morning. So I could feel that spark, that tingle, that happened whenever he touched me.

It hit me like a blazing meteor. There'd been no spark when Cooper had kissed me because all of my sparks were for Tyler. My friend Tyler who somehow, while I'd been distracted by thoughts of Cooper, had become more than my friend. He'd become the person I could depend on when something went wrong. The one I wanted to share good news with. The person who made me feel cared-for and valued whenever he came up to visit. Yesterday, I'd thought I was hungover. Really, I'd been melancholy, like some lovesick historical romance heroine pining for her hero. All I'd been missing was a voluminous silk gown and a basket of mending to sigh over.

By Carl Sagan's bushy eyebrows, I loved Tyler Young.

"Hey." My voice was low and wispy. My breath stuck in my chest.

But Tyler wasn't looking at me. He was staring at those garish pink peonies.

He gripped his fist so hard I heard a faint snap, and a tiny something plinked on the wood floor.

"Never mind." His Vans screeched as he turned on his heel, flung open the stairwell door, and pounded down the stairs.

"Wow," Ben said, fanning himself. "Angry Tyler Young is one scrumptious lump of man-flesh. It'd be worth pissing him off just for the make-up—"

"Shut it, Ben."

I walked to the stairwell door and picked up the piece of black plastic that had fallen from Tyler's hand. It was a tiny gun or maybe a blaster like the one I'd worn with my Princess Leia costume the other night. When I could get myself together enough to talk to him like a reasonable person and not some melancholy spinster with embroidering to do, I'd take it down to him.

I hoped he didn't need it right away.

———

"LOOK, I'm sorry about the punch." Alicia frowned as she squeezed her pregnant belly against the cafe table. "That's new," she muttered.

I pulled the table toward myself to give her some breathing room. "The punch?"

"At the party on Saturday. Didn't you invite me for coffee to yell at me about it? Everyone else has. Apparently, Sunday was pretty miserable. Poor Jackson was still recovering on Monday."

"Poor Jackson?" I snorted. "He made the foul stuff." I'd popped more than the recommended dose of ibuprofen. To hell with the bottle's warnings about heart attacks. My heart could kiss my ass. It'd led me astray for the past three years.

"He forgot he wasn't twenty-two anymore." She smiled, her eyes going soft and fond.

Tyler used to look at me like that. Before I'd broken him and ruined our friendship. He hadn't come upstairs Tuesday or yesterday. And I hadn't had the courage to visit him downstairs. That was what I needed Alicia's help with.

The server set down Alicia's herbal tea and my caramel latte with a heart in the foam. Ugh. I swirled my spoon through it until it looked like Jupiter with its striped cloud formations.

"I didn't invite you here to complain about the punch. Though Jackson should issue a formal apology for trying to poison us all. I need to talk to you about…about Tyler."

"Tyler? Is he okay? I didn't see him drink the punch."

I gripped Alicia's hand just as she was about to pick up her cup. "Forget the punch. I—I think I love him."

Thank Bernoulli I'd stopped her from drinking. From the shocked expression on her face, she'd have done a spit-take for sure. "But you have a crush on Cooper."

"Shh." The cafe wasn't the closest one to the office, but Cooper Fallon's fame spread far beyond the Synergy office. "I thought I did, but I don't." I leaned closer to her and whispered, "He kissed me at your party, and I didn't feel anything. It was like kissing Jackson—not that I've ever done that—or, or Ben. Not that I've done that either. But there was no magic at all."

"You mean, not like when you kissed Tyler?"

I covered my face with my hands and nodded.

"How does Tyler feel about it?"

I peeked between my fingers. "Before the party, he said he wanted to be more than friends. And I shut him down. Then he saw Cooper and me. And the apology peonies."

"Apology—"

"He didn't take it well. I think I might have hit a sore spot." His words had been ringing in my ears since Saturday night: *You used me to get what you wanted. And the worst part is I let you.* I'd done to him just what his ex, Bella, had. "I haven't sucked it up enough to talk to him about it."

She arched a blond eyebrow. "But that's exactly what you have to do. You were the one who made Jackson come to Austin to grovel."

"I don't know that what I did was as bad as—"

"You have to talk to him. Otherwise, how will he know how you feel?"

She was paraphrasing my favorite song from *Enchanted*. Both Alicia and Giselle were right. I'd tell Tyler I loved him, and he'd take me in his arms and kiss me again like he'd kissed me at Alicia's wedding. My toes would curl, the sun would burst out from the fog, and woodland creatures would sing. Tyler and I would ride a white horse—or maybe just his blue Mustang—into the sunset.

I leaned across the table to hug Alicia. "You're right. You're right. I'll talk to him tomorrow."

She squeezed me back. "You two are going to be great together. You should come over for dinner one night next week."

That'd be perfect. Dinner with Tyler, my best friend, and the boss I loved like a brother. I was going to get my happily-ever-after after all.

25

FRIDAY NIGHT, I dragged up our porch steps and stuck my key in the lock. It was almost more effort than I could manage to turn it.

I'd been a coward. I'd waited most of the day, hoping Tyler would break his silent streak and come upstairs to see me. But at four o'clock, I'd marched downstairs and into the programmers' bullpen to find Tyler's cube deserted. Sam told me I'd missed him by just twenty minutes.

I'd thought about texting, but could you really tell someone you loved him for the first time over text? I hadn't read that in any of my romance novels. I'd find him in the office on Monday. After the long, lonely weekend.

All I wanted to do was crash onto my bed and binge-watch some romantic comedies. I pushed open the door.

Sylvia greeted me in the kitchen with words I never wanted to hear again: "We should talk." Lines of strain bracketed her eyes, and her mouth was set in a thin line.

"Is he okay?" I asked, slipping off my heels. Dad wasn't in the kitchen, and he wasn't in his recliner, either.

"He had a rough day. I gave him a sedative."

"A sedative?" I glared at her. "We didn't talk about that."

"He was agitated and asking to talk to Maggie. Is that what he calls you?" Her expression told me she knew it wasn't.

"No. That was my mother's name."

The older woman's eyes softened and she unclenched her jaw. "I assume she's...gone?"

"Yes." I wasn't about to go into the details with her, not after the week I'd had.

She squared up her solid figure. "He said he needed to see her. He pushed me to try to get outside." She tugged up her sleeve to show me a long purple bruise on her upper arm.

I blinked. My kind, gentle father had pushed a woman? Surely it'd been an accident. "That doesn't sound like Dad."

Her dark eyes filled with pity. "This disease, it takes away who your dad was. He'll do a lot of things that aren't like the man you knew."

Her words were a knife in my gut. Dad had cared for me all my life, most of it alone. He'd kissed my scraped knees, braided my hair, taught me to drive in his old Ford pickup. He'd cheered me when I'd graduated from high school and college, and he'd consoled me after breakups. I couldn't lose him. And I needed Sylvia to keep him.

"Are you okay? He didn't hurt you, did he?"

"No, honey. He's not the first patient to get a little rowdy. But this might not be the right place for him anymore."

"Here, with me, is the best place for him. I'm all he has." And Dad was all *I* had. I wasn't about to lose him.

She put a hand on her hip. "Do you want me to teach you how to give the sedative injection?"

The constriction in my throat blocked my words. I couldn't give anyone a shot, certainly not Dad. And he'd never hurt me. I didn't know what had gone on with Sylvia today, but I wouldn't need the drugs.

I shook my head.

"All right." She took her jacket from the hook by the back door. "I'll see you Monday."

"Thanks, Sylvia. Have a good weekend."

After she left, I sagged against the door. Not even romantic comedy was going to ease the blow she'd given me. I reached for the bottle of vodka from the cabinet above the oven.

————

SUNDAY AFTERNOON, I muted the commercial during the Raiders game. "Want some popcorn?"

"Sure." Dad smiled at me from his recliner.

I grinned back, set aside my paperback—in this one, the hero was a football player, so it was like we were really bonding over the game—and passed him the remote. Dad was having a good weekend.

I scuffed into the kitchen to send a package of popcorn for a turn in the microwave. While I waited, I opened a couple of beers. The headache I'd had yesterday morning from the vodka had disappeared. Dad had laughed at me when I'd dragged downstairs. When he'd asked, I couldn't tell him the real reason why I'd drunk all the vodka. Or about my fight with Tyler. Instead, I'd told him I'd had a rough week at work. Which was true. He'd given me an indulgent smile and told me I worked too hard. I'd kissed his stubble-roughened cheek.

That morning, I'd cleaned the house from top to bottom while Dad had caulked around the doors and windows. Then he announced he was going outside to clean the gutters—though he'd called them rain-catchers. I distracted him by turning on the football game.

I dared to let a little optimism creep into my heart. He'd just had a bad day on Friday. Spending the week with a stranger had been difficult for him. I'd thrown my share of tantrums at preschool when he went back to work after my mother died. Time with me restored him. It restored both of us. Maybe Jackson would let me work remotely one day a week. Sylvia was wrong. Tyler, too. Dad was still himself, and we could make this work.

The microwave beeped, and I carried our bottles of beer and the bowl of popcorn into the living room. Dad cheered as the Raiders made a first down. I nudged his hand with the beer bottle, and he took it from me, his eyes still on the television. "Thanks, Maggie."

I sighed but didn't bother to correct him. He and my mother must have watched football together, and she'd brought him beers once upon a time. When they'd been young and in love, before she'd been taken away from him too soon.

Could I ever find that kind of love, the kind that lasted beyond even death? Dad had loved my mother from their first touch. I'd tried to manufacture something like that with Cooper. I could see it now. I'd dreamed that the perfect fairytale prince would sweep me up on his charger and carry me away, and Cooper Fallon fit that role to a T.

But even as I'd crushed on him, I knew, somewhere in the depths of my heart, that he was only a fantasy. Like my romance novels, he was something to keep my mind off Dad, my job that other people with no more qualifications than I had sneered at, my lack of real friends.

And when someone who actually cared about me came into my life, I was so deep in the comfortable groove of my crush that I couldn't see it. I couldn't see him. I'd ignored all the signals Tyler had given me, not wanting to risk our friendship. But with the feelings between us, our friendship was already wobbling on its axis. Now it might be too late, and we'd careen apart into the emptiness of space.

"I miss you, Maggie." Dad's voice sounded younger than I'd heard it in a while, all his usual gravel gone.

My stomach tightened into a cold, hard ball. I put down my novel and looked over at him. He watched me, but his eyes clouded with memory, not seeing *me* but someone else. My mother.

I reached across the table and gripped his hand. "Dad, it's me.

Marlee. Mama—Maggie—has been gone a long time. You know that."

"Dead." A tear glistened in the corner of his eye and then rolled down a groove on his cheek.

"That's right, Dad. She died a long time ago."

"Weeks ago."

I sighed. "*Years* ago, Dad. I'm all grown up now."

He blinked the fog from his eyes. "Yes, you are, Sunshine. You look so much like your mother."

I smiled at him. I'd always thought she was beautiful. "How about we remember her with her meatloaf recipe for dinner?" According to Dad, my mother hadn't been much of a cook, but her meatloaf had been his favorite.

"That sounds good."

I searched the freezer for ground meat, but my mother's recipe called for a mix of pork and beef that we didn't have. After being indoors all day yesterday and today, a shopping trip in the fresh air would do me good. I kissed Dad on the top of his white head. "I'm going to the store, then. I'll be back in a few."

He grunted, his attention already back on the game.

The sunshine and crisp fall air outside encouraged me to linger on my errands. I spent a few minutes talking to Mr. Oliveras; he'd seen Dad with Sylvia and asked about his health. I told him only that Dad had gotten more unsteady, which was true. I picked up a fruity Zinfandel to go with the meatloaf and a bottle of vodka to replace what I'd drunk. Plus some cheery yellow chrysanthemums for Dad to set in the bud vase next to Mama's urn.

When I unlocked the front door, I was sorry I'd been gone so long. Even vodka wouldn't fix this.

"Dad!" I shouted into the empty living room.

The room was a disaster. Beer from our tipped-over bottles hung in pendulous drops from the edge of the end table and plopped into a pool on the wood floor below. Popcorn was scattered across the room from the back of the sofa to the brown shag rug in front of it. The footrest of the empty recliner was up. The cushions had been pulled from the sofa and were thrown haphazardly in a pile nearby. My heart pounded. Where was he? Had he been attacked? Had we been burgled?

I found the remote on the coffee table and muted the television. "Dad!" I shouted again into the silence.

I strode into the kitchen. I'd whack the burglar with my heavy bottle of booze. And then Tase him while he was down. I scanned the room, which at first glance appeared to be empty. But then I heard a sniffle under the table.

Squatting down, I found him under the kitchen table, clutching his knees to his chest. "Dad, what are you doing under there?" I whispered in case the burglar was still in the house.

His eyes met mine, and they were clear but red-rimmed. "She's gone."

"Who's gone?" A female thief?

"Maggie's gone."

The tension left my shoulders, and I collapsed from my squat to sit on the linoleum. The grocery bag clunked to the floor. "Yeah, Dad. She's gone. Can you come out from under the table?" How had he gotten under there, anyway, with his bum knee?

He scooted out using his hands and his good leg. I stood first and then pulled him to his feet and helped him sit in one of the kitchen chairs. "What happened?"

"I couldn't find her. I couldn't find Maggie."

I looked up at the wall behind her place at the table to find her photo. But the framed picture was gone. Huh. Maybe that's what he was talking about. I'd look for it later.

Dad rubbed his knee. The crawl under the table hadn't done it any good. "Does your leg hurt? Want a pain pill?"

"Please." The hopeless tremor in his voice sent a chill across my skin.

I fetched him a glass of water and his prescription pill and watched him swallow it. Seeing the deep lines around his eyes and mouth, I asked, "Do you want to go lie down while I make dinner?"

His smile was strained. "That'd be good."

I helped him to his room and tucked the blanket around him. I kissed his forehead, which smoothed out under my lips. "I'll come check on you in a bit."

"All right." His eyelids were already fluttering shut.

I cleaned the living room for the second time that day, and then I made my mother's meatloaf. While it baked, I researched early onset Alzheimer's Disease and dementia support groups on my laptop.

That night, I ate dinner alone and tasted nothing.

26

MONDAY MORNING, I carried the weight of the weekend into the office. I hadn't slept Sunday night, my brain running in exhausted circles and my chest tight with worry. Was I doing the right thing by keeping Dad at home with me? Watching him become someone I didn't know was breaking my heart. How much longer could I do it before I kissed my own mental health goodbye?

But only an ungrateful daughter would want to leave her ailing father. My single father who'd raised me alone since I was two. Who'd sacrificed everything—a second love, a social life, bigger dreams—for me. Even as I pushed through the revolving door at Synergy, I wanted to turn around and take the train back home just to hold his hand.

I couldn't, though. Not only did I have work to do and a paycheck to earn, but I had to make things right with Tyler. I'd wanted to call him so many times over the weekend, either to talk about Dad or to take my mind off him; I wasn't sure which. But I'd stopped, my fingers hovering over the screen. I always laid my problems at his feet. When was the last time I'd asked him about his life, his problems? Was I a terrible friend?

What if he didn't want friendship or the *more* I was ready to explore with him? Thinking about the angry words he'd spat at me outside Alicia's house made my gut clench the way it had the morning after I'd drunk all the vodka.

I'd just set my bag on my desk when Jackson strode off the elevator. He stopped at my desk. "Marlee, I have a problem."

"Good morning to you, too." Despite the clench in my belly, I couldn't keep the smile off my face. I loved solving Jackson's problems.

"I may have forgotten to tell you that Alicia has an obstetrician appointment at two, and I'd promised her we'd go shopping for baby furniture after that. So we have to reschedule all my afternoon meetings."

I tapped to open his calendar. "I'm on it. Don't forget that Cooper's leaving for Europe tonight. I'll try to find fifteen minutes in your schedule for him; otherwise, I'll set you a reminder to call him before he gets on the plane."

"You're a lifesaver, Marlee." He grinned.

"I doubt you'll be saying that at one-thirty when you've been back-to-back all morning and I'm pushing you out the door. Plus, you're holding down the fort for Cooper this week while he's in Europe."

His face fell. "Remind me why I let him make me a VP again?"

"Because you love programming, this company, and the people who work here. You're doing it for yourself, for Cooper, and even for me. Now go do your meditation while I untangle your calendar."

He saluted me. "Yes, ma'am."

Just like I'd predicted, he was tired and cranky by the time I shoved a granola bar and a cup of coffee into his hand and put him on the elevator to go meet Alicia.

When I returned to my desk, a new appointment had appeared on Jackson's calendar for the next day, and the subject line caught my eye. *Tyler Young interview for development manager.*

I bit my lip to hold in my squee and texted him.

Me: Yay! I'm so glad you applied for the

> manager position! Want to come up and talk about it?

Tyler: Sure.

That had been almost too easy. A ready-made excuse to talk to him. Though why hadn't he told me he'd decided to apply? Was he still that angry with me? I wished I hadn't let so much time slip by. I wished I'd had the courage to talk to him last week.

Usually, I met challenges head-on. Work challenges. But throw in some emotions, and I got all tangled up. Like, it'd taken me three years to initiate Operation Prince Charming. And I still didn't know what to do about Dad, who, if I was honest, had been declining ever since his accident. But I wasn't going to let three years or even another week slip by without telling Tyler how I felt about him. He deserved to know that I was ready for more if he still wanted it.

I had time to arrange myself at my desk, ankles crossed, skirt smoothed, before the stairwell door opened and Tyler's familiar sneaker squeak sounded. He'd cut his hair short, almost a crew cut. I missed the floppy waves, but I longed to run my fingers over the short, plush-looking hair over his ears.

He trudged to my desk. "Hey." Wary. We were going with wary. "So you wanted to talk?"

I nodded. How did I talk to this version of Tyler, the one whose always-smiling mouth turned down into a frown, who stood a couple feet farther away from my desk than he usually did?

"Let's go into Jackson's office. He's out for the day." I led the way and shut the door. I flipped the switch that lowered the blinds. "I'm so happy you applied for the job." Shit, I'd already said that.

He folded his arms and shrugged. "I figured it was worth a shot."

"And see? They asked you to interview."

"Yeah."

Wow, okay. I wasn't used to Terse Tyler. Maybe he just wanted me to get to the point. "Sit?" I gestured toward the sofa in Jackson's seating area.

Without a word, he bypassed the sofa to sit in one of the wing chairs. I perched on the sofa right next to his chair and tugged my skirt over my knees. "I'm sorry you saw what you saw at Jackson and Alicia's party. I—"

"You mean you kissing Cooper? Isn't that what you wanted? For me to see so I'd get the message and give up?"

I sucked in a breath. My skin had gone all prickly, and not in a good way. "No! I'd never want to hurt you like that. We're friends, and—"

"Are we? Friends? Because you haven't acted too much like a friend lately."

"I know, and I'm sorry about that. I was scared."

His eyebrows slammed down. "Scared of me?"

"Scared of how I felt and how that might change our relationship." I traced a flower on my skirt. "You see, I…I care about you." Crap, that wasn't right. I'd undershot it.

"I mean"—I looked up—"I think I'm falling for you." Why was this so hard? I'd read the words a thousand times in my romance novels. They rolled off the tongues of the heroines. My tongue stuck to the roof of my mouth.

He didn't say anything, and he kept his expression blank.

"Say something. Please." I twisted my hands together in my lap.

"I—I don't know what to say. Is this Operation Prince Charming Part Two? More pretending so Cooper will pull his head out of his ass and propose? What role am I supposed to be playing now?"

I laid my hand on his knee. "No role. No pretense. I have feelings for you, Tyler. More-than-friends feelings."

"But at your house, you said you didn't want that. That you

couldn't. And two weekends ago, you kissed him. How can I believe that—"

I sprang up from the sofa, bent over him in the chair, and covered his mouth with mine. I tried to infuse the kiss with all the longing, all the regret, and all the love I felt for him. It wasn't soft, not like the kiss he'd given me on the dance floor, or sexy, like the one we'd shared outside the inn after his erotic foot massage. It was hard and full of meaning and promise. A commitment.

He was stiff at first, his lips frozen. But I persisted, nibbling at his soft lower lip, caressing his shoulders and pecs over his T-shirt. I was sure I looked ridiculous, bent at the waist, my ass in the air, but I didn't care. I needed to show Tyler how I felt about him. That I wanted more than friendship. That I could give him what he'd said he wanted.

Little by little, he softened. I slipped my tongue between his lips and tasted him. Sweet and citrus fizzed on my tongue. His lemony tang was like coming home. I hummed. His hands landed on my back, and I melted onto his knees, into his lap. He sighed against my lips. "Mar—"

"Marlee!" Cooper's muffled voice came through the door. "Are you in there?"

I tensed. By all the moons of Saturn, why had he come looking for me now?

"Don't. If we're quiet, he'll think you've gone out," Tyler whispered. He brushed his lips against mine.

"I have to see what he needs." I raised myself from his lap, rubbing stray lipstick from my chin. I strode to the door and opened it. "Yes, Cooper?"

"We can't find the presentation you and I worked on before my East Coast trip. Do you have a copy?"

I sighed. It was on the server, but Ben wasn't fully familiar with our filing conventions. "I'll find it for you. Give me a minute to finish up—"

But he'd looked over my head. Curse him for being so tall.

"Hey, Tyler." Looking down at me, he smirked. "I think he's wearing your lipstick."

I fell for it. I rubbed at my upper lip. "I need a minute." I needed to make sure Tyler and I were okay. That he wasn't about to bolt on me again. "And then I'll find your file." I started to shut the door, but Tyler had come up behind me.

"I'm going. I'm sure you and Cooper have important work to do together."

"Tyler, wait—"

"No, Marlee. We're done."

His last word sucked all the light and air out of the room like a black hole. "Done?"

"You can't give me what I need. What I deserve. Or even your undivided attention."

"I—I'll come down when I've taken care of Cooper."

"That won't be necessary. I don't want anything more." He brushed past me, past Cooper, and headed for the stairs.

Cooper leaned on the doorframe. "So, looks like you two—"

"Not helpful, Cooper. I'll get that file for you now." I strode past him to my desk, my face frozen.

Ben hovered near my desk. "Sorry," he whispered. "I tried to—"

"It's fine." I unlocked my laptop and navigated to the file on the server.

It wasn't fine. I'd made Tyler feel second-best again. Like I was using him again. It wasn't Ben's fault, and, as irritating as he'd been, it wasn't Cooper's. It was mine. I'd made it clear from the start of Tyler's and my friendship that I wanted Cooper. And it'd take work to make Tyler think otherwise.

Fortunately, work was something I was good at. And I'd keep working until Tyler believed I loved him and no one else.

27

WHEN I WALKED in the door that night, Sylvia and Dad sat at the kitchen table in front of a children's puzzle—one of my old ones—with pieces almost the size of my palm. Sylvia had told me that doing puzzles would help Dad's memory. And yet, I hadn't remembered to buy him any.

Sylvia looked up from the puzzle and smiled. "You're home early."

"Uh-huh." I slipped out of my heels. I wanted a shower. And sweatpants. And ice cream. In that order. But I bent to kiss Dad's temple. "Hey, Dad. Where'd you find this old thing?" My heart twinged when I saw the picture on the front: Beauty and the Beast, dancing alone in the ballroom.

"Sylvia found it when she was looking for Maggie."

I looked up at her, alarmed.

She shook her head. "Your mama's picture." Then she pointed up at the wall behind me. "Found her, too."

I looked behind me, and sure enough, my mother had been restored to her place on the wall. "Where?"

She nudged a puzzle piece toward Dad. "Under his pillow."

A tiny piece of my heart broke off. Even after more than twenty years, he missed her so much.

"Done!" Dad snapped the last piece into place.

"That's great. I'll get you another one. Promise." I'd go out on my lunch break and buy it from one of the expensive tourist places if I had to.

"Eh, this one's okay," he said. "I'll probably have forgotten by tomorrow."

A bigger chunk of my heart fell off at that. Now I really needed that ice cream. With fudge sauce.

Sylvia had nursed any number of dementia patients, but her face drooped, too.

"Do you want to go home early?" I asked. "I can handle him now that I'm home."

"If you're sure?" She rose from her chair.

"I've got it from here. Have a good night."

She gathered her things and left. I locked the door and leaned against it.

"What's wrong, Sunshine?"

"Wrong? Nothing."

He beckoned me over, and I sat next to him as I had my whole life.

"I may be losing my marbles, but I can tell when my Sunshine goes dim. Something's bothering you. Is it that boy with the car? Tanner?"

"Tyler." I slumped in my chair. Now I was fourteen again and telling him about my first crush. He'd never been any help with boy-girl stuff. His relationship with my mother had been flawless, and he knew nothing about having his heart broken.

But I told him. I told him about my crush on Cooper, trying to make him jealous with my friend, and then about my friend's developing feelings for me that I hadn't been ready to reciprocate until it was too late. How Tyler had told me he deserved more.

"Why did I screw it up so bad?"

His eyes were clear when he said, "I think I gave you an unrealistic view of relationships."

"No, Dad. You showed me what a relationship should be." I

started to break up the puzzle, starting with the flowing hem of Belle's golden ball gown.

He put a hand over mine, stopping my busy fingers.

"When I met your mother, I was still a young man. Younger than you are now. I had a job, spending money, friends. We'd drink beers after work. Maybe do a little—" He made a smoking gesture with his thumb and index finger.

"Dad!" I did *not* want to hear that.

He chuckled. "The last thing on my mind was getting serious with a girl. And then I met Maggie. She was beautiful and smart and funny."

I sighed. "And you fell in love."

"No." He ducked his head. "I knocked her up."

"Oh my God! Dad!"

"But I did what was right by her, and we got married."

"And then you fell in love."

He hummed. "We were partners working toward a common goal. Raising you. And we were so happy when you were born." He gripped my hand again. "We both loved you very much."

I rubbed my pendant. "Didn't you love each other?"

"We did, in a way. Not the way they talk about in the storybooks." He broke off a piece of the puzzle from the other corner, the Beast's furry paw. "I wanted to show you, maybe even show Maggie and myself, that it was possible. True love. So I read you love stories."

"What about that magical touch? Handing her the towel by the pool?"

"I wished it'd happened that way. I always wished we'd fallen in love like that."

Another piece of my heart snapped off.

"Do you regret it? Do you regret…me?"

He looked up, his blue eyes clear for once. "No, not ever. I only wish you'd had more time with her."

So do I. I broke up the rest of the puzzle and scattered the pieces into the box. When I looked up again, Dad's eyes were cloudy.

"Where was I going with that story?"

"Doesn't matter, Dad." I knew where he was going with it. Sam, who wasn't even interested in love, had given the best relationship advice. As much as I loved reading about insta-lust, love based on friendship was the best kind of love.

I stood and set the puzzle box on the pink shelves by the back door so he and Sylvia could build it again tomorrow. The telescope case caught my eye.

"Want to do some stargazing later tonight? It's clear out." Looking at the stars would improve both our moods.

"Whatever you like, Maggie."

I sighed and checked the time. Too early to start dinner. My pencil skirt dug into my stomach, and my shoulders ached under my bra straps. My sweatpants called to me from upstairs.

"How about some SportsCenter? I bet they'll have a preview of the football game."

"Okay."

I led him to his chair and flipped on the television. He leaned back, and his eyes went glassy. Maybe he'd drift off to sleep.

I snagged my shoes, jogged upstairs, and took my time changing into comfortable clothes, remembering the desperate kiss with Tyler and then his unyielding posture after. You'd think after all the romance novels I'd read, after all the romantic comedies I'd devoured, I'd know how to grovel. But I'd fucked it up. Had I ruined our friendship, and the possibility for more, permanently?

Even my yoga pants and worn sweatshirt scratched and irritated my skin. I deserved the discomfort after what I'd done to Tyler. Maybe if I texted him, he'd come over and give me a grovel mulligan?

Just as I turned to go downstairs and start dinner, a clatter rose from outside the window. Had Tyler read my mind and come over with his video game system? My heart pounding, I ran to kneel on the window seat.

My heart stopped.

Dad was splayed on the porch steps below. The telescope case lay at the bottom of the stairs. One leg stretched out at an unnatural angle. His head rested on the top step. The sunset spread a rosy glow over his face, but his eyes were closed. His body was still.

28

THE NEXT FEW hours flashed by in a smear of images and sounds.

Red and blue flares across the curious faces of our neighbors. The blare of the siren as we inched too slowly through the rush-hour traffic. The smell of disinfectant and shock in the emergency room, and then disinfectant and fear on the surgery floor. The flicker of over-bright fluorescent lights on eighty-four white vinyl floor tiles. The hard plastic chair, worn smooth by other anxious, waiting, terrified fidgeters. Looking up at every movement, hoping not to be called and told my world was ending.

Later, the *beep, beep, beep* of the heart monitor kept my heavy eyelids from closing. From the relative comfort of the stiff vinyl chair in Dad's hospital room, I watched the rise and fall of his chest through half-open eyes. Once a minute, I checked his slack, gray face but avoided looking at the shaved patch in his white hair and the bandage that covered the twelve stitches in his scalp. I wasn't as worried about his leg—we'd been through that before —but I willed his heart to keep pumping and that monitor to keep beeping and Dad to stay with me and not leave me because I'd been selfish and careless.

I curled up in the unforgiving chair, curved my fingers around his limp hand, and waited.

————

SUNLIGHT SHINING red through my closed eyelids woke me. I sat up and blinked. The steady beep of the monitors brought back where I was and what had happened the evening before. Dad's chest rose and fell, and his eyelids were blue-tinged. I stroked his motionless hand, taking comfort in its warmth.

I stood, stretched, and walked to the window. Outside the hospital, the early-morning rays gilded the rooftops in a soft pink. Cars crawled along the freeway, headlights on. A white BART bus trundled along in the HOV lane, reminding me of where I was expected to be.

I turned my back to the window and shot off a couple of texts to Jackson to let him know what was happening. I sent off another text to Ben to ask him to find a temp to cover for me for the rest of the week. Last night's surgeon had told me they'd want to monitor Dad for a few days. I eyed the cast on his leg. He'd broken the same one, which, I supposed, was lucky. His good leg would support him through rehab.

My eyes trailed up to his face. Asleep, he looked younger. Except for his white hair and the pallor of his skin, he looked like the dad who'd raised me, who'd held my hand through all my vaccinations, who'd made me chicken soup—from a can, of course—when I was sick, who'd bandaged my scraped knees when I wiped out on my bike. We were quite a pair, alone and broken as we were.

I'd be his good leg for as long as he needed me.

————

THE BEEPING of the monitors made me want to shred my itchy skin.

That, or the lack of caffeine.

Each time one of the nurses suggested I take a break, go for a walk, grab a cup of coffee, I'd refused. It'd been my sloppiness, my lack of care, that'd allowed this to happen. Why had I lingered upstairs? Why had I told Sylvia to leave early?

Why did I always let everyone down?

I looked down at my phone for the hundredth time that day. I already had Tyler's contact information pulled up. My finger hovered over the text icon. *I should tell him I'm sorry.*

But then what? Assuming he responded, what would I say?

That I wanted to try? How could I, with Dad needing more care?

He deserved more. More than I could give right now.

That I didn't want to try, then, and he could be free.

The icon blurred on my phone. Damned tears. I blinked them away and rubbed at the one that made a dash for my cheek.

I needed to be strong. For Dad. No distractions.

I tossed my phone into my purse on the windowsill. Outside, the blue shadow of the hospital building stretched across the highway below. Dad had slept all day.

The door banged open, and Jackson's voice echoed into the room, drowning out the beeps at last.

"Marlee, are you in here?" The second-biggest bouquet I'd ever seen—Cooper's peonies still held that honor—walked into the room. I could just see Jackson's eyes and mussed dark hair peeking over the top of the colorful gerbera daisies. Alicia, following behind, shushed him.

Jackson set the flowers on the small table between Dad's bed and the unoccupied one. A groove of concern divided his eyebrows. "Are you okay?"

Hoping I hadn't smeared my mascara, I hugged him, filling my nostrils with his familiar scent of soap and leather seats. "I'm fine. And the doctor says he'll be okay. Though he hasn't woken up yet." That was my worry. The last time, after he'd fallen off the ladder, Dad had woken up right after the surgery.

I'd give every romance novel I owned just to see his eyes blink open.

Alicia stepped up, and I hugged my friend. The November chill still clung to her coat, along with the scent of Earl Grey tea. Her slender hands pressed into my back, and I leaned against her.

"Wait." I pulled back and glared at Jackson. "You can't be here! You're scheduled in meetings all day!"

His face broke into an unconcerned smile. "That's what's great about being the flaky founder. I can blow off those meetings and dump it all on Cooper. He stayed up late to take the calls from Amsterdam."

Even Cooper was helping me. Warmth spread through me at the reminder that I wasn't alone.

I smiled back at Jackson. "I never thought I'd say this, but I'm glad you're shirking your responsibilities."

He massaged my shoulder, and a little more of my tension drained out. "Though I'm worried about—"

Alicia interrupted him. "The team will be fine without you for a few hours. Even down one. Or two. *You*, on the other hand"— she squeezed my other shoulder—"need our help."

I pretended to roll my eyes to hide the tears that welled up. I turned to the window to blink them away. "Thanks."

Jackson said, "Whatever you need. You've always been there for me, and now it's my turn to help you."

That only made the tears come faster. I sniffed and said, "In that case, would you mind getting me a cup of coffee?"

Alicia said, "And some fruit and yogurt. I bet you haven't eaten in a while."

Since lunch yesterday. I'd refused to let myself feel anything as selfish as hunger.

Jackson patted my shoulder. "I'll be right back." The door shut a few seconds later.

Alicia walked over to Dad's bedside. "His color is good," she said. "Maybe he'll wake up soon."

"I hope so. I'm—I'm worried."

She turned to face me. "Of course you are. It's tough to see a loved one…"

"Oh!" Guilt stabbed me. She'd lost her sister to cancer several years before. She must've hated hospitals. "You don't have to stay with me—"

"Course I do, Marlee." She stroked my arm. "That's what friends do."

"You're going to make me cry again."

"Crying is okay. Trying to hold it in, trying to do it all yourself, that's not okay. Let's sit." Stepping aside so I could take the chair by the bed, she sank into the other chair and passed a hand over her rounded belly.

Easing onto the unforgiving vinyl, I watched her. "You know, just before he—he fell, Dad told me he and my mother weren't in love when they got married. They were pregnant."

"Oh." Alicia's forehead creased. "How do you feel about that?"

"Not wonderful. Surprised. I always thought they had this perfect marriage, you know?" I touched my pendant.

"People can still love each other and not be perfect," she said. "Jackson and I love each other very much, and we still argue."

"How did you—how did you know Jackson was the one for you?"

"Well, as you know, he's not perfect. And there were lots of reasons why we shouldn't be together: we worked together, we lived in different cities, our personalities and lifestyles were completely at odds. But"—a smile floated onto her face—"I realized I was miserable when we were apart. And happy when we were together. I was a better person with him. He felt the same way."

I was miserable now, all right. And it wasn't only because Dad was injured and in the hospital.

When I'd danced with Tyler at Alicia's wedding, I'd been so happy I'd forgotten about my silly crush on Cooper.

Sitting on the lawn outside the Civic Center, eating the best tamales in San Francisco, the setting sun gilding our skin, turning us rose gold. We'd both laughed that day. And he'd given me his handkerchief when I teared up at *Hamilton*.

"Maggie?" The hoarse whisper came from behind me. I whirled to look at Dad. His eyelid twitched. I blinked hard to be sure it hadn't been my own eye twitching. When I opened my eyes, his blue-gray ones looked back at me. His face was still pale, but seeing him awake made the band constricting my lungs ease.

I slid my palm under his to avoid the tubes attached to the back. "I'm so glad you're awake."

"Maggie." His eyes were unfocused.

He could call me Minnie Mouse for all I cared. "It's Marlee, Dad." I wiped a tear from my cheek.

His fingers twitched in my palm, and I gripped them. "I'm glad I found you, Maggie. I missed you."

"I missed you, too."

His eyelids closed. But he'd been awake. I sniffed.

A heavy arm came around my shoulders, and for a wild moment, I thought it was Tyler. But it was Jackson. He pressed a warm cup into my hand, and I gripped it.

"He woke up. That's great. It'll be smooth sailing from here," he said.

Jackson may have been a genius about programming, but, sadly, he knew next to nothing about Alzheimer's Disease. He couldn't have been more wrong.

29

"SYNERGY ANALYTICS. Ben Levy-Walters speaking."

Okay, so I hadn't been able to go two full days without calling the office. Dad was napping as he'd done most of the morning in between the nurses' check-ins. I figured talking to Ben would keep my mind out of the dark place where I wallowed, worrying about when Dad would be well enough that we could both go home.

I turned toward the window so I wouldn't wake Dad. "Hey, Ben. It's Marlee."

"Jesus, Marlee." He gusted out a breath that crackled out of my phone. "How'd you do it?"

"Do what? Is everything all right?"

"N—wait. Why are you calling me? How's your dad? Are you okay?"

"He's better. He woke up yesterday. He wasn't exactly lucid, but he'll get there." If I said it enough, it'd come true. At least, that's what I told myself. "I just wanted to check in, see how things are going."

"Don't worry about the office. We're fine." But the high note of tension in his voice made him a liar.

"Tell me about it. Maybe I can help."

Another sigh. "The temp agency sent someone truly awful. I had to send her home early yesterday and then talk to the agency this morning. They had no idea at all what we needed, or even what we do. How did you ever work with them?"

My already-tight chest ratcheted down another notch. *My fault.* "Did you get it straightened out?"

"The new one, Angelique, she's perfectly acceptable. But she's not you."

The constriction in my chest eased for just a second. Until he said the next thing.

"You probably could've handled it when the director of development came up here looking for Jackson."

Uh-oh. "Why'd he need Jackson?"

"Something broke in this morning's build, and everyone's looking for someone to blame. No one knows how to fix it. And now half the developers are off chasing bugs and the other half are sitting around, waiting for it to get fixed. The director is *pissed.* So is Weston," he whispered.

Was the bug something I would've caught in my morning code review? "Where's Jackson?" I didn't recall that he had any commitments off site today.

"Not here. And he's not answering his phone."

I had one brief stab of anxiety before I remembered that it'd been a long time since he'd missed work for a hangover, a Formula One race, or that thing he'd done my second week on the job. That was Old Jackson. New Jackson, the one who was a better man for Alicia, didn't disappear.

Jumping Johannes Kepler. He was on his way to see Dad and me.

"Send me an email with a description of the problem. I'll look into it, see what I can do."

"Marlee, you can't."

"Of course I can." Hurt pride made my voice too sharp. "I have a degree in computer science. I'm just as qualified as any of our junior programmers to try to fix it. As a matter of fact—"

"No," Ben broke into my tirade. "That's not what I meant. All I mean is, you can't worry about the office right now. Your dad is your priority. He needs one hundred percent of your attention while he's injured."

"But he's…" I looked back over my shoulder. Dad's eyes were closed. "He's resting."

"Then so should you. He's going to take all of your energy for a while. Everyone here understands."

My shoulders curled inward. He was right. I couldn't do it all. Not well, anyway. I couldn't do my job while Dad was here, needing me to make decisions on his behalf, needing my support. Everyone at work—including Jackson—was a healthy adult. They could take care of themselves. Dad couldn't. At least not right now.

"Call downstairs to—to Tyler Young. He'll fix it." It was the first time I'd said his name since Dad fell. I still owed him an apology.

"He would if he—never mind. We miss you. But we'll be fine."

"Promise? Because I'll be back. Better than ever." Just like Dad. "Don't run the place into the ground without me."

"I don't know…" His voice held a curl of humor. "If I have to deal with that development director again, I might just burn the place down."

"Order some cookies for the team. But nothing with nuts. And when I see Jackson, I'll ask him to offer a prize to the person who finds the bug. That ought to get results."

"You're the best, Marlee. Take all the time you need, okay?"

"I will."

They needed me. But right now, Dad needed me more. And I couldn't help anyone if I burned myself out.

There was a knock at the door just before Jackson walked in holding two cups of coffee.

"Morning," he said brightly. "How's Will?"

I took the cup he offered. "He's fine." I'd keep saying it until it was true. "But your department isn't. I need you to turn right back around and go clean up the mess at Synergy."

"What mess?"

I glanced at Dad—still sleeping—then took Jackson's elbow to escort him to the elevator. As the doors opened, I said, "Your phone is off again. And as much as I love you, you can't be splitting your time between the office and me. You can't do it all."

Something we both needed to learn.

Something Tyler had tried to tell me with his stories about his grandfather and his nursing home pamphlets. He was wrong about the nursing home—wasn't he?—but he understood what I was going through. And he'd driven all over Oakland to visit memory-care facilities. For me.

As I walked back to Dad's room, I pulled my phone out of my pocket and pulled up Tyler's contact card. He grinned at me in the jacket and tie he'd worn to Alicia's wedding. I'd snapped it early in the evening, before we'd danced, before he'd kissed me. I'd thought he looked perfect, but now the picture looked off somehow.

I searched my photos for another picture of him. This one was right. He wore a T-shirt, his favorite Galaga one. Judging from the date on the photo, I'd snapped it at some Synergy party last spring. His grin was open, bright.

Wait.

I scrolled down to the one from the wedding. Compared to the earlier one, his smile looked forced. Was it only because he was wearing a suit, or was it something more? Was it because of Operation Prince Charming?

It'd been his idea. I'd have been fine going together as just friends. Tyler was the one who'd proposed the whole fake-date thing. Because he knew I wanted Cooper and he...he cared enough to help me get what I wanted.

He cared. Even then, he must've wanted more, but because he was a better person than I was, he'd done what he thought I wanted. For me. Until he'd woken up and realized he deserved more. More than me.

In Jackson's office, he'd said he needed my undivided attention. Between my responsibilities at work and my dad, could I give that to him?

I leaned against the wall next to Dad's door and covered my face. *Not right now.*

Tyler deserved more. So I needed to back up. Back off. Return to what was safe, what I could manage: friendship.

I tapped out a text: *I'm sorry. Our friendship is important to me. What can I do to make things right between us?*

Our friendship. Could we salvage it after what I'd done, how I'd treated him?

I sent the text and waited until it showed *Delivered.* Then a few minutes more until it said *Read.* And then five minutes...ten. When the nurse came by, I followed him inside Dad's room.

The rest of the day, whenever Dad slept, I checked my phone. But the text sat there, read, with no response.

———

"HEY, GUYS." Jackson strolled into the hospital room Friday afternoon. It was a better day for Dad. He and I were playing cards, and I was losing. I wasn't sure if it was my anxiety about my upcoming meeting with the social worker or Dad's addled rule-bending that had moved my pile of M&Ms to his paper cup. I welcomed the break, but—

"Why aren't you at work?" I lay down my cards and went to hug Jackson where he loitered by the door.

"It's nice to see you, too," he said, smirking. "With Cooper gone, I was practically the last person left on the sixth floor. But if you don't want this"—he held up a familiar red coffee cup—"I'll just drink it on my way back to—"

"No. Gimme." I snatched the cup from his hands and inhaled the nutty, caramel flavor. "Thank you. And thanks for visiting us. It means a lot." I tried to infuse my gaze with every bit of sincere affection and appreciation I felt.

"Is everything okay at the office?" I asked. "Did you fix the bug?" Ben had refused to give me any scoop, sticking to his line about focusing on what was important. And I had. But I still wanted to know what was happening with my friends. Especially Tyler.

"Yeah. Amazing how motivated people can get over a bottle of whiskey and bragging rights. Sam found it."

Sam? My money would've been on Tyler. And I'd been half-hoping Jackson would say his name so I'd hear something about him. The silence was starting to get to me. I could practically feel the hostility radiating from that *Read* icon.

In a low voice, Jackson said, "Take a walk. Go get an early dinner. Or something chocolate. I'll keep an eye on your dad."

He knew me well. I whispered, "Actually, I have an appointment with the social worker. I should be back in half an hour?"

He nodded and sauntered over to Dad. "Hey, Will." He shook his hand. "Jackson Jones. I'm Marlee's—"

Dad stopped him. "I know you. You're her boss. You drive a race car, and Marlee's always having to clean up your messes."

Jackson ducked his head. "That's me. Can I take over for her?" He sat in the chair I'd vacated and picked up my cards.

Thank you, I mouthed to him.

As I left, Dad said to Jackson, "Marlee and I were playing for candy, but you'll play for cash, won't you, John?"

Oh, boy.

In the social worker's office, I started to wish I'd stayed up in Dad's room. Getting shellacked at cards was much better than being on the losing end of an argument I desperately wanted to win.

"Why wouldn't I be able to take care of him at home? I've taken care of my dad since his injury." They'd said I couldn't do it then, too. But I'd made him do all the exercises the physical thera-pist had recommended. I'd hefted him into the truck to take him to doctor's visits. And I'd seen to it that he'd taken his medications.

Her eyes softened with something too much like pity for my

taste. "Your father's mental health has deteriorated significantly since his prior accident. The nurses reported that he's been uncooperative."

"With *them.*" I tried to keep the defensive tone out of my voice. "My dad would never act like that with me."

She stared at me, a challenge. "He wouldn't." Disbelief flattened her tone. "He's never been difficult with you?"

"Of course not." I jutted out my chin.

She stared directly into my eyes. "What was he doing the night he fell?"

I looked down at my hands, twisting the bottom of my pink cardigan into a rope. *Great Galileo.* "He was taking the telescope outside."

"And if he goes home with you, how are you going to keep him from doing it again? Are you going to install keyed locks on the inside of your doors? Watch him every minute? What about when you go to work?"

"We've hired a daytime nurse."

Her eyes were a warm brown, and although she wasn't much older than me, their expression told me I wasn't the first stubborn daughter she'd encountered. "What about when you need to work late, or go to the grocery? Or you need five minutes to yourself?"

Each question was a knife in my heart. I'd failed Dad when I'd done exactly those things. They were going to take him away from me. I blinked hard.

"We can recommend several home-like facilities where he'll be comfortable, and you'll be able to visit him whenever you'd like. Every day if you want." She paused until I turned my eyes from my lap to her face. "They have specialized memory-care units. They know how to care for your dad. They have enrichment programs to keep his body and mind active."

Better than that ratty old *Beauty and the Beast* puzzle. I remembered the pamphlets Tyler had brought me. He'd been trying to talk me into the same thing. "He won't be lying in a bed all day? He won't be"—I swallowed—"restrained?"

"No. There will be safe places for him to walk. Gardens. Art classes. Music."

"It sounds expensive." I bit my lip.

"It's not cheap. But there are programs to help pay for it."

"And it's what's best for my dad?"

"It is." Her brown eyes might have been soft, but her firm jaw told me she wouldn't budge on this.

"Think about it," she said. "Go visit some facilities. I've made a list." She handed me a printout, and I took it. I folded it twice and slipped it into my back pocket.

Tears prickled in my eyes, and I blinked them away. I needed help. I knew that. But Dad and I had taken care of each other since my mother had died. How could I let go of him now when he needed me most?

Outside Dad's room, I took a deep breath and rubbed my sweaty palms on my jeans. I pushed the door open and walked inside.

"You're back," Jackson said too brightly as he jumped up from the chair.

Dad slipped his hand into the pocket of his pajama shirt and grinned at me. "Sunshine! Did you have a nice walk?"

"Yes, Dad." I returned his smile. "I'll just take Jackson to the elevators. Be right back."

I took Jackson's arm and returned to the hallway. As we strolled, arm-in-arm, to the elevator bank, I said, "The social worker says he needs to go to a—to a nursing home."

"Ah, Marlee. I'm sorry." But he didn't seem surprised.

"I'll need a few more days off to sort things out. I'm going to have to sell our house."

"Whatever time you need. Ben's found us a great temp. I wonder why you were always so cursed with the terrible ones?"

"Just unlucky, I guess." We stopped in front of the elevators.

"Thanks for being understanding. I'll come back to work as soon as I can. No more than a week."

"Can I give you some advice?"

I looked up into his chocolate-colored eyes. "Lay it on me."

"In the immortal words of Ferris Bueller, 'Life moves pretty fast. If you don't stop and look around once in a while, you could miss it.' Taking care of your dad is an admirable thing to do. But you can't forget to live your own life."

"Thanks." Tyler had tried to tell me the same thing. They were right. I had a good job, and soon I'd find a place to live and start the next phase of my life. Even though some of my other relationships were giant trash fires, I had good friends. And I could still visit Dad every day and know he was well cared-for.

As the elevator button lit up, he said, "By the way, there's something I need to tell you about your dad."

My heart raced, and my palms went clammy. "What's that?"

"He cheats at cards."

30

SUMMERS when he wasn't teaching, Dad worked construction, and sometimes, he'd taken me with him to his jobs. Too little to help, I sat on the toolbox in the bed of his pickup, read books, and watched him. He hefted piles of two-by-fours on his shoulder and carried them around the jobsite like they weighed nothing. Even burdened with a tool belt and lugging a nail gun, he climbed scaffolding, nimble as an acrobat. His muscles strained as he levered cast-iron tubs into place. And six days after his fall, broken leg and all, it took two brawny nurse assistants to wrestle him into a wheelchair to take him to physical therapy. He wasn't called Will for nothing.

When he returned, I waited, ready for battle. The late-afternoon sun cast golden beams across his hospital bed. His eyes were sharper that day, and he'd called me Maggie only a couple of times.

"I have good news for you." The tubes were gone, replaced by yellow-green bruises and a bandage, and I held his hand. "They're releasing you tomorrow."

His face brightened. "We're going home! I can eat decent food again. Will you make your mother's meatloaf?"

Biting my lip to stop its trembling, I cleared my throat. "You're not going home, Dad. You're going to a new place. Bayside Gardens. They'll help you rehab your leg."

His face fell, but then he nodded. "I'll go home after my leg's better. The doctor said six or eight weeks."

I took a deep breath. "I'm selling the house. I'm moving into an apartment, and you're going to stay at Bayside. Permanently." I squeezed his hand, willing him to understand and not hate me. "They're going to take better care of you than I can. They have art programs and concerts. Bayside even has a library and a telescope you can use."

"You're putting me in a *home*? I'm only fifty-three!" His face flamed red. I was glad they'd removed the heart monitors; he'd have set off an alarm.

"Dad—" I covered his hand with mine, but he snatched it away and crossed his arms. "Dad, you have Alzheimer's Disease. I can't give you the care you need at home."

"I'm fine," he said. "Everyone forgets things."

My chest constricted. Maybe *I* needed the heart monitor. "You're fine today, but you've had some pretty bad days lately. You were having a bad day when you fell, and I couldn't take care of you. I'm afraid your health is going to get worse, and I need to keep you safe."

He looked toward the window. "I don't want that. I want to live in my house and sit in my recliner."

I wanted that, too. More than anything. But I was done lying to myself, and I certainly wouldn't lie to Dad.

"I'm sorry. I wish you could. But this is the right thing for you. For both of us."

He was silent for a minute. Then, still looking away from me, he said, "I'm tired. I'm going to sleep now."

Chills ran over my skin. I stood, willing myself to keep it together for another minute. "Okay. I'll see you tomorrow."

He said nothing, but a tear glinted golden on his cheek.

———

THE NEXT AFTERNOON, I started packing up our lives.

Dad and I both cried that morning when they wheeled him into the ambulance to go to Bayside Gardens. Although he kept asking where they were taking him, he remembered he was angry about *something* and it was my fault.

His tears were frustrated anger. Mine were liquid guilt.

The nurses told me to wait a few days before visiting him to allow him to settle into a routine. Since I was too much of a mess to go to work, I vowed to be productive at home.

The real estate agent I'd spoken with had practically salivated over listing our house. The next neighborhood over had become increasingly gentrified, and she was convinced that our neighborhood was next. My eyes had widened at the price she'd tossed out. Properly invested, it would cover whatever part of Dad's care the aid programs and his savings didn't.

So I packed up our home. I'd already finished the kitchen; most of it would be going with me to my new place near the office. I'd cleaned out the shed, including the Christmas lights he never got to hang.

Then I started on Dad's room. I'd already taken his clothes and his favorite photographs to Bayside Gardens. But a ton of photos of him and my mother remained, and each one stabbed my heart. I wrapped them in newspaper and nestled them into a box with the photo albums. One day I might be ready to look at them again.

Even worse was the secret stash of my mother's things I found in the corner of his closet. The twenty-five-year-old clothes and shoes went into a bag for a thrift shop. Her hairbrush, still holding a few golden-brown threads, went into the trash. We'd both been obsessed with my mother for too long; I couldn't let those memories weigh me down in my new future.

A local charity would cart off Dad's bedroom furniture, along with his threadbare recliner. I'd probably have to slip the guys a fifty to haul it away. I couldn't imagine that even Oakland's poor would want it.

I'd hoped my room would be easier on me than his.

My books had all gone into a box for donation to a local literacy group. I vowed that from that day on, I'd read more realistic stories. I'd join Alicia's book club that read only horrifying domestic suspense and depressing family dramas. That was real life, not the romantic, rosy world of my former favorites.

My old dolls were going to the charity, as well. I hoped some little girl would love them as I had. I sent a wish into the box with them that their new owner would pretend the dolls were Malala Yousafzai or even Beyoncé and living for themselves, not looking for a prince to marry.

When I got to my jewelry box, before I set it inside the moving crate, I reached behind my neck and unclasped my necklace. The pendant lay across my palm, the diamond chips winking in the lamplight.

I wouldn't live her life. She'd gotten trapped in a marriage she didn't want.

I wouldn't live Dad's life, either. He'd pined for a lost love that'd never existed.

I had to live my own life.

I was done with fairy tales. No more dreaming of a prince on a white horse. I didn't need rescuing. I needed a lover who was also a friend. Who'd call me on my bullshit whenever I spiraled into romantic fantasy. Who supported me. Someone who needed my support, too.

If only I'd seen what was right in front of me instead of what I'd imagined, I wouldn't be sitting alone, sifting through reminders of my own foolish decisions and missed opportunities.

I opened my jewelry box and dropped the pendant inside. I'd ruined everything, and there'd be no happily ever after for me.

31

TWO DAYS LATER, as I stepped off the elevator onto the sixth floor, I could almost convince myself that my world was back to normal. I'd left my boxed-up home behind to rejoin the routine at Synergy.

I frowned at my desk. The temp had moved my things. I took a minute to slide my pen cup into its place on the corner and square up the file rack so I could reach it without looking. I tossed a celebrity magazine into the recycling bin under my desk. When the space looked the way it should, I unpacked my laptop and powered it up.

Cooper was back in his office. His low voice was the only sound in the early-morning silence on the sixth floor. A month ago, I'd made a pass at him in that office, and he'd shut me down. It felt like something a different woman had done years ago.

Straightening my spine, I strode to his door and knocked on the frame.

"Marlee! Glad you're back. How's your dad?" he asked, setting his phone face down on the desk. "Jackson said he wasn't doing well."

I gave him the brief version, but his face still creased in concern.

"I'm sorry. I knew he had some lapses from time to time, but I didn't know it was that bad."

"He's safe now. That's what's important." I scanned him from his golden hair to his crisp lavender dress shirt. "How are you? How was Europe?"

"Fine. Same." He fluttered his hand.

Only Cooper Fallon could return from two weeks in London and Paris and say it was fine. "Okay. Well, I'm sure I have a mountain of work waiting for me. See you later." With a dorky wave, I turned to go.

"It's good to have you back."

I smiled, glad to be back to our normal level of awkwardness.

Ten minutes later, Ben strode in, shaking out his rain-spattered coat. His mouth was pulled tight into a harried frown, but he stopped at my desk.

"Hey, Marlee, you're back!" He darted a glance at Cooper's door, but then his face relaxed into a broad smile. "Is your dad okay now?"

As I had with everyone except Jackson and Alicia, I'd given him only the basic information about Dad's accident. "He broke his leg. He's healing in a nursing facility. I—he—he'll probably be there permanently. He has Alzheimer's." I had to own Dad's condition now and the new reality it forced on me.

His whiskey-brown eyes were kind, and worry lines bracketed them. "I'm so sorry about that. Are you okay?"

My lip trembled, but I forced out, "I will be."

He reached over and rubbed my arm. "Let me know how I can help. When you're ready, we'll go out for drinks and talk. Okay?" He held my gaze until I nodded.

I had more time for friends now. I'd be sure to take him up on his offer.

Twenty minutes later, Jackson bounded onto the floor. Without saying a word, he came behind my desk and pulled me up into a hug. His powerful arms around me assured me that everything would be okay in time.

We disengaged, but he held onto my hands. "How are you doing?"

"I'm okay, boss. Ready to work."

He shook his head. "No, really, Marlee. No bullshit. How are you?" His gaze held mine.

"It was…rough sending Dad there. I haven't seen him yet. The nurses told me to give it a couple of days."

"Want me to go with you? We can go tonight."

"I'm planning to go after work, and I appreciate the offer, but I need to do this myself." I pressed his hand. "You understand?"

He squeezed back. "I do. But tell me what I can do to help."

"I'd love to do some work to take my mind off everything."

"Then I have just the thing for you. We're two weeks away from our holiday party, and I *may* have dropped the ball."

I rolled my eyes. Jackson always offered to help with the annual holiday party on the first weekend in December, but his responsibilities usually fell on me. Picking up the pieces of the company party and ensuring the event went off without a hitch would keep my mind off my first Thanksgiving outside my childhood home. "Of course I'll help."

"Great! We have a meeting at lunch with the party-planning committee."

"But it's not on your calendar," I protested. "You have a meeting with—"

"You'll move it, right? Oh, and we'll need lunch brought in."

"I'm on it. But, Jackson, now that I—now that—" I took a deep, calming breath. "Since I don't have to rush home to Dad anymore, I'd like to take on some programming work. Officially." His smile froze on his face, and I hurried on. "I want to keep supporting you, but I want to work on some other projects, too."

His smile relaxed, but not fully, as if he was holding something back. "I may have something for you. Give me a few days to work it out." His lips pinched together. "I should—"

The ringing phone on my desk—his line—interrupted him. "That's your nine o'clock call," I said. "Better get in there."

"Thanks, Marlee, you're the best," Jackson called over his shoulder as he jogged into his office.

For a minute, I believed him.

———

MY FOOT JIGGLED ALL during the planning committee meeting. Stupid foot. It wanted to stop wasting time planning a party I didn't care about and run down to the fourth floor.

Tyler and I hadn't spoken or texted for over a week, and it was time for us to talk. Okay, it was time for me to grovel. Again. Because my grovel sucked the first time. This time, I'd be sure to do it where Cooper couldn't find me.

Once the meeting ended and Jackson was safely in his next conference call, I told Ben, "Be right back." I opened my desk drawer and pocketed the tiny black plastic gun. I didn't need the ruse to talk to him; we were friends, and it should've been perfectly normal to visit him at his desk.

It *should've* been. But he'd always come up to me.

I was a terrible friend and an even worse more-than-a-friend.

With the excuse in my pocket, I trotted downstairs. When I reached the fourth-floor landing, I straightened my white blouse where it tucked into my black pencil skirt and smoothed my hair.

Pushing open the door, I emerged into the sea of cubicles. They had low dividers to encourage collaboration, and the developers had decorated them to reflect their personalities. A giant pair of high-top sneakers hung from a string over the nearest one. A few rows over, a shelf displayed a glittering row of soccer trophies. I looked toward the windows where the senior developers, including Tyler, sat, and headed that direction.

But Tyler's cube was all wrong. It had been emptied, and it looked like it'd been done in a hurry. While the desk surface was clear, it showed streaks of dust where piles of books or papers might have been moved, and a few pushpins were scattered across it. The docking station was empty, and the big monitors were powered off.

The top shelf was bare except for dust and a Princess Leia figurine, her hand outstretched. Clear spaces in the dust surrounded her.

Had he moved cubicles?

I turned around and spotted Jackson's sister, Sam, in a small cube nearby. She gazed at her screen, a pair of noise-canceling headphones dwarfing her petite features.

"Sam." When she didn't answer, I walked up to her cube and gently touched her shoulder. She jumped.

When she saw it was me, she grinned, the crooked one that reminded me of Jackson's. She took off her headphones. "Marlee! What're you doing down here? Are you a programmer now? I bet you can take Tyler's cube."

"I came down to look for him. Do you know where he's gone?"

"Tyler?"

I bit my lip to keep from saying something that betrayed my anxiety. "Yes, Tyler."

"Home. Somewhere in Texas. Austin, maybe? Or Dallas? He said he wanted to spend some time with his family."

His family? They were jerks to him, especially Raleigh. I'd encouraged him to go home for the holidays, but he was a week too early.

"He's been working remotely for the past week. He said he'd probably stay through Thanksgiving. But if he was just going home for a couple of weeks, why'd he take all his stuff? I've been wondering if he's"—she dropped her voice lower—"looking for another job. He had a sport coat with him one day last week. The day he left early. I didn't want to say anything to Jackson, though. It wasn't really my business."

"Oh."

"Are you okay? You look pale."

"I'm fine. Thanks." I stared at Princess Leia. What was she telling me?

"It was weird that he took all his toys."

"His toys?" The few times I'd been down here, I hadn't paid attention. I certainly hadn't cataloged the contents of his cube.

"He has a whole collection—Yoda, Obi-Wan, Darth Vader, Chewbacca, Lando Calrissian, Boba Fett, Jabba the Hutt. He only left Leia here. Maybe because she's broken. He was about to throw away Han Solo, but Grant asked for him." She pointed at a different cube, and I spotted the action figure leaning against a potted succulent.

I walked across the aisle, pulled the tiny piece of plastic out of my pocket, and fitted the blaster into Leia's hand. She wore the same white gown and braided hair as I had on Halloween. But even tiny Leia looked stronger, surer, clear-eyed. She knew what she wanted, and she went after it. And she was smart enough to want the right things.

"Hey, you fixed her. I'll email him and let him know. Or maybe you should email him. He might want her back now."

My belly burned like it'd taken a blaster shot. No, he didn't want her back. That much was clear. If he had, I wouldn't have had to find out he'd left from Sam. I sniffed.

"Hey, are you okay?"

"I'm fine. The dust is making my eyes water." I kept my back to Sam, but my voice was high and strained.

"Oh. Okay. I don't have any tissues, but there's some in the bathroom."

"Thanks."

I picked up Princess Leia. She'd kissed both Luke Skywalker and Han Solo. Fortunately, she'd figured out she and Luke were better as friends before they'd become lovers. Leaving out the he's-actually-her-brother squick factor, I'd always thought she'd made a mistake. Han Solo didn't really love her back; not in the way she needed. Luke was the one who was always there for her, honest and true.

Just like Tyler.

Until I'd screwed it all up.

And now he was gone. For how long?

My knees wobbled, and I grasped the back of his chair. *Breathe.* Marlee Rice, executive assistant to the co-founder, couldn't lose her shit in the middle of the cube farm.

Even if my heart had just crumbled to dust in my chest.

———

ON MY WAY down to the lobby, I texted Alicia. *Can you talk?*

My phone rang as soon as I stepped off the elevator. "Hey."

"Hey," Alicia said. "I guess I was expecting you to want to talk, but I didn't think you'd find out so soon."

"You didn't think I'd find what out?" I pushed open the door to the courtyard, which was cold, damp, and deserted. I shivered.

"Oh. Nothing."

"No. We've been friends too long for that. What do you know?"

She was silent for a moment. "You can't tell anyone. No one knows yet."

"No one knows *what*, Alicia? Is Tyler okay?" A tiny droplet of water landed on my cheek. It wasn't exactly rain; more like the fog had started to liquefy.

"He's fine. He's good, I hear. Jamila saw him. They met down in Austin. I wouldn't know, except she asked me for a reference. She offered him a job, and he accepted."

"He accepted? You mean he'll be working at Jamila's office in San Francisco?" That wouldn't be so bad. He wouldn't come up to my desk every day, but we could meet for lunch a few days a week.

"No. The job is in Austin. She's opening a second office there."

"Austin?" It didn't compute. He'd just moved from Austin less than a year ago. He'd said it was his dream to work for Jackson in San Francisco.

"I'm sorry, honey. I'm sure he'll call to tell you about it. I hear it's a great job. Director-level, and he's not even thirty. Jackson's working on a counteroffer, but I don't know that Tyler will take it. He had to have a reason to ask Jamila for a job."

My face was wet, and I couldn't tell if it was rain or tears or both.

"Marlee, are you okay?"

"Fine."

"You don't sound fine. Do you need to put your head between your knees?"

"No." But standing wasn't working out for me. I squatted right there in the courtyard in my heels and my skirt and no coat. I hoped no one was watching me lose it.

"Talk to me. Or I'm going to come over there and make you talk."

I gripped my phone as if it could save me from drowning. "Before my dad fell, Tyler and I—I told him how I felt. But he didn't believe me."

"You told him what?"

"I love him, okay? Like, not friends-love like I love you. Love-love, like you love Jackson."

Her inhale was loud. "You love him."

"But he—but I—Cooper was there, and it was awful. And then my dad went into the hospital, and now this."

"Oh." She was quiet for a few seconds. "You know what you have to do, right?"

"I have to call him. I should've done it before, but I—"

"I know. You had a lot on your mind. He'll understand."

———

HE DIDN'T UNDERSTAND.

At least, that was the conclusion I had to draw. Seventeen texts and six voice mails—including one that I left after one too many glasses of wine where I *may* have sung "I See the Light" from *Tangled*—without a response was a pretty clear message.

But the clearest was his two-word response at the end of my one-sided text conversation.

Tyler: I can't.

32

HEADING the party planning committee meant I was too busy to think—much—and too busy for self-pity. Mostly.

Asking me to rescue the party had been one of Jackson's more brilliant ideas. Not that I'd admit it to him.

With all the calls I'd made, the food I'd tasted, the venues I'd visited, and the auditions I'd listened to, I hadn't had time to mope about my first holiday alone in my new apartment without Dad.

But I didn't spend Thanksgiving alone. Bayside Gardens had invited the residents' families to a meal. And while Dad still wasn't speaking to me over selling the house, throwing away his beloved recliner, and putting him into the nursing home, several times he'd gotten confused enough to be friendly. He'd called me Maggie and told me how nice I was to cook for all of his new friends. He looked healthy and well fed, and for that I was thankful.

After the meal, Alicia and Jackson picked me up and took me to their place for the long weekend, where I played video games with Sam and Noah. It was almost as good as having a family of my own.

And the week between the holiday and the party, I was definitely too busy to think about Tyler. I hadn't seen him in twenty-five days—not that I was counting—since he'd stormed out of Jackson's office. I hadn't cuddled up inside Tyler's sweater, which didn't even smell much like him anymore, every time I'd felt lonely or sad. That would've been pathetic.

Which I totally was.

So I'd resolved to do something about it. My groveling had been ineffectual, and I'd figured out why: in romance novels, the groveling was always preceded by a grand gesture, performed by the character who'd most wronged the other. That was me for sure. I had to prove to Tyler I was sorry before he'd accept my grovel. You'd think someone who'd read as many novels and watched as many rom-coms as I had would've thought of this. But I'd had a lot on my mind.

I'd already asked Jackson for time off, and I was planning to fly down to Texas after Christmas. Like in *When Harry Met Sally,* I'd lay it all on the table and tell him I wanted to be more than his friend for the rest of our lives. If—and I knew it was a big *if* after how I'd treated him—he forgave me and still wanted me, we'd kiss on New Year's Eve, and it'd seal us together forever.

Yes, I knew Texas was a big state, and I'd have to find him first, but I wasn't above using Alicia for reconnaissance. Jackson would be no help; he was still pissed at Tyler for giving his official two weeks' notice the day before the holiday party.

The night of the party, I smoothed the wrinkles from the flared skirt of my black cocktail dress. *Not nervous at all.* He probably wouldn't even show. Most likely, he was still down in Texas. But a tiny hope burned under the draped neckline of my dress.

To distract myself, I surveyed the tables in the main room of the party boat we'd rented for the company holiday celebration. Once everyone was on board, we'd cruise the bay for a few hours while the employees and their guests ate dinner and danced. Somehow, the committee and I had made it look like we hadn't thrown it together in only two weeks.

White linen draped the tables in the large function room. The darkened windows reflected a hundred tabletop candles. Vases of white roses and sprigs of blood-red berries topped each surface. Buffet tables stretched across the middle of the room, and soon they'd be loaded with hot food. The servers, holding trays of appetizers and glasses of wine, circulated among the early-arriving guests. I'd spent too much time planning the party to be hungry for the lettuce boats, crab beignets, and tiny avocado toasts I'd so carefully selected. It wasn't because I was too anxious to eat.

After I'd finished approving the table settings and reviewing the schedule of activities, I stepped out onto the open deck. My stomach pitched like the waves below. Maybe it was because of the boat's motion, or maybe it was nerves about possibly seeing Tyler again. Since we were still docked, I guessed the latter.

Alicia stepped off the gangway, stunning in her white evening gown. The beaded overlay on the bodice drew the eye from her bulging belly, draped in flowing fabric. She gripped Jackson's sleeve—as usual, he looked delicious in a tuxedo—and dragged him toward me. Jackson's sister Sam followed them. She wore a black sweater over black slacks. In the dark, she'd have been invisible except for her pale skin.

"Marlee, everything looks wonderful!"

I set down the tablet with my checklist and hugged Alicia. "*You* look wonderful. How are you feeling tonight?"

She hugged me tight and whispered in my ear, "I had my first Braxton-Hicks contractions today. But I'm keeping it on the down-low so Jackson doesn't freak out. He'd make me pack my go-bag and practice racing to the hospital."

I stepped back and beamed at her. "That's great!" Seeing Jackson's concerned look, I continued, "Great that you're feeling so well. Jackson, you look fantastic as usual. Though, let me—" I rummaged in my bag and pulled out a lint roller. I squatted and rolled it over the bottoms of his pant legs. "I guess you were getting some love from Tigger before you left."

He bent down to take the roller from me and whispered, "Have I got a surprise for you tonight." He winked.

A surprise? Could it be Tyler? I watched Jackson run the roller over his ankles, hoping he'd enlighten me.

But he only straightened and said, "Tigger's been a little anxious about all the changes for the baby. He and I bonded while we were waiting for Alicia to finish getting ready."

Sam stepped into our circle. "Hey, Marlee, I haven't seen you for a while. Just so you know, I emailed T—"

Jackson flung an arm over Sam's shoulders, startling her into silence. "Remember what we said on the ride over. We're not talking about that deserter tonight."

I smiled weakly at Jackson. Saying Tyler's name wouldn't stop me from thinking about him. Though I appreciated the effort.

"But I thought she'd—"

"Don't we all look nice."

I hadn't noticed Cooper's approach. He shook Jackson's hand and then Alicia's. He extended a hand to me, and I shook it. For the first time in three years, I didn't try to turn it into a hug or linger too long with his hand in mine. I didn't pretend there were sparks. All my sparks were for the one person missing from our group tonight.

The ship's captain's voice crackled in my earpiece. "Ms. Rice, it's time to push off. Is everyone on board?"

"Give me a minute to confirm," I murmured. I whirled and strode to the gangway, where the party coordinator stood with a tablet similar to mine.

"Has everyone checked in?" I asked her.

"All but one"—she scrolled through the list again—"Tyler Young."

He wasn't coming. I stroked my necklace, a plain crystal pendant. "Let's give it another five minutes, and then you can tell the captain to go ahead."

She flashed me a smile. "Sounds good. You go enjoy yourself, now."

I tried to give her a bright smile, but my face was too stiff. I stowed my tablet in my bag, removed my earpiece, and handed it to her, along with my bag. "Thank you. I'll go mingle. Come find me if you need anything."

"Will do," she said, all chipper efficiency.

I turned and walked back toward the bright lights of the party. Although I'd spent weeks planning it, from decorations to music to food, and I knew almost everyone there, something was off. Meandering through the clumps of Synergy employees and their plus-ones, I exchanged a few words here, shook a hand there, but I couldn't settle into any of the conversations that swirled around me. Tyler had always stuck by my side at these things, ready to make a goofy joke, smooth over a cutting word.

When the deck heaved and I wobbled on my sparkly heels, disappointment sloshed in my belly. He hadn't come. I wished I were anywhere but stuck on a boat and expected to have fun and be nice to everyone for the next four hours. I needed a drink.

I moved toward the first server I saw and took a flute of champagne from his tray. I'd just lifted it to my lips when I heard a familiar baritone.

Jackson's voice boomed over the speakers. "Good evening, everyone. Welcome to the annual Synergy holiday party." I froze. *This* was off-script. Cooper was supposed to give the speech. What was Jackson doing?

Cooper must have had the same thought because he stood stiffly at the side of the stage watching his friend, his thick eyebrows at a perplexed angle.

Jackson continued, speaking into the microphone he'd taken from the band's singer. "Don't worry, we'll save the speeches for later in the evening, when you've had a lot more to drink." A group of programmers whooped.

"But I'd like to thank someone, someone who's had a lot going on lately but who still made time to put together this fantastic party. Marlee, come up here."

A blush burned from the scooped neckline of my dress all the way to my hairline. I wished I were closer to an exit so I could disappear, but hands already reached toward me, tugging me toward the stage. I forced my feet toward Jackson, praying that my high heels wouldn't trip me up. On the way, I passed Alicia, who shrugged, just as confused as I was.

Jackson welcomed me to the stage with a grin and another wink. "Three weeks ago, we had no venue, no caterer, and no music. Once again, Marlee—and the rest of the planning committee—have saved the party from my overcommitment and under-delivery." Everyone laughed, and the drunk developers hooted. I'd have to call some cars at the end of the night.

When the applause died down, he said, "Marlee, I think you should lead us off in the first dance." He snagged Cooper's arm. "With our COO, Cooper Fallon."

Now the blood drained from my face. Six weeks before, I'd have been in heaven. That night, I'd rather have gnawed off my own arm than spend three awkward minutes dancing with Cooper. His plastic smile said he felt the same.

"Let's give them some encouragement," Jackson boomed through the microphone. The party guests whooped and clapped, and the band struck up "Almost Like Being in Love."

I squared my shoulders and reached for Cooper's hand. "Let's get this over with," I said through a too-bright smile. I led him down the step onto the dance floor and put one hand on his shoulder. The other, which I still clasped with his, I lifted near my shoulder. A Sam-sized person would have fit into the cushion of air between us.

Cooper placed a wooden hand lightly on my ribs and led me into a starched quickstep. The other guests made space around us. Mr. Weston stood near the stage, his expression too blank to read. Our dance wouldn't do anything to dispel the nasty rumors that'd crept through the company since the Halloween party. Oblivious, Jackson beamed at us from the stage like a proud papa. Ugh.

"Well, this is awkward—" I began.

At the same time, Cooper said, "Marlee, I—"

We both stopped speaking, and then we laughed. His rock-hard shoulder eased under my fingers. "You go first," he said and twirled me out. As I spun back into his arms, I remembered dancing at the wedding. I'd been paired with Tyler then, but I'd wanted this. Why did I always want what I didn't have?

Tyler's dancing had been fluid, fun. Dancing with Cooper was like dancing with a marionette. There was just no comparison.

"Jackson means well. I'm sure I'll forgive him. Someday." I grimaced. "I—I meant what I said to you. I'm sorry I made things uncomfortable between us. I hope we can be good friends."

He smiled down at me. "There's nothing to forgive. I'm dancing with a beautiful woman, a smart woman who found me the world's second-best assistant."

"Where is Ben tonight?" Between party prep and searching for Tyler, I hadn't yet seen him.

The corners of Cooper's mouth tightened. "At the bar. He brought—never mind."

My back was to the bar, so I couldn't see what he was talking about. By the time he turned me the right direction, so many couples had joined us on the dance floor that I couldn't find Ben. I hoped he was having a nice time, whoever he was with.

"He deserves to blow off some steam, you know. You're not the easiest guy to work for."

Cooper's posture went rigid. "I have high expectations of everyone—"

"I know you do." I stroked his shoulder. "What I've learned recently is that you can't put anyone on a pedestal. Not even yourself."

He started to say something just as the song ended. He closed his mouth, pulled me into a hug, and whispered in my ear, "Thank you," before he kissed my cheek.

My dad would've kissed my cheek with more passion. Cooper's kiss was a dry brush of lips I wanted to flick away. Still, he'd meant well. I hugged him back briefly, breathing in his minty scent. "Anytime."

The band struck up another song, and as I turned to leave the dance floor, Sam blocked my path. "I know I'm not supposed to talk about him, but Jackson's dancing with Alicia, and he can't hear us." She stepped closer so she didn't have to shout over the music. "Tyler's here. But when Cooper kissed you, he ran out that door." She pointed toward the double doors that led to the exterior deck.

"He's here?" I couldn't have heard her right.

"I tried to tell you earlier. He said he didn't want Princess Leia back, but he'd see all of us tonight."

He didn't want Princess Leia back. Well, if that didn't tell me how he felt, I didn't know what would. Still, he was here. And that meant I had one more chance to make things right between us.

"Thanks." I pushed through the crowd to the exit and looked right, then left. The moonlight glinted on the light-brown hair of a familiar form for a moment before he disappeared around the curve of the stern.

Despite my strappy heels, I raced to catch him before I lost him. Again. I thanked Pythagoras and whoever invented the sextant that we were on a ship with no way to escape.

I rounded the curve of the boat to find nothing but empty deck chairs. Huffing out a frustrated sigh, I clacked toward the front of the boat. When I reached the middle of the ship, a lone figure leaned his elbows on the rail, facing the moonlight-dappled waves. This time, my sigh carried with it all the relief I felt to find him alone, waiting for me. Or so I hoped.

"Tyler!" I called out and trotted to his side, skidding to a stop on the sea-sprayed wood. He gave me a quick glance but returned his gaze to the water.

So that was how it was going to be. Groveling would be required. I was ready.

"I heard you went home."

"Uh-huh."

"Is your family okay?"

"Yeah."

"I hope you punched Raleigh. Or at least gave him crap."

He shrugged. "It was good to see them. It'd been a while."

I tried to smile, but my lips wobbled. "I'm glad you went, then. Did you have a nice Thanksgiving?"

Still gazing out over the ocean, he said, "I did."

"I went to see my dad in his new place. Bayside Gardens. You tried to give me a brochure for it. I remember it on top of the stack before I—" I shivered in the icy wind and hugged myself to hold in the warmth. "I wish I'd listened to you then. They had a nice meal for the families. There was turkey."

That earned me a response. He turned to face me. "You put your dad in a nursing home?"

I cringed at the accusing tone of his voice, but then I shrugged a shoulder. "He—he fell. He broke his leg and needed rehab. And —" I hadn't told anyone this, but Tyler would understand. "And he hit his head, and it seemed to make his condition...worse." I rubbed my arms and stared out over the waves.

"I'm sorry," he said. Almost unwillingly, he asked, "Are you okay?"

I couldn't look at him. "I moved into an apartment. I'm selling the house. Dad's mad at me. Mostly because I gave away his recliner." I laughed, but there was no humor in it.

Beside me, he gripped the rail.

"I—I missed you, Tyler." I reached toward the sleeve of his coat but lost my nerve and pulled my hand back without touching him. "I could have used a friend."

Tyler whirled toward me, his eyes glowing in the string lights. "Marlee, that's exactly what you do to your friends: *use* them. You used me to get closer to Cooper. And from what I saw in there, it worked. So since I've served my purpose, I'm done being used. I can't be your friend anymore."

The pain in his eyes killed me. "No, it's not like that. We were just dancing."

He tapped his fingers on his thigh, but the rest of him was still.

"Jackson made us. Cooper doesn't mean anything to me. I only—"

But Tyler strode away from me, back toward the music and people. I launched myself toward him, tottering in my stilettos, until I could grab his sleeve. I latched on and dug my heels into the deck, pulling him to a stop.

"I don't want him. I want you." There. I'd said it at last. But he was an obelisk, all dark, cold stone, frozen in front of me.

"The way you wanted me after the wedding? As a consolation prize when you can't get your first choice? I deserve more than that."

Even in the moonlight, his pain was clear in the lines around his eyes, in the tense set of his mouth. What could I do to smooth away that pain? I reached a hand toward his cheek.

He pulled away and stormed toward the party again. I sprinted as fast as my heels would let me—Tyler and his damned long legs—until I caught him and planted myself in front of him.

"I agree. You deserve...you deserve everything. There's no question about who's first for me. There's only you. I love *you*, Tyler. Only you."

Now I'd done it: I'd laid it all on the table. If this were a romantic comedy, he'd take me into his arms and tell me he loved me, too, just before he kissed me.

"You love me?" His face was blank, not a dimple in sight.

"I do." I swayed toward him, ready for our kiss.

Tyler stood still long enough for what I'd said to settle between us, to drift to the deck and soak into the wood like so much spilled beer. His glasses reflected the party lights, opaque.

"I need a minute," he said.

"A-a minute?" To do what?

He lifted a hand, but instead of tucking a piece of hair behind my ear or stroking my cheek, he brushed my hand from his jacket sleeve and smoothed the fabric. Then he stepped around me and marched through the door into the light and noise of the party.

33

ON A BOAT full of happy drunks, it was hard to find a spot to be alone. After Tyler's minute had stretched to two, then three, then five, I'd slunk away and settled on a deserted upper deck with just enough room for a few wooden benches exposed to the moon, the stars, and the wind.

I huddled on a bench with my feet up, my arms curled around my shins, and my chin resting on my knees. My hair, torn free from its French twist, flew around my head except where it stuck to the wetness on my face.

No wonder the boat had been easy to reserve on short notice: it was bone-chillingly cold out on the water in December. And now I was stuck. We'd been cruising for only an hour and a half, maybe two—no way to tell with my phone in my bag down below—so I was trapped on the ship for at least two more. Shivering in the wintry cold. At least passing out from hypothermia would end my private pity party.

Not that I deserved release. No, from the way I'd acted over the past three months—hell, the past three years—I'd earned every miserable minute. I'd been unwilling to see what was real, and now fate, Karma, whatever, had called me out on it.

I hugged my legs and shuddered. The stinging wind slapped

my cheeks and made my eyes water. No, I was done deluding myself: they were tears. Tears of loneliness and heartbreak. Tyler would move to Austin, and I'd stay in my solitary apartment. *Maybe I should get a cat.* No, it would probably hate me, too, the way Tigger had. Even a creature with a brain the size of a walnut knew better than to love me.

At least on the upper deck, I could see the stars. I turned my gaze to Orion. He'd chased a girl who didn't love him, and her angry father had stabbed out his eyes. My one-sided crush on Cooper had kept me from seeing Tyler, who might have cared for me. Once. Not anymore.

I tracked across the sky from Orion to Perseus and Andromeda. Seeing the lovers usually gave me comfort, but tonight, their happiness punched me in the gut. Not every girl chained to a rock had a handsome hero to rescue her from a monster attack. No, in real life, if the girl couldn't slip her own bonds, the monster got her. And even if she did manage to escape, there was no guarantee she wouldn't screw up the relationship with the handsome hero who came her way.

Something heavy hit the ladder behind me. For a second, I hoped it was just a happily drunk partygoer who'd toppled into it. But, no, the clunks continued in a rhythm. Footsteps. Someone was coming up and would find me with mascara and snot running down my face. I swiped under my nose.

Wind-tousled hair came into view over the edge of the deck. One more rung, and moonlight glinted off a pair of glasses.

Tyler.

Great. He'd chosen my spot to hide out in, too. I supposed it was big enough for two to sulk.

I cleared my throat as a warning. Surely he'd reverse when he saw who occupied the space. But he didn't; his shoulders emerged over the rim. He was stronger than I was, and I didn't mean physically. He'd be able to walk past me, as he'd have to do to reach the other side of the upper deck, probably without even glancing at me. More hot tears rose, ready to betray me as a pathetic jerk who hadn't known my own heart and didn't deserve the love of this man. I rotated on the bench so I faced away from the ladder and wiped at my cheeks with shaky palms. Looking up toward the zenith, I found the familiar pattern of Pisces.

Tyler's solid body settled next to me, close enough that I could smell his citrusy, outdoorsy scent and feel the warmth radiating off him. I refused to look at him; I had enough vanity left that I didn't want him to see my red, mascara-smudged eyes. My teeth rattled together.

"Are you cold?" he asked.

I didn't trust my voice to speak, but I nodded.

He left my side for a few seconds, and then something heavy and scratchy settled on my shoulders. Nowhere near as wonderful as the jacket he'd lent me at the wedding, warm from his body and soaked in his scent. But it blocked the wind. I pulled it tighter around myself. Eyes still upturned, I cleared my throat and said, "Is that some magic they teach you in Texas? Conjuring blankets out of thin air?"

"No," he said, chuckling. "The benches up here have them stored inside."

I hazarded a look, and, sure enough, there was a hinge on the seat where I perched. I rolled my shoulders, trying to ease the tension the shivering had worked into my body.

"What are we looking at?" he asked.

I glanced at him. His gaze was fixed on the star-spattered sky.

"I was looking at Pisces." I wiggled a hand out from under the blanket to point. "That big square is Pegasus. And then below it, there's a small pentagon. That's the head of one fish. There are two, connected by the tails. You can follow that string of stars down to the bright one—Alpha Piscium, it's a double star—and then back up—"

He interrupted me. "I know Pisces."

I looked at it again, and the pattern clicked into place. "Your tattoo! On your shoulder."

"Yeah." He was silent for a minute. "My high school swim

team all got tattoos together. I guess I had water on the brain, so I decided to get my astrological sign."

"Really? Me, too. I'm February twenty-first."

"March fifteenth."

"So we're both dreamers."

"Romantics," he said.

We sat in silence for a minute. Under the blanket, I shivered.

Romantic. Old Marlee had read romance novels and seen love everywhere. New Marlee knew that not everyone got a happy ending. Including, apparently, New Marlee.

I scooted to turn my face away from him. Meanwhile, my stomach churned and my thoughts whirled. Why was he sitting next to me? Was this friendship? Or had he taken pity on me when he found me up here, half-frozen? I didn't need his pity. After all, I still had some pride despite how I'd acted earlier.

"Look, I—" I began.

"Did you—" he said at the same time.

I leaned my head onto my knee and looked back at him, everything but my eyes hidden by the blanket that covered my shoulder. The moonlight gilded the tips of his hair, and the stars reflected off his glasses. His white shirt gleamed under his dark suit coat and tie.

"You first," I said.

He tapped his finger against his knee and said, "Did you mean it when you said you love me?"

I resisted pulling the blanket up over my face. I'd said it out loud. There was no avoiding it. "I did. I do."

When he touched my back between my shoulder blades, I twitched. "And not like friend-love, like you love Alicia?"

It would've been so easy to take the escape he offered. But I couldn't lie to my friend. "Well, there's that, too. But I mean romantic love. I-want-to-jump-your-bones love. I-want-to-live-happily-ever-after-with-you love. I was even planning a grand gesture to try to show you and then beg for forgiveness."

"A grand gesture?"

"I was going to go to Texas for New Year's. Find you wherever you're going to be. Grovel like no one's business. And kiss the hell out of you if you'd let me."

"Marlee." He leaned around so his face blocked my view of the horizon. "Listen to me. I don't want something out of a fairy tale or a romance novel. No white horses. No boom boxes. No running through airports. No songs. No fucking Prince Charming. I want what's real. Is this real?"

I shivered under the blanket. "By Lord Kelvin's frozen left nut, do you think I'd be up here sniffling"—I wiped at the tears on my cheek—"and shivering my ass off if what I felt wasn't real? My heart ripped out of my chest when you left. And again tonight, downstairs, when you walked away from me. I'm crying all my makeup off because I love you and b-because you don't love me."

I scrubbed my face against my knees to hide my ugly-crying face. I hated crying, and between my Dad and Tyler, I'd done way too much of it lately.

"Hey. Hey." He rubbed my shaking shoulders.

"I don't want your pity. You should g-go downstairs to the party. Where it's warm. Be with Sam and the other developers. Say g-g-good-bye." Maybe my heart would freeze up here, and it wouldn't hurt so much that my friend was leaving.

"I don't want to be with them. I want to be with you. And I'm warm enough for both of us." He scooted closer and put his arms around me.

"What?" When I lifted my head, I saw I'd left a pale smudge of makeup on my black skirt. *Great.*

"I love you, Marlee. Since that day at the party when you were soaked in beer."

"But you—" He loved me? "You walked away. Why didn't you say anything downstairs?"

He twisted his lips in a wry smile. "I was so angry that day in Jackson's office. But I read all your texts and listened to your voice mails while I was in Dallas. The song was a nice touch, by the way. Tonight, I'd hoped we could talk. Face to face. But then I saw you looking cozy with Cooper, and I—I lost it. I didn't want to be second best. I won't be." The starlight illuminated the fierce set of his jaw.

I shook my head. "You're not. Never."

"Then when you said you loved me"—the other side of his mouth curved up now—"all I could think of was that I had to tell Jackson I wasn't leaving Synergy. Not leaving you."

"You're…not?"

"Definitely not." His eyes sparkled in the starlight. "It took longer than I expected because they're giving me the promotion. And not as a manager. As a director."

His smile was contagious, and the corners of my mouth tugged up.

He leaned toward me, his breath warm on my chilled skin. "Can I kiss you now, Princess?"

I rocked toward him and pressed my lips to his. He was right. He was warm and soft, all the things I wasn't as a human popsicle stuck up here on the windblown deck. But when he cupped my cheek with one hand and slipped the other under the blanket to rest on my back, I started to thaw.

"I understand skin-to-skin contact is the fastest way to warm up another person." I may have read that in a romance novel or two.

"I'm willing to give it a try." He whispered it in my ear, raising the hairs on the back of my neck.

With trembling fingers, I slipped loose his tie and unbuttoned his shirt. He sucked in a noisy breath when I pressed my cold fingers against his warm chest. "Fuck, you are cold."

"You really have to start believing what I say if we're going to make this work." I slipped my icy hands around to his back, making him shiver.

"Skin-to-skin contact, huh?" His smirk was my only warning before he lifted me off the bench and into his lap. My knees bracketed his hips, and he tugged the blanket to cover us both.

Sitting on his thighs, I touched my lips to his. It should've been weird, kissing my friend, who'd laughed with me, who'd wiped my tears, who'd come to see me every day at my desk to talk about nothing. Or maybe that wasn't weird at all, to be in love with my friend. To have all that, plus kissing, too.

My zipper scritched down my back, and Tyler's nimble fingers followed. My dress sagged down my shoulders, and Tyler kissed down my jaw to my neck before he ducked his head under the blanket. "There she is." His hot breath cascaded over the tops of my breasts. A tingle shot down between my legs.

"What?"

"Your pink bra. I worried when I saw you in this black dress. It didn't seem like you."

It'd be too cheesy to tell him I didn't feel like wearing bright colors when he wasn't around. "It's a-a formal event." Words became difficult as he nibbled along the edge of the rose-pink lace.

"You're beautiful in whatever you wear. But I can't wait to get this dress off you."

"It's mostly off now." Pushing my chest at his face, I rubbed my aching core against the front of his pants and felt an answering stiffening. I dropped my hands to his belt and fumbled for the buckle.

He stilled and put a hand over mine. "Not here, Princess. Someone might come up."

I bent to whisper in his ear, "I promise I'll be quiet." I squirmed against the bulge in his pants.

"I don't want you to be quiet. I want you to scream out my name when I'm inside you."

Remembering what I'd seen under the sheet the morning after I'd slept beside him, I nipped his earlobe. "Yes, please." The Tyler in my bedside drawer wouldn't hold a candle to the real thing.

His voice was strained when he said, "And that's why we can't do it here."

"No?" I nibbled down his neck to his collarbone, which I licked down to the hollow at the base of his throat.

He swallowed. "No." But he didn't stop me from grinding

against him. I hadn't tried to get off fully clothed since high school. But it seemed to be working. The friction between his slacks and my panties made me gasp.

When I moaned his name in his ear, he lifted his hips and ground back. His fingers dug into my ass while I gripped his too-short hair. His breath was hot in my ear. "Almost there?"

I let out a frustrated grunt. The angle was wrong. "I need—"

"Tell me what you need, Princess."

"Your fingers."

He exhaled like he'd just run up a flight of stairs. "On your clit or inside?"

"My clit."

He shifted one of his hands from my hip along the leg opening of my panties. His thumb delved inside and swept up to right where I needed him. I gasped. "That's it."

It didn't take much. One, two, three vibrating passes with the pad of his thumb, and I clamped my open mouth on his neck to muffle my cry. His thumb stilled as I pulsed inside, and he lifted his other hand from my hip to my back, pressing me against his chest. He made soothing sounds and rubbed my back until I slumped against him, shuddering.

"Warm enough?" He kissed my temple.

"Yeah." My muscles were loose and languid, like I'd just had a massage. "Did you…?"

"Oh, ah, not yet."

"Give me another minute, and I'll—"

"No." He clasped my hand, which had started to wander south. "As much as I want your hands and your gorgeous pink lips on me, I'll wait until we're alone. I'd rather not have my first act as a director to be caught with your hands in my pants."

I leaned back. "Your hand was in my pants."

He lifted his hand to his mouth and popped his thumb inside, sucking it clean. "Totally worth it."

My eyes widened as my mind raced to images of him sucking

me clean. I leaned forward to whisper in his ear, "I'd make it worth the risk."

He shivered, and I doubted it was because of the wind whipping the flag above us. But his hands went to my back and zipped up my dress, tugging it back over my shoulders. He leaned back against the railing and turned me so my back rested against his chest. The blanket covered us both. "For now, let's just enjoy the cruise."

"Did you want to go back downstairs?" He looked fine, if a little sweaty and rumpled. I'd most likely cried off all my eye makeup and kissed off my lipstick. And I didn't even want to look down at my dress to see the creases. But if he wanted to rejoin the party, hold my hand, and undo that stupid dance with Cooper by dancing with me the rest of the night, I'd do it.

"No. I've got everything I need right here."

And so did I. Unlike Andromeda, this princess wasn't waiting for a rescue. She was grabbing her destiny with both hands and never letting go.

———

"BEST HOLIDAY PARTY EVER." Tyler held my hand as we stepped off the gangplank onto the dock. I'd insisted on waiting until we'd docked and everyone but the catering staff had left the ship. I wasn't about to let my coworkers see me after I'd scrubbed off my melted mascara with a damp paper towel in the head and finger-combed my hair. Forget beachy waves. My hair was wind-whipped and tangled like I'd been in a turbine.

Reunited with my phone, I answered Alicia's *where-are-you* texts and offers for a ride.

Me: I'm fine, and Tyler's driving me home 😊

I looked up with a wry smile. "Thanks. I did it all myself while you were living it up down in Texas."

He unlocked the door of his Mustang and opened it for me. "I'm sorry. I—"

I placed a finger over his lips to stop him. "It's important that you see your family. I'm glad you did it, and"—I swallowed—"I hope it means you can spend the rest of the holidays here with me."

He put his arms around me and touched his forehead to mine. "I want to spend as much time as possible with you. Starting right now."

I kissed his lips briefly—it was freaking cold, and not even Tyler's suit coat was keeping me warm now—and slid into his car. He shut the door behind me, got in on his side, and cranked the engine and the heat. I shivered when cold air blasted out of the vents.

"Want to see my new place? It's not far from here."

He gripped my frigid hand and kissed my knuckles. "The heat works?"

"I think we can make plenty of our own," I said in my sultriest voice.

He raised his eyebrows.

"Too cheesy?"

He kissed the icy tip of my nose. "I love it when you're cheesy." Then he nosed around to my ear and told me exactly how he planned to warm me up, using filthy words I'd never heard from my friend.

I could've sworn he had heated seats in that Mustang.

A quick drive later, I unlocked my apartment door. With Tyler pressed against my back, I couldn't remember if I'd washed the dishes or tossed my pajamas into the hamper. So far, only Alicia had seen my apartment. Would he like it?

I stepped inside and flicked on the light. "So, this is—"

A second later, I was pressed against the door. He gripped my hands, planted them on either side of my head, and kissed me again, slowly at first and then building to a dance of tongues and nipping lips. When he released my mouth to kiss down my throat, I was done for.

Nothing had ever felt as good as his fingers in my hair, his lips on my skin. Who knew that the back of my neck, right along my hairline, was an erogenous zone? Two people: Tyler and sex-starved Marlee, that's who. He tangled his fingers there, and I shuddered.

I pawed at his chest. He'd taken off his tie and placed it, rolled-up, in the pocket of the jacket I still wore. Finding the buttons of his dress shirt, I worked them open by feel while his lips found mine again in another open-mouthed, citrus-flavored, needed-him-more-than-I-needed-to-breathe kiss. Oxygen was overrated. All the important nerve function was happening in the lizard part of my brain.

When I was able to push his shirt open, I groaned into his mouth.

"What?"

"Undershirt," I growled.

"It was cold tonight. I dressed for it. Unlike you in that tease of a dress." He dropped his dress shirt to the floor and tugged the tee over his head. "I'll admit I secretly hoped I'd have to give you my jacket." He reached for it and slid it off my shoulders.

I ran my hands over his bare chest. All that bare skin that I'd glimpsed the morning I woke up in his bed was mine now. Mine to touch. Mine to lick. (I licked.) I rested my cheek against the center of his chest where his heart beat, strong and steady if a little fast. "All I hoped was that you'd come back for the party. I was so afraid—" My voice broke. I'd been afraid he'd never want to see me again. That he wouldn't come to my party. That I'd go all the way to Texas for my grand gesture, and he'd tell me to go away.

"Marlee." He leaned back and waited until I met his gaze. "I was scared, too. Scared I'd fucked it all up by asking for too much."

I swallowed. It'd taken so much courage for him to ask for

what he wanted, to risk something he held precious: our friendship. "Now we have it all."

"We have it all." The dimple was back, and it was mine to kiss. So I did.

"Bedroom's back here." I linked my fingers with his and led him back to my new bed. The pink bedspread and throw pillows were gone. Now I had a simple white comforter. I hadn't decided yet on a color scheme for my new bedroom, so it was plain. Except for—

"Is that my sweater?" Tyler reached around me to snag it from its place on the second pillow.

I shrugged. No hiding it now. "I missed you."

He laid the sweater on top of my dresser and turned to face me. "You'll never have to miss me again."

My heart slowed at his words, and warmth filled me up like I'd just finished a yoga class. I sat on the bed and, without breaking eye contact, eased back until I was lying down, my legs hanging off the side. "Show me."

His hot gaze dropped from my eyes to my body, cataloging every part of me. A throbbing started at the juncture of my legs, and I pressed my thighs together to relieve it.

"Need something?" I'd never heard him growl like that.

My eyes flared, and I nodded. "Condoms are in the drawer." *Please, please, please don't let them be expired.* How long ago had I bought them in a flurry of hope that—no. I wouldn't let him come into the bedroom with us. Tonight, it was just Tyler and me.

"Oh, it'll be a while before we need one of those." He knelt on the carpet and slowly ran his fingers up the insides of my thighs, inching up my skirt. "That is, if you're okay with me down here?"

I squirmed, desperate for his touch. "Uh-huh." Words were hard.

He stood, and I groaned. "I thought you were going to—"

He chuckled. "Oh, I am." He reached for one of the pillows and wedged it under my head. Then he knelt again between my knees. "Watch."

Oh. *Oh.*

He tugged my panties down my legs and off before he gently pushed my knees farther apart. He gazed at my center, and his tongue darted out to wet his lower lip. "Beautiful," he murmured.

"What's that?" Yes, I'd heard him the first time, but I wanted to hear it again. Doesn't every woman dream of finding a guy who thinks her naked body is beautiful?

He grinned. "Your pussy is gorgeous, Marlee. Pink and swollen and dripping for me."

By the ten-thousand-degree surface of the sun, I had it bad for Tyler's dirty talk.

"You seemed like such a nice boy."

Those hazel eyes of his went dark. "I'll show you nice." There was a puff of hot air before his mouth descended on me, his tongue exploring, his teeth abrading, his lips soothing. Propped on the pillow, I watched his face delve between my thighs, a look of concentration on his face I'd only glimpsed the few times I'd watched him code.

And as good at coding as he was, he was even better at cunnilingus. Soon, he pressed a finger inside my entrance, and I arched my back.

"Still good?"

His warm, nimble finger and his talented tongue were so much better than my vibrator—even The Tyler. "Stop and I'll slap you."

"Maybe later." His smile was wicked.

While he slowly pressed in and out with his finger, he trailed his tongue up. I fisted the sheets in anticipation.

"You like that?"

I nodded, frantic.

He circled my clit with the tip of his tongue. When he touched the sensitive nub at last, the first wave of pleasure washed over me, and I cried out.

"You do like that." His stubble scratched the inside of my thigh.

As he alternated circles with the tip and licks with the flat of his tongue, continuing to drag his fingers in and out, I climbed higher and higher. I twisted my fingers into his hair now, urging him to stay where I needed him.

My ragged breaths turned to groans as I spiraled up to catch the orgasm that bobbed just out of reach.

"I've got you, Princess."

His hand stilled, pressed into me, and the orgasm caught me and shook me in its teeth. He held me through it, whispering soothing nonsense into my skin as every muscle inside me clenched and released and multicolored stars danced behind my eyelids. When I blinked my eyes open, he'd come up to lie on his side next to me, silhouetted by the lamp behind him. Propping his head on his hand, he watched me as my breathing slowed. He still wore his glasses and pants. He draped his other arm across my waist.

I could hear the smile in his voice when he said, "I could look at that face all day."

"You mean my O face?" I turned it into the pillow.

His hand left my side and two fingers nudged my chin up so I faced him again. He smoothed a lock of hair from my forehead. "Just your face. O or otherwise."

His tenderness was melting my insides. Why had I pushed him away? I could've had this man over and over by now, the man with the nimble fingers who'd just spun the starry skies around me.

My interior muscles clenched again, wanting more, needing to be filled with more than his fingers. I moved a hand to the front of his pants and felt him straining toward me. I trailed a finger along his length. "Want to see it again?"

"God, yes."

Rolling to hover over him, I planted a kiss on his lips that tasted like me and trailed down his neck, pausing right at the dip in his collarbone, at the center of his citrus-and-cedar scent. He hummed and closed his eyes.

Encouraged, I licked down to his nipple, which already stood upright, waiting for my teeth to graze it. When I nipped it, he moaned.

I smiled into his skin and continued lower, crouching to skim the hills of his abdominals, one by one. My fingers went to his belt buckle, pushing the leather through the metal as, with my tongue, I drew an orbit around his navel.

Sitting up, I unhooked his pants and drew the zipper down, careful not to catch his straining erection in the teeth. This was it. I was going to see how The Tyler compared to my Tyler. I kissed his happy trail right above his waistband before I tugged off his underwear and pants. Showing restraint that surprised even me, I pulled off his socks before I let my gaze fall on his cock.

Holy *Gray's Anatomy*. The Tyler was monstrous. Not to mention purple. Tyler himself, although more modest, was gorgeous: veined, flushed, and oh-so-erect. I trailed a finger up from the base to the head and across the slit, smearing the moisture beaded there. He was silkier. Warmer. And he jumped under my touch.

Reaching back to my zipper, I pulled it down until the dress fell from my shoulders and puddled on the floor. My bra joined it a second later. I stood naked before my friend and lover.

His face went slack. "Jesus, Marlee."

"What?" Had he imagined—expected—me to look different? Maybe I should've left the dress on.

"Even better than I imagined," he said on a breath.

I stepped to the nightstand and pulled out a condom packet from the box next to The Tyler's pouch. I dropped it on the bed and knelt over his thighs. "You imagined this?"

"Only every night. And weekend afternoons. And once or twice at the office. Whenever you wear that swingy skirt. The one that I can never tell if it's white or pink."

The corner of my mouth lifted. "It's oyster pink. I may have imagined you, too." Someday I'd tell him about The Tyler. Maybe we could all play together sometime. Not tonight. Tonight was just for very-real Tyler and me.

His cock strained toward me, eager and glorious. I wrapped my fingers around it and tugged experimentally. And then more confidently when he groaned and his shaft hardened further in my hand. I looked up into his face to check that I was doing it how he liked. He blinked hard.

"Baby, stop or I'll come in your hand."

So I was doing it right. "I came in your hand. And your mouth." I bent and licked him from root to tip. But before I could repeat the action, he cradled my chin with his palm.

"I want—I want to come inside you the first time. Is that okay?"

I kissed the side of his cock. "I'm on board for that. First time, second time, third time. We have all night to get creative."

His dick jumped. Before I could kiss it again, he ripped the packet and rolled the condom down over his length. "It's up to you, Princess."

He meant it was one thing for him to bring me to orgasm with his fingers and his tongue. And for us to be naked together, even for me to have given him those few intimate licks. But this was different. Joining our bodies was a step beyond friendship, even friends who'd messed around a little.

I'd already given him my heart. I'd give him my body, too.

On my knees, I walked up to straddle his hips. I lifted up and guided the tip to my entrance. He watched me, those hazel eyes dark and hooded, as I sank slowly onto him. I was ready and wet, and I'd had lots of practice with The Tyler; still, I took my time as I lowered over him until my hips met his. We both sighed, complete.

"Just a second." I wanted to capture this moment, this memory. Etch it onto my brain so I could take it out and resavor it. I clenched around the fullness and smiled at his sharp intake of breath. Would this be my last first sex? I hoped so. I'd never thought Tyler was a Prince Charming, but I knew now he was perfect for me. Better than the fairy tale.

Slowly, I began to rock my hips. He stayed still, letting me direct the action. He rested his hands on the swell of my ass, squeezing a little, either to steady me or to keep from ravaging me with his hands. I trailed my fingers over his pecs down to his abs. "Is this okay?"

"So good." He squeezed his eyes shut, but they flew open a second later like he didn't want to miss anything. "You focus on you. I'm doing great."

I stopped moving and slapped my hands onto my thighs. "No."

"No?" He blinked the haze from his eyes.

"We're not doing that. You're not going to put your own pleasure, your own happiness, second anymore. We're partners. We do what's good for both of us."

His playful dimple disappeared. "Marlee." His voice cracked on my name. He ran his hands from my hips up to my back and urged me down onto his chest, wrapping me up in an embrace. He kissed my temple. "No one's ever—" He heaved a sigh.

"I know, baby. But it's time you realize you deserve more."

His arms, his body, tightened around me. It was just under my cheek, so I kissed his tattoo.

With one athletic bunching of his muscles, he rolled us so I was on my back and he hovered over me, still inside me. "I can't —I can't be gentle. Not right now." His eyes had gone from dark to wild.

The thrill started from the place we were joined and shivered all the way to the ends of my hair splayed on the bed. "I don't want gentle. I only want you. Just as you are."

He levered down to kiss me, thorough and demanding like a duke in one of my historical romances. But like the heroine, I was feisty, and I kissed him right back, making my own demands.

Lifting, he watched my face as he pulled out and thrust back in. The second time, pleasure flashed inside me like a pulsar, rhythmic. A few thrusts later, I warmed inside and curled around him. "Don't stop."

"Never, Princess." He bent and nipped me right where my neck joined my shoulder. Then he rolled his hips, brushing against my swollen, sensitive clit.

I went full supernova. Clenching every muscle, I clawed at his straining ass and cried out his name. He rammed inside one more time and stilled, a look of bliss frozen on his face. But instead of collapsing on top of me, he planted a kiss on my forehead, another on the tip of my nose, on my lips, my chin. He peppered kisses on every part of me he could reach. "I love you, Marlee."

I giggled when he tickled me with a kiss on my ribs. "You're just saying that because of all the endorphins."

He stopped kissing me and pushed up again. "Nope. I love you. With or without the endorphins."

I smiled. "We'll see."

He pulled out, gripping the condom. "Be right back."

A minute later, he returned, smelling like my floral hand soap. Lifting the covers, he slid into bed beside me. "I still love you, Marlee."

"Haven't you ever heard of afterglow? Endorphins can last for hours." I snuggled up next to him and tangled my legs with his. "The real question is, will you still love me when I'm cranky?"

"Like, when you're about to get your period and you snarl at everyone, including Jackson?"

"What?" I moved my feet back onto my side of the bed.

His blissful expression dimmed. "Oh, I mean, I totally didn't notice that. But if I did, I'd bring you chocolate and still love you."

I wrinkled my nose. Tyler did often bring me chocolate right before my period started. Holy Edwin Hubble.

He tugged me closer. "Remember that time we were right up against deadline and the power went out in the building?"

"That construction crew down the street accidentally cut the power. And the internet connection."

"The rest of us just sat around staring at our screens,

wondering if the batteries would run out before the power came back, knowing we couldn't compile without the network. But not you. You got on the phone to the power company, to the ISP. You marched downstairs and told us to keep working. Even Jackson was afraid of you that day. You were like…thunder. Or a vengeful goddess."

I buried my face in his neck. "I knew how important that deadline was. I'm sorry I was a bitch."

"No, sweetheart." He hitched my leg over his and pressed me against him. He was already half-hard again. "You were magnificent."

I rolled him to his back and straddled him. "I'll show you magnificent."

We made love again, more gently this time. After, we burrowed under the comforter, our legs tangled and my cheek resting on his chest, our breathing synchronized and slow, my limbs loose, like we were two fish in the ocean.

Tyler brought my hand to his lips and kissed my thumb. "I can't believe this is real," he whispered, like if he spoke louder he'd break the spell.

I tilted my head to look up into his eyes, shadowed in the darkness. "It's real. I love you, Tyler. I want you to be my plus-one at weddings. I want you to stop at my desk and flirt with me every time you come up to see Jackson. I want you to come upstairs just to see me. I want to hold your hand in the elevator when we leave every night. Together."

His smile, the special one he saved for me, gleamed in the moonlight coming in through the window, and his arm wrapped around me. "Friends. And lovers."

"Lovers. And friends."

The best of both.

TYLER

MARLEE'S FACE WAS PALE, but her square chin jutted out in that stubborn way I loved—as long as it wasn't directed at me. We sat in my car, parked in front of her father's nursing facility. She'd wanted to visit before we left for Dallas, but I knew it was hard for her. Since we'd been together—six months now—she came to see him a few times a week, sometimes with me, sometimes alone.

I gripped her hand. "Ready, Princess?"

She'd been a princess since the first moment I saw her, dressed in her girly-pink work clothes and handling the executives as if they worked for her. Then, when we'd finally gotten together on the party boat, it'd slipped out. She hadn't seemed to mind. And now she was my princess, I'd do whatever she asked of me: toss my coat over a mud puddle, climb a tall tower, fight off a dragon, all for her.

She turned to face me. As usual, seeing her brown eyes soft and sad almost stopped my heart. She gave me a wobbly smile and squeezed back. "Ready."

We got out of my low-slung Mustang and met on the sidewalk in front of the hood. Hands joined, we walked in together. Marlee chatted with the receptionist and signed us in while I scanned the lobby. As usual, it was clean and bright but empty. No one sat on the sofa or the pair of straight-backed chairs. Bright-yellow sunflowers in a blue vase lit up the drab room. Like my Marlee.

The receptionist unlocked the secure door and walked us through. On the other side, one of the patient care directors met us. I knew her face, but I couldn't remember her name.

"Hi, Liz." Marlee remembered. Once she'd finally admitted that her dad needed more care than she could provide, she was on a mission. She'd done her research, chosen the best place for him, and monitored every aspect of his care. She chatted up the nurses every time she visited.

"He's having a good day today," Liz said, answering the question I knew Marlee couldn't bring herself to ask.

The tension in her shoulders released.

Liz said, "We've been trying a new therapy with him this week. He's in there now. Would you like to see it?"

"Can we?" Marlee asked.

"Of course. Let's go."

Liz led us through the facility and then, surprising me, outside through another secured door, along a covered walkway, to a corrugated metal building, not much larger than a shed. She used a keypad to open the door.

The interior looked like my dad's workshop at home except lower tech. Hand tools hung on pegs on the walls, and three wooden workbenches took up the middle of the room. Fluorescent lights hung from the ceiling to illuminate each workspace. The sweet smell of sawdust filled the air, and despite the humming dust recovery system, dust motes and tiny curls of wood danced in the beams of light shining through the high windows.

Two men stood with their backs to us across the room in front of a manual lathe. One was the beefy nursing assistant we often saw with Marlee's dad; the other, turning a chair leg on the lathe, was the man himself.

Will Rice had stabilized over the last few months. He still had bad days like the one when he'd wandered off and we'd found him at the transit station, but he had good days, too, when he knew Marlee. I always reintroduced myself since I never assumed he'd remember someone he'd met since his illness; my experience with Grandpa had taught me that. I hoped Will wouldn't decline as fast as Grandpa had.

Liz patted Marlee's arm and left us. I massaged Marlee's shoulder where it met her neck, where the tension had started to build again. I wouldn't push her, though. She had to do this on her own terms.

She rolled her shoulders back and approached Will where he worked the lathe. He stood on his good leg and used the weaker one on the foot pedal. The scrape of the blade on the wood covered the sound of our footsteps.

"Dad?" Her voice was too soft to carry over the grinding of the lathe. She cleared her throat and tried again, louder. "Dad."

Will stopped the machine and looked at Marlee. A smile split his face, so similar to her own.

"Sunshine!"

Her back was to me, so I couldn't see her face, but her posture relaxed. She reached up to hug him, and his sawdust-covered arms went around her. When he released her, dusty handprints marked the back of her pink shirt.

I approached and stuck out my hand. "Mr. Rice, it's good to see you. Tyler Young."

"I remember you, Tyler. I can see you're taking good care of my girl."

So it was a good day. "I try, sir. We take care of each other." In fact, we were moving in together next month, but I wasn't about to tell Marlee's dad *that*. Bum leg and all, he was strong.

"Let's take a walk," he said.

The assistant handed him his cane, and we all strolled out into the sunshine. The facility sat on a hill surrounded by rolling lawns. A few residents worked in a vegetable patch nearby.

"I'll hang out here," I said, pointing at a bench. I'd give Marlee and her dad some time alone on his good day.

She flashed me a dazzling smile. "We won't be long. I know we need to go."

"Take as long as you need. I'll get us to the airport on time." I gave her a wicked smile. What was the point of having a muscle car if you couldn't flex those muscles every once in a while?

Giving me a last lingering look, she turned away with her dad. They ambled arm in arm, with the assistant following a discreet distance behind.

I sank onto the bench and tilted my face up toward the sun. There was less fog over here in Oakland, and I always enjoyed visiting on clear days. Maybe next year, when we'd banked enough cash, we could buy a place on this side of the bay, or maybe in one of the suburbs away from the city lights where we could see the constellations at night. I loved it when Marlee told me the stories of the stars.

My phone pinged with a text.

Raleigh: Still coming tonight?

Worrying was unusual for Raleigh, my overconfident asshole of a brother. He was the reason Marlee and I were heading to Dallas later that day. I'd held her to her promise to be my date to his wedding. I'd missed his bachelor party—Marlee's new programming project had kept us in San Francisco all week—but I'd heard from my next-older brother, Lincoln, that it was a rager. We'd be there for the rehearsal dinner tomorrow night.

Me: Wait, that's this weekend?

After all the shit Raleigh and my other brothers had given me, he deserved a little ribbing.

The dots appeared while he typed, then they disappeared and reappeared a few more times. I'd really yanked his chain.

Raleigh: Not funny

Me: Seriously, everything OK?

From the group texts with my brothers and sister, I'd gotten the feeling Raleigh was getting cold feet. Of course, he'd projected it onto Bella to make it seem as if *she* was the nervous one. But I knew that couldn't be true. Like all my brothers, Raleigh had been the big man on campus in both high school and college. Girls couldn't resist him. I couldn't imagine Bella backing out on him.

Raleigh: Just get here, and everything will be.

I smiled. I'd have to play some prank on him. Something small, though, like showing up in red socks or claiming my tux had gone missing, just to harass him some more. He made it too easy.

Me: We'll be there late tonight. Can't wait for everyone to meet Marlee.

I knew they'd love her almost as much as I did. I pocketed my phone, turned my face up to the sun again, and closed my eyes.

We'd been up late last night packing. I'd bought Marlee a carry-on full of romance paperbacks to replace some of the ones she'd discarded. Like I'd told her at the holiday party, we were both romantics. And I'd do everything I could to keep the romance in her life.

We'd stayed awake even later to make love. Exhausted or not, we couldn't keep our hands off each other. I'd never had a friendship that'd turned into love. But adding intimacy to friendship with Marlee? Every time we touched was pure magic.

I must have dozed off because the next thing I knew, Marlee

was squeezing my shoulder. "Let's go, big guy. A speeding ticket will only make us later for our flight."

I opened my eyes to find her face blocking the sun. Its rays radiated out from her dark-honey hair, making it sparkle. No wonder her dad called her "Sunshine." I glanced behind her. Will and the assistant were gone. I stretched out my hand, as if to let her pull me up, but I pulled her down onto my lap instead. I cradled her cheek and kissed her pink lips. She stroked the back of my hair, short now thanks to my pre-wedding haircut, and I twisted my fingers in her long silken strands. I could've kissed her there on the bench in the sunshine for hours.

Reluctantly, I disengaged and rested my forehead against hers to catch my breath. The last time I'd gone home to Dallas, we'd almost broken apart. But this time, she'd be at my side through what was sure to be pandemonium like everything involving my family, which was one of the reasons I lived two thousand miles away. But with Marlee by my side, we'd get through it together.

I plucked a long gray hair off her shirt. "Subha's been in your drawer again."

She brushed her lips against mine. "What can I say? She shares my passion for discount designer clothes."

I thought Subha shared my passion for Marlee, but I wasn't going to argue. The only thing my cat—our cat—loved more than nesting in her drawers was sitting on Marlee herself. The morning she'd cozied up to her coat had been the beginning of Subha's obsession with her.

I pushed Marlee to her feet and then rose and linked my hand in hers. We walked toward the parking lot. "Good visit?"

She sighed. "Yes. Moving him here was the best decision."

"Not the *best* decision." I squeezed her hand. "That was agreeing to be my date to Jay and Alicia's wedding."

She grinned up at me and slid her arm around my waist. "You're right. Let's go, wedding date."

We ambled down the path, on our way to another wedding

together. And someday soon, I'd ask her to be my wife, and *that* would be the best decision of our lives.

———

THANK you so much for reading *Friend Me!* Please consider posting a review on Amazon or Goodreads.

Not ready to let go of Marlee and Tyler? Join my newsletter at michellemccraw.com/Friend to download an extra-smutty bonus epilogue!

Read on for a sneak peek at Sam's story, *Trip Me Up.*

TRIP ME UP (SYNERGY BOOK 3)
EXCERPT
CHAPTER 1

SAM

Not everyone would sneak her dog into a fundraising luncheon. Her adorable, hardly-ever-barks, absolutely—well, mostly—nonshedding dog.

But, to my mother's never-ending disappointment, I'm not everyone.

Everyone wishes they had your advantages.

Everyone should marry someone who fits into their social circle. By that, she meant wealthy.

Everyone wants to be a Jones.

But at some point over the past twenty-five years, she should've realized that I'm a little...different.

"Bilbo Baggins," I hissed, lifting the white tablecloth of a large round table.

"Sam!"

Grimacing, I dropped the tablecloth and whirled toward my younger sister. She looked down at me from her sky-high heels, one hand on her hip and the other holding a pink cocktail that matched the baby pink of her silk dress. She always looked so effortless at these things. "What are you doing?" she whispered.

"Um, looking for an earring?"

Natalie squinted at me. "You're not wearing earrings."

"Oh. Then I guess I'm looking for two of them."

"Pearls. You should be wearing pearls." She scanned me from head to toe, and I nudged my huge black tote bag behind my back. "That suit is so two seasons ago. Didn't Mother send you a new one?"

I stared at the round toe of my low-heeled shoes, remembering how I'd dropped the lurid pink dress at the donation box. This suit wasn't so bad. I'd bought it back when I still had new-clothes money, and it was my favorite color, black.

Natalie's voice was gentler than I'd heard it in a while. "Next time, tell her what you want."

"What I want is not to be here," I muttered.

"Oh, really? How would Dad have felt about that?" She stared at me for a moment and sipped her pink drink before she spun on her sparkly sandal and stalked off.

I sucked a breath into my suddenly too-small lungs. I hadn't been thinking about Dad, who probably would've been too busy working to come to this event, even though it was named after him. I was only here because Mother insisted that her family be here, picture-perfect.

And that reminded me I needed to find Bilbo Baggins before she did. Where could he have gone? He wasn't usually shy. He wouldn't hide under a table. Unlike me, he'd be out in the center of the action, making friends. I turned in a circle, scanning the room.

A long buffet table took up one side of the high-ceilinged museum space. Mother usually hated the idea of people holding food, but dining tables wouldn't have fit with the large sculptures. The other side of the room had smaller tables serving hors d'oeuvres. Maybe he'd gone to beg for a chicken wing. Not that Mother would ever serve messy chicken wings, but Bilbo Baggins didn't know that.

I'd taken one step in that direction when a silky-soft but steely hand clamped around my wrist. "Samantha, *what* is that?"

Frantic, I surveyed the area nearby. Had she seen him?

Pale, French-tipped fingers plucked at the strap of my tote bag. "Why didn't you leave your school bag at the coat check?"

I turned slowly to face her. "Mother, that's where I've got my wallet and keys." And my dog, too, before he'd made his grand escape.

Her red lips turned down. "What happened to the bag I gave you for your birthday?"

"It didn't match my suit." I waved my hand at my black pantsuit and white shirt. I didn't mention that when I'd sold the flowered fuchsia purse on eBay, it'd covered Bilbo Baggins' annual vet visit plus his heartworm preventative and allergy medications.

"Don't get me started on that suit," she muttered, brushing a speck off my shoulder. "Now, where is your date?"

"My date?"

"Yes, remember, I told you William Winford wanted to meet you."

"You didn't mention it was a date."

Her blue eyes, paler than mine, shifted to my collar, which she straightened. "He's very well respected. And brilliant. From what I hear, he's tripled his trust fund."

Don't let her get started on trust funds. "What's his line of business, drug kingpin? Weapons runner?"

Her mouth formed a shocked, red *O*. "Samantha Renee Jones, you know we don't associate with people like that."

"Mother, it was just a jo—"

"You can trust your family not to expose you to people like that."

My lips parted. She wouldn't actually bring up my horrifying mistake here, would she? My heart raced.

"Samantha." She laid a hand on my sleeve. "You need to trust the people who love you. We'll help you find a partner who can support you."

"I can support myself." Maybe I made shitty decisions about

men, but I didn't need her to match me up with a partner. I had a plan for my life. I crossed my arms. "The last thing I need is a partner."

"But you need security. I've seen that hovel you live in. That's not—"

"Mother." My oldest brother's big hand settled on the shoulder of her jacket.

"Ah. Jackson." Her voice went all soft at my brother's name, the way it never did when she said mine.

He bent to kiss her cheek, but his crooked smile was all for me. "I need Sam for a minute."

"But I was going to introduce her to William Winford. You know, the *investment banker.*" She pursed her lips at me.

"She can meet your guy later. I have someone else in mind."

I narrowed my eyes at him. My brother didn't pimp me out or try to use me like some pawn in his business game. But he betrayed nothing under Mother's gaze.

"All right. I'll find you later, Samantha. With William." She stalked off, her heels clacking on the wood floor.

"What the hell, Jacks—"

"You didn't happen to bring that oversized rat you call a dog here, did you?" He flicked my tote bag.

I sucked in a breath. "Did you see him?"

"Over by the charcuterie table."

"Oh, no." With Jackson right behind, I scurried toward the table filled with platters of meats and cheeses. I squatted and pulled up the cloth draping it, but the space under the table was empty. "He's not here."

"Sam, why would you bring your dog to Mother's party?"

I stood and patted my tote like Bilbo Baggins could've magically reappeared where he belonged. With my dog against my side, my hands had stopped trembling, and my heart rate had eased from hummingbird speed down to frightened rabbit. "I don't know." But I couldn't help glancing at the giant banner of my larger-than-life dad's face by the museum entrance.

His smile drooped. "I hate it, too, Samwise. But people pay big bucks to come here and eat cheese, and the money goes to a good cause."

Dad's favorite cause, he didn't have to say.

"I know, but—" The Jones Foundation events were the worst. People wanted to talk about books, which I didn't read, or Dad, which made my heart ache like he'd been gone only a year and not fourteen. "Why can't they just write checks and leave me out of it?"

He shrugged. "Like it or not, you're a Jones."

I couldn't escape my name, not here in San Francisco. But someday—a year from now, if I could turn around my dissertation project—I'd be able to break out. I'd find a research professorship somewhere far away in the middle of the country where Mother wouldn't go. South Dakota or Iowa or even Arkansas. It didn't matter to me where, as long as it didn't have any designer boutiques or donors. All I needed was a computer lab and an apartment big enough for me and—

"Bilbo Baggins," I hissed again, low. With his giant ears, he should've been able to hear me even under the noisy luncheoneers.

"Look, we'll divide up and search. You cover this half of the room, and I'll check over by the buffet table."

"What if he ran outside?" There were foxes and hawks, maybe even coyotes, in the surrounding park.

"That dog would never leave you, Samwise. He just went looking for a snack. We'll find him."

The inside of my nose burned a little as I reached out and squeezed my brother's arm. "Thanks."

"Don't worry about it. This is much more entertaining than talking to stuffy literary types. Hey, remember how we used to hunt for gnomes in that game we made together?"

"Gnome Dome? That was years ago." Ancient history. "And Bilbo Baggins is a lot trickier than the gnomes we programmed."

"But he's pretty predictable around snacks." He winked before heading across to the buffet.

I turned back toward the hors d'oeuvres tables. He had to be over there, begging for a treat. I scanned the floor. No sign of his black fur.

A laugh, rich and deep, caught my attention. It wasn't the polite chuckle people used to signal their usually false amusement at these things. It was pure and unrestrained. And loud. I glanced over to see who'd violated the social contract.

He was big and…and glowing, like he was on fire on the inside. His hair was the same color the sky had been when we'd had the wildfires last summer, a deep russet. Golden freckles coated his skin. He had the physique of someone who played one of those sports where you carry a ball on a field, broad across the shoulders and tapered below. Someone who'd look more natural in a fur-lined cloak and gripping an ax than wearing a charcoal-gray suit and holding a—

"Bilbo Baggins!" I skidded to a stop in front of the Viking.

"Excuse me?" With one oversized, freckled hand, he cuddled Bilbo Baggins closer against his chest. He walloped me with a pair of blue eyes. No—I wrinkled my nose—they were green. Flecks of gold lit them like sparks. Even his lashes were red. Was there a Norse god of flame? Because this guy was a bonfire, toasty warm but also popping with danger.

I looked right and left, but we were outside the nearest circles of conversation. I edged closer. More softly, I said, "That's my dog. Bilbo Baggins."

"This guy, here?" He looked down into Bilbo Baggins' bulging brown eyes. Bilbo Baggins flicked out his pink tongue to lick the man's clean-shaven chin, then squirmed in his grip. "He looks more like Toto than a Hobbit."

I couldn't arch an eyebrow like Natalie could, but I raised both of mine. "And does that make you the Wicked Witch of the West, kidnapping my dog?" Movie references, I could do. This guy looked more like a linebacker than a librarian; if we stayed in the shallow water, I wouldn't have to betray my literary ignorance.

A smile spread like honey across his face. "Kidnapping? More like safekeeping. It appears that Bilbo Baggins was ready for a quest."

My stomach hollowed. I couldn't even meet Bilbo Baggins' eyes. "I know I shouldn't have brought him. It's just that—" I pressed my lips together. I couldn't tell this stranger that I needed my tiny dog to fend off the emotions that threatened me here.

"Hey, hey." He waited until I looked up again. "It's okay. He's safe now. See? I've got him." Bilbo Baggins sighed and pressed into his chest.

I wished I could've snuggled up to him, too.

The man chuckled. "Sure, there's plenty of room for you both."

"Shit, I said that out loud, didn't I?"

"'No legacy is so rich as honesty.'" He glanced around the room. "Though you couldn't tell that from this crowd."

I tilted my head to the side. "That sounds like Benjamin Franklin."

"Shakespeare, actually."

"Oh." Despite his appearance, despite his assessment of the fundraiser attendees, he was one of the literary types. "I'll take Bilbo Baggins back now."

His red eyebrows crunched together, but he extended Bilbo Baggins toward me, and my dog swam his tiny, fluffy feet right into my arms. I snuggled him close against my chest. Too close, I discovered when he let out a belch.

"You didn't happen to feed him cheese, did you?"

The Viking uncurled his other hand and showed me a crumpled napkin holding a single orange cube. "Just one or two pieces."

I grimaced. "I'm going to get him out of here before he sh— before he has gastric distress, I mean." I wrinkled my nose. "He doesn't tolerate dairy."

"Sorry about that. He seemed to like it." His voice, like his laugh, was low and rich. I didn't blame Bilbo Baggins for running to him. Hell, I'd like to snuggle up against this man while he fed me snacks.

A hint of stinky cheese smell wafted into my nose. I scooped Bilbo Baggins into my tote.

"He does like cheese, right up to the moment his little intestines let loose." Was that too much information? Probably. When I was nervous, my mouth was more unrestrained than Bilbo Baggins' bowels after eating Muenster.

He winced. "I really am sorry."

"It's okay. It'll give me an excuse to leave early." But my feet stayed right there in front of the friendly giant who'd rescued my dog.

"I'm Niall Flynn." He stuck out his right hand.

"Samantha." My hand disappeared into his much larger one, his fingers so long that they brushed the sensitive skin at my wrist. My heartbeat quickened, and I sucked in a breath.

"Oh." He grimaced. "Sorry. Rough hands."

It was true. Calluses roughened his palm and each of the fingers that covered the back of my hand. Most of the men at these things did nothing more strenuous than click a mouse, and their hands were smoother than mine. Maybe Niall was an athlete. Every once in a while, a pro sportsballer would join up with the foundation.

"It's okay. I—I like it." I eyed the way his suit coat sleeves stretched over his biceps. My friend Marlee would tell me to go for it. To have a drink with him. To flirt with him. But I was no Marlee. I must've been in the computer lab when they gave the lessons on hair-tossing and small talk. On the conversational scale of light banter to deadly serious, I generally came off as an eleven —intense.

Realizing he was still gripping my hand, I tugged it out of his grasp. "Well, thanks for saving Bilbo Baggins from being spiked by someone's heel."

"Wait." He was studying me, a slow perusal of my face, like some people looked at art, not like the mental math most people did when they looked at a Jones.

I blinked. "Do I have something on my face?"

He shook his head, and the intensity left his expression. "Sorry, I—I guess I was just surprised to find someone like you here."

"Someone like me?" I wrinkled my nose. "What's that supposed to mean?" What had he figured out about me in our ten minutes together?

"Someone…real. And yet not. It's like you're going to turn into a woodland creature when the sun goes down." His face went red, even the freckles.

"Like in *Ladyhawke?*"

"Yeah, like—"

"Niall! There you are." A woman about my height, with curly dark hair and tawny skin, gripped Niall's sleeve. A volley of clicks behind her told me she'd brought a photographer. I cringed and turned my back to the sound. "What are you doing hiding over here? We need to get you out and circulating."

"I was talking to Samantha." He held out his hand toward me. No way was I getting pulled into his photo op. Each click of the shutter added to the cold weight in my belly. How could I have been so wrong again? He wasn't a gentle giant. He was some minor celebrity here to dump some cash for library programs in exchange for publicity.

Or worse, he was like Stephen, luring me into his trap, waiting to spring it. Somehow, he'd connected me to the Jones family even though I hadn't given him my last name. Blast that ridiculous family portrait they stuck on an easel for these events. I'd been ten with my straight dark hair in a zigzag part, a closed-mouth smile hiding my braces, and eyes too big for my face. Now my hair was back in a low ponytail and the braces were gone, but I still looked like that prepubescent kid too clueless to know she was about to lose her dad.

The woman's gaze turned on me, even more penetrating than Niall's had been. "What's your last name, Samantha?"

"Gabby," Niall said, "I need another minute with Samantha." I didn't usually like my full name, but the way it rolled out in his low voice made me shiver. Or maybe that was a warning tremor from Bilbo Baggins. What could Niall need another minute to do? Brush the dog hair off my suit for a photo? Once, I'd been willing to be arm candy, smiling for pictures I didn't want, all for the sake of a guy. Never again.

I put up my palms in front of my chest like I could push them both away. "It's cool. We're done. Nice meeting you, Niall." Without another word, I strode toward the exit, leaving Niall and his entourage in front of the charcuterie.

When we reached a grassy patch outside the museum, Bilbo Baggins leaped from my tote bag to rid himself from the evil cheese, staring at me like I'd betrayed him. "That was your new friend, Niall, who poisoned you," I said as I cleaned up the mess. "And he totally wasn't worth it. He's just like Winford Whatsit. Wants to use me like an ID badge for getting into shitty parties like that." I shook the plastic bag of dog shit at him. "I'm no one's golden ticket. I'm getting my doctorate and getting out of here. Understand?"

Bilbo Baggins cocked his head.

"I know. You get it." I tossed the bag into the trash and spread sanitizer gel over my hands.

As I clipped the leash to his collar, my phone buzzed from the outside pocket of my tote. Dr. Martell's pattern. He usually respected my weekends. Maybe he'd forgotten about some tests he needed graded.

"Hi, Dr. Martell."

"Samantha. I thought I'd get your voice mail. Didn't you have some party this afternoon?"

"I—I'm all done." I led Bilbo Baggins to a bench and sat down, easing off my heels.

"Good. Good." I could practically hear his brain switching

back to research mode. I'd always liked my adviser's focus on what was important.

"We need to talk about your research. Monday morning, nine a.m., my office."

My stomach gurgled like I'd eaten the bad cheese, too. "I know it hasn't been going that well, but—"

"Don't worry, Samantha. It's an opportunity."

The last opportunity he'd given me had taken me down a rabbit hole, and I was still trying to steer the project back in the right direction. "An opportunity."

"You'll love it. See you Monday."

There was no question in his voice. He oversaw not only my stipend but also my doctorate. Without his signature on my dissertation, I'd be the Ph.D.-free version of Samantha Jones, unable to get the research position I needed to escape. "Okay."

I dropped the phone into its pocket. "Let's go home, Bilbo Baggins." I toed back into my shoes and stood. Passing the row of black Mercedes and Bentleys and Jackson's garish yellow Lamborghini, I trudged toward the nearest bus stop.

Trip Me Up will be available in paperback in November 2021.

AUTHOR'S NOTE

So…this lighthearted romantic comedy had some very serious elements in it, namely dementia, Alzheimer's Disease, and the challenges caregivers face.

Marlee would not have been able to give her father the care he needed—or pay for it—without legal tools known as advance directives. While I'm not a lawyer and am not giving legal advice, if you're a caregiver or someone who may need care, you should consider looking into these tools and deciding if they're right for you.

- A medical power of attorney or healthcare proxy designates a person to make medical decisions for you if you're unable to do so. You can find templates online.
- A financial power of attorney designates someone to make business or financial decisions for you if you're incapacitated. Again, you can find templates online.

Alzheimer's Disease and dementia can be agonizing for caregivers. If someone you love has one of these conditions, I'm sorry. If you need help and information, check out the Alzheimer's Association (alz.org) or your country's healthcare resources.

If Marlee and Will's story touched you, you might also consider making a donation to an Alzheimer's or dementia research organization. I hope someday we can find a cure, and this story will be obsolete.

ACKNOWLEDGMENTS

This book has been a trip, y'all.

First, thanks to the many, many people who supported me through it. First, author Katrina Kittle and her 12-step writing program, who helped me focus and finish this book. Also, my many critique partners, especially Lauren Accardo, Dr. Bella Ellwood-Clayton, and Rebecca Thomson, who provided feedback and loved Marlee even when she was a selfish bitch. Thanks to Maureen Moretti, who believed in this book and in me. She asked me to add what is now one of my favorite scenes, the one in the bridal shop with the Dragon Lady.

As always, thank you to my Twitter squad of RChat cheerleaders, especially Meka James and Coralie Moss, who listened to me vent and then told me to suck it up and publish the damn book. Your support has been invaluable.

Finally, thanks to my family, especially my mom and dad. They'll never read this book, which has too much sex and not enough murder, but they've supported me on my path to becoming a writer since I was just an oddball kid who always had her nose in a book. Thanks to my husband and kids for your forbearance when I snarled at you to give me five damn minutes of quiet while I wrote down the words in my head. You'll never read this—please don't!—but I appreciate your support throughout my writing journey.

CREDITS

Edits

Angela James

Proofreading

April Bennett, The Editing Soprano

Cover Design

Avery Kingston

ABOUT MICHELLE

I write steamy contemporary romance featuring characters who unashamedly love science, engineering, and technology and also lots of sex. My novels have been finalists in the RWA Vivian Contest, the Contemporary Romance Writers' Stiletto Contest, and the Windy City Romance Writers' Four Seasons Contest.

A native Texan, I now live where my family considers me a Yankee, but I'll never stop saying y'all.

For updates about my upcoming books and more free reads—plus guaranteed puppy pics—please subscribe to my newsletter at michellemccraw.com. You can also follow me on Facebook, Twitter, and Instagram.

- facebook.com/MichelleMcCrawAuthor
- twitter.com/MMOWriter
- instagram.com/MMOWriter
- amazon.com/Michelle-McCraw/e/B08Y77D69B
- goodreads.com/MichelleMcCraw
- bookbub.com/authors/michelle-mccraw

ALSO BY MICHELLE MCCRAW

Synergy Series

Work with Me

Friend Me

Trip Me Up

CPSIA information can be obtained
at www.ICGtesting.com
Printed in the USA
FSHW011634230721
83499FS